BODIES
of
WATER

Also by J.S. Borthwick:

The Student Body
The Down East Murders
The Case of the Hook-Billed Kites

BODIES
of
WATER
J.S. BORTHWICK

St. Martin's Press
NEW YORK

The Church of the Apostles, the sloop *Pilgrim*, and all the characters and events described in this book are imaginary.

Map and text illustrations by Alec Creighton

Design by Glen M. Edelstein

Library of Congress Cataloging-in-Publication Data

Borthwick, J. S.
    Bodies of water / J. S. Borthwick.
        p.   cm.
    ISBN 0-312-04269-8
    I. Title.
    PS3552.0756B64   1990
    813′.54—dc20
                                   89-78091
                                        CIP

First edition

10 9 8 7 6 5 4 3 2 1

To Katie and Clare, Nicholas, Malcolm and Louisa,
James Alexander II, and the Gump.

CAST OF PRINCIPAL CHARACTERS

Sarah Deane . . . .   Teaching fellow, Bowmouth College

Alex McKenzie, M.D. . . . . .   Doctor of internal medicine

Tony Deane . . . .   Brother of Sarah, crew on *Pilgrim*

Grandmother Douglas . . . . . .   Grandmother of Sarah and Tony

Mary Donelli-Larkin . . . .   Assistant professor, Bowmouth College

Amos Larkin . . . .   Associate professor, Bowmouth College

David Mallory . . . .   Owner and skipper of *Pilgrim*

Gracie Mullen . . . .   Secretary on *Pilgrim*, sister of Billy

Andrea Elder . . . .   Cook and deckhand on *Pilgrim*

Thanks are due, again, to Mac and Rob, my medical information team. I am also most grateful to Kathleen Waterman, Innkeeper of the Isleboro Inn, for island details; and to Sandy Nevens for a conducted tour of Isleboro. In addition, thanks are due to Rick Steadman of Wayfarer Marine, Camden, Maine, for advice in outfitting the *Pilgrim*. Any errors made in describing her equipment and layout are on my head, not his.

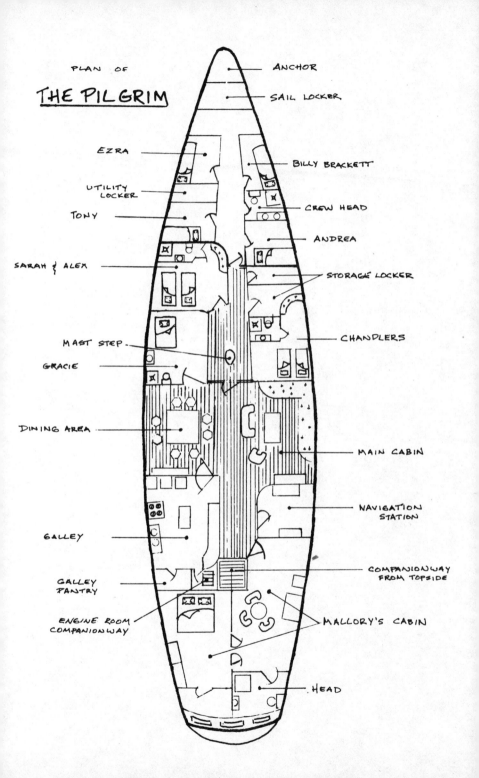

PLAN OF

THE PILGRIM

ANCHOR

SAIL LOCKER

EZRA

BILLY BRACKETT

UTILITY LOCKER

CREW HEAD

TONY

ANDREA

SARAH & ALEX

STORAGE LOCKER

MAST STEP

CHANDLERS

GRACIE

DINING AREA

MAIN CABIN

NAVIGATION STATION

GALLEY

COMPANIONWAY FROM TOPSIDE

GALLEY PANTRY

ENGINE ROOM COMPANIONWAY

MALLORY'S CABIN

HEAD

BODIES
of
WATER

ONE

"O Death, old captain, it's time! Raise anchor,
We tire of the land, O Death, let us be underweigh!"
—Baudelaire, "The Voyage,"
translated from the French

SARAH DEANE PUT DOWN THE THREE SHEETS OF HER letter and sat up cautiously in her canvas lawn chair—cautiously because the chair, mended with wire and random bolts, was apt to snap apart with undue motion. Sarah was a thin, tense young woman with large dark eyes, high cheekbones, and short, rather tumbled dark hair. Now she pushed her sunglasses up on her head and squinted at the man beside her who sprawled comfortably in another badly maintained chair, a Boston Red Sox cap tilted over his eyes.

"It's about Tony. My parents say their prayers have been answered—at least for three months." Then, since there was no response, Sarah lifted her letter and rattled the pages at her companion, Alex McKenzie.

Alex sighed and turned slightly in his chair to face and perhaps discourage Sarah from reading the letter aloud. He had been happily drowsing over a medical journal and at the same time enjoying a fine eighth inning from Fenway Park, courtesy of a portable radio by his chair. The Red Sox led by three runs over the hated Yankees. It was Saturday afternoon in late June and the weather had settled into a long hot spell, hot for mid-Maine, meaning the lower eighties. Already Sarah and Alex had twice dragged their chairs to follow the shade of the large maple behind their house, an old farm converted to a two-family rental.

"Don't you want to know what prayers? Hey, Alex, do listen." Sarah poked at Alex, using the toe of her foot to connect with Alex's ankle. "I've got an offer you can't refuse."

"Try me," said Alex, whose attention was now divided between a case of pancreatitis in the *New England Journal of Medicine* and the possibility of a Yankee pinch hitter.

"Well, you know we haven't had any vacation. Just a stray weekend looking for a house—which we probably won't find for years. So my mother has an idea that'll kill two birds with one stone."

"What two birds did she have in mind?" asked Alex, frowning over the pathologist's report of the autopsy and a Yankee double to left field.

"Listen, will you. For once, we both have some real time off this summer. After this session I don't have to start teaching again until after Labor Day and you said yesterday that you had three weeks saved up. You don't want to spend all your free time reading medical journals and listening to baseball."

"There are worse ways of taking a vacation. Besides, any idea that kills two birds scares me."

"It's my brother, Tony. You know he's been at loose ends."

"Your brother *is* a loose end."

"Alex. You like him; you've even said he was charming."

"I said he could turn on the charm. If he wants to."

"But my parents have been really worried."

"So, relax, you said their prayers have been answered. Though," he added, "I can't picture them on their knees over Tony."

"Alex, concentrate. Boston's still way ahead, so you can listen to me. You see, Tony just blows here and there, his latest girlfriend walked out on him last month when he was ski bumming in Vail; before that, he was tending bar in Louisiana, and last winter he'd been working as some sort of dockhand at a marina near Sarasota. I mean, how long can you bat around from job to job before you're forty and haven't a life that makes any sense? I know that makes me sound as antique as my grandmother, but really."

"I think Tony can bat around forever. Why not? As long as there's a boat to sail, or snow to ski on."

"It's mother. She says we might be a good influence."

"My God, what a terrible expression."

Sarah persisted. "Her idea is for us to spend time with him to prove that you don't have to be absolutely corrupt just because you have a regular job. She thinks teaching English and practicing medicine aren't as threatening as if we were, say, politicians or junk bond traders."

Alex flung down his medical journal, sat up, and shoved his baseball cap to the back of his head. He was a tall man with black hair, threatening black eyebrows, and a long, thin mouth that finished in a humorous twist. His chin was notable. He shook his fist at Sarah. "I knew if I lived long enough, someone would try and turn me into a role model. Are you saying that your brother, Tony, who I admit can be personable, shall come—in the flesh—and disturb the sanctity of whatever house we manage to find? Are you out of your skull? Here we are, ready for domesticity, and you are actually suggesting that brother Tony will move into our nest like some freewheeling cuckoo."

"Alex, how completely selfish. It would be only for ten days, or at the most, two weeks."

Alex picked up his journal. "Oh, that's okay. You frightened me; I thought you meant for life. Two weeks I can stand. But we haven't an extra room in this place. He'll have to sleep in the bathtub." Alex indicated the rather ramshackle building from which he and Sarah hoped to escape, life with six medical students in the other half of the house being less than tranquil.

"Not stay here. On a boat." Sarah picked up a sheet of her letter. "An eighty-foot cruising sloop. Our own cabin. Privacy, comfort, and a crew and a cook. Everything handsome, as Jane Austen might say. Tony, along with his job as a dockhand, has been doing some sailing for a local Daddy Warbucks named David Mallory, and this Mallory has actually gotten Tony to sign on as crew this summer when he brings his boat to the northeast to cruise off the Maine coast. It seems Mallory has taken to Tony."

"People often do, to their cost."

"No, usually to Tony's cost. His friends come apart at the seams or get into something illegal before he knows what's happening. Anyway, here's the point. Tony can ask two guests— people who know how to sail and would enjoy showing David Mallory around. Mallory doesn't know anything about Maine waters."

"So this Mallory can buy some charts and the *Cruising Guide to the New England Coast* and do very well." Alex bent over the radio. "Someone's scored a run and I've missed it."

"What is it with you today, Alex? Mr. Negative. Tony suggested us, and my mother's all for it. We wouldn't be going as real crew. Just to help when needed. Of course, you'll be the helper, because I don't know anything about a big boat. And Mr. Mallory has a regular crew besides Tony and will add a couple of other guests when he hits Maine."

"Hits Maine may be a good description. Why, we don't even know this guy. Imagine being bottled up on a sailboat with someone who may turn out to be a psychopath or a lush or directing a seagoing pimp operation. Not to say anything of this unknown crew and the unknown guests."

"Alex, shut up and listen. David Mallory is apparently very much respected in his community, and besides, Tony's had plenty of opportunity to find out if there's anything funny about him."

"Tony worked for that zombie on lead guitar who also 'liked' Tony, and the zombie turned out to be an addict and got thirteen years for possession and intent to sell. Tony's damn lucky he didn't get hauled in, too. Give me another reason."

"Tony says he's been on three shakedown cruises and that Mr. Mallory doesn't fracture when anything goes wrong. And Mallory can really handle a boat, *and* he likes Tony's music."

"Strike one."

"You do, too."

"Alone. Without the amplifier and his support groupies."

"Mr. Mallory went to college in Maine—a Bowmouth College graduate, no less. What more can you want?"

"I don't want at all."

"One thing."

"Ah."

"Mallory is religious and says grace at dinner. He's going to be supervising the distribution of Bibles and tracts for his church to little out-of-the-way coastal missions and churches."

"Oh, God."

"Exactly. But Tony says he's low-key, not into sin and transgression. Besides, you love to sail and you keep saying you wish you had something longer than a fourteen-foot catboat."

"I wasn't planning to jump to eighty."

"But my parents think it's a terrific chance for us to contribute to Tony's stability, something like that. I don't buy the idea, but at least we can see if he has what they call 'life plans.'"

"I'd say Tony finds the unexamined life well worth living."

"Okay, okay, but how about it? Two weeks on the bounding main. If the man is a nut, we can always jump ship."

"He doesn't have to be a nut. Think of sitting in a fog-bound harbor for five days with a perfectly decent, utterly dull religious zealot who goes on about the textual differences in Genesis and Leviticus, or a well-meaning goof who talks about the Dow Jones and whether industrials are off and gold is up in London and the yen is killing the dollar in Tokyo. Or worse, someone who has ideas about how to practice medicine, or how to teach freshman English. We'd have to be polite and well-behaved— all against nature. If you're dying to restructure Tony, we could charter a thirty-foot something and ask Tony to swab the decks."

"Tony has a job now. He can't join us. We have to join him. That's the deal. We can meet David Mallory when they put in to Camden, talk to Tony, pool our vibes, and then decide."

"All right. For now. But keep an escape clause."

"And look at these." To cap her argument, Sarah reached down to the grass and fished two photographs from the envelope. "Mother sent these from Tony as a sort of come-on."

The first picture showed a very large sailboat riding at a mooring, beyond a line of palm trees. The day must have been hazy, and this, plus the soft blue-green of the hull and the distance of the shot, combined to give little detail.

"Not too clear but the lines aren't bad," said Alex, interested in spite of himself. "Good bow, sensible stern. Looks a little like a Hinckley strung out."

"And here's Tony and Mr. Mallory."

The second photograph was a close-up, the two men standing by a bait shack. Sarah could read a sign over their shoulders saying FRESH BAIT, NIGHT CRAWLERS, CIGARETTES, 7-UP AND COKE. Tony was wearing what Sarah realized must be the yacht's official costume—a green rugger shirt with a circular logo on the pocket, obviously new knife-creased khaki trousers, and equally new moccasins. For years, Tony had worn ones patched and held together with duct tape. Tony's black hair was cut and his ragged beard was trimmed. Altogether, Sarah thought her brother looked less derelict than she had seen him in years.

"Positively wholesome," said Alex. He turned his attention to David Mallory: a tall man, up there with Tony's six two, powerful-looking, with a light brown lionlike head sporting a modish long haircut, a tawny mustache, a big chin, a broad smile, a green and yellow Hawaiian shirt, white shorts, and . . .

"White shoes," said Alex.

"So?"

"They shine. Plastic. Or white patent leather. Those slip-on kind with the gold chain across. Like a snaffle bit."

"Come off it. You can't tell what kind of shoes he has from the picture. I think they're sneakers."

"They glow; they gleam. Never trust a man with white patent-leather shoes with gold trim. I learned that at my father's knee."

"My God, Alex, the man's in Florida. You know, guava jelly, oranges, alligators, Travis McGee. Florida has jai alai and tropical clothes. People down there wear shoes like that."

Alex shrugged. "If we went to Florida and I bought shoes like that, you'd say plenty."

"I don't believe we're having this conversation. Tony says David Mallory is an experienced blue-water sailor. The Bahamas, the Caribbean, South America, the Atlantic. His shoes are irrelevant."

"So what would you do if I bought a pair?"

"I'd burn them, of course," said Sarah crisply. "And I'll write mother and Tony tonight."

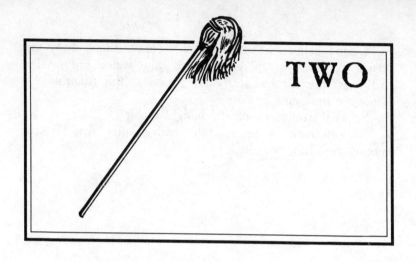

TWO

THE QUESTION OF WHETHER DAVID MALLORY WORE
white plastic shoes with gold snaffle bits was not a problem for
Tony Deane. Unless someone came aboard a boat with jewelry
that threatened to catch in the rigging, or teetered about on
high heels, Tony paid no attention. And David Mallory did not
wear jewelry or high heels. Their association had begun when
Mallory turned up at Tony's place of employment—Ziggy
Mancuso's Marina—shortly after Tony's arrival from the Colo-
rado ski slopes. Tony had been hired to sail with Mallory and
three business buddies in one of Ziggy's old Coronado Thirties—Mallory's new sloop *Pilgrim* having not yet come off the
ways. So Tony had taken the four men out, had paid proper
attention to safety and comfort, allowed each passenger a trick
at the tiller, and kept a watchful eye out for the sudden cat's-
paws of wind that told of a coming breeze.

Mr. Mallory had proved to be not only a knowledgeable
sailor but also a sensitive helmsman. The fact that David Mallory had said grace over the picnic hamper and that the buddies
had turned out to be the elders of a church somewhere near

Sarasota had not shaken Tony, because Mallory hadn't turned heavy. Not like Tony's grandmother, who, on his visits, would lecture him in her sweet elderly voice on matters of Faith and Grace—or the lack of them—so that afterward he often had to settle down to some serious beer drinking at a local bar before he could juggle himself back into his usual state of equanimity.

So here was this job. Three months' crew duty aboard the *Pilgrim*, with the possibility that Mr. Mallory might exercise his option for Tony's services for an additional three months.

Tony signed the contract. He put his full name, Anthony Sinclair Deane, on a paper that would no doubt be considered binding in any court of law. He stood forth as a trapped man for all the world to see: trapped into a job demanding a haircut, new sneakers, clean shirt, and a generally deferential posture.

It was curious, moreover, because Tony, after taking his last exam and tossing his diploma into a corner of his closet, had to this moment managed his life so as never to have to work at one job for more than four months running. Tony had, in fact, developed the art of the human tumbleweed to a fine point: blow here, drift there, pick up a few bucks, lose a few bucks. Play banjo here, sail there. He had done carpentry, painted houses, sold popcorn at Fenway Park, hot-walked racehorses at Gulf-stream Park, held an orange flag on a highway crew. Beholden to none, committed to nothing, a balloon without a string. Until now.

Tony's arrival in Florida had been without portent of serious things to come. He had washed up mid-winter, as he had in the past, on the Gulf Coast, just north of Sarasota, at Ziggy Mancuso's Sun 'n' Sea Marina and Motel.

"Hang around," Ziggy had said, "if you feel like working. Just don't wreck a boat or lose a customer. If you've got a woman, keep her off the dock and out of the boats." Ziggy had other helpers, stray characters with leather faces who stopped around for a while and then floated off on payday in a cloud of bourbon or zonked on the drug of their choice. One of these hired hands had recently been mixed up with two guys Ziggy called "south-of-the-border kilo-cowboys" and had been brought back to the dock encased in a black plastic bag. "Name of the game," said Ziggy, yawning.

But for Tony, a pretty good life. When the last charter boats had been tied up, sluiced and pumped out, fishing gear stored, sails dried on the sail charters, there was time for Tony to sit with Ziggy drinking beer and enjoying the welcome evening breeze that blew across the Gulf. The two men would lean against the wall of Ziggy's bait shack and listen to the wind rattle the ragged fronds on the palm trees overhead and talk about the world of boat chartering and the problems of running a motel that served as much as a pad for drugs and random fornication as it did as a winter resort. Ziggy's reputation for well-maintained charters and Tony's knowledge of boats made them into something of a winning combination, and Ziggy was the first to admit that business had picked up when Tony joined his outfit.

Then into this best of all possible worlds came Gulf Coast real estate mover and shaker David Mallory. Despite the fact that Mallory was undeniably rich—excessive wealth in Tony's eyes being the primordial sin—he seemed a decent sort of man, friendly and cheerful, not averse to joining Tony and Ziggy in their evening beer sessions and talking over the day's fishing. Over the past few years, Mallory had become an occasional customer of Ziggy's and had hired Ziggy's boats to take out friends and business clients. One evening, he told Ziggy he was sick of marinas that took advantage of the large boat owner, fleecing them for every possible service, and that he appreciated good service with no frills. He had backed up his words with the arrival of his beautiful new eighty-foot sloop, *Pilgrim*. Ziggy had put in a heavy-duty mooring for her and dedicated the entire length of one of his long slips to her care. And, ever the prudent businessman, he had posted an across-the-board raise in rates for charter and motel, to stay in effect for the duration of the *Pilgrim*'s stay.

And this same David Mallory had taken hold of the question of Tony's employment—and Tony's immediate future. So that David was, as Sarah had told Alex, an answer to Tony's parents' prayers.

His mother and father were, as Tony tried to remind himself, "supportive," but sooner or later in almost every letter, with Wagnerian repetitiveness, the leitmotiv sounded.

"What," wrote his mother, "is the *good* of your B.A. from a place like Dartmouth—it was your first choice, remember, dear—if you don't seriously make an effort . . ." And here followed the usual suggestions on the matter of useful employment.

Tony's father wrote shorter letters and often included true-life stories about young men and women who had floundered and sunk without a trace and then, suddenly, at the edge of middle age ("you're twenty-five now, Tony"), these same persons rose up, hauled themselves off the beaches and ski slopes, out of rock groups, off city curbs, out from under viaducts, and, presto, became doctors, lawyers, city planners, foresters, genetic engineers, or even, his father added—as a sop to Tony's love affairs with the ocean and the banjo—turned into maritime historians or orchestra conductors.

But now, without Tony moving a muscle, David Mallory had pushed Tony into the world of salary schedules, withholding tax, and comprehensive health benefits. Whenever Tony felt a wave of uncertainty over the idea of steady employment, he had only to look at the *Pilgrim*. Built in Virgina to Mallory's particular specifications and delivered in early May, her first appearance as she nosed her way toward Ziggy's Marina had sold Tony into slavery. He forgot his scruples and stood ready to polish, to haul sails, to grind winches, to do any service for such a beauty—because the *Pilgrim* was the ultimate. Long, slim lines, a wonder of polished teak and stainless steel, of new bronze and gleaming brass. A sloop that graced the waters she sailed upon.

The matter of guests joining the *Pilgrim* had come up the afternoon after Tony's transformation by haircut and beard trim. David Mallory sat with Tony on the foredeck as the *Pilgrim* bobbed softly at her mooring. Mallory sometimes seemed to have all the time in the world, and that day he talked about how Tony thought the new mainsail was breaking in, whether the roller-furling genoa needed adjusting, and then brought out the newly arrived charts of Maine. Tony, tracing the familiar coast with a finger, pointed out Penobscot Bay and Camden harbor and mentioned that his sister taught at a college near the coast and her boyfriend—or whatever you called a thirty-five-year-old live-in physician—was an avid sailor and had grown up sailing Maine waters just as he, Tony, had.

Mallory followed the subject with questions about Tony's past—his family, his college, and about his sister and her friend.

Tony gave a brief, not very up-to-date summary of Sarah's life at Bowmouth College, and the few facts he knew about Alex, and then since David seemed really interested, he told him about summers in Maine spent with his Grandmother Douglas in Camden. "She's always been totally in the nineteenth century, and since my grandfather died last year, she's been even more so. Everyone has to measure up, only none of us do. Especially me. Although," Tony reflected with a grin, "Sarah moving in and living with Alex without being married has Grandmother pretty steamed."

Then somehow the conversation drifted around to the fact that David had no real sailing friends in the northeast and that he'd always wanted to explore the Maine coast. And the *Pilgrim* had lots of extra room; besides the crew's quarters, three complete guest cabins, each with its own head, and so, "how about it, Tony? I'm not too old for new friends. Would your sister and this Alex McKenzie like to take a chance and go cruising with us? A week, two weeks, whatever they can fit in? It'd be great to have someone along who *knows* the waters—all those islands and coves with the ledges probably not marked on the charts. Why not write and feel them out."

And Tony, who had been meaning all month to write his parents a letter, agreed to include the invitation to Sarah at the same time. David nodded and then pointed to the harbor entrance, where a modified thirty-foot Hatteras fishing boat belonging—through seizure—to the marine patrol was nosing around a beacon.

"Remember a couple of weeks back those men who went out from Ziggy's dock and the one who came home in a body bag?"

Tony said yes, he remembered. Those things happened; customers chartered a boat and returned in a horizontal condition. David frowned and his bass voice sounded a regretful note. "I just found out the men weren't fishing. Not for fish, anyway. Cocaine. Six one-kilo bags. That's not much these days, so they must have been in the middle of a transfer or a sell. Well, one got caught in the cross fire. Shot in the head. Someone muscling in on the deal, free-lancing."

"Yeah," said Tony. "Ziggy said it might be a drug deal."

"Well, Tony, I'm not just chatting up the Florida drug problem. The thing is, we've all got to be concerned. Human loss, families blown apart. Crime. Absolutely out of control. Crack, all the trendy new stuff."

"Yes," said Tony politely. "I try not to think about it."

"So I'm asking you to. Now hold it"—this as Tony scowled and raised his shoulders. "Friend of mine in Sarasota—actually works on the narcotics squad for the local sheriff's office—wants me to keep an eye out when we sail. I've been sworn in as a deputy. Nothing overt, reporting Florida registered boats perhaps."

"You mean me?" asked Tony unhappily. "To help? Look, that's not what I want a part of."

"Not a part. Just if you see something offbeat, tell me, I'll pass it on. Ever lose a friend through drugs?"

"Yes," said Tony. "I mean, who hasn't? At college and in some of the music groups I worked with."

"Then you understand. They tell me the whole eastern seaboard is turning into a big floating drug conduit and funding has been cut for coast-guard surveillance. I had to square with you before we pulled out. If you don't want any part of this, we'll shake hands and tear up the contract. And no hard feelings."

But Tony remembered one of his college roommates who ended up dead in a Florida motel, and a woman he'd almost fallen in love with who had jumped out of a window in Manhattan. "Okay," he said. "If I see something. But I won't be able to sell this invitation to Sarah and Alex as a vacation if it's really a drug hunt."

"But it *is* a vacation and it is *not* a hunt. All I'll do if anything turns up is call the police and they'll handle it. Okay?"

So Tony, who for a moment had felt the cold breath of the law on the back of his neck—it hadn't been that long since his lead guitar had been hauled off to prison—nodded. "Okay," he said.

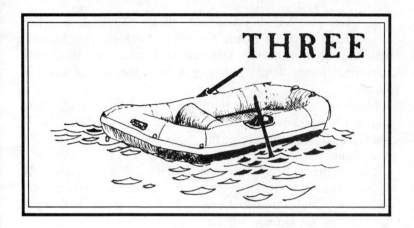

THREE

OVER A PEACEFUL SECOND CUP OF MORNING TEA, Sarah considered the things she had to do. Only five more days to go until July twentieth and the end of the first summer session at Bowmouth College. There was next year's thesis work to outline, a final typing of a paper for her graduate seminar on the novel, and the correcting of her own students' finals. Then, freedom, sun, soft ocean breezes, and Alex cut loose from the hospital grind. No classes, no students, no conferences for her; no patients, no beepers, no night calls for Alex. The summer billowed out in Sarah's imagination like a rosy cloud: the cruise and Tony, then home to find some charming, underpriced house near the college. Both of them ready for September with their batteries recharged.

There was Patsy, however. Sarah pushed her feet against the back of her Irish wolfhound, who rolled over and bared his teeth in appreciation of spinal massage. Patsy, no matter how mellow this David Mallory proved, would not be welcome aboard a sailboat, nor did Sarah like the idea of putting the enormous dog in a kennel. Alex's mother and father might have taken him but they had just left for Denmark, and her own parents were off to the Canadian Rockies. Her friends? After all, what are friends for? But who, no matter how great an animal lover, would welcome a beast the size of a small pony?

Mary, of course. Mary was animal crazy. Mary Donelli, former teaching-fellow colleague and now just fledged Ph.D. Mary, who was spending the summer doing research at Bowmouth and had recently moved into an old farmhouse on a hill near the college with one Professor Amos Larkin. Of course, Amos was, if nothing else, unpredictable, often a little frightening, and although he now kept two goats, had never been known to mention the lack of a dog in his life.

Well, nothing ventured. The farmhouse, as the crow flew, was only two meadows and a field away, the weather was clear, and Sarah was bursting with early-summer energy. She jumped to her feet, fastened on Patsy's leash, and took off. As she scrambled through the brush and over the wandering stone walls, she reflected on the oddity of Mary Donelli, the English Department's newest assistant professor, who had yearned after what was Bowmouth College's most notable drunk. She had through a series of accidents managed to rehabilitate him and then joined with him in writing a new biography of Jonathan Swift—their joint passion.

Mary was home, hunched into a hammock under an oak tree, a copy of the newest Anne Tyler novel in her lap. "Hi, you caught me enjoying myself." Mary pulled herself into a sitting position and indicated a wicker bench. She was a short, round-faced woman with large brown eyes, quizzical black eyebrows, and dark hair that tended to escape from whatever tether she had arranged for it. "I've just corrected a batch of exams, figured the grades, and Amos has gone out for supplies. I'm doing a pasta special. Enough for you, too. Call Alex. Celebration. We're getting married the end of next week."

Sarah exclaimed and offered best wishes while Mary grinned. "We Italian ladies are very pro family. Amos has his son from his first marriage coming back next week—a redhead just like him—remember he was snatched away by the grandparents when his mother died and Amos began imitating a whiskey sponge. Now that Amos is on the straight and narrow, Grandma and Grandpa have discovered that eight-year-old boys aren't the easiest things in the world to have around. I think being Mrs. Donelli-Larkin will make me seem more motherlike than the single housemate. To the grandparents, that is, and to Terence—that's his name. So what's up? You have a glitter in your eye, so I suppose you want me to do something."

So Sarah told her about the cruising plan. "Of course, we don't know the man, but Tony likes him, and my parents think Tony's on a permanent drift through life and they have this idea about life at sea. Anyway, if we go, we need a place for Patsy."

Mary showed herself willing. "If Amos says yes."

"What should I say yes about? Not that horse you call a dog. How are you, Sarah? Goofing off, like Mary?" Amos Larkin, a wiry redheaded man, leaned an old black Raleigh bicycle against a tree and dropped a bulging knapsack in Mary's lap, hung a summer jacket over a chair, loosened a tie, and growled about a faculty reception he'd been forced to attend. "When I drank, no one wanted me for any of these damned things. It's enough to drive someone back on the bottle. So what's this about Patsy?"

"He likes children—I think—and Mary says your son is coming back. He could spend the summer trying to ride Patsy. And congratulations, Professor, to you and Ms. Donelli."

Amos Larkin flung himself into a dilapidated wicker chair. "We're making me an honest man. Or Mary an honest woman. Will you and Alex hold our hands or be a congregation? The priest thinks I'm a great hazard to a holy and domestic life. A damaged forty-one-year-old taking advantage of this fine twenty-six-year-old flower. Alex can stand by with the oxygen and you can see that Mary's hair doesn't fall apart."

Sarah, after more congratulations and a telephone call about dinner to Alex, told Amos about the invitation to go sailing, adding that she was afraid Alex was habitually suspicious. "Being a doctor makes him see symptoms. He's down on this man Mallory because he wears white patent-leather shoes with gold chains."

"I wouldn't even eat a hamburger with a man who wore shoes like that," said Amos.

"Then you're just one more stuffy East Coast male. Talk about open-mindedness. You should lose tenure."

Later that night, Mary and Sarah and Alex and Amos sat on the farmhouse porch drinking espresso and rocking in old high-backed chairs that Mary had found at an auction. The night was warm, a whippoorwill called counterpoint to a bullfrog down by the pond. Peace and good fellowship seemed total when Alex said to the evening air, "There's more to this cruise than meets the eye."

"What do you mean?" demanded Sarah.

"I ran into George Fitts."

"Murder," said Mary. A suitable response, as George Fitts was a senior member of the local state police's CID, and his presence seemed to act as a sort of preambulatory Venus's-flytrap attracting homicides in settings where none such had seemed possible.

Alex examined his coffee cup and took a careful sip. "George asked what I was up to, and I told him that Sarah and I were thinking of sailing down east with her brother and one David Mallory."

Sarah swiveled around to him. "You don't have to finish. I'll bet that David Mallory is a well-known terrorist from Panama or a cocaine dealer, and that he's going to arrive in Camden harbor with a body in the bilge. And would we mind very much pretending we didn't know about this body but go sailing with him and report back to George by smoke signal. Right?"

"Sarah," said Amos Larkin, "why are you wasting your time with English literature when you have such a feel for detective work?"

"Sarah's feel for detective work last winter almost killed her *and* her friends—particularly me," said Mary. "Go on, Alex, I'm partial to George. After all, he didn't arrest Amos when it was obvious that Amos was as guilty as hell."

"And to think we're being married next week," said Amos. Alex put his coffee cup down on the porch rail. "Here it is. George has been working with the marine patrol. Drug smuggling is way up. The coast of Maine is tailor-made for hiding in, holing up in uninhabited islands, sneaking off in the fog."

"The coast of Maine," recited Sarah, "if stretched out straight would reach from Portland, Maine, to San Francisco. It has over three thousand islands. I learned that in fifth-grade geography, but we're still not going on a drug-hunting voyage. Not me. Not you, Alex. And I hope not Tony."

"So ask Alex what he's gone and done," said Mary. "He's just sitting there waiting for you to stop sputtering."

"George said he'd been getting reports from all along the Atlantic seaboard, and in particular has been working back and forth with the Florida police. Not Miami, but the west coast, Sarasota region. George and the Maine Marine Patrol helped them with two very productive busts last year. The Florida end has asked the captains of certain pleasure boats with police connections to keep their eyes open. Not to *do* anything. Just observe and report."

"Don't tell me, let me guess," said Sarah.

"It's written on Alex's face," said Mary. "This hospitable David Mallory has a police connection."

"As it so happens." Alex peered across the darkening meadow and then looked over at the goat shed, from which came a plaintive baa-aaa. He turned to Amos. "Are you thinking of goat farming instead of literature? It might be restful."

"It might indeed. I'm feeling my way with goats. I find I like them. Who knows where it will lead—cows, pigs, even llamas. A horse. But as I tell my students, don't change the subject. Sarah is ventilating and her eyes are flashing."

"And my teeth are grinding." Sarah tipped her rocking chair forward and put both feet flat on the ground. "Alex, what *have* you told George?"

"George told *me* that Mallory is some sort of Florida deputy and he wanted his guests to know that he'd keep a look out. That's all. Absolutely all."

"I'll bet."

"Nothing more. David Mallory, as a sort of service to his church—it's a mission church—helps fund and distribute religious material—Bibles, Sunday school stuff, pamphlets. The church maintains a number of small vessels—Mallory calls them the Apostle boats—along the Atlantic coast. They put in to various islands and small ports, and distribute material. It's mostly done by lay volunteers with a paid skipper. Mallory on his new sloop, the *Pilgrim*, coordinates the whole thing, this year from the Maine coast. Well, I suppose it's a good cover for idle observations."

Sarah rocked violently once or twice and then twisted her chair to face Alex. "Damn! What could be worse. This was supposed to be fun. I've gone and bought white trousers and a jacket. What I'll probably need is a face mask, black grease-paint, and a snorkel. Oh Alex."

"Not to worry. It will be fun. Rest in peace. David Mallory is the chief observer, and he and George are very firm about not wanting Tony, or you, or me to *do* anything. Recreation is being stressed; we're to have the use of a dinghy for exploring."

"You're suddenly all in favor of the thing," said Sarah. "You still haven't met this Mallory. Have you forgotten about the escape clause and that you might hate the sight of the man?"

"But George has been cooperating with the Sarasota police for a couple of years and Mallory is vouched for. The Church of the Apostles seems to be on the up-and-up."

Amos Larkin tipped dangerously back in his rocking chair. "Could the names of these Apostle boats be *Simon Peter, Andrew, James, John, Bartholomew, Thomas, Matthew,* and *Thaddaeus*? Who else?"

"There was another *James* and another *Simon, Philip,* and, of course, *Judas Iscariot*," said Mary. "I didn't go to Holy Name High School for nothing. How about it, Alex?"

"On the nose," said Alex. "Except no *Judas*. This isn't a new idea. Bible, missionary ships have been around a long time."

"And this David Mallory's boat is a sort of floating motherhouse?" asked Sarah.

"We'll find out when we meet him. Next weekend in Camden harbor, if the wind holds for them. George said the

Pilgrim made it to Baltimore last night. One other little wrinkle."

Sarah closed her eyes. "Go on. The face mask, the snorkel?"

"No. Perfectly simple. And sensible. George suggested that we both learn to use the marine radio. Said everyone who goes cruising should. A practice session. You could call Mary and Amos here and have a nice chitchat about Patsy and his kibble diet, remembering that cruising boats with radios can hear every word, so keep it clean."

Mary smiled sweetly. "What fun to hear from dear Alex and dear Sarah, who are playing games at sea while Amos and I teach a bunch of grouchy summer students the meaning of metaphor."

Amos pushed himself out of his chair and paced up and down the porch. He stopped under the lighted window, his sharp chin and the bridge of his nose illuminated, his red hair showing like a flame. Sarah remembered when she had first seen him how shocked she had been to hear that he was only forty, because he looked a dissolute eighty. Now he looked an honest forty-one, a bit weathered perhaps, but a healthy-enough specimen.

Amos turned and looked down at the others. "I'm glad, Alex, that you and Sarah are off on the bounding main, but this Mallory as a deputy sheriff is a phenomenon that would give me pause. And the very idea of George Fitts and the police intruding on this celebratory evening is enough to cause chills."

"The police do have that effect," agreed Sarah. "And what do they want with an amateur sailor like Mallory as a helper? They all—particularly George Fitts—loathe, despise, and want nothing to do with amateurs. I remember George wanting to chop me up when I mixed into his nice homicide investigation."

Alex nodded. "George said the Florida police cooked this one up, that he himself is reluctant, that Mallory is an amateur, but he can't prevent a sworn deputy from keeping a weather eye out or sending word that a vessel from Colombia is hiding behind an island. In short, George sees some tiny merit in Mallory's eagerness to look for bags of cocaine being passed from ship to shore and will not throw a wrench in the scheme."

"You mean he won't rock the boat," said Mary.

"Our friend, the detective, is not happy," said Alex. "At least as far as I can tell with a man whose expression never changes. George usually goes after what he wants without frills—and he considers Mallory a frill." He stood up, leaned over, and kissed Mary. "We'd love to see you two married. I'll make a police doll for a wedding present and you can stick pins in it."

"While you're at it," said Sarah, "make one for me."

FOUR

DAVID MALLORY WAS NOT WEARING WHITE PATENT-leather shoes. The meeting took place in Camden harbor at Wayfarer Marine, where the *Pilgrim* had docked the afternoon before. David and the first mate, a man with a wide smile and a boxer's nose, named Ezra Coster, were now busy with minor repairs and equipment checks; Tony had gone on an errand. Sarah, even as she walked forward with her hand outstretched, could not help a glance at Mallory's feet. Moccasins. Proper dark brown leather Bass-type moccasins, the kind with deck-gripping soles.

Nothing about the man suggested a life on the tropical fast track. In fact, it seemed to Sarah that David Mallory had outfitted himself from top to toe as the perfect East Coast type in an admix of L. L. Bean and Brooks Brothers, with touches from one of the nattier marine catalogues: blue oxford-cloth button-down shirt (sleeves rolled, shirt open), white duck hat with green-lined brim (weathered and slightly stained), khaki pants, tortoiseshell half glasses fastened on his head with a navy blue stretch band. As he shook Sarah's hand with what her father called "a decent grip," she noticed that to the perfect New England sailing look was added a gold signet ring with a worn heraldic design and a sporting-type watch with a cloth band.

"Looking me over, Miss Deane?"

Sarah jumped.

David Mallory smiled broadly. "Don't blame you. You're thinking about being cooped up with a man you've never met. I could bore you to death, couldn't I? Going on about diesel engines or the church and being saved. Drive you and Alex here right off the boat."

Sarah pulled herself together and gave an answering smile. David Mallory seemed to have summed up their apprehensions in one short speech. Except about looking for drug boats.

"And the police matter," said David Mallory, lowering his voice. He could read her mind. Alex could do that sometimes, and Amos Larkin, when sober, had often been one thought ahead of her. This clairvoyance was always disconcerting because it made her ideas seem secondhand. With Mallory it was eerie—or did it suggest an immediate empathy?

"It's entirely my problem, as I've told Tony," said David, not letting go of his smile. "I just wanted to level with both of you and still be able to do something about the drug situation. The Sarasota police suggested it, said it might fit in with some of my mission visits, so they checked in with your police and Sergeant Fitts. I agreed to be an extra set of eyes. You and Alex have nothing to do with it. Now come and see the *Pilgrim*. She's my very great joy."

It was well done. Or too well done? No, stop it, Sarah told herself, remembering the energy she'd spent in the last few years suspecting the wrong people and at the same time being on agreeable terms with assorted villains. Now Tony, who had just returned, came up and hugged her: a short hug. He seemed a little on the defensive about appearing in public in his new guise as a neatly dressed citizen. She remembered all his proclamations about the artificiality of clothes, but she said nothing and instead launched into a review of family news and then pointed to the *Pilgrim* and exclaimed.

The *Pilgrim* lay against the dock, a blue-green shining whale of a boat. The sloop was a standout even at a marine facility where forty-, fifty-, and sixty-foot sloops, schooners, yawls, and ketches lay snugged into adjacent wharves or nodded at nearby moorings.

Camden harbor was a small seafaring paradise. Masts spiked the skies, and boats of all sizes twisted about the harbor, and like little water beatles, small outboards buzzed too close to mooring lines, ran into docks, departed laden with supplies, or steered by children in orange life jackets, circled with the sheer delight of motion on the water.

Sarah knew Camden harbor from childhood summers—but as a child on the fringe. Now she was, if only for two weeks, part of the yachting scene, and all she could think of was the cost of it all. She said as much to Tony, but the family socialist was dazzled. "The *Pilgrim*'s something; she just cuts the water in half, stiff when you need it, sensitive as a dream in a light wind. God, I mean it, she's awesome. And good old Camden Harbor; remember I used to sail my Widgeon across everyone's bow?"

Sarah smiled a bit reluctantly remembering how Tony's sailing had caused shouts and shaken fists and several near collisions.

Alex, standing aside with David Mallory, listened with half an ear to the latter's detailed description of some trouble they'd had picking up markers leaving Marblehead. The rest of his attention was taken up watching the reunion of brother and sister. Tony was dark-haired like Sarah, much taller, an elongated version of her, as if the brother had been rendered by Velázquez with something of the interior fragility of his subjects but not the angst. Tony moved slowly; his gestures were short, half-finished, while Sarah, expostulating over some piece of news, made quick sparrowlike moves, her hands opening and closing, her head bobbing, her feet shifting. She had Tony's high cheekbones, his deep-set dark eyes, the dark brows, the determined lifted chin, and although Tony's features were pretty well obscured by the black beard, any casual observer could be sure the two came from the same family.

Then Tony excused himself and went forward to the bow to work on the anchor chain, and David Mallory came forward to collect Alex and Sarah for a tour of the *Pilgrim*.

Sarah certainly had no notion about the quality of certain shipboard appointments, but Alex was making complimentary noises about self-tailing electric winches, hydraulic systems, and eight-cylinder diesel engines, so she assumed that everything was as it should be. She left them to a discussion of something called a Datamarine speedometer and devoted herself to those aspects on deck that concerned comfort. Everything seemed a marvelous mating of function and luxury: aesthetics. Teak trim varnished to a glowing chestnut, the silver of the aluminum mast, and the cockpit itself aside from the wheel and the compass—two items Sarah was able to identify—displayed teak holders for binoculars, for sunglasses, for drink glasses and was furnished with cushions that matched the soft blue-green of the hull. This color was repeated in the sail covers, the canvas spray dodger that protected the companionway, and in the awning that stretched over the cockpit, giving shade from the July sun.

She made her way cautiously down the companionway ladder to the main cabin below—a kingdom of muted browns. The floor—Sarah knew it was called the cabin sole—and the trim and bulkheads were rubbed to a satin finish. A brass ship's clock sweetly chimed eight bells which Sarah, remembering her crash course in seagoing lore, made it to be twelve noon. Sunlight filtered from large portholes and two translucent hatch covers and shone on the brass of the cabin lamps, the barometer, and the two mounted heaters. Everything was a miracle of order and saved space.

Alex and David Mallory arrived for a tour of the sleeping area. Mallory led them forward along the passageway, opening doors and showing the three spacious guest staterooms, each with a tiny head and shower. Sheets, with PILGRIM written in flowing script on their hems, were turned down over the navy blue blankets that covered the twin berths. Forward past the guest cabins, said Mallory, lay the crew berths, the crew head, areas for stowage and the anchor locker.

Back amidships, David produced his housekeeping and secretarial assistant, who emerged from the recessed dining area: Gracie Mullen. A quintessential secretary, Sarah decided. She had steel-gray hair clamped flat about an elliptical face, a vanishing chin, and a body built on the lines of a hairpin. She wore a sensible blue dress piped in white, sensible navy canvas shoes, and gold-framed glasses clinked against a little enamel daisy watch that clung to her inadequate bosom. And Gracie had busy hands; they slid along the seams of her dress and came clasping together. Eager hands, thought Sarah, hands anxious to serve. Or was Gracie one of those souls who take the problems of the world on their narrow shoulders and try to solve them? In this case, the problems of the *Pilgrim* and its crew.

"Gracie is my right arm," said Mallory. "I met her in Maine at a northeast Bible conference and I bless the day. She remembers and worries about everything, the supplies we need, churches we must visit, the appointments I would forget. She even understands the plumbing. Anything you need, go to Gracie."

Gracie shook hands and in an unexpectedly melodious soprano voice spoke her welcome.

Mallory and Gracie moved to the main cabin area and indicated the chairs and a long sofa. "Fawn tweed, so sensible and goes with everything," said Gracie. "I helped make the choice."

"Of course, we had to have space for books," said Mallory, "so we fitted shelves around the tape deck and the compact-disc system and hid the video components because I don't like electronics hanging out. And see here." Mallory began to move happily around the cabin, opening louvered doors, showing a revolving bottle holder, wine rack, a game shelf—backgammon, cards, a chessboard—then forward by the companionway ladder, lockers for binoculars, lockers for dry clothes, for wet clothes, for emergency supplies, for cold-weather supplies.

"And the galley," announced David, crossing the dining area and with a flourish folding back a hinged door.

The galley—Sarah had the impression of an overgrown doll

kitchen—was enchanting with its two stainless-steel sinks, its refrigerator, its four-burner stove fixed on gimbals so that cooking utensils remained level no matter the angle of the boat.

"Now both of you come and see my cabin," said David. "Home away from home, office, bedroom, and a duplicate communication center. I like to work late and have everything at hand without going back and forth into the navigation station."

They slid through a passageway to starboard side of the companionway and came to a louvered door with a bronze handle and lock. David opened the door. "We're under the afterdeck but as long as you're under six foot four, you can stand up. "I had my cabin made to specifications: Head room, big ports, only one berth, and the fitted desk center."

Sarah stood in admiration. A crimson Oriental carpet, a wide port bunk covered in a crimson comforter, crimson curtains, and fitted compartments, sliding panels, ingenious rotating tables, and pull-out chairs. The port side was taken up with a walnut desk that followed the curving line of the stern. It was set with a small typewriter, a mini word processor and printer.

"And," said David, "the raison d'être. The sop to my conscience for enjoying myself so much. The Church of the Apostles." He leaned over and slid a deep drawer from under his bunk. Bibles—Bibles without end. Leather, cloth, paperback, oversized, and miniature. Children's editions. Mallory bent down and picked up a large volume.

"Not just the standard fare. The New Testament, large-print version for people with partial vision. And this folio is in braille. Our church tries to reach out-of-the-way communities because not every church has the means to provide special editions."

"And casettes and videotapes," said Sarah, awed by the collection.

"Absolutely. The living Word. From time to time, we'll stop at an island, or meet with one of our Apostle boats to make distribution calls for local churchs."

"Which Apostle?" asked Alex.

"Actually two. Summertime is especially busy on the northeast coast. Let me see. This month it's *Matthew* and *Simon*

Peter. We rotate the ships to give the crews experience with the whole coast."

Here, David Mallory dropped his voice. "And you can see why such an operation makes such a good cover, though *operation* is hardly a way to describe the Lord's work. But, it may help with this infernal drug business. Come over here to the stern portholes."

Sarah and Alex moved obediently to a series of four portholes that, spaced closely, made up a window that wrapped around the stern of the *Pilgrim*. David Mallory pulled aside a heavy red curtain backed with green. "Keeps the sunrise out of my eyes if we're anchored east and west," he explained. "I sleep like a cat and there's no point in waking up any more than I have to. Now look across the harbor."

Sarah peered through the salt-speckled glass. A small sailboat drifted past, followed by a large motor launch churning up the water and making the harbor boats rock and sway at their moorings."

"No, there, over by the public landing," said Alex. He turned Sarah's head so that her nose flattened against the glass.

And then she saw it. Or rather, them. A black motorboat with a high curved bow on which was written in enormous white letters MARINE PATROL. This vessel, like a seagoing collie, was herding a blue-hulled pleasure boat with a flying bridge toward the town wharf.

Mallory shook his head. "You wouldn't believe the idiocy of the people. It's in the morning paper. Quite a haul. George Fitts mentioned it when I called this morning, and I told Alex when I was showing him over the foredeck. Now come on and try a cold drink." David ushered Sarah and Alex back through the passageway to the main cabin and slid open a cupboard filled with ranks of glasses, each with the *Pilgrim*'s name and the figure of a hooded man with a staff. "What will you have? Name it. Rum, vodka, gin, a chilled Chablis perhaps. I have no scruples about drinks at noon on a hot July day. At church meetings, I stick to soft drinks, but not when I'm on my own."

Forty minutes later, on the crest of tall rum sours, Alex and

Sarah debarked, Mallory waving them off from the cockpit. Then, just as they moved up the dock, knee-high to the open portholes of the *Pilgrim*, Sarah heard it: a sound just above the noise level of the harbor. A high laugh with an uncertain vibrato. A laugh that trailed off in a sort of cackling noise. Then a voice in a slightly lower register gave a returning lower pitched laugh. A moment later the second voice, quite clear, "not to worry. Not about those shits." And again, this was followed by the lower laugh now descending into a chuckle.

"Alex, what's that?"

"What's what?"

"Someone's laughing. Or two someones. From the *Pilgrim*, or inside it. First a high laugh, a cackle, then a sort of funny low chuckle cackle."

"I didn't hear a cackle."

"Hush, maybe it will do it again."

They stood still for a minute, bent toward the *Pilgrim*. Nothing. Nothing except they saw Mallory, who must have been watching them, leave the cockpit and make his way to the bow."

He shouted across to them, "Forget something?"

"No," said Alex grinning. "Sarah's just hearing things."

Sarah, unable to kick him in public, called, "Thought I heard a siren, another police boat."

Mallory waved, a genial dismissing wave, and Sarah and Alex moved up the dock gangway.

"There *was* a sort of a cackle and you almost gave us away. Honestly, Alex. And someone saying something about 'those shits.'"

"Cackle my foot. You're hearing things and I'm not trying to give you away, there's nothing to give. Mallory had better be warned that you're apt to hear things that go bump in the night . . . or day.

"I couldn't tell about the second voice, whether it was a man's or woman's, but the first was definitely a woman's. Or a counter tenor's. A little of out of control. It was like Grace Poole. Which is a coincidence."

"What is? Mallory's Gracie and this Poole?"

"Grace Poole was supposed to have the weird laugh that Jane Eyre kept hearing, but it was really the mad wife, only Jane didn't know Mr. Rochester was married, let alone had a mad wife in the attic, so she thought the peculiar ha-ha and cackling was Grace Poole's."

"If you think that synopsis is going to make me read *Jane Eyre,* you're wrong. And I think you're just ready for something creepy."

Sarah subsided and remained silent through the drive back to Sawmill Road and their house. Then as they made the turn, she turned to Alex. "David Mallory said that he couldn't believe the idiocy of those men that George Fitts just nabbed in Camden harbor. What I want to say is, I'm beginning to wonder about the idiocy of Alex McKenzie and Sarah Deane in getting mixed into this whole scene. And Tony. Being led into this like pet poodles on a leash."

"Not pet poodles. And it was your parents' idea."

"Okay, not poodles, then. But how about turkeys? Or shits? What is going on, anyway? I'm not talking about the laughing and cackling but the whole business. David Mallory must come from another century, because he kept lowering his voice in a conspiratorial way, as if he didn't want to offend a female with delicate feelings, so I've missed bits and pieces. Something he was talking to you about on deck. I didn't read the morning paper, but I gather there was a police bust. George Fitts in action. And bodies . . . in body bags. Tony told me that body bags are all over the Florida coast; no one thinks a thing about it."

"Which means *he's* trying not to think about it."

"Anyway, I understand that these drug fellows were trying to pass themselves off as yachtsmen enjoying the ocean-cruising scene with stops at popular island harbors. Only they must have blown it or the state police wouldn't have been on the welcoming committee."

"Blew it is right. Mallory told me when you were below decks that something phony stuck out all over. Those people made sailing mistakes. Anyone who tries to cruise the northeast had better do his homework, or use a pilot. Two boats, one fetched up on a ledge, the other grounded out in shoal waters. A crew member spoke Spanish in public and that suggested southern connections, and then there was the cash. Rolls of cash paid for everything, for a cottage with dock, for boats, for motors. And to top it off the crew never asked for a yacht club mooring or dock use."

"Do you have to use yacht club facilities?"

"No. But people who cruise are always looking for a good safe mooring. Yacht clubs along the coast often maintain a few moorings for visiting yachtsmen, and so do marine supply places and some inns. It's a sure bet that if you cruise for more than four days, you'll hit bad weather and want to hunker down for a day or so. These birds not only avoided any outfit that had moorings, they tried to avoid contact with the harbor master. Always anchored at the outskirts of the harbor, and any fool knows that being tied up to a fixed mooring is the way to rest in peace. You don't have to set a watch at night to see if the anchor's dragging."

"There must be some pretty sharp Marine Patrol people to pick up all these nuances."

"The cash really did it. One sure way to make a New Englander's hair stand on end is to flash money. No questions, no asking if there was anything cheaper. No discreet use of the credit card or the personal check. Now if you will simmer down about weird laughs, I'll tell you that I had a message from your grandmother. A command performance."

"Tony told me. She wants you, me, Tony, and David Mallory for one of her family inspection luncheons. She'll gently tell Tony he's wasting his life, and work us over about getting married—or not getting married. And quiz David Mallory."

"I'm game. I like your grandmother. She has character."

"Alex, I love you very much, but we won't get married simply because my grandmother goes into a fit over the jellied consommé."

"In the annals of marriage, it wouldn't be the first time a grandmother flogged a couple to the altar."

"Not this couple; we'll go on our own steam."

"Right. And I love you, too, my beloved. As the good book

says, your hair is like a flock of goats and your teeth are like a flock of ewes that have come up from the washing—"

"That would certainly wow Grandma, except she distrusts that section of the good book. But you'll make time with David Mallory and the Church of the Apostles. And my hair feels exactly like a flock of goats. Have you a comb?"

FIVE

THERE FOLLOWED A WEEK OF SOCIAL BUSTLE AND EN-
tirely too much food. It began with Mary Donelli's prewedding
festivities and ended in the curtained gloom of Sarah's grandmother's dining room.

The Donelli-Larkin nuptials (as they were referred to in the
local paper) were inserted between the first and second summer
terms of Bowmouth College, since the principals had to be on
deck in a classroom on the following Monday. Sarah found herself in the role of chief assistant, driving back and forth between
motels and inns with the numerous members of the Donelli
family and explaining to anxious relatives that yes, Amos Larkin
was over forty; no, he wasn't Catholic; no, he hadn't been di-
vorced, his first wife had died; no, he had not killed her; yes, a
priest would give the service at the church; and yes, it was a real
church and Mary knew what she was doing. The wedding took
place on Saturday at Our Lady of Good Hope, under benevolent skies. Neither bride nor groom turned pale or garbled the
responses, and Mary, at the end of the dinner following, hurled
a bouquet of daisies at Sarah's head and pointed at Alex.

"Okay, you two holdouts. Go thou and do likewise."

Although the cruise on tap for early Monday brightened the horizon, the Sunday luncheon at Grandmother Douglas's house in Camden loomed as an oppressive sequel to a wedding. "I love her," said Sarah, "but she doesn't make it easy. After all that Italian joie de vivre, Grandma's high moral profile will be hard to take."

"Mallory ought to leaven the loaf. He seems to know what to say on every occasion. Having him at lunch will take the heat off me. Your grandmother sees me as the Don Juan of mid-coast Maine."

"Tell her about the patients you've saved. Derail the marriage lecture."

Alex found, however, that he didn't have to derail Mrs. Douglas. Seating arrangements found David Mallory on his hostess's right and Tony on her left. Sarah and Alex faced each other over an expanse of polished mahogany, while at the far end of the table sat a retired vicar, stooped and gray, and his look-alike sister. These two, having established that Alex and Sarah had no garden, whispered back and forth at each other about earwigs, aphids, leaf mold, and slugs.

Sarah sat in a condition of numbness in the almost stifling dining room. The windows were half-hidden by maroon brocade curtains and the general dimness was accentuated by the maroon and gray flocked wallpaper and a series of oil paintings in ornate gold frames that, suspended from a ceiling wire, leaned oppressively toward the diners. Sarah, feeling like a victim of some heavy enchantment, ate her way through ham scallop and a compote of stewed fruit, all the time trying to keep her attention on her grandmother's conversation with Tony and David Mallory.

The latter had not alarmed her grandmother by arriving in his Florida costume; his light gray suit, foulard tie, and polished shoes could cause nothing but approbation. In fact, Tony in his new pants and shirt, Alex in his new tan linen jacket, she in her best navy and red cotton skirt looked like ads from one of the more chaste New England catalogues directed at conservative buyers.

Her grandmother, remote from fashion in an indeterminate gray voile garment with a lace collar, remote from life beyond her own walls and garden, presided at the head of the table as a white-haired, almost ghostly presence. And yet her voice, insistent, high-pitched, each word articulated with care, forced attention.

At first, Tony seemed to be trying to counter his grandmother's lecture on the fruitful—and godly—life; then he sank into silence and occupied himself with second helpings and the crumbling of bread. David Mallory fared better. He took up the conversation after the jellied consommé, and Sarah, who had feared that he might tell her grandmother about his planned extracurricular drug-traffic assignment, was much relieved to hear the talk take a religious turn. Relaxing, she half-listened to phrases like, "Of course, as a mission church, there is no congregation or service as such. . . . We have guest speakers . . . lay workers. . . . We encourage the young people to lead a meeting. . . . Yes, I was raised as an Episcopalian . . . prayers, a Psalm every night. . . ." From this point, Grandmother Douglas and David Mallory launched into a discussion of the Psalms. Quotation followed quotation, and David Mallory in his fine deep voice spoke of one of his favorites and recited a few verses. Sarah couldn't make it all out, something about the Lord being great and all the trees of the wood rejoicing and the fowls of the air singing among the branches. His voice murmured on and on, Grandmother Douglas nodding her white head, her thin finger tapping the table, as David wound it up with a series of "Praise the Lord with trumpets, lutes, and harps."

"Thank you, Mr. Mallory," said Mrs. Douglas. "A man's voice gives them so much resonance. Your favorite, you say?"

David Mallory smiled and said yes, a favorite among many favorites, and as Mrs. Douglas gripped the arms of her chair and prepared to rise, he offered her an arm and they made a stately recessional out of the room.

Instead of disappearing immediately for her nap, as was her custom, Mrs. Douglas beckoned to Tony, and they moved to what had once been the conservatory but was now a rather sparsely furnished sun room. In about ten minutes, Tony, rather red in the face, returned alone holding an envelope. "To be opened later. Another lecture I'm afraid. On direction and moral purpose. Sarah, she wants you now. Another envelope, I'll bet."

Sarah found her grandmother sitting erect at a spindle-legged desk overlooked by a tall rubber tree. Mrs. Douglas put down a pen and folded a piece of blue writing paper and slipped it into a waiting envelope. Then she rose stiffly and beckoned. "Come down through the garden with me to the shore. I will need your help. I rarely walk that far anymore. I'm afraid the rose bushes are dreadfully overgrown and the day lilies are completely out of control."

They moved together, Grandmother Douglas leaning on Sarah with one arm and on a cane with a carved parrot head. Step by faltering step down the sloping lawn until they stood at the edge of a narrow beach guarded by two huge white pines. Mrs. Douglas shaded her eyes and frowned across the harbor where one of the coastal schooners moved, sails full, against the horizon.

"It's quite strange," she said. "I never expected to be old. Inside I feel as I did when I first came to Camden and looked over the harbor. When I came here with your grandfather to plan this house we stood down on the beach and watched the sailboats and thought we would live forever, that life was our gift."

Concerned, Sarah peered at her grandmother. She started to speak, but her grandmother pressed her arm for silence and turned away from the ocean, a flip of wind catching the hem of her gray dress, showing her gray cotton stockings, her black laced shoes.

"Speaking of Psalms as we have been doing at luncheon, I remembered that line—from the One Hundred and Second: 'My days are like a shadow that declineth; and I am withered like grass.' It is just possible that I have been too severe with life, but it is far too late to change. But," she added, "I do wish you, Sarah, happy sailing. Remember living is hazardous, but as Saint Paul writes, suffering trains us to endure. Now, my dear, it is time for my nap. I have just had a rather difficult discussion with Tony, and I almost never entertain, and then only family. A stranger, even such an affable man as Mr. Mallory, is a strain. I have left an envelope for you on my desk."

Sarah took her grandmother's arm and they returned to the house, where the housekeeper was waiting to help her grandmother with the stairs. Sarah leaned over, brushed the tissue-thin cheek with her lips, and tiptoed out of the room.

Returning from the sun room, she slipped her grandmother's envelope into her handbag and went outside to join Tony and Alex and to say good-bye to David Mallory, who was returning to the boat.

"Well," said Tony, as they walked slowly to Alex's car parked by the old stable, "that was certainly depressing. But her mind's as sharp as a knife. Feisty as ever on her favorite subjects."

Sarah nodded. "Her doctor says she's remarkable, which is what doctors always say about old people who are hanging in there. She's not strong, but, after all, she's eighty-nine."

"I looked in my envelope," said Tony. "She's written out a long Bible quotation and told me she's asked her lawyer to make out a check for tuition at a graduate school if I'm accepted somewhere. Talk about pressure. Or plain bribery. But believe me, I'm not going to tie myself into the academic zoo again. Look at you, Sarah, thinner than ever, sort of twitchy, always carrying around a batch of papers to correct. But Grandma did add a fifty-dollar bill, with no strings."

That night after a late dinner, Tony, Alex, and Sarah stretched out in lawn chairs. The evening was warm and the marsh below the meadow buzzed with late peeps and cries. "What's in your envelope?" asked Tony. "I'll bet it's Saint Paul telling you it's better to marry than burn. What do you suppose he meant, sizzle with passion or sizzle in hell?"

"I suppose I'd better see," said Sarah. She reached in her handbag, brought out the envelope, and slipped a finger under the flap. A folded sheet of her grandmother's best Crane paper with her monogram, and underneath that a smaller second envelope. Enclosed in the letter was a check made out to the Bowmouth Graduate School of Arts and Sciences. Sarah held it up to Tony. "She must have called our bursar, because it's enough to take care of a year's tuition and thesis guidance." The note itself did indeed refer Sarah to Saint Paul's first letter to the Corinthians, followed by several verses from the Proverbs. Sarah sighed. "Always the last word."

"In the beginning was the Word, and the Word was with Grandmother," said Tony.

Alex reached for the paper and held it to the light that came from the kitchen window. "Proverbs Thirty-one. About the virtuous wife whose price is far above rubies and it ends with 'Many daughters have done virtuously, but thou excellest them all,' and then, 'Favor is deceitful and beauty is vain: but a woman that feareth the Lord, she shall be praised.'"

Sarah rose from her chair and stared into the distance where the rising Camden hills made a denser darkness. "I feel blighted."

"But think what she could have put in," said Tony. "All those dire warnings. I had the one last year about 'Woe to the rebellious children.' What does the other envelope have in it?"

"On the outside Psalm Ninety-four, verse seventeen. 'Unless the Lord had been my help, my soul had almost dwelt in silence.' And I know exactly what that means. Grandma has wrestled with her conscience, which has come out ahead, so she's free to tell me what she thinks about my living with Alex. And I am *not* going to read it." Sarah stood up, jammed the second envelope into her skirt pocket, and moved to the edge of the lawn where a dark tangle of burdock, vetch, and loosestrife marked the edge of the meadow. "Not only blighted, but full of aphids, earwigs, and slugs."

Alex joined her and put his arm around her. "Kiss me; unblight yourself. Cheer up; tomorrow we sail. Anchors away. Have you packed those frivolous white pants and a yachting jacket?"

Sarah reached up and pulled Alex's head to kissing level and held him close for a moment and then took his hand and they started back to the house. "You're right," she said. "Enough gloom and doom. Rejoice, rejoice, O Israel. I have packed a sort of sailor jacket with a silk tie to go with my white pants. Vanity, vanity."

Back in the house, they found Tony, who had gone ahead in

search of a bottle of beer. He had settled down at the round oak table in the middle of the kitchen. His expression was one of a person of probity ill-used by the world.

"It's like I'm caught between a rock and a hard place. Grandma spouting Scripture and Mallory with his Bibles. And having to wear a shirt with a boat's name. I feel kept."

"But Tony," protested Sarah, "you asked for it."

Tony sighed. "Yes, and Mallory really doesn't shovel it out. I just know sometimes what he's thinking, that he's playing I Spy with his little inward eye."

"What sort of church is Mallory's?" put in Alex.

Tony tipped back in his chair and blew a low note on his half-filled bottle. "Sort of a funny affair, the Church of the Apostles, but David says that's because it's a mission church. I even went to a meeting once."

"A convert?" asked Alex with interest. "Born again?"

"I did a music job for their annual church picnic, kind of a luau. David has this huge beach house with thatched palm-roof shelters and a pool and everyone ran around with Frisbees and volleyballs."

"And you played 'Amazing Grace'?" asked Sarah.

"As a matter of fact, yeah. I did a few bluegrass numbers, then some spirituals, revival hymns. Antique stuff. I sort of winged it, played chords and bass lines. Everyone linked arms and swayed to 'Amazing Grace.' On fruit punch. With nothing in it. Christ, I thought, I'm not going to make it all summer on fruit punch, but on his own, Mallory serves hard stuff. And beer."

Alex regarded Tony with disfavor. Good time Charlie. "You should try coal mining, Tony. Maybe roughing it on an eighty-foot sloop on fruit punch won't seem too bad.

Sarah intervened. "Alex, you wouldn't want to spend the next two weeks on a soft-drink diet. Tony, has Grandma said anything more to cheer you up?"

Tony spread open the blue sheet of writing paper.

"Psalm One Hundred one," said Tony. "The Godly life."

"The Godly life should be within reach," said Sarah. "A

cabin on an eighty-foot sloop, a salary, new shoes, and three meals a day—cooked by someone else. The clean shipboard life with Captain Mallory and his Apostles and Saint Gracie, the Immaculate Conception. Grandma should be delighted."

Tony grinned. "You should see our new cook. She came aboard this morning, flew in from Florida. She worked for Mallory last year but I'd never met her. And she is something; I mean she is really something. Grandma would not be delighted."

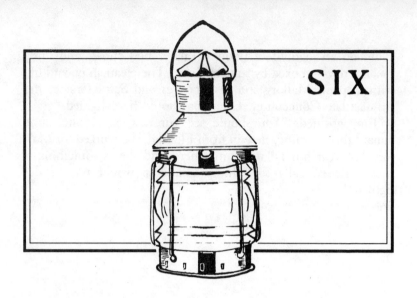

SIX

ALEX MET THE NEW COOK AND ALL-PURPOSE DECKHAND the next morning. He had made a run to Camden and down to the Wayfarer Marine dock to help load luggage while Sarah delivered Patsy to the Donelli-Larkin homestead. Alex wasn't sure what sort of woman would turn out to be Tony's idea of *something*, but when he met Andrea, he decided the word was inadequate.

Andrea Elder stood on the deck above the forward hatchway directing the loading of stores. She wore the same green shirt as Tony, with PILGRIM written across its pocket; her khaki shorts and her moccasins were the same cut and make. But Andrea fitted into her shirt and her shorts in a way that suggested spray paint, and the sight of her on deck was enough to cause several men working on a sloop tied aft of the *Pilgrim* to look up from time to time and make audible comments on the subject of deckhands, cockpits, and night watches.

Yes, Andrea *was* something. And although her attitude as she stood with note pad and pencil was entirely businesslike, her presence shouted sex. Fair with wispy, almost white curls like a

Botticelli angel, a tilted nose, full lips, rounded chin, little ears, and deep gray eyes heavily lashed—eyes open and inquiring, as if wondering why anyone should pay her attention. Alex remembered Marilyn Monroe tripping through the train station with her ukulele case in *Some Like It Hot*. This updated new woman model brought back visions of fun in an upper berth with sweating males.

Andrea spoke in a husky lisp, calling for first Tony, then Ezra, then Billy—the third male crew member, as yet an unknown quantity—to take this carton to the freezer, that box to the galley storage, these packages to a locker. Every now and then, she paused, ran her hands over her waist and up over her breasts, pausing as if surprised to find anything so warm and prominent on her body. From time to time, she lifted her arms to the back of her neck to pull her hair free of its collar, so her back arched and her chin lifted, her whole posture offering bodily delight. Then, impatient at some delay, she took hold of a carton and breathing in so that her shorts slipped a few inches down her hips, she lifted it, and carried it herself down the companionway to the galley.

Alex looked over at Tony, ready to make some pleasantry about his grandmother's warnings. But Tony, easy, laid-back Tony, was stumbling about the deck, reaching blindly for cartons, his eyes never leaving Andrea until he disappeared below.

Alex turned to Ezra, another crew member, to see whether he was in any way affected by what could only be described as the presence of a potent sea goddess. But Ezra, whistling under his breath, was busy with the business of the boat. Alex guessed he was somewhere in his early forties, a smooth-shaven, wiry man with dark hair, trimmed as if he had just finished military service. He had a wise-looking, triangular Irish face that fitted with his smashed nose, and a perpetually amused expression. He moved with a tense grace, tossing cartons, coiling lines, tightening sail covers, shaking out slickers and rain pants and hanging them over the *Pilgrim*'s lifelines. Everything about Ezra suggested competence. And a damn good thing, too, Alex told himself, what with Tony being knocked flat over Andrea.

Then there was the other crew member, Billy Brackett, who turned out to be the young half brother of Gracie Mullen. Alex accepted his languid hand, and then Billy, without making any answer to Alex's greeting, returned to the loading. From the look of faint distaste on Billy's face, Alex guessed that each carton arrived in Billy's hands as an unpleasant event; he got rid of it as soon as possible, making few trips down the hatchway. If Andrea seized a package from him with an exclamation of impatience, Billy let her have it with a slight shrug of his narrow shoulders.

Billy had a cap of pale red hair and a fairness that bordered on transparency. Unlined cheeks gave no hint of an underlying beard, and his thin legs and slender arms were hairless and white, the lack of color surprising in one who had been at sea for at least three weeks. Alex, not usually given to unearthly intimations, felt that Billy carried with him an almost palpable aura of corruption, that behind him could be heard the whistle of a scythe and the beating of dark wings.

Alex shook himself and as an antidote turned for a quick glance at Gracie Mullen, the efficient nonpareil. She, looking fresh in peach cotton, stood by the mast and with a clipboard in hand checked off items. Andrea might have been a piece of nautical furniture for all the attention Gracie gave the woman. In fact, if she looked at anyone, it was to frown at her brother, Billy. Alex waved at Gracie, shouldered his duffle, and made his way below.

Sarah delivered Patsy with leash, bowl, and security blanket into Mary Donelli's hand and settled down to a cup of tea and a piece of surviving wedding cake.

"How in God's name can anyone eat cake at eight in the morning?" demanded Amos Larkin, coming into the room and putting his briefcase on the table. "So, Sarah, you're off on the high seas, bringing the Word and spying on the drug trade."

"None of the above, and certainly not spying," said Sarah. "David Mallory's just supposed to keep an eye out. Frankly, I think he's a bit inflated about his police role and being a deputy."

"I will never understand the police mind," said Amos, reaching absentmindedly for a piece of cake. "From what I've seen of him, George Fitts is not one for sharing his professional pleasures even with other members of the constabulary. Why would he even allow himself to talk to a roving Florida sailboat man?"

"George has his little ways," said Sarah. "But I agree, he doesn't usually allow the laity into his magic circle. It's probably an affirmative-action program. Well, when I make my practice radio-phone call, I'll fill you in on our adventures."

"I have never liked the telephone," said Amos, pulling up a chair to the table, "and I believe I will detest the radio-telephone."

"You won't be able to fill us in on anything worth saying," said Mary. "Everything you say is blasted all over the coast, but I'll call in with little messages, such as Alex is being sued for malpractice and you've lost your fellowship. Things to brighten your day."

Amos stood up. "Good-bye, Sarah, may your anchor be fouled—whatever that means."

Sarah and Mary watched Amos slide his briefcase over the handlebars of his bicycle and hurtle down the dirt driveway to the main road and career out of sight. Mary sighed. "Honestly, sometimes I think he is more of a menace riding a bike sober than he was driving a car drunk. Then he just crawled into things."

"Like you," said Sarah, remembering the description of their first meeting.

"I keep thinking what a terrible invalid he'd make if he racks himself up. Always in a red-haired rage. All right, Sarah, go along and a pox on the police. And just think of how many enemies George Fitts has made. He's probably lying out in our field out with a telescopic rifle and detonator."

Sarah laughed, a not entirely untroubled laugh. "And anti-personnel bombs are being planted in our grocery supplies."

Alex met Sarah at the dock, helped her stow her gear, and then escorted her to the Waterfront Restaurant for lunch, where Sarah described her last remarks with Mary.

"Sarah," said Alex in an exasperated voice, "quit the talk about enemies. The only bomb we have to worry about is right there aboard the *Pilgrim* preparing our dinner. I wonder if David Mallory has a low sex drive or she didn't wear shorts and a T-shirt when she worked for him before. Tony is unstrung."

"Tony always falls for new and exciting females but never for too long. I hope he doesn't go overboard—not a pun—over this one."

"I don't care if she's Cordon Bleu, anything she cooks is going to be overlaid with sauce à la sex. If Tony wants to hang on to this job, he had better gird up his loins and pay attention."

"I think that's exactly what you don't want him to do. And, it's hardly a subject we can talk over with David Mallory. Or with Tony—he'd eat me alive."

David Mallory, however, had not needed outside suggestions. When Sarah and Alex returned to the dock for the appointed departure time of two o'clock, David and Andrea were on the foredeck in earnest conversation, and even at a distance of fifty feet, Alex could see that there had been a costume change: from size six to size eight. The shirt now draped modestly over Andrea's slender shoulders left only a fold here and there to suggest the riches beneath. The shorts were loose and longer and the buttocks no longer defined.

Mallory came over and welcomed them aboard, and, as he conducted them to their cabin, said in a low voice, "That girl has no idea of the effect she has on the normal male. Tony is almost useless. Fortunately, I had the boat uniform made up in several sizes because of possible crew changes. Andrea is a first-class cook—she's done some of my church picnics for me, in a coverall, I may add—but she always seems to be an absolute child about her body. I've just had a fatherly but explicit talk with her, which I hope she won't misunderstand and think I'm a dirty old man."

Alex sat down on the port bunk and nodded. "She's an arresting specimen, I must say."

"Men," said Sarah. "No one has even suggested that the poor woman has feelings, a brain, and is probably a very competent sailor."

"That's my point," said David mildly. "No one suggests it because the other, shall we say attributes, overwhelm her real talents. She's done offshore racing as well as cooking. I suggested to her that she let these talents speak for her. Now I'll leave you to unpack. We'll cast off in about fifteen minutes, and Alex, I can use your help. Sarah, come on deck and see us out of harbor."

There was just time for Sarah to open drawers, look into lockers, and test the mattress on her bunk before she was called topside for the departure. The decks were clear, the sails uncovered, and David Mallory, sunglasses in place, white canvas hat tilted over his brow, stood by the wheel. He waved Sarah to a place in the cockpit, leaned forward, pressed a button in a cockpit recess by the wheel. There was a heavy rumble, David listened intently as the engine warmed, then, hand on the throttle, called, "bring up those fenders, make ready to cast off." A series of cylindrical fenders in blue-green canvas slip covers that had dangled between the *Pilgrim*'s hull and the dock, were hauled aboard, and Mallory shouted, "cast off the spring line, cast off bow line" then, "cast off stern." The lines were thrown and caught. David shoved the gear shift into forward, and the big bow of the *Pilgrim* turned first toward the harbor and then, the diesel engine thrumming, swung toward the open sea.

Having asked permission to go forward until it was time to hoist sail in the outer harbor, Sarah now stood, hair blowing, one hand around a stay, feet braced as the increasing size of the sea swells made the ship rise and fall as she nosed out past the sheltering harbor into heavier seas. At such a time, with the brisk southwest wind, the sky azure, the harbor entrance and the horizon filled with sailboats that, like great white seabirds, bowed to the wind, Sarah thought that the scene was magic and the *Pilgrim* was alive and flying. She looked back across the harbor, where she could make out the turret of the old Douglas house and remembered her grandmother standing yesterday there at the beach edge, her white hair spun like floss around her head, the hem of her gray dress lifted in the wind. Perhaps, now, at the end of her life, Grandma might wish to stand on the deck of this boat, feel the surge under her feet, and not have a single reproving thought as the harbor diminished behind her.

When the work of setting the sails was over and the big pale green genoa jib had filled with air, Sarah established herself in a corner of the cockpit with a chart and asked where they were going.

David Mallory pointed to the chart. "We're taking it easy. A short hop. Gilkey Harbor on Islesboro, just off to the northeast of Camden harbor. A chance to settle into sailing, go over the charts, and practice picking up the markers. I've arranged with the Islesboro Inn for a heavy-duty mooring. Now, Sarah, you can take the wheel."

"Does it go in the opposite direction like a tiller? I mean if I push to right—I mean to starboard—does it go left? Or is it like an automobile?"

"Never say automobile on shipboard," said Alex, climbing down from his place on the deck. "Not on a sailboat, anyway. There's a pecking order. Sailors like to pretend when the wind dies down that they haven't got motors hidden away. Stinkpots are looked down on."

Mallory beckoned to Sarah. "How about taking the wheel and seeing if you can pick up the next marker on a course for Islesboro. Alex tells me to head for the lighted bell buoy lying south of Ensign Island."

Sarah, standing at the pedestal with the wheel in her hands, with the need to keep the sails filled and stay on course, found that the idea of drug dealers could not intrude on the demands of wind and water, on a perfect afternoon.

"Look at your wake," said Alex. "You're weaving. Hold her steady, watch your compass."

"Like this," said David, taking the top of the wheel. "Don't overcompensate. That's it. Fine. You're a natural helmsman. Or helmsperson."

"No," said Sarah firmly. "I'm not, but I probably can be trained to aim at something. Otherwise, I'm a subnormal athlete."

David Mallory murmured something in protest, talk subsided, and they flew on rising wind to Islesboro.

— 48 —

SEVEN

DAVID MALLORY, COMPLIMENTING SARAH AGAIN ON her sailing aptitude, turned the wheel over to Ezra, and, with Alex by his side, checked off marker after marker as *Pilgrim* threaded her way between Ensign and Job islands. And now Gracie emerged as a tourist guide. She sat down next to Sarah, two volumes on her lap, and began to read about the wonders of the island.

From one cruising guide, she picked out the information that they now had a marvelous view of the Camden Hills, and from the other that the Islesboro Inn, their destination, had many chimneys and yellow awnings. "It was built in 1916 as a summer cottage," she added.

"Cottage, as in enormous house," put in Sarah, but Gracie was now busy scanning with her Instamatic camera. In the soft summer light, the passing scenery was enchanting. The dark spruces, long rock sequences, and occasional beaches of Job Island yielded to the southern reaches of Islesboro, where houses—cream, white, or finished in shingle—began to appear by the shore. The *Pilgrim* left barge-shaped Minot Ledge to starboard, slipped past a spruce-capped thimble called Thrum-cap, and then Gracie stood up searching for the first sign of the inn's yellow awnings.

The *Pilgrim* came floating in on its blue and green genoa, and just when it seemed as if the big sloop might fetch up on someone's front lawn, Ezra swung her into the wind, Tony rolled in the genoa, and David Mallory and Andrea stood by the bow ready for the mooring. Then the mooring line was on deck and *Pilgrim* was safe, her nose nodding gently into the wind.

"We're in," Mallory called. He stood, boat hook held vertical, like some triumphant gondolier. At that moment, Sarah saw Billy come up behind Gracie, who was still busy with her camera, seize her around the waist, and shove her forward as if to push her into the water. Gracie gasped, her camera swung loose around her neck, and she grabbed unsuccessfully for a stay. Then Billy, as his sister pitched forward, caught and steadied her. He chuckled, and Sarah knew where she had heard that laugh before. Something cold crept down her spine.

"Relax, Gracie," said Billy. "Just a joke, okay?" But Gracie, her mouth open, her face white, just looked at him.

Mallory, busy in the bow, had missed the whole scene. "All right," he called in a jovial voice. "Time for guests to stretch their legs. Sarah, why don't you and Alex take the Avon raft into shore for some exploring, and then we can all meet for drinks on deck at six."

Alex and Sarah tied the rubber raft up to the Islesboro Inn's float, dodged behind a screened tennis court, and made for the road that passed by the front of the inn. For a while, they hiked in silence, turning off on a gravel road that led back to the shore. Alex strode along, binoculars slung over his shoulder, cocking his head every now and then toward birdcalls. Sarah managed something between a fast walk and a slow jog. Then, after Alex had stopped, listened, and identified a boreal chickadee, Sarah pointed out a gap in the trees that showed a slice of the harbor. The *Pilgrim* rode gently at its mooring, easily the largest and most impressive vessel in sight.

"It's a bit of a mixed bag, isn't it?" she asked.

Alex lowered his glasses. "What is?"

"Well, there's Billy, the odd man out in the perfect ship's company. Scaring his sister like that, almost sadistic. Then the perfect boat, the perfect skipper. The special mooring. Mallory's noble mission looking for drug boats, which as far as I can see, he's not doing."

"First, yes Billy's a weirdo, maybe not a very nice one. Second, oh malcontent, Mallory was wise to arrange the mooring. The *Pilgrim*'s a big baby and he doesn't want to worry about dragging. And we've just started; there's been no time for Mallory to scan for suspicious boats. Or he may be doing it without your permission."

"Okay, but what about all the rest of it?"

"I don't follow; what's your beef?"

"Everything seems, well, so laid on."

"Just because you've had one very fine day with the wind in the right direction and the boat in top shape, don't go jumping to ideas of perfection. The wind's bound to shift—it always does—and we'll be slammed by a northwest blow or be socked in by a pea-soup fog and you'll change your tune."

"I am waiting for the hitch."

"One day, madam, you've just had one day."

"Yes, Alex. Subject closed."

The subject of too much perfection came up again, however, when they returned aboard and went to their cabin to make ready for dinner.

Their cabin was its own kingdom, repeating all the comforts of the general living quarters. Every inch of space was managed for maximum use and comfort. Little drawers, designed to stay closed if the boat pitched, when lifted slightly, slid forward, and teak rails held objects safe on every top surface and along the bunkside shelves. Daylight filtered into the cabin from a large, translucent overhead hatch cover and from two very large portholes above the port bunk, while ship's lamps depended over two comfortable chairs fitted into the space at the foot of the twin bunks.

Sarah pointed out the reading lights and the tiny built-in radio-tape decks with earphones fitted in over each bunk. "All the amenities. And look at those." She nodded at their bunkside tables, on each of which lay a small navy blue leather Bible with the image of a pilgrim stamped in gold in its lower corner. "Bible and bathroom, body and soul all cared for."

"Running hot and cold," said Alex, ducking into and then emerging from a small doorway forward of the bunks. "Our own head, no people groping their way past your berth to the john in the middle of the night. A shower stall, sea toilet, sink, and huge towels."

"With PILGRIM written on them?" asked Sarah. "Honestly. And look at those." She pointed to a hanging teak bookcase across the cabin bulkhead. A row of just-published hardbacks, including a Jan Morris travel book, a Margaret Drabble, and a Lewis Thomas—for Alex, no doubt, along with a new Stephan Jay Gould—and for general excitement, the just-out John Le Carré and a Jane Langton, plus a row of older mysteries, including a Rider Haggard and John Buchan's *The Thirty-Nine Steps*. For those times when real meat was wanted, there was a copy of the *Odyssey* and Boswell's *Life of Johnson*. In a rack below the bookcase was a lineup of current magazines.

"Blimey," said Sarah. "Where are the fruit baskets and the chocolates, the telegrams and Fred Astaire and Ginger Rogers and the sixty-piece orchestra?"

"Well, here are the chocolates, anyway," said Alex. He opened a drawer and indicated several little boxes labeled HAR-BOR SWEETS. "It's time you got away from the mainland. Your past life as an amateur detective has poisoned you. Enjoy, live it up, for tomorrow . . ."

"We die?" finished Sarah. "And I've never been a detective; I'm an accident crime-prone English teacher, as George Fitts would be the first to say. I intend to reform, read novels and roll in the monogrammed sheets and sail away to the land where the Bong-Tree grows."

"And there in the wood . . ."

"A Piggy-wig stood. Yes, okay, I've said that I'm thinking about wedding rings. So should you be. Serious thinking."

Sarah sat down suddenly on her bunk. It was as if former promises and plans had risen from the bottom of the sea to remind her of what had gone before; as if two long-gone shadows had suddenly darkened the cabin with their warning presence. For a moment, Sarah held her breath and closed her eyes and with an effort pushed the faded figures of those two young men back into the past where they belonged. Then she shook herself slightly and stretched out a hand to Alex.

"You know I'm scared of the idea. Marriage. I've been on the edge of it twice before and you know what happened. They're both dead. Pres and Philip both."

"Sarah, you didn't kill them. It was bad, dumb luck. Their dying had absolutely nothing to do with you. I know that somewhere beyond your rational self, you think that you're sort of a fatal attraction but that is—if you'll pardon my saying it—a lot of crap. No wait, listen. Attraction, yes. I'll go along with that. Fatal? I say bullshit."

Sarah sat silent for a moment. The shadows receded and the cabin was once again a glowing, comfortable space. She stood up and kissed him. "All right," she said, trying for a light touch, "you just keep yourself safe and I'll be thinking about weddings."

"Good, but think later. There's a gong. As in drink and dinner gong. I feel as if I should climb into a stiff shirt and black tie."

"The Fitzgerald experience. And the eyes of Doctor T. J. Eckleburg upon us."

Not the T. J. Eckleburg but the questionable Billy Brackett. He stood in the corner of the cockpit staring down into the shadow of the companionway, so that anyone coming on deck met his gaze—a gaze without eye contact, without significance. And Sarah remembered Fitzgerald's description of Doctor Eckleburg's blue eyes "dimmed a little by many paintless days under sun and rain," which brooded over a valley of ashes and a small foul river. Billy stood unmoving, head slightly tilted, one arm slipped around a stay as if for support.

David Mallory jumped down from the main deck, where he

had been fiddling with some sail stops: the genial host in action.

"I know you've met Ezra; have you met Billy Brackett? Gracie's brother, or half brother."

"We had the same mother," murmured Gracie, giving Billy a worried look. "Mother married William Brackett, Sr."

"Yes, Gracie," said Mallory, waving away a possible genealogical detour. "Billy's been on his own for quite a while, but Gracie caught up with him in Florida. Felt he needed a change, fresh air, get his health back on track. So here he is, a crew member without too many duties, can help when he feels up to it. We'll leave the real muscle work to Ezra, Tony, and Andrea for the time being. Get you back in shape first, right, Billy?"

Sarah studied Billy to see how this description of his physical state was hitting him—and what reaction to Mallory's avuncular arm now across his shoulder. Not much reaction. A faint smile on the young man's face, the curving posture, the light blue eyes fixed on some undefined horizon.

David Mallory, with a nod at Gracie, went on with his thumbnail biography. Billy had apparently spent the summers of his youth on this very Islesboro, Billy's father having a house on the island. Billy's father was now dead.

"As is Mother," said Gracie. "It's very sad."

David, undeflected, sketched in other events of Billy's past, his leaving college (the college unnamed), a long illness (also nameless), Gracie to the rescue, her idea of taking Billy on the cruise. Then, Mallory standing, glass raised, called to everyone to join him in a toast to celebrate the beginning of the cruise.

Finding the description of Billy's life less than gripping, Sarah looked about and saw Gracie, brows contracted, watching Billy, her busy hands squeezing a cocktail napkin into a moist ball. Yes, Billy worries Gracie, said Sarah to herself, but now the arrival of drinks broke off further judgments.

The drinks were served in the cockpit under the green canvas awning while Andrea passed little toasted crab puffs and spiced carrot sticks. She was now a picture of stylish modesty in a loose yellow coverall, her blond hair pulled back and held into a knot by a thin gold chain. The bar scene was handled by Ezra, wearing white trousers and the green *Pilgrim* shirt. He stood, braced against the slight harbor swell, shaking up David's favorite rum and crushed lime drink in a competent manner, once winking in a companionable way at Sarah when she accepted her frosted glass.

Then dinner at 7:30. The table, pulled out from some inner recess, was set with handsome white plates rimmed by a running *Pilgrim* script and a full complement of silver and wineglasses. Andrea and Ezra brought steaming pots of mussels, bottles of white wine, and a crusty loaf of French bread to the table. Tony filled the glasses, and then—obviously used to the routine—the members of the *Pilgrim* bowed their heads. Alex and Sarah followed suit, Sarah withdrawing her hand guiltily from her napkin.

David Mallory in his rich deep voice asked a blessing on their repast and on their voyage to come and gave thanks for the pleasures of new friends—Alex, Sarah—and the presence of old companions and wound up with that old standby, "Bless O Father Thy gifts to our use."

They began their excellent dinner, although Sarah, as she let the first mussel slip down her throat, wondered about red tide. Hadn't there been a warning in the papers, no clams, mussels, whelks, carniverous snails (whatever they were) or other shellfish to be taken on certain parts of the coast? She paused in mid-mussel, thinking that this was perhaps a new and imaginative way of doing away with guests, when David Mallory turned to Andrea.

"Marvelous, what did you do to them? Not from a red-tide area, I hope?"

Andrea shook her head. "From east of Blue Hill, guaranteed. I checked particularly." She went on to describe cooking the mussels in butter, shallots, and vermouth, and told them to be careful of the pearls. Her soft lisping voice and downcast eyes would have done justice to a Victorian maiden whose parents had kept her at home through her school years. Sarah watched her through the subsequent course of fettuccine, eggplant, and tossed salad. She tried to reconcile what Alex had told her about Andrea to this vision of virgin restraint. Tony, Sarah saw, was increasingly afflicted with her; he was unnaturally silent, rotating his wineglass and mashing his fettuccine and folding and refolding his napkin.

After Alex and David began a comparison of voyage books starting with Shackleton, Sarah decided, rather reluctantly, to try Billy Brackett, at her left. She had noticed that he wasn't eating, just moving his food about on his plate. An expert since childhood on pretending to eat unwanted food, Sarah admired from the corner of her eye the deftness with which he covered fettuccine with two or three unopened mussel shells. Well, since he wasn't eating, he might talk, although she felt it might be like conversing with a shade who had floated in from the underworld.

"The *Pilgrim*'s a beautiful boat, isn't she?" Certainly a safe remark.

Billy looked at her and then let his glance slide over her shoulder. "Of course. Are you surprised? If you are, you don't know David Mallory. Persona perfecto. Six-inch foam mattresses, matching upholstery. Hotel Splendide. Designer soap and chocolates and your own Bible. High life on the bounding main. And gourmet meals."

"Are you enjoying this particular gourmet meal?"

"No. But I can look as if I enjoyed it, can't I?"

Was he drunk? No, he sat quietly, not swaying, not fumbling, his articulation clear. Drugged? Possibly. Yet he seemed to be saying more or less what she herself had been saying to Alex only a short while before. With a side glance, she took in the thin face, the transparent skin that looked almost like an X-ray film, revealing the skull beneath. And at Billy's throat at the edge of his shirt, a glint of silver: a silver metal chain. A crucifix? Sarah wondered. A Roman Catholic presence in the midst of all this hearty Protestant zeal?

"The secret," said Billy in his high whistling voice, "is to create the sense of fork and knife in motion. To reach for the wine or water glass. Masticate."

"And hide fettuccine under mussel shells."

"Exactly." Billy seemed faintly pleased. "And slip these egg-plant strips under the lettuce leaves. No one thinks about lettuce not being eaten—it's a throwaway food—but the eggplant takes time to prepare; people are worried if you don't eat specially prepared food."

"Do you do this for all your dinners?"

"All dinners prepared by alien hands. I have a nice protein drink that gets me through the day. Safe food for safe people."

"What do you mean, 'alien hands'?" Are you expecting a Borgia in the galley?"

"Ah, the Borgias, what fine family feeling. Now I will crumble the French bread—bread is another throwaway—and it will cover some of the mussels. Then I will raise a wineglass to my lips and pretend to take an appreciative sip. So, no more questions. I want to think."

Sarah subsided. As a dinner partner, Billy wouldn't win a prize, but it had been interesting. She looked across the table and saw Gracie Mullen leaning forward, watching Billy, her lips forming a concerned oval. Then, meeting Sarah's eyes, Gracie smiled and returned her gaze to her dinner plate, a plate almost as untouched as Billy Brackett's.

From Billy, Sarah turned to Ezra, on her right, and found him ready for talk. She began with sailing. She rolled out the subject and listened as he expounded on marine novels that made sense because the writer had actually been at sea. She tried other gambits—home, birthplace, family—but found the subjects tossed lightly back with a quip, a humorous allusion, then a blank wall. Born in Ireland, lived all over, especially around the U.K. Nothing much in his life to brag about, liked his job, hoped he was good at it. Liked working for Mr. Mallory, always knew where you stood, got respect. At first, Sarah thought she could hear, as she slogged on with her questions, the accent becoming thicker, but perhaps that was the wine. Ezra didn't stint himself.

As he talked on, however, Sarah found herself listening carefully—though not that hers was an ear noted for picking up finer points of U.K. accents—and decided she'd caught a major shift. The Irish-American singsong had taken on a burr and the heavy sound of Yorkshire, well known to Sarah from Public TV's "All Creatures Great and Small." Then as Ezra reached again for the wine bottle, Sarah heard the voice slide south to Liverpool and then travel along to Cornwall. She sat tense, trying to pick out each shift of vowel, each hard or soft consonant, trying to remember some of the finer points of a course in linguistics. The man seemed to have no vocal root or core to him—a verbal mishmash.

"And so," Ezra went on, the voice moving to London and having trouble with its haiches, "I 'ear you're an Hinglish teacher."

Sarah felt that a shifting accent didn't seem like a signal flag but it was worth a small probe.

"You don't sound a bit Irish now. Did you live in London?"

"Ah well, now," said Ezra with another of his sly winks, "I'm a bloody fraud. You've got an ear on you, but it's like this, you see."

"Like what?" demanded Sarah, hearing the voice return to the auld sod.

"'Tis a fraud I am. I was only in Ireland 'till I was twelve or so. Father was a salesman, sold a line of machine parts, and the job kept him moving. Yorkshire, Cornwall, London, stretch of time in Scotland, then to the States. I don't have any accent· you can hang your hat on. I'm a chameleon, see. Pick up voices. You should hear me in the south. It's a fair treat to see the folks trying to decide if I'm from Alabama or Louisiana."

"Some people do pick up accents," agreed Sarah, not satisfied but thinking that too much was being made of the matter. She swiveled to the other end of the table and discovered that the conversation there had stopped and Mallory had been listening to them.

He leaned over and clapped Ezra on the shoulder. "This guy's an embarrassment. Goes right into native song and dance wherever we are. In Florida, he's just off the boat from Cuba and before you know it, he'll sound like an old Maine salt."

With this, the talk became general with the exception of Billy, who appeared to be studying the port cabin bulkhead.

Andrea said that she wished she could do accents, would have liked to have tried college acting. Gracie said that once she'd taken a public-speaking course so as to overcome nerves connected with making reports. David Mallory speculated on the ability to hear certain vowel combinations shown by philologists who could pick up seven or eight linguistic influences. From there, the talk rambled into comparisons of regional pronunciations, and then Sarah turned to Andrea and asked her whether she'd really been interested in college theatre.

Andrea became shy and tentative. The evening had turned cool and she had wrapped herself in a long, soft white cardigan and looked like a twelve-year-old angel in a Christmas play. She shook her head apologetically. She'd only gone to junior college, hadn't been that crazy about structure, mandatory courses, hadn't had a good self-image. Spent a lot of time batting around wondering who she was. Maybe it'd been a mistake, maybe it was time to go back now that she was mature, could handle structure. Time to do some reading. Real reading.

"The kind, you know, you always put off, unless you're an English major." (Here a shy little smile with eye appeal.) There were, she knew, a whole bunch of novels, those *great books* about which her family was always bugging her. After all, her parents had been pretty neat about a lot of things for which she'd never given them credit.

Sarah smiled and nodded but inwardly muttered to herself. She could not believe that Andrea was about to flower before them as a lover of literature as well as a dutiful daughter who now realized the value of her parents' advice.

"I brought *War and Peace* and *Anna Karenina* and Dostoevski," said Andrea. "Dad said start there and everything would fall in place."

"Your parents bug you about reading?" asked Tony, obviously finding this idea attractive. "God, I know what you mean. Can't take you for your own person. Probably haven't read a new book since *The Scarlet Letter*. I mean, some books are almost dead to contemporary experience."

"You don't think I should give in and read *War and Peace?*"

asked Andrea, raising her dark gray eyes and lowering her lashes at Tony. "I'd like to be up front with them about it."

"Oh sure," said Tony. "The Russians are mostly okay. But just to be dragging through someone else's reading list. Are your parents pretty heavy? Do they really stress you out on achievement the way mine do?"

Here Tony turned away from Sarah and she could hear him murmuring to Andrea, explaining, giving an instant and inaccurate life history of the Deane family while sympathetic little bubbles rose from Andrea. Sarah had not decided whether to leap into the fray and defend her family and her memory of Tony's childhood as a most-favored only son, when Billy surfaced again. Sarah had to lean close because his voice did not carry over the general rumble of voices. Billy spent no time on general amenities.

"Why did you come on this cruise?" Sarah noticed that although Billy still avoided direct eye contact, he had shifted his gaze from her shoulder to her brow.

"I was invited. By David Mallory, because Alex knows the Maine coast and my brother is part of the crew. I don't see Tony very often; it's a chance to catch up."

"I don't think you're going to see Tony very often on this trip."

This was a fair prediction, but Sarah wasn't going to discuss Tony's present preoccupation. "I'm enjoying myself. Aren't you?"

"Certainly. Isn't that what I'm meant to do? Shall we talk about books? You're an English teacher. We could combine two subjects. Sea books. Man against the elements. Man against the leviathan. Do you teach those? *Moby Dick?*"

"Yes, *Moby Dick. Two Years Before the Mast*—Dana's boat was called the *Pilgrim*, did you know? And Conrad, of course."

"Of course. All that business about immersing yourself in the destructive element. Such bad advice; I try to avoid destructive elements."

"The idea was to keep afloat in it."

"I don't try. *The Secret Agent* is my favorite Conrad novel."

"Which isn't about ships and the ocean."

"What's the difference, really? Are you also interested in bringing the word of God to the benighted and playing drug spy?"

"I'm only interested in sailing with Alex and Tony."

"And Uncle Tom Cobbleigh and all. Change of subject. Slightly. I used to learn nautical poetry. When young. Not the 'Give me a tall ship and a star to steer her by' stuff but 'Yo ho ho and a bottle of rum, fifteen men on a dead man's chest.' Real blood and guts in iambic pentameter—or is it anapaestic?"

Sarah was starting to wonder whether Billy was stoned and suicidal as well as being ill and possibly psychotic to boot. Anyway, she didn't have to work very hard at a rational conversation.

"When I was very small—a prodigy in fact—I learned all the brave battle poems. My father's copy of *Golden Numbers*. 'The Burial of Sir John Moore.' 'The Burial of Moses.' Lots of burials. 'We buried him darkly at dead of night/The sods with our bayonets turning.' Stuff like that. But then I moved away from battles, put away childish things, went for the classics. You know Keats, that great beginning of 'Ode to a Nightingale'?"

"Yes," said Sarah warily.

"All about 'how a drowsy numbness pains/My sense as though of hemlock I had drunk,/Or emptied some dull opiate to the drains. . .'"

"Are you saying that Keats wanted to take drugs?" demanded Sarah.

"Didn't he? Don't you? Don't we all? Aren't we all a little besotted—what did he say, 'half in love with easeful Death'?"

"Why don't you just leave Keats in peace," said Sarah crossly.

"All right. How about Baudelaire? Do you know 'The Voyage'? My French is rusty, let's see if I can translate that bit near the end—

> '*les hardis amants de la Démence:*
> The fearless lovers of madness,
> Flee the great herd shut up by fate,
> And find refuge in the great opium!
> —That's the eternal bulletin from the whole world'"

"How interesting," said Sarah, as unpleasant images of skulls, death, dope, and corruption jostled in her head.

"I like these lines," said Billy. "'O Death, old captain, it's time! Raise anchor,/We tire of the land, O Death, let us be underweigh!' Anyway, it goes on to suggest that we drink poison to revive and dive into the great unknown. Hell or heaven. Who cares."

"Don't you care?" said Sarah.

"What do you think? What do you care? For instance, do you think I'm on this cruise for my health?"

"Aren't you?" said Sarah. "Haven't you been sick?" Perhaps she should let Billy talk about it. Sick people often wanted to ventilate. The poetry had certainly suggested some of the things on Billy's mind. That is, if he had enough of a mind left with which to work.

Billy seemed to consider. He leaned back against the uphol-stered bench and studied his artfully arranged plate. "What's sick, what's well? Yes, I suppose I am. Sick. For better or worse, till death us do part. Sick. Infirm, debilitated, off-color, indis-posed, not quite the thing, in a fragile state. What an incredibly boring topic."

He paused, picked up his knife and balanced it for a moment on his forefinger and then let it drop to the table. "Incredibly boring," he repeated, and since Sarah, after murmuring that she was sorry, was silent—what was there to say—Billy simu-lated a sip of wine and went on. "Don't be sorry. For me? Don't be ridiculous; you don't know me. How about you? Perhaps you're here for your health. Along with brother Tony's health and Dr. McKenzie's health. Physician heal thyself. Or how about Captain David Mallory?"

Here, Billy dropped his voice an octave and spoke in the voice of David Mallory. It was uncanny, the voice, intonation, the ecclesiastical baritone together with the lifting of the chin and stretching of the mouth into a benevolent smile. Sarah felt the hair on her arms rise.

"David Mallory," continued Billy in David's voice. "The man of the Good Book. I will lift up mine eyes unto the hills whence cometh my help and I will dwell in the house—make that the boat—of the Lord forever. King Arthur Mallory or Mallory's King Arthur and his nautical round table." Billy paused, cleared his throat, and said in a high, tentative, familiar woman's voice, "And our servant Gracie, now, Billy, behave yourself and what fun we're having here on the great big ocean doing all these good works. Gracie, shall we call her Morgan le Fey, Hail Morgan Full of Grace, Blessed Art Thou. And Ezra? Sure and begorra, we've a man from auld Erin? Gawain the Green Irish knight? Calls himself an Irishman, a 'tis a foin laugh I'm after havin'." Billy dropped the brogue and said in his own voice, "And Billy, Will the Brackett. Shall I be Mordred. More dread. Quite a cast, right out of the Old Vic. Ta rah rah boom tee ay."

All at once, Sarah had had her fill of young Mr. Brackett. Whatever Billy was on or whatever was wrong with him, she had put in enough time for one evening. So he knew Baudelaire and could imitate the crew; it wasn't enough to keep her listening, although she did think that properly harnessed, Ezra and Billy might turn their hands to a two-man show—if Ezra could control his vocal roller coasting. She turned away and to her relief saw David Mallory hold up a bottle of brandy and call on everyone to move along to the sitting section of the main cabin and discuss plans for the morning.

"Gracie, Ezra, and I have church-related calls to make. Billy, too, if he cares to come." David deferred to his secretary, who sat, blue and white pumps neatly together, her blue and white flowered dress tucked neatly about her. She was sniffing, not drinking her brandy. Now she put the glass down carefully and slightly expanded her meager flowered chest with its little daisy watch and assumed an expression of alert efficiency. "The new pamphlets with the color-coded index. I have them all bundled with the children's cassettes, *Tales from the Old Testament*. And the fall schedules, of course."

David turned to Alex and Sarah. "Would you two like to spend the morning exploring? I can arrange for bicycles."

Sarah nodded. It was high time for brisk exercise, for mental regrouping. Alex spoke in favor of the bicycles and it was settled. Ezra excused himself to go on deck and check the mooring and the riding lights, and Andrea returned to the dining area to clear the table. Billy, rising slowly and seemingly without the assistance of bone or muscle, started to follow her and stopped. He was moved aside by Tony, who vanished after Andrea, and the listeners could hear dishes being clattered together. Billy subsided against a cushion and closed his eyes. Sarah suddenly felt she had to go to her cabin and be quiet. All the earlier fuss of packing and leaving home combined with her first day on the water and the strain of meeting new people propelled her out of her seat. She stood up, said good night hastily, had her hand patted by Gracie—"So glad you're with us"—a grin from Ezra, and an unexpectedly knowing look from the half-opened eyes of Billy. David Mallory rose and ushered her out of the main cabin, then detained her in the passageway.

"Billy, I hope he hasn't been bothering you." David leaned down to her, speaking in a whisper. "I was glad to see him opening up, talking to you, but he doesn't always make a great deal of sense."

Sarah agreed. "I had a little trouble following him, but he didn't really bother me." She searched for something positive to say. "He does seem very bright. He knows a lot of poetry and he can imitate anyone's voice. Have you heard him do Ezra?" She thought she could omit his re-creation of David's voice.

David grimaced and shook his head. He and Sarah were so close in the passageway that, with the whispering, it felt as if they were engaged in some shipboard conspiracy. "Yes, he's loaded with talent, but he's not entirely stable. A tease. Loves to joke, plays games with people. I'm afraid you can't believe much of what he says if he's in one of his moods."

Sarah, thinking with increased longing of her cabin, her bunk, those monogrammed sheets and soft blankets, listened with impatience.

"Don't misunderstand me," David went on doggedly. "We welcome anyone with sensitivity, anyone who takes an interest in the boy. He's been, well, so disconnected, from life, and then, not being well. . . . I had hoped that perhaps Tony might be a role model, but they don't seem to have much to say to each other."

Sarah remained silent—with difficulty. Lord, Tony as a role

model. Well, she could hardly go into Tony's lack of qualifications as an example for wayward youth. Mallory was his employer.

Fortunately, David seemed to have run out of steam. "Just don't take Billy seriously," he finished rather lamely, and then added, "I think he was an English major—when he was still in college—so he sees you as someone he can be open with. And now I know you're dying to go off to bed."

Sarah admitted this, pleaded the day's fatigue, and hurried forward toward her cabin. As she undressed, she struggled to put down a rising sense of irritation, but whether it was from Mallory's little homily on Billy, or Billy's strung-out recitals, or from Andrea, or, perversely, the marvelous dinner, she did not know. And why was Andrea part of her discontent? Inwardly, she scolded herself. Just because Alex thought Andrea was a sexpot, did she, Sarah, have to go along with it, to question the girl's every look, every word? Hadn't she herself pointed out that Andrea probably had a fine working brain encased in that splendid body? And Tony could always be guaranteed to raise hackles. She, Sarah, should settle down to something as worthwhile as *War and Peace*, and then she and Andrea could sit up on the deck and groove about Moscow and the Bezukhovs, the Rostovs, and the Bolkonskis.

This resolve resulted in Sarah picking up the copy of the *Odyssey* from their cabin collection and ignoring the Jane Langton she had wanted to read. However, this scholarly choice that went on and on about pillage and usurpation did not bring peace. Even the wrapped chocolates in the shape of little sailboats in her cabin drawer suggested an old mystery favorite, *The Poisoned Chocolates Case*. Strychnine, wasn't it, inserted into the bottom of the chocolate with a syringe? She turned over her half-eaten chocolate, looking for a puncture at its bottom.

"Good stuff," said Alex thickly through a chocolate-filled mouth. He had followed her to the cabin and, untouched by the *great books* influence, had settled down with *The Thirty-Nine Steps* while the radio gave out with the eighth-inning news from Fenway Park.

For a moment, Sarah studied Alex, with his strong bone-shaped face, his long mouth, dark eyebrows, good chin. Alex, so happily unlike Billy Brackett. He lay on his bunk under the navy blue PILGRIM blanket, the light blue sheet turned over the top. Sarah saw that he wore his new white cotton pajamas piped in red—he usually slept in the buff but had made the purchase from some sense that he might be called topside in the middle of the night; as had Sarah, who now lay swathed in pink checked pajamas, a costume she thought more suitable for the sudden abandoning of ship than her usual granny nightgown.

The muted light from the bunk lamps shone on the teak bulkhead and the pristine pillows. The *Pilgrim*, rocking gently at its mooring, transferred the motion in velvet undulations to the bunks, so that Sarah felt she was being cradled in the arms of some giant nurse. Above her bunk, the porthole formed an oval frame for the night sky, a sky strung with stars. She put down her book and knelt under the porthole. Two sloops in black profile, their riding lights high in their rigging, marked out the edges of the harbor. In the sky, the Little Dipper poured itself into the Big Dipper. And was that Draco bending his head over Vega? Nothing seemed real, to belong to the earth, neither time nor place. Not herself. Not Alex. Turning back to the cabin, she saw them both as alien dummies in their still-new, creased pajamas under their new monogrammed bed covers.

She sighed and turned back to the *Odyssey*, but reading the references to Lotus Eaters and Circe acted like a burr in her brain by bringing her back to the possible enchantment of the *Pilgrim*'s passengers. Billy was clearly over the edge, but what about the rest of them? The enchantment of her brother, for instance. Not that she begrudged him Andrea—or Andrea him—but how long had he known her? Twenty-four hours. Well, she supposed they would very soon, tonight perhaps, be enjoying one bunk, kicking off the monogrammed blankets and sporting in the fitted sheets. So be it, but she hoped that the bulkheads were soundproof. To that end she knocked sharply on the cabin partition that divided them from the crew's quarters.

"Are you looking for secret panels?" asked Alex.

"Testing the wood. I'm interested in the seaworthiness of various materials."

"Like hell you are," said Alex. He switched off his light and, reaching across to Sarah, caught her hand and pulled her, unresisting, into his bunk.

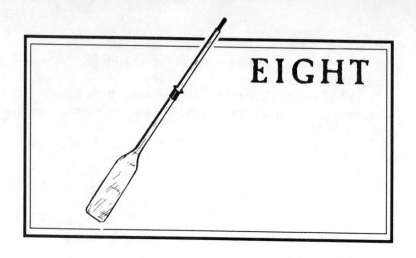

EIGHT

THE NEXT MORNING AFTER BREAKFAST, SARAH JOINED Alex on the forward deck with a second mug of coffee. "Tony," she said, "has turned himself into a walkie-talkie on one frequency: Andrea's."

"So I notice," said Alex. "But David's being understanding."

"Too understanding. Sometimes he has to repeat himself before Tony even turns around. What if he calls to abandon ship and Tony's in such a fog he doesn't hear?"

"David probably thinks Tony will pull out of it, get used to her. Doesn't want to start yelling at your brother the second day out. But it's not your problem."

Sarah considered for a minute and then said, "Andrea's too good to be true."

"What's that supposed to mean?"

"I don't know. Maybe it's all too good to be true. Except Billy, who may be too bad to be true. And Gracie, she's in a disapproving fidget over Billy."

"Protect and preserve me from literary ladies."

"It's just that . . ." She rose to her feet and watched a small outboard that buzzed past the *Pilgrim*'s bow, missing the big mooring ball by inches. Then holding on to a stay, she peered over the rail—and hastily backed away. "Jellyfish. Yuck. As big as a cauliflower, all brownish red."

Alex joined her, looking down into the water with a pleased expression. "Now that's something worth talking about. Lion's mane or *cyanea capillata*. Biggest of all, sometimes run to as much as eight feet across. But this one's a good size."

Sarah made a face. "Good enough size to take care of any interest in swimming. Does it sting?"

Alex, happy to move the conversation into another vein, launched into a lecture on medusae, lobes, tentacles, and mouth arms, winding up with an enthusiastic summary of sea nettles and sea wasps and problems of tentacles that kept their stinging power long after being beached.

"But not to worry," he added, "even the Portuguese man-of-war sting isn't that dangerous. I don't know of any really documented fatalities in New England unless the reaction is an allergic one. The man-of-war only turns up accidentally off the Maine coast, so you only have to worry about the lion's mane, and it's relatively harmless."

"I love the expression *relatively harmless*. People say it about bears and rattlesnakes."

"So relax. No bears or rattlesnakes in the North Atlantic. The only thing that might get you swimming here is hypothermia."

"Or sharks," added Sarah. "I'd forgotten about sharks."

"Keep forgetting. Sharks won't bother the *Pilgrim*. Mallory wouldn't let them. Let's go below for our radio lesson."

The navigation-station door stood open and David Mallory stood with Gracie, ready for a tutorial.

"Everyone should know how to call the marine operator," he said. He smiled up at Sarah and Alex. "How about it, Sarah, would you like to make your practice call?"

So Sarah was instructed in the mysteries of marine radio, when to depress the button and talk, when to let it up and receive. She was placed before the instrument and gave *Pilgrim*'s call letters of Whiskey Romeo Delta 6677 and Mary's telephone number, and presently heard Mary's voice responding to the operator's "Stand by for a marine radio call."

"Mary, hello, we're having a good time," said Sarah tentatively.

"I can't hear you," said Mary.

"Push the button to speak," said Alex.

"A good time," repeated Sarah.

"Bully for you," said Mary.

"Wonderful meals, lots of fun," said Sarah.

"Great."

"How is Patsy?"

"Patsy," replied Mary, "has just finished two of Amos's socks and the handle of his briefcase, and tries to sleep on our bed. It's been just groovy hearing from you and now there's someone at the door."

David Mallory finished the call for Sarah. "Camden Marine, this is *Pilgrim*. Finished with my call. WRD 6677 over and out."

The operator was chirpy. "Thank you, *Pilgrim*, have a nice day."

"Does everyone on the ocean," asked Sarah, "get wished a nice day?"

"Or a nice evening," said Gracie. "Those marine operators are just marvelous. They'll make calls and relay emergency information."

"That's all there is to it," said David. "As I told you, I've a duplicate system and a little portable battery set in my cabin, so we're set for any emergency. Which I sincerely hope we won't have. Now, I've arranged the bikes. Go on and explore. Ezra will take Billy and deliver church publications—we've arranged for a delivery van—and Gracie and I have a car waiting. We're going first to the other end of the island, a new congregation, Church of the Island. Tiny group, but growing. They have a program for the handicapped."

Then, thought Sarah, if Mallory is busy all day, I might even have a chance to see Tony alone, catch up on his life.

But it was not to be. David Mallory waved at the inn, a welcoming white building that looked over a sloping lawn. "They don't usually serve lunch but I've made special arrangements. One-thirty, you two and Gracie. Tony's going to work on the deck and Andrea will be off buying groceries. Put some fresh clothes in a bag and I'll have Ezra leave them at the desk for you."

Sarah made herself smile. "How nice." She turned her attention to the motor whaleboat that now was being lowered from the stern davits for the shore-bound church party. Several stacks of cartons marked PRAYERS FOR THE SEEING-IMPAIRED and SELECTIONS FROM THE NEW TESTAMENT IN BRAILLE stood on the *Pilgrim*'s deck. These certainly did more than any perfect stateroom or gourmet meal to underscore the honest purpose of the *Pilgrim* and its crew.

For a few minutes, Sarah watched while Andrea, Tony, and Ezra in fireman's brigade fashion lifted and swung and stowed the cartons in the whaleboat. Watching the activity, Billy Brackett sat on the afterdeck, his legs dangling over the side. Once when Tony dropped a carton, Billy unexpectedly laughed; a high, jagged laugh, like a giggle gone out of control, which stopped as suddenly as it had begun, and Billy's mobile face tightened like a drum skin after the little explosion. Billy had a voice for all occasions, as he had amply proved; but, Sarah wondered, did he also have several laughs? Before she had time to consider this possibility, she saw Billy suddenly stick out a foot as Tony came across the deck. Tony sprawled forward, the carton shooting out of his arms, and for a moment Sarah thought her brother was going to turn and shake the life out of Billy, but then, red-faced, he tightened his shoulders and turned away.

Later, as she and Alex rowed the Avon raft to shore, Sarah remarked that Billy was not only weird but absolutely dangerous. "He's the kind that pulls practical jokes that hurt people just for the pleasure of it all."

"Stay clear of him, then," said Alex. "But you should be reassured about the *Pilgrim*. The whole Bible operation looks pretty solid, part of the perfection you're complaining about. So relax and and concentrate on having a nice tough bike ride."

"I do need exercise, all that food." Sarah, who had asked for the oars, gave an extra pull, spun the Avon in a circle, and flopped down onto the rubbery raft floor. Recovering, she pulled hard and bumped against an Islesboro Inn float.

"Bicycles?" queried Sarah. "David said he reserved them."

"He arranged for two to be left at the inn for us."

Sarah allowed Alex to lead the way, identify himself to a personage at the desk, who indicated the front of the inn, where two bicycles stood with tags marked PILGRIM. New bicycles. All-terrain numbers with fifteen gears, plus helmets hanging from the handlebars and water bottles fastened to the frames.

"Don't say it," called Alex as they wheeled down West Shore Drive. "You'd feel a lot better if the bikes were old, rusty one-speed clunkers with coaster brakes. Right?"

"Right."

"Don't give up, maybe you'll have a flat or the derailer will fall apart."

Sarah, not deigning to answer, sped away, and for an hour or so they both devoted themselves to speed. Heads low, backs level, they shot around Shipyard Point Road, spun around Dark Harbor, over to East Shore Drive, back to Main Road and to the end of County Road, turned, and, panting, ended up at the Alice L. Pendleton Memorial Library. Locked. "Open afternoons," said Sarah, reading the notice.

"You need a book?" asked Alex, who was examining a map of the island. "The *Odyssey* isn't holding you?"

"I like to visit libraries."

"Come on, we haven't much time. We've got to make it back to the Islesboro Inn by one-thirty. If we get moving, we can do a spot of bird-watching."

"You do a spot. I think I'll keep spinning. See you for lunch."

Alex nodded agreeably and each took off with renewed vigor. Sarah, with no particular destination in mind, turned her bicycle and headed down on the Main Road that sliced through the middle of Islesboro.

It was almost her last ride.

Sarah saw the truck coming down behind her like a missile. At first, aware that the road gave a free view of any vehicle and that she was well on the margin, she did nothing except keep a resolute straight track. The truck, a green pickup, was almost on her back, almost grazing her shoulder, before she realized that she might be tossed into the air. And killed.

She turned her wheel savagely, an acute turn that caught her tire in the sandy edge of the road, which sent the bicycle spinning and over, and Sarah into a spread-eagle dive into the overgrown ditch.

Alive. Unhurt. Only a few scratches, a line of grease from the grazing bicycle chain, a torn pocket on her shorts. She picked herself up slowly, hauled the bicycle from a mass of alders, and with trembling hands pulled the chain back on its derailer. For a moment, she stood gripping the bicycle handlebars, her whole body shaking as if buffeted by a strong wind. Yet she had no real sense of shock. It had happened too fast.

In fact, it was only after she had pushed her bike back on the road and seen her island map spread flat on the pavement, the dirty marks of a tire track diagonally across it, that she realized how narrow a miss she had had. An accident? One of those ubiquitous pickup trucks that rocket around the islands and coast of Maine with hee-hawing occupants. Put the scare into the tourists, screw them, trash them, send them home.

Except. Except Sarah could swear that one of the faces she had seen in a thousandth of a second flash, turning toward her from the truck window at the last minute, was Billy's. Billy the semi-invalid who should be helping Ezra; Ezra, that perfect first mate. Ezra and Billy who were church-bound with inspirational material. Was the face like Billy's in the driver's seat or in the passenger seat? Who was the driver? She'd been too frightened, too busy getting out of the way to notice. Did Mallory own, or had he hired, a green pickup? Did Ezra or Billy own a green pickup? David had said something about a van. What the hell was going on? Or was it her own brain that was going on? On and on, right off the rails.

No, be logical. Billy might be up for tripping people but would he—or anyone—choose a pickup truck for a practical joke. Or worse, select murder by pickup truck as an efficient way of doing someone in. Billy was very bright; that had been established. And if Ezra was in charge of a murder, she thought the affair would be well conceived, private, and adroit. And certainly without spaced-out Billy as an adjunct. The whole idea was ridiculous because hit-and-run was a messy, never-certain affair. It had to be some horrible practical joke.

But. But why not some research? Basic research. A judicious private telephone call or two. She needn't tell Alex, who felt that she was always overreacting. However, after the close brush with the truck, she felt like action, something more substantive than just riding aimlessly around making herself a target for another near miss. And the telephone? Wasn't there one near the Dark Harbor Shop where she and Alex had considered ice cream cones? Okay, she was due back in that direction for lunch, anyway. The trouble was, she told herself, a suspicious nature like hers revived without much nourishment.

Back in Dark Harbor in the telephone kiosk, Sarah caught Mary on her way to a faculty meeting.

"You called this morning," Mary said, "and I'm in a hurry."

"I'm on a regular pay phone. Listen, I just want to quiet my nerves and get some reassuring information. First hit the alumni office and see if a William Brackett went to Bowmouth and if he did, what happened to him. It's a long shot, but he spent summers on Islesboro, so he might have gone there. Then for the hell of it, get me a rundown on David Mallory. Did he really go to Bowmouth, what kind of a record, activities? The works. And keep it quiet."

"You don't want much. I've got a class to teach at two and the Record Office probably doesn't have an open season on old grads."

"I'm counting on you."

"I thought Mallory was Captain Marvel. Are you having moist palms, because I really am up to my ears."

"Mary, please. Mallory probably *is* Captain Marvel and I'm more interested in Billy. Humor me. I'll try and call you after your class. Maybe around four."

"Have you forgotten? Your call goes through the department switchboard. You might as well send out announcements."

"Think of something. Wing it."

"Wing yourself. Good-bye, I've got to go."

"Thank you, Mary." This to the sound of a slammed receiver.

Sarah was about to set off again when she decided that there would be no harm in finding out whether David Mallory and company really visited churches or whether they were busy hiring pickup trucks to knock off or frighten boat passengers. She looked through the island directory and dialed the first church listed there—St. Anne of the Ocean, nondenominational.

The answering voice responded to Sarah's question about the availability of inspirational material for the blind by telling her that the word *blind* was incorrect. "It's the seeing-impaired and, such a coincidence, we expect delivery of cassettes and several braille New Testaments today. We give them out for loan a week at a time, and we have volunteers who can instruct you in braille should you need it. May we have your name, dear?"

"Dora Spenlow," said Sarah without hesitation. "I'll be in touch," which bad and unplanned pun she hoped the voice would forgive.

Now she felt better, at least reassured about the legitimacy of the *Pilgrim*'s mission. As she pedaled back toward the inn, she again considered the possibility that she simply had been caught in some crazy game of chicken—with herself as chicken. One of the island wild men—with or without Billy—egged on by his buddies and a few beers. This last idea reinforced by a line of smashed brown bottles along the road.

She arrived back at the inn before Alex. Collecting her bundle of fresh clothes from the desk, she made her way to the ladies' room, which, miraculously, boasted a bathtub, and after considerable splashing and scrubbing, she managed to transform her disheveled self. Dressed, she gave a satisfied look in the mirror. Short dark hair neatly laid to rest, fresh white shirt, blue batik skirt, straw slip-on shoes, the whole entirely suitable for genteel summer lunching. And, except for a developing bruise along her chin, she would not be taken for a near-miss hit-and-run victim.

Not that she intended to neglect the subject, because she certainly needed to let someone know about a rogue pickup truck, especially if the driver or passenger happened to be Billy Brackett.

They sat, David Mallory's special guests, the only ones in the dining room, at a table overlooking a terrace and a border of flowers that complemented the inn's yellow awnings: daisies, blue salvia, lobelia, white impatiens, sweet alyssum. Beyond lay the harbor, and riding at her mooring, that perfect sloop, the *Pilgrim*.

And, thought Sarah, here we are, the perfect quartet of summer visitors. Alex, unnaturally formal in a seersucker jacket and his best paisley tie, and Mallory, on Gracie's right, massive and solid in a blue linen blazer, flushed and affable with a morning spent at good works. Gracie sat upright in a hostesslike posture, her gray hair in neat undulating waves, her white pop beads circling her neck, her angular figure draped in a pale cotton dress printed in a salad pattern of laced lettuce leaves.

Over a cup of chilled melon balls, David and Gracie chatted about the beauty of the island, the sadness and courage of the seeing-impaired, the marvels of braille, the happy invention of cassettes. The subject of two new guests—"old and dear friends, the Chandlers"—was introduced by David. They would be joining the *Pilgrim* on Thursday. "Flip and Elaine, such fun people."

Then Gracie, chirping up like a well-trained sparrow, asked about the bicycling. Had they enjoyed their morning?

Sarah, before Alex could answer, remarked that the bicycling had been terrific and that she'd almost been killed.

There was an appropriate pause, Alex dropped his napkin and scowled at her, David put down his spoon, and Gracie gasped.

Everyone spoke at once. Alex: "What the hell do you mean?" David: "Sarah, are you joking?" Gracie: "Oh dear, oh dear, oh dear."

"Not a joke and I'm still furious. Some yahoo in a pickup almost ran me down. Cowboying around, being funny I suppose."

She returned to her melon balls, while everyone reiterated concern. But when she raised her head and reached for the iced tea, Alex shot her a look that asked her as clearly as if he'd said it aloud, What have you been doing that you shouldn't? Sarah carefully selected a blueberry muffin from the basket on the table and considered. All right, might as well go all out, bring it to a boil.

"One of the men in the pickup—they were going by so fast that it was just an impression—looked like Billy, though I suppose it could have been anyone. I don't even know if that person with Billy's face was driving." Sarah carefully broke her muffin apart and buttered it. Then she sighed and said, "I'm sorry, Gracie, it was only a flash, it could have been a hundred people."

It was Alex who came to a boil. He stepped hard under the table into the middle of her instep. Sarah, choking on a bite of muffin, reached for her napkin. David shook his massive head, slowly, like a grieving lion, while Gracie, her face crumpled with distress—or was it anger—gave out a continual counterpoint of "Oh no, oh no."

"Billy was supposed to be with Ezra," said David. "I arranged a Sunday school van for their deliveries. Where would he find a pickup truck? Yes, I know Billy has friends here on the island, but remember Ezra was in charge and would never let Billy take a casual ride with local hoodlums."

Sarah was interested. She'd thought the word *hoodlum* had passed from the active language. She gave an encouraging nod. "It was just a face turned toward me. Perhaps I was mistaken."

"Perhaps you were," said Alex unpleasantly.

Sarah was saved from answering by David Mallory, who launched into yet another resumé of Billy's health, Gracie's concern, and a history of Ezra's trustworthy work in the service of David. This recitation, with many examples from life, lasted well through the salmon mousse.

"Naturally," he concluded, "we are worried about Billy. Gracie agrees, as I said last night, that he *is* unstable and entirely too casual about responsibility. But the bottom line is that I'm sure Billy would never do anything so foolish, so frightening."

"No indeed," said Gracie between tightened lips. "Billy is not aggressive; in fact, I can hardly persuade him to do anything, help with the meals or help keep us shipshape. Of course, he has his little jokes, nothing serious."

Jokes like pushing you and tripping Tony, Sarah said to herself. She looked over at Gracie and found her visibly fighting for control. Why, she really was in a state about him—or afraid of him.

"It may be a mistake; it was over in a minute," said Sarah, satisfied that if Billy's job of helping distribute church material included putting her on ice (as the Mafia put it) or just scaring the hell out of her, she had put him—via sister Gracie and Captain Mallory—on notice. Notice? Notice of what? Well, that she, Sarah, wasn't floating around in a fog of summer happiness. She was alert, ready. If not for head-on combat, bike against pickup, at least with pretty good avoidance reflexes.

David was still shaken. He spoke seriously of what he was doing on the *Pilgrim*, the alarming drug traffic around the islands, cocaine, crack, new compounds. He wanted Sarah and Alex to know that they were under no obligation to continue the trip if they had any reservations about the dual purpose of the cruise. There might be unforseen hazards, et cetera, et cetera.

Here, Sarah and Alex broke in and reassured him. They were passengers on the *Pilgrim*, for better or for worse, for the long haul. Although, Sarah added to herself, if Billy turned out to be part of the problem, the term *long haul* might be an understatement.

"Thank you both. I know we have a great many happy days ahead of us. The weather is marvelous and the report is for more sun and good winds." David smiled at each in turn, a warm, all-embracing smile. He reached across to Sarah's hand and gave it a squeeze, then touched Alex lightly on the shoulder. Very graceful, thought Sarah. She let her eyes move away from David's meaningful gaze and fix on the green lawn beyond the dining room, where someone was setting up croquet wickets. It was easy, looking at that stretch of lawn and the harbor beyond, to empty her head of anything but the comfort of a good lunch in pleasant summer surroundings.

She turned back to the luncheon table and found that the subject had turned to the possibility of swimming. Alex and

Sarah, said David, might enjoy an afternoon hike and cooling off on one of the beaches. The water was warming up; it had been in the middle sixties for the last few days. In fact, the church business wasn't quite wound up and he'd like to spend a second night in Islesboro—perhaps at a new mooring. They could sail around in the late afternoon and choose a quiet cove. Alex looked at Sarah, who had been wondering how she was going to work a second visit to the pay phone to call Mary.

"Swimming is a marvelous idea," she said. "I brought my bathing suit just in case."

Later, as the two walked down the path from the inn, Alex said, "You don't like swimming that much in cold water and offshore Maine water is frigid. And you didn't bring your bathing suit; it's hanging up on a hook back there on the *Pilgrim*. And why go on about a near accident and seeing Billy? *Did* you see him?"

"I honestly don't know. When you're about to be knocked into a ditch, you just get a flash. What I want to do is find myself near the telephone around four, so let's go swimming if the water's really in the sixties, then diddle around until it's time to call Mary. I'm hoping she's found something out about David Mallory. And maybe Billy."

"Sarah Deane, private eye. Ease up. So Billy is a problem— yes, I saw him trip Tony. Ask Gracie about her brother. Or better, go to David; he's been asking for your understanding in the matter. Remember the police and George Fitts have a complete profile on Mallory, and you know George. Complete means complete. George is satisfied and that's like satisfying Robespierre."

"Oh, Billy is a very long shot, but I'd rather do the checking by myself through Mary. Gracie is in a sweat about him and it might look like I'm sticking my nose—"

"You *are* sticking your nose."

"As for Mallory, I just thought Mary could rummage around in the Bowmouth College files and see if there's anything George might have missed. Student activities, fraternity-house records."

"Student riots and cocaine rings, you mean. Lay off, Sarah.

The man is an honorable citizen of the sovereign state of Florida. He's the pride of the Sarasota Chamber of Commerce, a prime candidate for a Church, God, and Country award."

"What you mean is that he's a Red Sox fan and can sail a boat and you're having a fine time. A blue-water sailor is above reproach. Remember what Tony said about being kept."

"And remember, my beloved, what you answered him. You said he asked for it. This cruise was your idea—a way to spend time with brother Tony. Have you even started to talk to him?"

"I'm having trouble breaking through the Andrea barrier."

"Okay, he's distracted, and he won't thank you for even saying hello to him, but keep trying. And I know you well enough to realize that this sudden revival of your detective instincts is a reaction to a close call with a pickup truck. You're just casting around. I think a swim will do wonders for you. The colder, the better. Let's try down there." Alex pointed ahead to a small path that led to a little sheltered cove with a pebble beach.

The ocean, as David Mallory had pointed out, was only semifrigid, and if the swimmer kept to the eight inches at the surface, moderate pleasure was possible. A tiny beach, away from cottages, allowed skinny-dipping. Alex took two snorting, shouting plunges, and then climbed out and dressed, intending to check for migrating warblers. Sarah paddled about in the shallows, then having reached the desirable state of numbness, she slithered up to a rock and put on her clothes. Alex emerged from a tangle of shore brambles, claiming a Cape May, two parula warblers, and "too many yellow rumps."

Together, they wheeled their bikes back to the road and turned toward Dark Harbor and the public telephone. "Just let me get this one call out of my system," shouted Sarah, passing him with a burst of speed, "and I'll be a model passenger."

Mary, when reached in her office in the English Department, reminded Sarah that she had a student appointment in five minutes.

"Okay, fine," said Sarah. "If there's nothing, I won't bother you again. And paraphrase if the whole department is plugged in."

"There is nothing. No William Brackett in the last fifteen

years and nothing much about Mallory. I didn't have alot of time and the Records people aren't dying to let me play around with their microfilms. Mallory has a B.A., a B-plus average, liberal-studies program, took a semester off his sophomore year, some sort of work-study deal. Abroad, somewhere or other. Headed the winter carnival follies one year, and at no time absconded with funds."

"Terrific."

"Isn't it?" What else? His picture in the yearbook is a little out of focus, he played soccer on the j.v., debate club for two years, drama club all four years, outing club. No takeovers of the chancellor's office, no record of molesting faculty children or starting fires in classrooms. As far as I can tell. Dullsville."

"How about church activities, chapel polisher?"

"He must have found God later. Nothing religious."

"Well, if anything turns up . . ."

"You're sunning yourself on a yacht, eating high on the hog, living the good life. Listen, come back to school and try teaching Intro Lit in the middle of a heat wave. Relax. Enjoy. Lay off."

"Best to Amos."

"He needs it. He got into a patch of poison ivy the other day and looks like something from *Journal of the Plague Year*."

Sarah hung up and reported to Alex, who was scanning a tree with his binoculars.

"Crossbills," he announced. "White-winged."

"No William Brackett at Bowmouth and David Mallory had an exemplary undergraduate record."

"Poor Sarah."

The rest of the day was uneventful. Sarah spent the late afternoon lying on the deck of the *Pilgrim*, turning the pages of the *Odyssey* and letting her mind drift with the soft afternoon wind. For a while the *Pilgrim* floated down wind out in the open ocean. Then she was turned back toward Gilkey Harbor and Ames Cove—home of the Tarratine Yacht Club. "Good holding here according to Alex—and the cruising guides," announced Mallory, "and not too far off shore."

The *Pilgrim*'s great anchor was dropped well off the club float, and the bow swung slowly into the dying air. Andrea and Tony brought drinks, cheese, and biscuits to the cockpit and took themselves off to sit on the forward deck. Sarah had just settled on the cockpit cushions when she found herself being watched by Billy Brackett. He had come up the companionway and draped himself across the hatch cover. He was dressed rather nattily in white trousers and shirt with large blue stripes. A cotton sport jacket hung loosely from his shoulders, but somehow the clothes emphasized the fragility of the man, and Sarah was reminded of pictures she had seen of Devil's Island inmates after they had completed a long sentence.

"I have been scolded and threatened, you wouldn't believe," said Billy in his high sibilant voice. "Sister Gracie is annoyed and our captain thinks I have been up to no good. Threatening Sarah, the fair maid from the Good Ship Lollipop."

"Well, have you?" demanded Sarah, twisting around and confronting Billy face-to-face.

"Why would I?" asked Billy softly. "Or why would I not? But King Arthur is not pleased, and I'm being sent off to a church supper to ponder on my possible sins. Ezra is to go as watchdog—a function he does not always perform to perfection. King Arthur will join us later with blessings and words from on high."

"Did you try and scare me? Almost kill me?" repeated Sarah. "And if you did, why in God's name?"

"The atmosphere aboard is infectious," said Billy, unfolding himself and rising to stand on the deck. "Already, you are invoking Our Lord. Never mind who did what. Since you are unmarred, remember that academic flowers like you need shaking up every now and then."

Ezra now emerged, dressed in his shore clothes and holding a denim sport jacket. "Okay, Billy, move it. We're supposed to be there by five. Opening prayers and introductions. Tony's rowing us in."

"All that jazz," said Billy. "As the poor monkey said, 'There are liars and swearers enow to beat the honest men and hang up them, praise the lord.'"

"What?" said Sarah, but now Gracie stepped forward and with a grim expression examined Billy and then, wordlessly, lifted and adjusted the set of his sport jacket. For a moment, Billy endured her ministrations and then pushed her off with a slight grimace.

"You behave now," said Gracie, and the two men, one after the other, climbed down the hanging ladder into the Avon raft.

Sarah turned and settled herself to enjoying drinks with the diminished company; David, Alex, and Gracie. Tony, returned from delivering the two men, huddled in the bow with Andrea.

David Mallory was putting little lumps of Brie on water biscuits. "I let Billy and Ezra off the job. Saint Ann of the Ocean asked if we could have someone stay for the church supper. These little congregations are struggling and it's always good for their people to know that someone beyond the island is interested in their work. Although," Mallory added with a shrug, "I don't think Billy's interest is exactly overwhelming. I'll be joining them for a general meeting at eight."

"I don't see how you have time to keep an eye out for drug deals with all the church work," said Alex.

"Today it's so beautiful," said Sarah, "I don't really believe that there are nefarious characters in the harbor delivering cocaine to one another in little boats."

Mallory shook his head sadly. "I wish I didn't believe, either. But this evening, the church comes first. The entire membership is supposed to discuss upcoming needs."

"Church suppers were fun," said Sarah, sipping her rum and lime. "Grandmother Douglas used to take all of us children. Baked beans, cole slaw, a hundred different kinds of pie."

David smiled, his big, happy family smile. "Then we'll have to find a church supper for you."

"That was pretty transparent," said Alex as he and Sarah went below to their cabin before dinner. "You wanted to row in and race over and see if those two were really eating beans and squash pie. Hoping to catch Billy in a green pickup truck knocking off children on tricycles."

"No such thing. I'm not a ghoul, though I think Billy might

be. But you know," she added thoughtfully, "I find it hard to believe in this drug business and David working for the police. Is David really working a double play, the arm of the law and the hand of God?"

"Ms. Deane, if David Mallory decides to use you for shark bait, I will only be able to stand around and cheer."

NINE

DINNER BROUGHT A RETURN OF THE CONCERNED David Mallory—even heavier than the model seen at lunch. He worried Sarah's bicycle incident like a dog with a rag. He fussed over her suggestion that Billy might have been a partner to it; told her that he intended to verify Billy's every move that morning.

"As I intend to do," said Gracie. She paused, a slice of curried lamb—another Andrea triumph—on her fork. "But, I can't always be my brother's keeper, we're different generations, we've grown too far apart."

Mallory nodded at Billy Brackett's empty place. "My talk with him was not very reassuring; he seemed to take the whole subject as a joke. Black humor seems to be his specialty, but I have a gut feeling that he didn't pull that stunt."

"Of course he didn't," said Gracie angrily.

"Gracie, dear," said Mallory, "We think we can judge someone, and then every so often, we make a mistake. You know I took him on because I really believe the sea changes people."

Sarah nodded; it was a piece out of her mother's letter about

Tony. "That's an old idea, when boys shipped before the mast and came back men. It sounds like Conrad," she added, remembering her dinner conversation with Billy.

"Things are elemental at sea," insisted Mallory. "In a storm, there's no time for posturing. You have to face up or go under."

"Maybe on a little tub with a torn sail or a leaky old *African Queen*," said Sarah. "But on the *Pilgrim*, everything is luxury."

"And state-of-the-art technology," put in Tony, surfacing briefly while Andrea went to bring on the salad.

"Still, a boat is a boat," said Alex. "And a storm is a storm."

"Exactly," said David. "And I'm sure at some point Billy will be tested. And Tony. Not now, I hope, with all of you aboard, but when we sail home. Autumn sailing in the hurricane season off Hatteras can scare even old salts."

Sarah finished her last bite of lamb and thought maybe this was part of Mallory's missionary activities, taking hold of drifting young men, giving them a dose of shipboard life. The persuasion that the sea made for sea changes seemed imbedded in some people. But from Sarah's view of yacht life, they might all be on a floating resort. All that gear—electric winches, roller reefing jibs, hydraulic this and that, radar, loran—my God, they could probably go to the moon. Life on the *Pilgrim* kept them away from the gritty land world, and what was a gale at sea to the drug and fast-track jungle on shore. Cruising was pure escape. And Tony, he wasn't being retooled by life aboard; Andrea was his polar star. As for Billy, Sarah wondered if he even noticed whether he was on sea or land. She woke up to the dinner-table scene to find Gracie sitting in stony silence and David still on the subject of Billy. He must be really worried. And if he was *that* worried . . .

David had gone from heavy to ponderous. "I know I'm too easy with people, but I always start out assuming trust."

"We all do that," said Andrea, who was occupied dealing out a salad of bib lettuce and avocado. "I mean you just can't go on being a human if you don't trust anyone."

This was too much. Goody Two Shoes, you are not real, grumbled Sarah to herself as she pursued a slippery piece of avocado around her plate.

— 86 —

"I've been messed up a lot," put in Tony. "Trusting, I mean. Last year, my lead guitar into hard stuff."

"Don't anyone stop trusting on my account," said Sarah. "I'm sorry that I mentioned Billy." And, she thought, now I *am* sorry. If David and Gracie start following Billy around, he'll just become more difficult. It would be a lot better if I'm written off as an excitable female who can't keep her balance on a bicycle.

Tony unexpectedly assisted this idea. "Though I wouldn't put anything past Billy, Sarah isn't the greatest bicyclist. I mean, she doesn't always pay attention to where she's going and she once ran into a hydrant and broke two front teeth."

"I'm always thinking of something else when I'm biking," Sarah explained, grateful for the shift of subject.

Tony smiled a brotherly, condescending smile. "It's okay, you've probably got all sorts of great books on your mind, like Andrea here."

Sarah nudged the conversation toward books and found that Andrea had indeed launched herself into *War and Peace* and was full of Prince Andre Bolkónski, and the problems posed by that upstart Buonaparte. Sarah recommended the *Odyssey* to the group at large, David said someday he hoped to read Gibbon, and Alex said you wouldn't believe how dated *The Thirty-Nine Steps* was but that he was having fun with it.

David rose before dessert. "Time to be off. No, Tony, you don't have to take me in. I'll take the Avon and then I can collect Ezra and Billy. It might be late." He reached into the hanging locker and pulled out a navy poplin jacket and inserted a flashlight in the pocket. "How about some poker for all of you tonight. Did you know that Tony and Andrea are cardsharks?"

So it was cards. Gracie pleaded sinus trouble and retired. Alex was reluctant, as he wanted to read. But Sarah spoke for poker; it was a chance to do something with Tony.

Andrea played seriously and did not take chances. As dealer, she stuck to five- or seven-card draw and kept her chips neatly stacked in piles of five. Tony, in character, chose exotic forms with several cards wild, bluffed, raised every bet, and played with abandon. Sarah lost almost every hand and Alex endured.

However, the game was only camouflage. Sarah could almost

feel an erotic current running from Tony to Andrea. Where was Miss Modesty Two Shoes tonight? She had taken off her loose cotton sweater and now bloomed in a low-necked handkerchief-thin blouse. She breathed and her shapely breasts moved softly under the fabric, little beads of moisture sat on her upper lip, and the tiny pink point of her tongue reached up to touch them. From time to time, she tilted her head over her cards, pressed them to her bosom and sighed as if telling Tony that the decision to raise or fold was difficult, whispered that she had forgotten whether one-eyed jacks were wild, and wondered aloud whether it was wise to draw to an inside straight. Once she dropped a card, and as she stooped for it, a golden chain slipped out of her blouse and a beautiful dark red stone set in a whorl of gold swung to and fro like a pendulum. She straightened, picked up the pendant, and for a moment held it in the hollow of her hand, and then let the chain slip slowly through her fingers so that the stone slid down again between her breasts. Sarah thought she had never seen such a nicely played moment.

Tony, immune to jewelry but not to sex, perspired. The game wound up in a crescendo of error and misdirected attention.

"I think we'd better call it a night," said Alex in a cross voice. When he agreed to do something, he wanted to do it well, but one attentive adult can do little with three otherwise-occupied players.

"What a waste of time," he complained as he and Sarah reached their cabin.

"Don't you want sit on the deck and look at the moon?"

"The deck is fully occupied by those two. I'm too old to share even that much space. Besides, the deck is wet, the planking is hard, and privacy is zip. I like love on a mattress."

"Andrea may not have been after him before but she is now."

"And he's after her. Perfect agreement. Male and female created He them. As long as Tony can still recognize port from starboard, let him get on with it."

"A bulldozer couldn't stop either of them."

"Undoubtedly. But take heart. Tony plays cards. It may lead

to bridge, the stock market. Middle-class happiness just around the corner. Tell your parents to relax. He'll be applying to business school next."

Sarah fell asleep almost as soon as her head struck the pillow. The bicycling, the near miss with the truck, the salt air, the gentle rocking of the vessel, all combined to knock her out cold. Only a persistent banging and bumping in the middle of the night brought her reluctantly awake. Alex was sitting up.

"What's the matter?"

"The anchor may be dragging. I'll go up and see." Alex, barefoot, slipped out of the cabin.

He came back almost immediately. "Ezra," he said. "Came back in the Avon raft with Mallory. Lost his footing on the ladder. Maybe his church buddies gave him something stronger than hot coffee. Young Billy seems to be absent without leave."

"What?"

"Mallory wasn't surprised. Apparently, he left the church supper early. Ezra and then David went after him, but he'd slipped off. Probably looking for some of his island friends. David's betting he'll turn up somewhat damaged in the A.M. Said keeping Billy up to the mark may take some doing."

Sarah retired feeling that this news about Billy was hardly earthshaking. A more perfect candidate for jumping ship, she had never met. She hoped he stayed jumped.

Ten minutes later, she lifted her head. "It's still bumping. That can't be the raft."

"The boat may have swung around and caught the Avon, or the wind has switched. Someone's moving it, anyway."

"Good," said Sarah sleepily. She turned over and burrowed under her blanket. Her porthole was open and the sloop, even an eighty-foot number, was like a drum, reverberating to every thump. She listened to the muffled thud of footsteps on the deck, the scrape of something being drawn along the hull—the Avon raft no doubt—another scrape and a thump, a hose splattering, more footsteps, then a hatch closing somewhere.

Sarah reared up again. "Noisy bunch."

"You don't just step on board and go to sleep on a boat. You have to secure everything, hose out the Avon, saltwater shouldn't sit in it. Everything shipshape."

"Certainly," said Sarah, pulling her pillow over her head.

Then quiet. And sleep.

Sarah was still half-asleep when she became aware of the steady thrum-thrum of an idling diesel engine and footsteps above her head, then the splash of the mooring dropping off and the rise and fall of the sloop as she moved out into choppier waters.

She reached for her watch: 6:30. Had Mallory said that they'd be making an early start? She saw Alex's bunk empty and heard the sound of water running into the washbasin and then he opened the door of the head and leaned out. "We're underway early, maybe looking for a new cove for tonight."

"Why?"

"Don't know. Change of scene. Mallory doesn't need our permission to make an early start."

Sarah reached for her bathrobe. "Am I hungry. The ocean may not change character but it makes you eat like a bear."

Breakfast, even on a slightly rolling sloop, was spectacular. Ezra was on deck taking the ship out of the cove. "Good for him to handle *Pilgrim* without my breathing down his neck," said David, who was unwrapping steaming hot cinnamon buns from a blue and white checked napkin. Andrea had struck again: feather-light tomato omelet, tiny sausages, fresh orange juice, the works.

Sarah, sitting between Alex and Gracie, took a long, satisfying drink of her tea and reached for a roll. Then she remembered.

"Billy?" she asked.

"No show," said David. "I've been on the horn to the deputy sheriff here, the constable, and the harbor master. Told them we'd be heading for Crow Cove for the day and night. All I can do, can't run over the whole island chasing Billy down."

"Good riddance," said Tony, emerging from the galley.

Gracie looked at Tony with disapproval, and reminded David that Billy had friends on the island. "Have you called any of these? Billy is so careless about telling us his plans."

"Yes and the constable put me in touch with some of the summer colony and with a Mrs. Parker, who'd rented him a room one summer. No one's seen him. They'll run a check on Billy's friends. So-called friends. I think it's probably a bunch who'd cut and run if they thought Billy was in any sort of mess."

Gracie, wearing an expression that mixed distress and irritation, said, "He's worrying us to death, that's what he's doing."

"Now, Gracie," put in Mallory, "we'll do our best to find him, but if he won't be found, that's that. We have a cruise to take and work to do. Now about this afternoon . . ."

But the passengers were never to know about Mallory's plans for the afternoon. The *Pilgrim* gave a sluggish roll to port, swung back to starboard, and Sarah had to grab her plate to keep it from ending in her lap. Gracie wasn't so lucky; she tilted her coffee down her chest, and rose gasping. Alex jumped to her aid with napkins and cold water. Mallory, at the moment *Pilgrim* changed direction, had raced for the ladder and swung himself on deck, and Sarah heard him call, "Ezra, what the hell?"

Gracie, released by Alex, scurried toward her cabin, one hand clutching a sodden, stained blouse. Tony disappeared topside, and Alex started for the companionway. "See if I can help," he called.

"Me, too," said Sarah, not to be outdone.

"But not me," said Andrea, emerging from the galley. "I've got enough to do down here." Sarah noted that with Andrea's hair tied up in a crimson scarf, her perfect body wrapped in a blue apron, her face flushed, she was absolutely enchanting. And anyone who could appear enchanting at 7:30 in the morning after cooking breakfast for six in the limited space of the galley was one of nature's miracles. Sarah not only gave Tony up for lost, she felt that Tony was damn lucky to have caught the attention of this goddess.

On deck, David was angry, his face dark. The first time I've seen him really lose his happy family look, thought Sarah, and then corrected herself. The first was when she told him about Billy and the pickup truck. Now David was gesturing with a fist toward the stern of the *Pilgrim*. "Damn lobster rope or warp—whatever they call it. Heavy nylon. Caught in the prop. We must have been dragging the whole trap and now it's snagging on the bottom. We can't make headway unless we get it loose."

Ezra, who had been hanging over the stern with a boat hook, looked up. "I'll get into the Avon and see if I can free it."

"Right," said Mallory. "Tony, go down there with him and see if you can hold the dinghy steady while Ezra tries to unravel the mess. And break out the wet suits. You and Ezra may have to go overboard and cut the line out of the prop. No, Alex, thanks, nothing you can do. Just a hell of a nuisance."

"You were taking off early," said Sarah, centering on what she felt was question one.

David forced a smile. "The best-laid plans of mice and men. Thought I'd get a jump on you all. Get a good start on the day and make it to Crow Cove—it's less busy than Gilkey Harbor—drop the hook early and have more time for seeing the rest of Islesboro. Perhaps have a picnic after I finish with my church business. And give Billy a whole day to think on his sins and come back. I'll leave word at the yacht club and with the constable about our location."

Alex nodded his understanding. "Happens all the time on the Maine coast. Everyone catches lobster warp in the prop sooner or later. I hope they don't have to cut the trap loose."

There followed the efforts to free the lobster trap, Tony and Ezra sitting in the Avon raft by the stern of the *Pilgrim*, jabbing with the boat hook, reaching and pulling. Then Mallory, the man of God, saying loudly, "Oh Christ, the damn thing's wrapped itself into the prop; we may have to go back to the harbor." He looked up and saw Sarah smiling. "Sorry about the language," he said, but Sarah didn't think he looked in the least sorry.

"Quite appropriate," she answered, but now Tony passed up from the stern a tangled seaweed mess of lobster warp and in the middle a dingy-red-and-black lobster-pot buoy heavy with molasseslike deposits, barnacles, and cinging strands of seaweed.

"Jesus," said Mallory, switching expletives. "Someone find a swab. I won't have my deck crapped up like this." Mallory strode to the stern, where voices and thuds continued. "Okay, Ezra, what's the propeller look like? Can we get going here?"

Ezra reared up from the Avon raft, looking in his glistening wet suit like some ill-favored creature of the deep. "Sorry boss, can't get a good fix on the prop. It may be bent, but it's free of warp, anyway. Had to cut the trap free; some lobsterman's going to be out for your hide. Let's go back half speed to the harbor and I'll get a light under there. Too much current here to work."

David was silent for a minute, then grimaced. "Okay, we go back. And this time, I'll take the helm. Tony, stow the diving gear. When we get in, make a thorough check, but I don't want the whole day shot because Ezra steered the boat into a lobster buoy."

"Wouldn't it be better to take it to one of the boat yards?" Alex ventured.

"No," said David. "We can manage this ourselves. If it's anything serious, then I'll go that route. Now you and Sarah go on down and finish breakfast."

"Captain Friendly is Captain Bligh," said Sarah as she and Alex settled back at the breakfast table.

"Aren't all sea captains a little headstrong when something goes wrong?" asked Andrea, slipping onto the bench beside Alex. Sarah thought her blooming fairness made a splendid contrast to Alex's dark, lean, and hungry look. "I mean there's Captain Nemo and who's the man who rolls ball bearings? Queeg?"

"It's a nice list," said Sarah. "There's Captain Ahab and Captain Kidd."

Gracie joined them, a basket of hot muffins in her hand. She was wearing a fresh yellow blouse decorated with little green spotted butterflies. "The coffee didn't burn me, Alex was so helpful, and you've forgotten Captain Hook."

Alex looked up. "The skipper on any boat has to have a certain amount of steel, otherwise he'd probably sink the boat in the first crisis. And I'd say Mallory's a perfectionist; he makes plans, gives orders, and he doesn't like foul-ups. Surgeons are like that. I'm always stubbing my toes on surgeons."

The *Pilgrim* returned to her heavy mooring in front of the Islesboro Inn. Ezra and Tony made preparations for the examination of the propeller, which David said crossly might take at least an hour. At this, Alex suggested, with David's permission, that he and Sarah take shore leave. "A quick hike, another chance to check some birds, stretch our legs. Tell you what, I'll see if I can pick up some lobsters for that picnic lunch. My treat."

David thanked him but said not to go just for lobsters. He was sure Andrea had something planned. However, Andrea said not yet, and Tony added, "Hey, yes, a lobster picnic. Andrea does a great potato salad." And it was settled. Andrea would start on the potatoes and augment with fresh fruit and brownies. Alex and Sarah would pick up lobsters at the nearest lobster pound.

They let themselves down into the Avon raft and Gracie leaned over the rail, her crimped hair slightly ruffled by the breeze, her white skirt blowing away from her angular knees— She looks like a worried Olive Oyl, thought Sarah.

"I heard someone say there's a new man that sells lobsters south of the inn, around by Thrumcap," called Gracie. "He has a tiny dock and a float. He's your closest. And keep an eye out for Billy, won't you?"

"We'll order the lobsters before the hike, and they'll be ready when we get back," called Alex, who was cradling a large blue-speckled enamel lobster pot between his knees.

"Are we being gotten rid of?" asked Sarah.

"You are so refreshingly predictable, Ms. Deane. Rid of for what? Are you afraid of arsenic in the potato salad?" Alex gave her a look of exasperation as he bent to the oars, pulling short, hard strokes against the incoming tide. Then he jerked his head toward the shore. "We're almost around the point. There's the float. We'll land on the beach near it."

And Sarah jumped from the bow, soaking her sneakers by bad timing and held the bow straight into the shore and together, they hauled the raft safely past the high tide line.

"You know, Sarah," said Alex as he finished a neat bowline around a huge spruce root, "one minute you're talking about Captain Bligh and think everyone is up to no good and the next that the moon is made of green cheese and all's right with the world. You are a hard woman to follow, but today, let's opt for the green cheese." And Alex made off down the shore, the blue enameled lobster pot in one hand.

"Wait up, where are you going?"

"To order the lobsters as planned."

Sarah caught up and they scrambled along the rocks, slipping on the seaweed, retreating into a bramble of rugosa roses and beach peas as the shoreline indented to admit a small stream. A steamy smell of decaying seaweed mixed in the salt-sharp air and Sarah suddenly felt full of life and vigor. To hell with doubt and doom. She was ready for a rousing walk and a wind-whipping sail to a beach for a lobster picnic, a picnic with her brother and their new friends, Andrea, David Mallory, Gracie, good old Ezra, even to welcome Billy when he came back. The sun fell warm on her shoulders and she was in charity with the world.

In this happy frame of mind, Sarah almost bumped into Alex, who was standing stock-still around the turn of a small cove that had partly hidden the narrow ramp that led to a small float.

"Move it," she said, giving him a little shove.

"Something's going on." Alex pointed to three men in a huddle on the float. Below the triple arch of their bodies, Sarah could see a sprawled figure, could see—she was that close—that the figure lay in a puddle of water; lay like a huge just-landed fish.

Somehow, without memory of the trip, Sarah followed Alex around the shore, down the ramp, and onto the float. The three men gave way, Alex put down the lobster kettle and knelt by the figure, turned the head slightly, and reached for a pulse in the neck.

Sarah peered over his shoulder and retreated. Billy Brackett had been found.

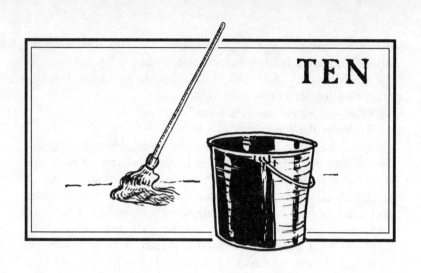

TEN

IN LIFE, ALTHOUGH BILLY BRACKETT HAD SEEMED UN-
sound in body and mind, there was about him, even in his most
languid moments, something that had commanded attention.
Now nothing was left but this sodden, sprawled puppet figure.
Sarah turned away from the group of men and backed up to the
end of the float, trying to force her brain to nullify what she had
just seen. Look at the dock, she told herself. Concern yourself
seriously with its construction, how it was joined, its flotation,
what kind of wood. Nails, pegs, bolts? Were splinters possible
for bare feet? How fortunate then that she was wearing sneakers.
Was that a dinghy tied up at the other end of the float. Or a
skiff? A punt? Or a scow? A pram? What was the difference?
Were they all rowboats? Was rowboat a generic name? What the
hell was Alex trying to do, revive him? She hadn't meant to
look, but Alex was turning the body to the side. No, now he
was releasing it, letting it roll soggily back to its facedown position. Oh, thank God, Alex was standing up, letting it alone.

One of the men said, "Hey, we've got to call someone," and
another man in a navy blue shirt went leaping up the ramp. Of

course, the rescue squad, the ambulance, the sheriff. The pathologist. The works. Oh damn it to hell.

She must have said it aloud, because one of the men turned around with a surprised frown, and Alex looked up, puzzled, as if he couldn't quite remember why she was there. The physician with the patient—or in this case a defunct patient.

Billy. Sarah forced herself to think about Billy. Poor Billy. How old was he? Twenty-six or -seven maybe. Tony's age. No family except Gracie. Did Billy have friends? Lovers? Women, men? Or would Billy have slipped out of life with no one giving a damn?

Slipped, was that it?

"Did he slip?" she called over to Alex, who stood scowling down at the prone figure. With a shudder she saw that Billy was naked from the waist up, his skin an awful blue-gray.

"Slip?" asked Alex stupidly. "What? Oh, I see what you mean. Coming back last night. Slipped in the water. He might have. Can't tell. I think he's been dead for hours."

"And he drowned. Oh poor Billy," she said again. And then, she remembered why they were standing on the float of a lobster pound. "Oh God, you'd better row back and tell Mallory."

"I'll call from the inn; it'll be quicker than rowing. I suppose Mallory or Gracie will have to identify him. Sarah, will you stay here while I call and then stand by until someone comes in from the *Pilgrim?* No"—this in answer to a look of horror—"you're not to do anything. Just stay put." Alex turned to the two men, who stood, hands hanging down, looking as if they'd been turned to cement. "This is Nick Johnson and Tom Banter; they'll stay here, too. They're the ones who found Billy."

So Sarah stood by. All day. Stood by on the dock while the rescue squad scooped onto a stretcher what was left of Billy. Stood by on the beach as the Avon raft and the motor whaleboat shuttled back and forth to the *Pilgrim* and the shore. Stood by with Alex while the constable called the mainland police, and then back on board the *Pilgrim*, waited and watched. A passing parade. David Mallory in shock. Gracie, who simply disintegrated, trembling, red-eyed, gulping. Speechless Andrea.

Tony quiet, comforting Andrea. Alex preparing a sedative for Gracie from the small medical duffel he always carried. Ezra efficient, fastening sail covers, since it was certain there would be no more sailing that day. Then sandwiches, Andrea bringing out paper plates, a salad, coffee. The Islesboro deputy sheriff on board, sitting stiffly in the cockpit, a revolver sticking out of a black holster, taking notes and looking overheated in his uniform. When, where, how? Then the police. The real police, the Criminal Investigation Department of the Maine State Police. In other words, Detective Sergeant George Fitts.

George Fitts by seaplane.

"Damn, why George?" asked Sarah. It was after one o'clock; the slight morning wind had moderated to a small breeze and the sun was bright. She and Alex were sitting on the deck beside the forward hatch cover with a plate of sandwiches and a thermos of lemonade.

"Why the police? It was an accident, wasn't it? He did fall in, off that float." She sighed. "But you know, after you stopped in front of me, and I saw him down on the float, well, I simply knew it was Billy. That he was dead. I mean underneath the shock, the surprise, I wasn't surprised. You know that saying, an accident waiting to happen. Well, Billy seemed to be on the edge, the edge of something final."

Sarah paused and took a bite from a poorly cut meat sandwich—Andrea had not come up with a gourmet spread for once, which was a relief. Close attention to food preparation, Sarah thought, would have been somehow unseemly.

"But still," she persisted, "if Billy drowned, why do we all have to go through this police question business? Wouldn't a few statements do it? I'm not being simpleminded, but I think it's bad enough that he's dead. After all, he was alone, he'd left the church meeting, he'd been drinking. All certified to."

Alex finished a handful of potato chips and reached for a sandwich. "Autopsy is a must. It's a rule. It's an unattended death—no witness."

"Well, don't you usually wait for the results of the autopsy before you sound general quarters?"

"I'm one of the medical examiners for the county, so I know

you can't sign a death certificate on the strength of Billy turning up with an incoming tide. Which he did."

"But he drowned."

"I can't tell that. He may have been dead before he hit the water. We'll have to call his Florida doctor, find out about his health record, which from his appearance was questionable. He may have been into drugs, he may have had a cardiac condition, a systemic disease. A hundred things. We'll just have to hang in here until the autopsy. Routine, routine. Ours is not to question why."

Sarah stuck out her chin. "Well, I question why."

"A still, small, unheard voice. The others seem glad George is here, someone to help them cope. Mallory seems shattered."

"I suppose he does feel responsible."

"Of course. Billy was one of the world's stray sheep, and I'd say that David thinks of himself as rather the shepherd sort. Anyway, he's very upset. As is Gracie, very naturally. Her brother. The others, too—Ezra, Andrea, and Tony, but they're not so vocal."

Sarah stood up, walked over to the lifeline, bent over the water brushing her hands free of crumbs. "Gracie must have had a time of it with Billy. I think it's made her almost schizoid. On one hand, she's competent, efficient, a place for everything and everything in its place."

"Except for Billy," put in Alex.

"Yes. So on the other hand, she has these protective sisterly responses and since she was so much older, she may have felt almost maternal. It's enough to make anyone go off the deep end. Trying to keep order, please Mallory, and knowing your brother's the one who fouls everything up." She shook her head, adding, "We're a funny bunch on this boat."

Alex was already on his feet and screwing the top on the thermos. He had a date with the local medical examiner at 2:30, which promised to take up much of the afternoon. "Funny bunch? How do you mean? I think we're all perfectly ordinary. Billy was the odd man out, but sick people are never quite like anyone else."

"Andrea ordinary?"

"In the category of attractive sexpot, yes."

"Okay, so she's ordinary, but how about Mallory? And Ezra?

"Mallory? Basically a conformist, and undoubtedly sincere about good works. Likes his work and loves his boat. Maybe is even a bit compulsive about sailing, which is probably a good thing in a skipper. As for Ezra, he's one of those sea dogs that's batted around. A seagoing rolling stone, if that's not an oxymoron. And Gracie, as you say, a type."

"I've seen her in a million old movies. The faithful aunt, secretary, practical, hard-nosed sometimes but keeps the glamour-puss star on an even keel. But herself has nervous episodes."

"Go back to the *Odyssey*. It might be restful, because I'm not pretending finding Billy Brackett has been easy for you—or for any of us. Maybe you can detach Tony from his beloved long enough for him to talk it over with you."

Alex departed by the faithful Avon raft, David Mallory seeing him off. Sarah saw what Alex meant by "conformist." Mallory was in a tan linen jacket, a dark tie, and spotless tropical-weave trousers, ready for any social, churchly, or constabulary appearance. Whatever the death of Billy Brackett demanded, Mallory would be properly dressed. Alex, on the other hand, wore his usual garb, faded denim pants and shapeless tennis shirt.

Sarah made her way back to the cockpit. Perhaps Tony *would* turn up ready to talk; when they were growing up, they'd always hashed over their troubles.

However, it was David Mallory who stopped, patted her shoulder, and said he was going below—to check on Gracie. "She's been hit very hard by this. I'll just see . . . ." Mallory's voice trailed off; he shrugged and made for the companionway.

Sarah, after waiting for twenty minutes or so for Tony to appear, gave up and went to her cabin, thinking that the *Odyssey* might indeed prove a calming influence. First, since the lemonade seemed to be acting like a diuretic, she stopped in their cabin head. But to her annoyance, the flushing operation proved balky. These blessed sea toilets. After pumping valiantly up and down with the designated handle, Sarah paused in her exertions. She had flushed it all right, closed the seacock, but now instead of pumping the toilet bowl dry, her efforts seemed to be having an open hydrant effect, water bubbling up and threatening to spill out over her sneakers. Desperately, Sarah reviewed the written instructions posted over the toilet. Open this valve, bring in fresh water, close the seacock, use toilet, open cock, flush with water, close cock, and pump dry. "BE SURE TO CLOSE THE SEACOCK. Failure to follow these instructions can flood head compartment." And, she supposed, as the water dribbled over the toilet seat's edge, the whole damned cabin.

Now frantic, as the water began to pour over the rim of the toilet seat like a miniature falls, she reached under the washbasin cabinet and shoved every valve back against the side of the boat, Alex having told her that this cut off the entire water supply, something they should do when leaving the ship.

That last action seemed to have stemmed the flow, but the water was now sloshing uncomfortably around her feet and little wavelets threatened to overflow the four-inch floor partition that separated the head area from their cabin. I'll have to find someone, Sarah thought. Not Gracie, who was supposed to be resting or being consoled by David or was knocked out by Alex's sedative. She'd have to go into the crew's quarters.

She opened the door that led forward to the forward crew area, hoping that Ezra might be available. She certainly didn't want to barge in on Andrea should she and Tony be happily wrapped around each other, as they well might since neither was on deck. Moving cautiously toward the bow along the narrowing passageway, Sarah became aware of an underhum of voices. A man's and an indeterminate female voice that rose and fell against the man's lower tones. Tony and Andrea? She thought not. And then as the sounds subsided, she stepped farther forward until she came abreast of a series of louvered doors. No nameplates. Well, perhaps she could just find a mop and bucket and try for human help later. There must be a utility locker somewhere, that door ahead on the starboard side; it was ajar.

She pushed the door cautiously and saw that she had found the crew's head and separate shower compartment. A pink lace bra was drying on a towel rack, several crumpled towels and a man's T-shirt hung on the top of the shower, and a can of shaving cream lay in the water-splattered sink. A unisex facility. She turned back to the passageway and was startled again by the same voices rising almost next to her ear. Coming from the next starboard-side cabin door. She raised her hand, ready to knock, when the door opened in her face and Gracie backed into her, whirled around, and gasped. Sarah had only time to see a gaping mouth and a puffy tear-splattered face when David Mallory loomed in the door space. In his right hand, he held, delicately between thumb and forefinger, a syringe.

A syringe complete with needle. Even in the subdued light of the passageway lit only by a translucent hatch cover, Sarah picked up the silver glint of the needle.

She had time to note this detail because Gracie and Mallory turned into twin pillars of salt, and for at least ten seconds, no one moved.

Sarah spoke first; said the first words that came to her mind. "Where did the syringe come from?" Because it was inconceivable that sister Gracie Mullen or good Captain Mallory were into drugs. Gracie, the perfect secretary, Mallory the perfect skipper.

Still no one moved. Sarah swallowed twice, looked from one to the other. Gracie shivered and then gulped.

David Mallory took charge. "Sarah. Oh, Lord. Well, I suppose I'm glad it's you. One of our family so to speak. Not the police. Though I'm on my way to them now. With this."

At which, Gracie grabbed at Mallory's sleeve. "Please, please, David. Don't. Let's work this out between ourselves. Please."

"Gracie, Sarah. Come back into Billy's cabin. Yes, it's Billy's cabin"—this to Sarah's look of inquiry. "Come in and sit down and see if you don't agree with me." Mallory released himself from Gracie's hold and gently pushed her inside the room. Sarah followed and watched Mallory place the syringe on the middle of the bunk's blanket. Then he repeated in a heartfelt voice, "I'm certainly glad it's you."

Sarah nodded. It was indeed her.

"I think you'll understand. Billy was undoubtedly taking

drugs, what kind I don't know. Perhaps even for pain, pre-scribed drugs. The police will let us know. Anyway, I decided I didn't want to bother Gracie in case she'd gone to sleep—so I thought it might be a good idea to see if Billy had an address book. Of course his cabin was supposed to be left as is and locked for the police, but I have a master key. As do Gracie, and Ezra. So, to make the story short, when I came along to his cabin I found the syringe. In plain sight above the bunk. And suddenly there was Gracie—who should have taken her sedative and been lying down. I guess she just couldn't rest and wanted to be the good angel. Gracie, do you want to tell Sarah what you wanted to do, why you came here."

Gracie, backed against the bunk—the cabin's narrow space now seemed overwhelmed by its three occupants—and began to shake her head, but Mallory took her hand and said that Sarah would understand, would be sympathetic.

She began. It was a stumbling recitation. "This horrible thing, poor Billy. I've been beside myself. It's all so terrible. I kept saying over and over, what can I do, what can I do. I felt absolutely useless. You know, all these men taking charge and me, Billy's sister, thinking there was nothing I could do. You understand, Sarah?"

Sarah nodded again. Certainly there were moments in the last hour, as the male representatives of the law boarded the *Pilgrim* and Alex rowed off full of manly purpose, that she had felt like useless extra baggage.

"I was beside myself, thinking, thinking. And then I felt I had to go down to his cabin. You see, I knew Billy wasn't well and I hoped he wasn't taking drugs, because he shouldn't take drugs. I mean no one should but, especially Billy."

Sarah waited, feeling the heat of the little cabin, thinking that in the warm sepia light they all must look overcooked, like people trapped in a toaster oven. Then Gracie lifted her head, words coming out now in little puffs and gasps, and went on.

"I didn't take the sedative because I knew I must do some-thing, at least go down to Billy's cabin and look through his things before the police did. We weren't supposed to come in here, but, as David told you, I have a master key, too. For all the cabins."

How reassuring, thought Sarah.

"Go on, Gracie," prompted David.

"I came down here meaning to throw away anything I found that would hurt Billy's reputation, like the syringe or any pills. But David was here. I didn't see him at first; he was sitting on the bunk. I went to open the porthole, but it was open already. I meant to throw anything I found overboard."

"Which I've told Gracie would be obstructing justice with a vengeance."

Gracie, face contorted, stamped her foot. "No one. No one wants a memory of Billy on drugs. It's enough that he's dead, that he drank too much at the church supper and drowned. Sarah, wouldn't you do the same for *your* brother, for Tony? For the peace of your own parents."

It was a telling shot. What if it had been Tony?

Gracie, now more coherent, her voice gaining strength and resonance, pressed her advantage. "You see, Sarah, it isn't so easy. What good can David do by taking the syringe to the police? It isn't as if it's going to lead them to some drug gang here in Maine. Billy probably got it in Florida."

David picked up the syringe. "I'll turn this over to Alex until the police arrive. He can keep it in his medical bag. Gracie, now go and lie down. I'm sure the police won't blame you for acting like a human being, and they'll be glad you didn't have a chance to throw it overboard." Mallory moved toward the door.

Then Sarah remembered why she herself was down in the crew's quarters. "David, do you know where I can find a mop? My toilet didn't turn off when it was supposed to, and I've about three inches of water in the head."

It was a successful diversion. Gracie, who seemed about to crumple, lifted her head. "Good heavens. Right away. Let me do it. That can be a terrible mess. Did you close the seacock?

"All right, Gracie," said Mallory. "If you won't lie down, keep busy. It will make you feel a lot better. Remember, we're all very shocked by this but we must keep functioning." With that, Mallory stepped into the passageway and opened a small door opposite from Billy's cabin and revealed a phalanx of brooms, mops, buckets, and brushes.

Gracie sprang at a mop and pail and, together with David, moved down the passageway, and Sarah heard her say, "All right, David, I know you're right. Tell the police. I lost my head. But I will not believe Billy was taking drugs."

Sarah, as was proper, should have gone directly to her cabin and helped with the mopping. Instead, she stood frowning at Billy's closed cabin door. Then, as if Herr Drosselmeier himself were winding her up and pushing a button in her back, she found herself reaching for the door handle, opening it—they had forgotten to relock—and soundlessly shutting it behind her.

Billy's bunk fitted into the starboard side of the curving forward hull of the *Pilgrim* with a locker beneath the bunk and a small hammock slung above it. The porthole was still open and Sarah wondered for a moment whether she should close it, but then remembered the police wanted everything left as it was.

Now that she was in the cabin, she found there was nothing really to see, no real imprint of the owner's strange and disturbed personality. In the hammock, a paperback—a spy thriller, with a woman screaming against the background of a swastika on the cover—and a tattered copy of poems by Ezra Pound. On the ledge over the bunk, three more books, *Confessions of a Porno Queen*, Malraux's *Man's Fate*, the poems of Wilfred Owen. A mix, like Billy himself.

Sarah, without any particular motive other than a vague idea of understanding a little more about Billy, moved over to the built-in chest, a narrower version of the one in her own cabin. The top, protected by the usual teak rail, held two bottles of sun-block cream, a bottle of calamine lotion, and a half-used tube of Anti-Ivy Corto-cream. Poison ivy on shipboard? wondered Sarah, but then remembered that trips ashore and beach picnics could be hazardous. When she herself even looked at poison ivy, she broke out. Next to the sun lotions, Sarah saw a transparent plastic bag with a jumble of foodstuffs. No wonder Billy didn't need to eat at dinner. Raisins, rice cakes, and a package of soybean protein drinks in vanilla and chocolate flavors. How surprising, a health food freak.

But now a tardy sense of shame overtook Sarah—or was it fear that any moment George Fitts might find her standing in a room presumably locked against intruders? She turned, about to leave, when she heard a click of metal under her sneaker. A key. One of *the* keys, the master keys. This must have been dropped by a dismayed Gracie when she discovered Mallory in the cabin. The key, which, of course, Sarah would return like a good citizen.

On deck, Sarah found Alex returned and collapsed on one of the cockpit cushions. His face was flushed and wet with perspiration. The wind had died, leaving the harbor at the mercy of almost ninety-degree heat. He saw her and shook his head. "What a bitch. What a way to pass a hot day. They've taken the body over to the mainland for the post—the autopsy. The pathologist will do it tonight. They'll call me about it later, because I'm going to duck the whole scene. George is in a huddle with the local law people."

Sarah sat down beside him, felt his forehead like a visiting nurse, and said, "Have you talked to David Mallory?"

"Yes, I have. And I want to hear nothing more about Billy as long as I live. What I want is a swim and forty iced drinks."

"It was a syringe."

"Yes, I know it was a syringe."

"Gracie was going to deep-six it. And anything else off-color she found. Protecting Billy's reputation. Or maybe she needed the syringe for herself. That's possible, I suppose. But she was very agitated. Mallory was fatherly and firm."

"Yes," said Alex, "he struck me that way. For your interest, the syringe was empty. And looked clean. As did the needle."

"Yes," said Sarah, sitting down beside him.

The syringe is marked in clear black letters: EPINEPHRINE, INJECTION USP 1:1000 FOR SC USE. And . . ."

"Wait a minute. SC?"

"Subcutaneous, under the skin. It also says to see the directions for I.M. or I.V. use—that's intramuscular or intravenous."

"And?"

"First off, epinephrine is hardly the drug of choice for addicts. It gives a quick rush, all right; it's a synthesized substance produced by the adrenals."

"Trust Billy to choose something different."

"It's used therapeutically as a vasoconstrictor and a cardiac stimulant, but it's certainly not in the popular class like heroin, cocaine, or the crack compounds. It has unpleasant side effects, so I can't imagine choosing epinephrine for a buzz, but who knows, I've had patients shooting anything from Windex to paint thinner."

"How about Billy using the empty syringe for taking a legitimate prescription drug. A painkiller in case he was in pain."

"Yes, Billy could have used a syringe—I don't say this one—to take an analgesic. Dilaudid, morphine, Demerol, something like that, and he could have faster relief from injection than by mouth. But adrenaline? For pain? And with that syringe?"

"What's the matter with that syringe?"

"Nothing, except it's specifically designed for giving an allergic person two doses of epinephrine. You inject yourself with half the stuff, and if you need a second dose, you rotate the barrel of the syringe for the second round."

"What if that was the only syringe Billy could get his hands on? He could rotate the syringe, couldn't he?"

"Yes, but it would be a nuisance. But then, syringes and needles aren't lying around for the taking. That's one reason I.V.-drug users share dirty needles; they can't find clean ones."

"So if you can find your own personal syringe, you're in luck. Is this epinephrine syringe easier to find than any other?"

"Sure. This one probably came from a kit. Allergic people often carry a safety kit with a syringe filled with epinephrine, a tourniquet, some antihistamine pills. Then if they get hives, begin to wheeze, have trouble breathing, they can take action."

"Not go find a doctor or an emergency room?"

"Often no time. Especially if you're off in the woods, up a mountain. Bee stings are the usual troublemakers and these kits are quite common. I have several friends who carry them."

"And leave the syringes around?"

"Undoubtedly. In the garbage, in their cars, their backpacks. Easy to pick up. And the prescription isn't too hard to get refilled. A little forgery goes a long way. Other syringes are around, insulin needles for diabetics, but those are a different size. And veterinarians give out syringes and needles to farmers and animal owners so they can deal with sickness and accidents."

"But we're not talking about horse syringes or diabetics."

"Right. Billy may have borrowed, stolen, picked up this syringe to use with a painkiller. Or he's an addict. Or allergic. The police will ask Gracie. And, now, listen, my darling Sarah, stay clear of this. Don't talk, don't discuss. Not with Tony. Not with anyone. As David quite rightly says, leave it to the police. If Billy was buying stuff, Billy may not be dead by accident. Or he may be. But you know drug people don't fool around."

"Poor Gracie, trying to protect Billy's good name."

"Hiding his bad one more like." Alex was silent for a moment, then stood up and stretched. "That's enough because, by God, epinephrine or painkiller or bee sting or none of the above, I'm going to flush myself into the deep blue sea. Then we'll have sanity hour. Take the Avon for a toot, drink deeply, and watch the moon come over the mountain."

"What mountain? You mean the Camden hills?"

"Who cares." Alex rose, disappeared down the ladder into the companionway, and reappeared almost immediately in bathing trunks, a towel over his shoulders. "Come on in yourself. Cleanse thyself. Purify, don't be a wimp."

Sarah watched as Alex strode purposefully to the bow and with one spring arched over the water and disappeared.

He rose gasping. "It's great. It's as cold as fire."

"Or ice," said Sarah, leaning over the bow rail. "Robert Frost. Watch out for those big jellyfish."

"No jellyfish for miles. Come on, come on." Alex splashed water up at her with one hand and took another dive.

Sarah couldn't resist. In minutes, she was in her bathing suit and in the water.

They splashed, they swam, they raced around the bow of a light-blue-hulled sloop manned by what seemed to be five children and three Irish setters. They paddled across to a pretty little yellow catboat with the name *Louisa* on her stern. Then, surfacing by the *Pilgrim*'s swimming ladder, they hung and kicked. Suddenly, Sarah said, "Where did you put the syringe?"

"Relax. It's not going anywhere. It's in my locked medical bag as David suggested."

Sarah rolled over in the water, did a surface dive, returned to the ladder, spitting out a mouthful. "I hate to think what's in this water."

"Ships and shoes and sealing wax and probably the flushings of many toilets. From many pleasure boats owned by honest environmentalists. Just don't drink it. I don't give a damn. I'm a new man. I can even listen to the report of the autopsy with a moderate amount of interest."

"Hey there." It was David Mallory leaning over the rail. "I'm coming in."

"Sarah, I'll race you around the *Louisa*," called Alex.

And the swimming party went on—joined by Tony and Andrea, Andrea in a bathing suit that could not have consumed more than five minutes of a seamstress's attention. She and Tony water-wrestled, splashed and dove and caught each other, while David circled the *Pilgrim* in long rhythmic strokes.

Cocktail time reverted to law, order, death by misadventure, drowning, or drugs. The life and times of Billy Brackett. Sarah hoped they would get on with it and over with it. Soon. "They" being the deputy sheriff, Tom Terhune, whom Sarah had secretly named Trigger Tom because of his full regimentals and filled holster; and at his side, his flip notebook open, George Fitts in a stiffly ironed Hawaiian shirt. He's gone native, thought Sarah; it was as if her grandmother had appeared in a bikini. George, with his bald head shaped like a light bulb, his face so unremarkable, so almost featureless—if that were possible—his voice so uninflected that Sarah in his presence was always put in mind of an extraterrestrial creature wearing a rubber coating to conform to earthly views of the human form.

In a sober ring around the cockpit sat the people of the sloop *Pilgrim*, all suitably dressed and combed, Gracie old-maidenly in a lavender and pink Liberty floral. Sarah, still in her yellow bathing suit, felt reproached. Over crab puffs—Andrea was in gear again—they went at the subject of Billy with hammer and tongs. His past, present, and lack of future. His known habits, his friends. There were apparently great gaps in Gracie's knowledge of her brother. For the past few years, she had seen him only after long intervals, but she denied that her brother took drugs and said that he had a history of food sensitivity. And was afraid of bees.

"The laboratory tests will help us decide cause of death," announced George. "Now I want general information, social habits, interests, as he expressed them to you. Or as you observed them." Not once did George refer to Gracie's intended syringe-disposal plan. He was being discreet, Sarah decided.

Gracie—perhaps in some sort of latent reaction—exploded with a mix of trivia and information. She explained and expounded. She brought out little anecdotes about Billy so that David Mallory finally had to reach over and pat her hand.

"Now Gracie, that will do. The sergeant here and Sheriff Terhune want facts, not stories."

But Gracie wasn't easily subdued. "It's the human things I remember. When he was little. He never ate properly and simply lived on raisins and health food and powders. He broke out when he ate certain things. And as I said, he was afraid of bees. He had to be so careful in the summer. He carried a bee kit. Sergeant Fitts, I've just remembered, he always had a bee kit, a little red plastic box. Maybe that's where the syringe came from. Maybe he wasn't into drugs, after all; the syringe came from his bee kit. David, did you find a bee kit?"

David looked grave. "No Gracie, no kit." He turned to George Fitts. "I wish I could say that I found the syringe in the bee kit and lay the idea of drugs to rest. But I didn't. Just the syringe. If it came from a kit, I'm afraid Billy may have used it for other things."

George looked up from his notebook. "I wasn't going to get into drug possibilities now, but I will tell you that the police didn't find such a kit. If any of you find one or remember seeing it aboard, I'd appreciate it if you'd let us know."

No one seemed to remember a kit, however, and Gracie began again. "Billy was a very private person. So hard to talk to.

Perhaps he did try drugs from time to time, I don't know. I'd be the last to know. And Billy never wore a necktie, did you know that? He said couldn't swallow with one on."

"Yes, yes, Gracie," said Mallory. "But let's stick to important things. I'm sure we all want this to be over as soon as possible."

George looked up from his notebook and studied Gracie. In Sarah's experience, George Fitts didn't just undress his victims; like a human CAT scanner, he penetrated into deep tissue and found imperfections, shadows, lumps, and fractures. And when George questioned, it was as if a laboratory technician drew blood for close microscopic analysis.

"Now Miss Mullen," George said in his toneless voice. "Why don't you just tell me about this one swallowing problem, and then we will take a few supplementary statements from the others."

Strange, thought Alex, who had been with George on a number of interrogatory occasions; strange because George usually avoided group scenes, preferring to skewer his witnesses separately and then compare privately their contradictions and evasions—or even consider the possibility that someone was actually telling the truth. But perhaps today this joint questioning among familiar faces allowed a letting go that might prove useful.

Gracie did seem encouraged and now held forth, and even David Mallory's most palpably knitted brow was no deterrent.

"Never a necktie. I mean even when we all went out to some restaurant. David has been so generous, and I remember in Savannah, or was it Charleston, anyway, Billy wouldn't wear a tie—or even a turtleneck, which everyone wears. Or an ascot. I told him that ascots are quite the thing with a blazer. Billy wouldn't hear of it. It was always as if he thought he was going to be choked in a necktie."

This interesting idea caused a discernible movement in the hearers, and David went so far as to reach over again and say quite firmly, "Get to the point, Gracie."

"But I don't know if there is a point. He said that he'd had a bad experience with a tie knot too tight and he couldn't get it off. He was afraid of not being able to breathe."

George folded his notebook. "As you say, Miss Mullen, these little things might find a place in an investigation. Not"— George bared his teeth in what passed as his smile—"that this is an investigation. Say a discussion. Sarah, I've run over your statement. Have you anything to add or can you remember an incident that might suggest that Billy used syringes for any purpose?"

But Sarah again denied any special knowledge of Billy. "Anyone could see he wasn't well; he said as much to me when we sat together at dinner. As Gracie said, he didn't eat anything. He said he had a nice protein drink that got him through the day. And he recited poetry, mostly about death, dope, and corruption, and asked me why I'd come on the cruise. He was disjointed, and I couldn't always follow what he was saying."

"You are not alone," murmured David Mallory.

"I just assumed he was an oddity. I'm afraid I wasn't interested enough to stick with it and try to understand, but I also had a sense that he really didn't want anyone to pay attention to him. Oh, and he could do a very good imitation of voices. Ezra's, for instance."

David nodded. "As I've said, he was loaded with talent but very mixed up."

George thanked Sarah, and she asked and got his permission to leave the group. She had meant to change from her bathing suit for dinner, but the weather was really too nice. The heat had eased, the sun, now lower in the sky, was kind, and a breeze had come up from the south. She reached for the *Odyssey* and made her way forward. A half hour of quiet reading would be blissful. She would turn her back to everyone and put her mind firmly on the problems Odysseus would face coming home to a wife after twenty years' absence. The mast would make a reasonable backrest.

Sarah lowered herself to the deck, stretching out her long, bare legs in front of her.

And jumped into the air yelling like a banshee.

ELEVEN

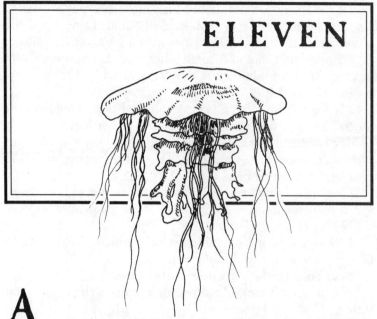

A YELL IN A QUIET HARBOR—MORE LIKE A SCREECH,
Alex told Sarah later—can release all sorts of energies. People
on the water are alert for emergencies. For rescue, for resuscita-
tion. For masts falling and sails blowing out. For collision and
calls of man overboard. They fling themselves into wild and
often random action.

But what is to be done about a woman in a yellow bathing
suit alternately clutching at her thighs and hopping along the
deck making squeaking noises of pain—Sarah had swallowed
her yell and was trying to stifle her cries. People sitting on the
decks of nearby yachts froze into position. A small dinghy with
a tiny outboard turned and began buzzing around the *Pilgrim*
like an anxious bumblebee. A man from the little sloop,
Louisa, stood up in the cockpit and raised his binoculars, and a
small child in a life jacket in a passing skiff began to cry.

Alex leaped out of the cockpit, stumbled over a lashed boat
hook, and splatted on the deck. Tony followed and tripped over
Alex. Ezra squared his shoulders, Gracie rose and wrung her
hands, Andrea slipped below saying something about the first-

aid kit, and Tony sat and rubbed his shin. David pulled Alex to his feet and together they took hold of Sarah. George and the sheriff stood at attention, the latter with a hand on his holster.

"Damn, damn, damn," Sarah whispered, her face drawn up in pain. "I've been burned. Or bitten. Damn."

"Bitten?" said Alex. "Where?"

"My legs. It must be a bee. A hundred bees. Goddamn, it hurts." She reached around to the back of her legs.

Alex grabbed her hands. "Hold it. If it's a bee, you may just rub in the stinger. Let me look." He turned her around and bent over the back of her legs.

"I'll say it's a hundred bees. You have a couple of lines of red across both thighs. No, don't touch. Is the pain subsiding?"

"Not so far."

"I think you've got something stuck on there. We'll have to be very careful about cleaning you up."

Sarah groaned. "It's a whole hornet's nest."

"No, it doesn't look like a bee or a wasp. Where were you sitting?"

"Can't you do something to stop it? No, I know you can't." Sarah leaned against him, breathing fast, half-crying. "I'm not trying to be hysterical but it bloody well hurts. I was just sitting there, against the mast. Out of trouble." She tried to smile.

"Lean on Tony, turn into the light, and I'll have another look." Tony now stood forth and offered a supporting arm. "I think Andrea's gone for the first-aid kit," he said.

"Let's see if I can find out what got you, then we can decide what to do. Bend down, Sarah. Tony hold her still." Alex knelt by Sarah's backside and examined the territory.

"Well," said Sarah. "Is it a hornet's nest?"

"What did you sit on? Besides the deck."

"A wet bathing suit," said Tony. "Mine. I put it up there by the mast to dry."

Alex pointed. "And that mop?"

Tony nodded. "That's the deck swab. It was in the Avon, on the bottom under the seats, and it belongs on deck. I took it out and brought it to dry along with my suit."

"And Sarah sat down on them, well almost on them," said

Alex. "She sat down on the deck, leaned against the mast and . . ."

"Put my legs across them, the suit or the mop or both, I guess," said Sarah. "At least I must have. But I was stung so fast I never noticed where I had my legs."

Andrea now reappeared and handed David a basin, a roll of cotton, and a white toolbox marked FIRST AID.

"I've brought something called "Afterbite," said Andrea. "And meat tenderizer and vinegar. I've heard you can use them for insect stings."

"Well, I'm available for any treatment you have." Sarah had pulled herself together. The pain seemed to have reached a sort of climax and leveled off, stinging like fire. That was it. Fire. "Fire ants," she said. "That's what it is. Fire ants."

"Not on board ship," said Mallory, shaking his head. "No way. Bees, I'll buy. Or how about a chemical? Some caustic chemical. Have you been doing any cleaning here?" He turned sternly to Tony.

"We swab the decks with Murphy's soap or the boat detergent, nothing dangerous."

"Lie down on your face," Alex instructed Sarah. "Let's see what we can do."

Sarah, felt that the position was a humiliating one, but the pain was great, so she did as Alex said, resting her face on her arm.

Alex bent over her legs frowning. Then he straightened and shook his head. "It's not a stinger, but if I'm guessing right, you sat on a jellyfish?"

"What! You're crazy."

"Not the whole thing, the filaments. Tony's bathing suit may have picked them up, just a few short strands; he may have bumped against a jellyfish swimming. Or the mop. You probably rinse it out in the ocean, don't you, Tony?"

"Yes," said Tony. "Sometimes, anyway. We swab out the Avon and the whaler and work the deck. Every morning. Actually we have three mops, plus a couple of brushes for the deck."

Alex now bent again over Sarah's upper thighs. "I'm right. Even with the urticaria developing—that's the rash—I can see a filament. And another. Little ones. It's not too bad. The problem is the treatment for these stings is always changing. I know fresh water activates the nematocysts which are the stinging cells and hot water increases systemic uptake of venom so I think I'll go with the vinegar. I've read a recent article that said it was acceptable. Okay, Sarah. Hang in there. Jellyfish stings hurt like the devil. What I'm going to do is try and lift off the filaments. Gently. I'll try not to make it worse."

"Good," said Sarah, lifting her head like a turtle.

"It's going to start itching as well as stinging but if you rub you'll just activate more nematocysts. And I'll give you something for the pain and an antihistamine."

Tony leaned over Sarah. "In Australia, they have something called a box jellyfish, which stings so hard, people drown in the water. They go into paralysis and shock."

"Thank you, Tony," said Sarah in a muffled voice.

"I mean, you're lucky, just a couple of stingers. I'm lucky, too, if they came from my bathing suit. I could have had it across my chest or stomach, which would be a lot worse than the back of your legs. Of course, these Maine jellyfish are wimps. No real impact."

Sarah put her head down on the deck. "Tony, I hope you don't come around if I'm ever really sick." As the pain and stinging receded in a small measure, Sarah became uncomfortably aware that George Fitts and Deputy Sheriff Terhune were now leaning over her backside with interest.

Alex set to work in earnest to lift the few filaments. Finally, he straightened. "There. Don't touch your legs. I'll make up a wet-and-baking soda compress so that you can sit down without too much misery."

Dinner that night began with David giving a prayer in memory of Billy and continued thereafter on a low key. Sarah, her thighs itching and burning, was sleepy with medication. The blight of Billy's death seemed to have infected everyone else with a general malaise. The food was once again excellent, a delicious veal affair with a lemon herb sauce, but they all sat munching as if it were so much sawdust. Even David's promise of tomorrow's sail to Bucks Harbor—police and weather permitting—did little to lift spirits.

"But will they let us go?" asked Alex. "The autopsy report should come in tonight. If it wasn't accidental death by drowning, they may want to question us again."

"The police know where we'll be," said Mallory. "Right now, I'm checking with one of our Apostle boats, the *Simon Peter*. I'd like to take on another crew member in Billy's place. Not that Billy was that useful—sorry Gracie, but it's true. We're losing Ezra for a day or so. He has to stop off sometime in Castine to pick up a delayed shipment of Sunday school material."

"How about the *Pilgrim*'s own distribution work?" asked Sarah, turning to David. Surely neither rain nor sleet nor sudden death could stop the *Pilgrim* from handing out braille Bibles.

"We can work out of Bucks Harbor and the Mount Desert area. The *Simon Peter* can take care of the southern Penobscot Bay islands. Gracie has been rewriting the schedule."

Gracie clasped her anxious hands together as if she were afraid that they might detach themselves and depart. In her evening dark print with the white collar and cuffs, she looked more like Olive Oyl than ever, thought Sarah.

"I think perhaps," said Gracie, "that Billy—I know he wasn't religious—might want the church distribution to go on as usual."

This sounded unlikely, even fatuous. Sarah slid a look at David and saw him shake his head. "Billy's strong point, if he had one, was not good works."

"Forget religion with Billy," said Tony. "He was a menace. All those cute practical jokes like tripping me. He talked about a ship of fools and told me once he wished we still had pirates."

This remark brought the little trickle of conversation to a halt. Gracie glared at Tony and bit her lip. Ezra rose and said something about checking the mooring, and David looked sternly at Tony.

Sarah glared at Tony. "You have absolutely no sense. Or sympathy."

"Right," added Andrea, suddenly Sarah's ally. "What's the

point of saying that. Billy was probably drunk or stoned and probably didn't know what he was saying."

"Though perhaps, *in vino veritas*," said David heavily. "Or truth in drugs. Well, we know Billy often wasn't himself."

There followed then a rambling discussion of Billy's condition, all of which ground had been much trodden over with and without the police. Then, with the appearance of dessert and coffee, Mallory seemed to brighten and went for diversion. He tried travel: a trip to Spain following with little anecdotes, the wine of the given area, a pension with bedbugs. Sarah remembering that the topic of the theatre had proved animating on another evening asked whether everyone had seen the *Phantom of the Opera*. The subject brought the crew to modified life. They talked of theatre, current shows, off-Broadway, on Broadway. Tony said that musicals were boring. He'd like to see some oddball combos. A rock tragedy. Charlie Brown as Dracula.

"*The Cherry Orchard* as a musical comedy," put in Sarah.

"A *Long Day's Journey* with a cancan," added David Mallory.

"*Oedipus* on roller skates," said Andrea.

"Or *Macbeth* as a tap dance with banjos," said Tony.

Gracie pulled at her hands. "Don't say that, it's unlucky."

"What's unlucky?" said Tony.

"That play, the Scottish one. We're on a boat; we might all sink or be lost in a typhoon." Gracie sounded quite serious.

"What?" repeated Tony. "Come on. *Macbeth*, *Macbeth*, *Macbeth*. Maybe as a tap dance with roller skates."

"Just don't ask for trouble," said Gracie. Sarah saw that the secretary's jaw had set and she had half-risen in her seat. Time to break it up.

"Let's plan a nude *Pinafore*," Sarah said. "That should keep everyone happy. Gracie, I'm so sorry about everything. Now I'm going to bed and to sleep, even if I have to lie facedown the whole night."

"I'll change your dressing," said Alex. "And then I'm going ashore for the autopsy report."

Tony, remembering that he had a sister who was under the weather, belatedly asked whether there was anything he could do. "Read to you, maybe? T. S. Eliot, ee cummings, a book on jellyfish?"

"Thank you, Tony, no," said Sarah. "But if you'll look for the *Odyssey*. I was reading it on deck when I was stung."

"You mean that old Modern Library book you've been carrying around? It went overboard. I saw it go after you yelled. You must have knocked it over. It sank."

"Oh damn. David, I'm so sorry. It was one of the *Pilgrim*'s books."

"Never mind, Sarah," said David Mallory in a soothing-to-the-invalid voice. "We'll pick up another copy in Northeast. They have a good bookstore there."

"You can read *The Thirty-Nine Steps*," said Alex. "Pure escapism. Or something more lofty. Lots of books aboard."

Sarah had no intention of reading John Buchan's old spy thriller, but when she had arranged herself prone on her bunk and Alex had put new wet compresses on her thighs, she found herself reaching for it and losing herself in the world of Richard Hannay.

She turned the pages slowly, floating along on the top of the narrative and hoping that Buchan wasn't going to drown any characters. Billy Brackett kept moving in on the story. She couldn't forget the sight of him as he lay sprawled and sodden on the float. She closed the book, trying to lose the image, or transform it, remodel the figure into something bearable.

Sarah's immediate experience with drowning—surely Billy had drowned—up to now had been through hearsay, art, and fiction. Grim pictures and descriptions, yes, but grim in a romantic, consoling sort of way. Winslow Homer's *Undertow*— the victims wet, and dead, certainly dead, but dead with a sort of sober dignity. And Steerforth on the Yarmouth beach remembered by David Copperfield as looking like the boy he had known at school. And Shelley. Sarah had always imagined Shelley with his head on one arm, bright hair streaming on the sand, eyes softly closed. And James Dickey's poem of the lifeguard searching in moonlit water, "And hold in my arms a child/Of water, water, water." And Sarah was asleep.

And almost immediately awake.

Alex was sitting on the edge of her bed.

"Billy Brackett wasn't drowned," he said.

Sarah, forgetting her bandaged legs whirled around on the bunk, groaned, and made a half-turn facing Alex. "But he *was* drowned, we saw him lying on the float. Those two men had just pulled him out of the water. How could he not be drowned?"

"Because he was dead before he went into the water. The autopsy showed that the whole respiratory system wasn't overwhelmed by sea water—I won't go into the details."

"Someone pushed him in the water?"

"No, hold on. They're guessing he might have been down at the water's edge, or wading in it, died, and just slipped under. Possibly he was disoriented, drunk, thought he was on the Inn float and was trying to find a dinghy to row out to the *Pilgrim*."

"But died of what? Did someone hit him?"

"He might have got into a fight with someone—person or persons unknown as they say. There was a slight bruising by the chin and a shoulder laceration, so he could have been hit, or fallen, or both. The blow wouldn't have been enough to kill him, but if you add it to what he had to drink, well, it would be enough to put him out for a while. People at the church meeting said Billy was on edge, spoiling for trouble, so when he left he might just have found it, even looked for it. But the bruise on the chin is just an accidental complication. The medical examiner is guessing, guessing mind you, that Billy may have died of a fatal laryngeal spasm, from an anaphylactic reaction."

"You mean?"

"He couldn't breathe."

"Why not?"

"Edema—swelling—in the throat and larynx. The lab people are adding the fact that Billy was drinking to the emerging profile of an allergic person, and they're wondering if he had a reaction that was violent enough to kill him. It must have happened hours before he was found in the water because his body had gone down to water temperature."

"An allergy? To food? Alcohol, bee stings?"

"To some material. Dangerous to him, something Billy was

sensitive to. The pathologist has a definite line on it, real evidence, and the lab is checking it out."

"I think everything was dangerous to Billy. Gracie said he was allergic. Maybe that's why he didn't eat anything. There was soybean powder in his room."

"Wait for the lab report. We'll know in the morning. Now, listen Sarah, it's late. Go to sleep. I'm turning in right now."

"Sleep! How can I sleep?"

"Yes, you can. I'll change your bandages and rub your back and whisper sweet iambic pentameters in your ears."

Sarah subsided. "That's why I love you Dr. McKenzie."

TWELVE

THURSDAY-MORNING BREAKFAST BROUGHT THE TWO new passengers, the Chandlers. Sarah—and Alex judging from his expression—had completely forgotten. Flip and Elaine Chandler described by David at the beginning of that luncheon at the Islesboro Inn as "such fun people." Surrounded by a clutch of boxes, monogrammed bags and duffles, they were ferried to the ship's ladder in the motor whaleboat. They came aboard almost apologetically, as if they knew they were intruders on the scene of death.

Sarah and Alex seemed to be the only ones surprised at the arrival; the rest remembered sailing with them before and welcomed them. Mallory kissed Elaine Chandler, clapped Flip Chandler on the shoulder, then lowered his voice and spoke sadly of "our recent loss."

There was no loose talk about Billy Brackett at breakfast; the Chandlers made sober and appropriate reference to the death and then began a nicely coordinated description of their summer, their visit on Islesboro, and their joy of being—at last—aboard *Pilgrim*.

Sarah, as the talk flowed around people and places unknown to her, was at leisure to inspect the couple.

She guessed that they were both in their mid-fifties, although so beautifully coifed and displayed that age seemed irrelevant. They were timeless. Elaine had hair the color of ripe wheat, pulled into a braided knot at the nape of her neck, a fine mobile mouth, dark eyes expertly lined, a broad forehead, and a beautifully elevated chin. Her throat was swathed in a saffron scarf, her arms ajingle with heavy gold, her long fingers enhanced by several twisted gold rings and one spectacular ruby sided with two large diamonds. She was wrapped in a mustard-colored cotton that showed her splendid mature figure to great advantage. Her voice was a musical yet penetrating alto, her diction impeccable.

Flip, his real name emerging in the general talk as Fleance, had a light tenor voice well suited to little anecdotes and crisp rejoinders. He looked like a Ralph Lauren ad, in an open-neck blue striped shirt, a blue linen blazer, white trousers, and espadrilles. He would, with Elaine on his arm, have been in place at any chic spot in the country—or out of the country. Sarah could picture the two of them on verandas of yacht clubs, eating from a hamper on the tailgate of a station wagon while watching a Maryland point-to-point, applauding politely at Wimbledon, joining a walking party along the coast of Majorca.

After breakfast, the Chandlers made their way to their cabin to unpack, and the silence about Billy was broken. It appeared that everyone knew about the autopsy report.

"It seems that Billy didn't drown," said David Mallory to the company at large. "Beyond that, I know nothing. The police are waiting on the lab tests. I'm afraid it will be drugs."

"I'm sure it was something he ate," said Gracie, "something he should have left alone and it made him sick."

"But does that explain the syringe?" asked Sarah.

"It could," said a voice from the top of the companionway—a voice like the cold flow of fog seeping into a warm and pleasant place. George Fitts. He climbed noiselessly into the cabin, made his way to the breakfast table, and sat down and carefully opened his notebook.

"The syringe," said George, looking neither to the left or right, "matches the sort that comes from a common allergy kit called Banabite. There are several makes around, particularly in the summer when people expect bee or insect bites."

"There," said Gracie, in a voice of vast relief, "I told you he had that kit and was afraid of bees. He was stung and was drinking too much and it killed him and he fell in the water. It's not drugs, even though David keeps saying it is."

"Billy walked into a bee's nest?" asked Tony. "A bee's nest in the middle of the night?"

"He'd been drinking," Andrea reminded him.

"About the drinking," said Sarah. "When I sat next to him that night at dinner, he didn't drink the wine, he faked it."

"He certainly has had too much on occasion," said Mallory. I've talked to him about it. But usually rum seemed to be his choice."

"Rum has a sugar base," said Alex. "Sometimes it's tolerated better than whiskey or wine by people with a food sensitivity."

"It doesn't take a hive of bees," insisted Gracie. "One bee sting can kill a person like Billy."

"It's possible that Billy was not stung by bees," said George.

"Well, what then?" Tony stared at George with obvious dislike, and Sarah remembered that Tony had never much love for men of law. In fact, since his lead guitar had been busted, he'd been almost paranoid on the subject.

"I'll see each of you again. Alone." George brought out a ball-point pen and clicked it. "We will wait until all the laboratory tests are in. Try not to speculate on what may or may not have happened, or you'll start imagining things about Billy that have no relation to fact and will only distort the case."

"Sergeant Fitts, I don't imagine things," said Gracie. She had been bustling with coffee; the news that Billy's syringe might have come from his insect kit seemed to have lifted a great weight from her. "I only tell what I know, and it's bad enough to know what happened. It's been a nightmare."

George studied Gracie for a moment, then inclined his bald

head in her direction. "Miss Mullen, I'll see you first. Next, Tony Deane, Andrea Elder, and Sarah, in that order. Ezra, I saw last night. Alex, please sit in and help with the medical end. When I finish, you can take off for Bucks Harbor. Keeping in touch as planned."

George moved fast. Gracie was disposed within less than fifteen minutes; Tony under ten; Andrea, a twenty-minute session. She returned from David's private cabin, which George had borrowed for his questioning, and reported her interview to the waiting group. "How well I'd known him in Florida, that stuff again. Did he swim in Florida in the ocean, and I said I'd never seen that much of Billy, and I didn't know if he had a syringe in a kit or out of a kit. Or whether he'd ever talked about wheezing or itching or having hives. I said he drank and I didn't know if he did drugs."

Sarah, still conscious of her own itching legs, made her way to Mallory's cabin and found Alex and George going over a sheet of paper with a long series of handwritten notes.

"This ought to interest you, Sarah," said Alex, picking up the paper. "Can you guess what this report says?"

"No," said Sarah crossly. "And I don't see why George needs anything more from me. I only knew Billy from Monday morning to Tuesday afternoon on this trip, and I've never seen him use a syringe. Which I've told you, George Fitts."

"But I haven't told you something," said George.

"What something?"

"Billy possibly went into anaphylactic shock as a result of an extended contact with a venomous jellyfish."

"As I suggested last night," said Alex. The lab report came in on the phone just before George started the interviews."

"But Billy's dead," cried Sarah. "Jellyfish don't kill you here. Or even in Florida. And this isn't Australia."

"Even peanut butter, or fresh lobster, or one yellow-jacket bite can kill if you're allergic," said Alex. "One man's poison."

"You mean the same sort of jellyfish I sat on, the kind that was stuck on Tony's bathing suit or the mop?"

"Yes," said George. "Most probably the lion's mane jellyfish, though there have been a few unconfirmed reports of Portuguese man-of-war this far north in the past two years. The labs have been examining the filaments. From Billy's body."

"And the lab people," put in Alex, "will look at Tony's bathing suit and the boat swab for good measure."

George clicked his pen in and out with authority. "That's why I wanted to go over Billy's activities in Florida with Andrea. She knew him down there but only remembers him swimming in a pool. Or occasionally wading in shallow clear water. But anyone who has ever swum in southern waters may be sensitized by coelenterates—jellyfish. Sensitized by being stung or by simply swimming in the area in which a jellyfish has released antigens. Taking everything together, including what Billy's sister, Miss Mullen, has told us, we have a picture of a wide range of possible allergies and sensitivities—to food, the sun, animal and insect venom. We're also considering, as Mallory suggested we do, the improper use of analgesics and illegal drugs."

George put both thumbs together, contemplated a cabin porthole for a moment, and then turned to Sarah. "Thought you'd like to know about the jellyfish, Sarah. After all, you're a victim in a way. I'm not telling the others yet for my own reasons." George folded the lab report and placed it carefully inside his notebook, leaned back in Mallory's desk chair, and addressed both listeners.

"Mallory tells me he's taking on a new crew member from the Apostle boat, the *Simon Peter*. He belongs to Mallory's church and has spent some time working with the Apostle fleet. The man's name is deTerra and he'll be here directly. He's originally from Maine, which may be helpful in sailing this boat. As a matter of routine, just to set everyone's mind at rest, because I know Billy's death has been disturbing, we've checked with the Florida police, who tell us that this deTerra is a good citizen."

"I don't see why the Chandlers couldn't fill in for Billy; they're right on board." But even as Sarah said this, she felt that the Chandlers would not fit happily into any scheme involving physical exertion.

"I have seen the Chandlers," said George in a disapproving voice, "and I doubt that either of them would be useful."

"But decorative," said Alex.

George pushed himself away from David Mallory's mahogany desk. "Now Sarah, get well and let me worry about jellyfish and syringes. I know that in the past you have demonstrated during a criminal investigation a certain amount of initiative and the result has been hazardous. For you, your friends, and for the police."

"I have no desire to spend a single minute on Penobscot Bay thinking about syringes or jellyfish," snapped Sarah. "I'm very sorry about Billy and there's an end to it."

"Just take care and watch out for pickup trucks."

"George, is that supposed to be funny? And who told you about the truck? I told everyone that I couldn't tell who was driving."

"Sarah," said George, "I never try to be funny, certainly not about someone being run off the road by a truck. Alex told me; David Mallory emphasized the incident, said that some of Billy's pals on the island may not be law-abiding citizens. Then Ezra told me—said Billy *had* slipped his leash during the Bible-distribution business. And Tony and Andrea mentioned it. In fact, Grace Mullen is the only one not to bring it up. Everyone else emphasized that Billy was an off-the-wall practical joker. Anyway, please take care." And with that, George slipped noiselessly from the cabin.

Sarah sighed. "Now I suppose George has put me in the same category as Gracie, an unstable female."

"I think George was trying to be friendly," said Alex mildly.

Sarah made a face. "With him it's hard to tell."

"You underestimate George Fitts," said Alex, pushing her ahead of him out of Mallory's cabin. It was a remark that Sarah would remember with some chagrin.

They found David Mallory signing off on the radio-telephone. "I called ahead to see about a Bucks Harbor anchorage." He shook his head sadly. "The name *Pilgrim* has now been splashed all over the local papers because of Billy, and I suppose the publicity will just about finish any attempt on my part to look for questionable boats. George suggested I cancel the idea unless something really alarming crosses my bow. I said for the present, I'll just concentrate on our regular Bible-distribution plans. All right, friends, we'll probably set sail by noon after we off-load the rest of the Islesboro church material. The wind's southwest and freshening."

"Could I go ashore, get some exercise, use the bicycle again?" asked Sarah.

"Your legs," reminded Alex.

"Much better."

"They didn't look it this morning. Take it easy."

Sarah smiled a tight smile at Alex, trying to send by telepathy the message there was something she wanted to do. "I'm just a little restless; the bicycling will do wonders."

"Not for a jellyfish sting, it won't."

"I think Alex is right," said David, "but if you want to go ashore for thirty minutes or so, why the Avon is all yours."

"I'll row them in," said Tony, appearing unexpectedly. "Andrea has an order of groceries coming down to the dock."

"Oh, do let us come with you." It was Elaine and Flip Chandler from their cabin. Flip carried a shoe box marked SLIDES, WINTER CRUISE, and Elaine a large photograph album in maroon leather. They were "Pictures at an Exhibition" on the hoof. Elaine in a raspberry crushed-cotton divided skirt and an ivory silk shirt; Flip in linen, a yellow paisley tie, and a panama hat.

"Hiking?" said Sarah dubiously. The couple moved in a mingled haze of after-shave lotion and perfume, the resulting essence rather that of old varnish.

"No hiking for the Chandlers," said Flip. "We're meeting the Gurneys, old, old friends. Just a hello and a good-bye at the inn. We heard they were coming in this morning from Hobe Sound, where they've been simply frying in the heat. We have pictures to show them, our last trip together to Portugal."

Elaine indicated the album. "Pictures are worth a hundred letters—which I never write. I buy these enormous photograph books, and we can do a whole year in half an hour, really catch up."

"I'll come with you, Sarah," said Alex.

"Oh," she said, a little dismayed. She had wanted to find a telephone without Alex frowning his disapproval.

One by one, they lowered themselves into the rubber raft, Tony at the oars steadying the craft and giving a hand to the Chandlers, who sat gingerly down on the rubber roll of the stern.

"Sarah, you don't look so great," said Tony, pulling away. "Why didn't you stay put? Andrea said she'd been stung in Florida and it took a couple of days to feel better."

"Of course, I don't look great," said Sarah. "But I need the air and Andrea isn't me."

"No way," said Tony, grinning.

"Tony," said Sarah, "I used to be very fond of you."

"That's your itchy legs speaking, sister dear. Andrea is trying to be helpful, and I'm showing decent brotherly concern. Alex, don't you think she should take it easy?"

"Yes," said Alex shortly, "but Sarah doesn't listen."

Sarah was about to retort when Elaine joined the chorus and Sarah had to submit to a stream of advice about rashes and sun and poison animals. This, in turn, stimulated Flip into a tangled tale of a trip to the Sonoran Desert and the discovery of a scorpion in his bedroom slipper. This tale finished only with the arrival at the inn float. The Chandlers clambered out—Flip first, and Elaine, trying to step and balance on the edge of the boat, dropped her album on the dock. Alex reached for it, but Flip was quicker.

"Oh, thank you, darling." Elaine beamed at her husband and then leaned down to those still bobbing about in the raft. "You know people ask me what I'd save in a fire, and I say the picture albums. Our whole life. Furniture and clothes, jewelry you can replace. Not photographs."

"What about the Pissarro, love, or the little Monet?"

"Those, too, but *after* the photographs." Elaine slipped her free arm under her husband's and started up the gangway.

"They are *not* real," said Sarah, clambering out on the deck.

"Neither are you," said Tony, "when you should be in bed. I'll meet you here in an hour. I'd like to come for your hike but after I pick up the groceries, I've got to help load church stuff on the *Simon Peter*." Tony pointed to a sturdy blue boat that was making its way from the outer harbor.

"Tony's right," said Alex. "You're not well."

"Well enough," said Sarah as they started up the incline toward the inn pathway. "I've got to call Mary again."

"For Christ's sake."

"For my sake. Please listen. I have this idea. Gracie—do you think there was more going on between them than just a brother and big sister relationship?"

"No, I do not."

"You see, I think Gracie looked at him once in a way that made me think he really bothered her—or scared her. Beyond being worried about an errant brother. She certainly doesn't like the idea that he may have been into drugs. She's been fighting Mallory on that at every turn."

"Sarah, for God's sake, he was her brother. Wouldn't you resist the idea that your brother was into hard stuff?"

Sarah held up her hand. "Yes, yes, of course. But what if, just what if Billy and Gracie were a team, a drug team working right aboard the *Pilgrim*, and after Billy was found dead, Gracie went down to his cabin to dump any evidence, any drugs supplies that might be around—but she found Mallory already there holding that syringe."

"Sarah, I can only assume that the jellyfish venom is affecting your brain."

"I said listen. Gracie is appalled to find David in the cabin, so she makes the best of a bad situation by saying she's come down to look for anything that might damage his reputation."

"I believe Gracie did what she said she did. It's the sort of thing an overwrought sister might do."

"She knew Billy was allergic; she knew Billy carried an insect-bite kit and probably that the syringe that came with it was a special sort. Well, if the syringe was safe in its kit, then it wouldn't hurt Billy's so-called reputation. But no kit. Only Mallory with the naked syringe ready to turn it over to the police. A syringe without a kit suggests drug use. To Mallory, to George, to everyone. It's easy to believe since one look at Billy and you start thinking about something illegal. And Gracie doesn't want anyone to start thinking drugs because her part in the business may turn up. I say she went down to Billy's cabin because she was afraid of evidence that might suggest she and Billy were in business together. Hidden drugs, or a list of suppliers."

"Are you saying now that Mallory cleaned the cabin of this so-called evidence and is now protecting Gracie?"

"No, I'm guessing that there wasn't anything to find, only the syringe which must have been overlooked. I think Billy had cleared the cabin. He was going ashore, remember. To that church supper. And he left early. Why? To wheel and deal, I'll bet. The Gracie-Billy brother and sister team makes sense, and now Gracie's going bonkers trying to cover tracks."

"Now you listen. Mallory seems sure the syringe is related to drug use. No epinephrine was found in Billy's cabin, no bee kit, no Benadryl tablets. Yes, it's possible that Billy could have lost his Banabite kit, he wasn't exactly the responsible type, but it's equally possible that he's been messing with drugs, as well as being allergic. Messing alone. As a single user. Without Gracie. So wait—please—for the lab reports and a medical rundown from Florida."

"One minute more. Here's my idea of how the team worked. Billy went ashore and picked out or met customers or drug suppliers—from some fake church group maybe or just around the area. Remember George told us that Billy 'slipped his leash' and left Ezra. Say he met his friends in the green pickup truck, has some fun trying to scare me—that's his idea of a laugh—and does his dealing. Gracie was the organization person, which was easy for her because she acts as housekeeper, in charge of space and stowage on the boat. She could use the cartons, slip it in a Bible. Cocaine doesn't need much room."

Alex took hold of both of Sarah's shoulders. "Now hear this, Gracie Mullen is Mallory's girl Friday, his right arm. You've seen those Bibles, the cassettes, the whole bit. Legitimate supplies to legitimate churches. Mallory supervises those Bible boxes; they're sealed and labeled. Tony, Andrea, and Ezra load them. Ezra and the rest distribute the stuff. Not just to one fake church that's working a drug scam. George tells me that David has made a donation of material to each—got that, sweetie—*each* church on the island, except the Catholic. They run their own supply system. Do you think Gracie ran a separate drug ring with Billy that took in the Episcopal, the Methodist, Congregational, the Baptist, the you-name-it church on the whole blessed island?"

"It's just something I feel in my bones."

"Your bones are crazy. I'll say it again. George checked the Church of the Apostles and its minions. Gracie is one of its minions. The church does good works. They distribute books and tapes. For free. For the meek, for the poor in spirit, for the merciful. Amen."

"You may have missed your calling."

"Blessed are the peacemakers. That's me. If you want to suspect someone, try the Chandlers. Feel perfectly free to consider them second-story artists. Or forgers. Because, as you said, they are not real."

"I take it back. I'm afraid they are. The Beautiful People at work and at play."

"Mostly at play."

"But I do want to call Mary. Gracie may have a Bowmouth College past. Remember David told us she first met him at a northeast Bible conference. In Maine."

"Poor Mary, pulled into Sarah's spiderweb."

"Good for her. She spends too much time wallowing in the eighteenth century. A little contemporary research will be a relief."

They recovered their bicycles and Sarah, trying not to feel her legs like flames, pedaled earnestly to the public phone booth in Dark Harbor. But Mary was not now at home. Amos was.

"Oh dear," said Sarah when he answered.

"How flattering," said Amos Larkin. "Is that you, Sarah? I was hoping our relationship had progressed to the point where you might ask about what sort of a summer I'm having."

"I don't want to bore you."

"You'd rather bore Mary. Well, bore ahead. I've just finished a batch of papers and I need something dull."

Sarah sighed. Alex thought she was crazy. Now Amos would join the ranks of the unbelievers.

But Amos sounded mildly interested. "I'm by nature suspicious. I think the worst of everyone. It's the Jonathan Swift world viewpoint. This Gracie Mullen and brother Billy Brackett, deceased, as a drug duo? Are you sure you're not reaching? What have you been reading lately? Not Jane Austen."

"John Buchan, *The Thirty-Nine Steps*."

"There you go. I knew there was an influence. Okay, I'll hit the computer center, because this Gracie Mullen rings a bell. She might have taken one of the adult-ed English courses. I tend to remember fools as well as the bright lights."

"I don't think she's a fool, but she's got this jumpy way of acting, sometimes tough, sometimes in pieces, and she looks just like Olive Oyl."

"I've always admired Popeye but I never could understand his interest in Olive."

"Anything you can dig up, Amos. I'd like to sic you on a gorgeous couple called Chandler, Elaine and Flip. Flip as in Fleance."

"Zounds."

"And odd's buckles. But never mind them. They're genuine, right out of *Town & Country*. No, I just want Gracie."

"You don't want much, do you? I may have to cancel classes."

"Thanks, Amos. And Alex wants to make sure you know I'm out of my head."

Alex reached for the phone. "Crazed by jellyfish. She sat on pieces of one."

"Life at sea was never easy," said Amos. "Mary can hit the registrar's files, and I've got a stack of old alumni mags in the barn. I'll put myself in the hammock and do some reading. I suppose it will be a relief from undergraduate essays on the meaning of *Gulliver's Travels*."

"Sarah," said Alex as they pedaled slowly back to the inn, "do you think you can bear it if you find that Gracie and Billy are not a deadly drug-dealing team?"

Sarah did not answer. She had the virtuous sense of one who has made an intuitive leap from the most fragile collection of evidence. Now it was only a step from thinking of Gracie and

Billy as a drug team to deciding that Gracie had somehow slipped a jellyfish down Billy's back. Gracie was metamorphosing from Olive Oyl to something closer to the Greeks. Clytemnestra? Medea? Yes, the more Sarah thought about it, the more she thought it was fear that Gracie had shown when she looked at Billy. And where does fear lead you? Anywhere.

THIRTEEN

S ARAH AND ALEX ARRIVED BACK ON THE *PILGRIM* IN time to watch the last loading of the *Simon Peter*. She was a stable craft built as a cross between a small tug and a large lobster boat, and now stood throbbing under her idling diesel engine, abeam of the *Pilgrim*.

David Mallory marched about the deck supervising, Gracie trotting at his side with a clipboard and pencil, while Ezra, Tony, and Andrea passed cartons across to waiting hands on the *Simon Peter*. Sarah, sitting on a hatch cover away from the action near the bow, saw that each sealed carton had been carefully marked. First the destination, color-coded: Vinalhaven, North Haven, Isle au Haut, Swans Island, Castine, Deer Island; then the names of the lucky church or meetinghouse. Some of these were familiar-sounding names, such as St. Paul's Episcopal, North Congregational, St. Peter of the Sea, Church of the Trinity; others were wild cards like Jerusalem the Golden Meetinghouse, Children of Zion, the Bible Bonding Society. Sarah saw that this last was marked on the side for two brailles, four large-print New Testaments, ten *Bible Tales for Children*, twenty *Happy Jesus Pop-up Readers*.

What efficiency. Mallory should work for the government, or the Army Supply Corps. Straighten out the mess there.

Elaine Chandler agreed. She sat down on the hatch cover next to Sarah, sweeping her skirt under her so that not a wrinkle would appear on rising—something Sarah had never mastered.

"My dear, have you ever seen the like, what a system. David knows where every copy of the Good Book is going, books for the deaf, the blind, the retarded, and probably for the unborn, not to mention the children's titles, like *Bobby and Bonnie Bear on Noah's Ark* or *Joseph's Coat Coloring Book.*"

"It *is* impressive," said Sarah as a box labeled TIMMY TEDDY SAYS HIS PRAYERS, was tossed from hand to hand.

Flip sauntered over from the bow. "Have you seen this object?" He held up a soft white stuffed rabbit with a pink bow around its neck and turned the key in its back. A childish mechanical voice squeaked its message into the air: "You shall have no other Gods but me; Before no idol bend your knee."

"Frightening, isn't it? Ten Commandments in easy rhyme for little ears," said Flip. "David is something else."

Sarah recoiled. However, as she was about to launch into a denunciation of plush rabbits, David joined the group. "Just about loaded. What do you think of Rollo Rabbit? Sarah, you object. It's going to far. Right?"

"I didn't say," Sarah began.

"Your face did. Never mind. Some children have no willing parents—or no parents at all—to read to them, have no regular Sunday school or Head Start program. We have toy animals who tell Bible stories. And this rabbit is something they can love and still hear a message. The Ten Commandments are pretty good rules."

"'Thou shall not commit adultery,'" said Sarah. "For toddlers? Or 'Thou shall not kill'?"

"We tell it on their level. Adultery is treated as falsehood, murder as hurt. 'You must never tell a lie; Do not make another cry.'"

"Oh David, you are too much," said Elaine. "I agree with Sarah. I think the Rollo Rabbit is awful. Absolutely too Disney. Couldn't you have had a brown animal, a decent one with proper eyes? A Steiff teddy."

"A Steiff animal of that size costs well over a hundred dollars, and kids want pastel colors—at least that's what my market-research people tell me."

"Market research," said Flip with contempt. "We are all sold a bill of goods by advertising idiots with the taste of orangutans. The sort of people who put plastic flamingos on their lawns."

"All God's children," said David. "Remember the kingdom of heaven and the eye of the needle. Now Sarah, how are you feeling?"

"Perfectly well," lied Sarah. Her legs were stinging from the earlier exercise but she wasn't going to admit it.

"I don't believe you, but you're a good sport. I won't ask you to look at another rabbit for the whole cruise. Elaine, I'll have a Steiff animal made up just for you. Now I came over to say that our new crew member, deTerra—Mark G. deTerra—is coming on board from the *Simon Peter*. Quite a guy, done some really imaginative things down in the Keys, not an easy area what with the tourists and the local population at odds. He's originally from Maine and tells me he's done some sailing along the East Coast."

Sarah, aware of a sudden movement at her side, turned and saw Elaine Chandler working to control a look of—well, what was it? Annoyance perhaps. Then her face went smooth.

"David, darling, I haven't met this man, but if he's the treasure you say, then I suppose Flip and I can help put out the welcome mat. Though frankly, I thought we were quite cosy the way we were. Let's hope he plays bridge." She yawned and rose to her feet. "Flip, my love, I must have more lotion on my shoulders or I'll have to stop wearing these sun tops. You know what the quacks say about those awful little brown spots. Sarah, I have the most marvelous sun block. It doesn't smell like the medicine cabinet, pure Giorgio. I'll lend you some." And the two Chandlers moved toward the stern at a leisurely pace.

Sarah couldn't help herself. "I suppose that remark is meant to mean that Elaine doesn't like the smell of my Sea 'n' Ski."

"Elaine is a bit critical sometimes," said David.

"I think she objects to the new arrival," said Sarah.

"She can adjust. It's just that they've heard me say he's a bit of a rough diamond." And David returned to watch over the last of the loading process.

Sarah sought Alex, who had gone to the bow with a book from the main cabin library, Roger Angell on baseball. "The new crew member approaches. Another man of God, or God-related."

Alex looked up. "As foretold." He patted the deck beside him. "If a wind blows up, we could use extra help to sail this big baby. Flip Chandler and darling Elaine are about as useful as . . ."

"As Rollo Rabbit, a creature you haven't met. It's a white stuffed rabbit, who, as Elaine might say, is too sick-making. It cranks out the Ten Commandments for little ears."

"I doubt if the Chandlers know the Ten Commandments."

"But Flip can be amusing," Sarah conceded.

"In a decadent way. There's more to Elaine."

"I think the reverse," said Sarah. "Flip can really make me laugh even if I think he's deplorable. Elaine is always posing. They're indoor people, lapdogs, but on their own turf, very sharp. I'll bet they're lethal at the bridge table, the kind of players that cue-bid clubs to tell you they have a six-card heart suit."

Alex pointed over to the dock. "There's our new man now. Tony's loading his stuff in the whaler. We'll be taking off in a minute. Why don't you take a rest; you've been much too active."

"I'm as strong as a horse," said Sarah firmly.

"Make that mule."

"You just want me to go below before I decide this new man is an ax murderer."

He did look rather like an ax murderer, Sarah decided on meeting him. Or a felon of some sort. Dark complexion, long, bony face, cleft chin, heavy brows, blue-black hair in a short businesslike cut. And his eyes, pale blue, as cold as ice. He was of medium height, gave the impression of great strength, and moved with the grace of a boxer. Muscled arms showed through his thin blue work shirt and ended in big wide hands, and his dungarees fitted as if they grew on him. Sarah felt that all her days of stumbling into crime had been building for this moment. Gracie and Billy Brackett faded in interest. Here was a dangerous man.

Mark deTerra was introduced to Sarah. He took her hand without interest, as if it were an unwelcome foreign object, and dropped it immediately. He was almost as brief with Alex but then gladdened at the sight of the Chandlers. On Tony and Andrea's arrival topside, he was short with Tony—"Glad to meet ya"—and delighted with Andrea, joking and talking of a "real live mermaid" on board, had heard a lot about her. Ezra, he greeted as an old shipmate with whom he had spent six days last year bringing the Apostle ship *Matthew* into dry dock.

Last of all, Mark deTerra turned his attention to Gracie, calling on her to remember a church conference in Tampa last year. Gracie nodded soberly and sat down on the other side of the cockpit. DeTerra made a few more cheery remarks to the crew in general and then disappeared below to stow his gear— Billy's cabin in the crew's quarters.

And now it was sailing time.

David at the helm kept the big wheel firm, and the *Pilgrim* leaned to leeward, her bow nodding and rising into and over the waves like a graceful mare released to pasture. Now they were free of restraint and the shore, free of stale harbor air and unmoving harbor water, of buzz and business. Of George Fitts and all his works. Of lethal green pickup trucks. Of poor dead Billy, now lying dismembered on some autopsy table. Free.

Sarah repeated the word *free* to herself as she felt again like a blessing the release of the open sea. What if this deTerra looked like Blackbeard or Gracie wasn't all she should be. Sarah felt the weight of the past two days slide from her shoulders. She lay on the windward deck, her head to the sky, listening as Tony, standing by the helm holding a chart open, called off the islands and the markers to David.

Free, she sang to herself. Deep water, a good wind, no shoals. Nothing mattered but the sun and the wind and that blue sky without a cloud or a shadow. A lovely boat on a lovely ocean.

This beneficent frame of mind lasted through luncheon.

They ate under sail, Andrea serving little compartmented trays to the guests, Tony, Ezra, and David taking turns at the wheel.

The Chandlers, flanking the new arrival, began the old game—beloved of highborn WASPS—of "do you know?" It was soon obvious that, despite Mark deTerra's familiarity with the whole Florida seaboard, east and west, and large sections of his native Maine, he did not know the "right people," had not gone to the right schools or colleges.

"Do you know the Murray-Scotts, Todd and Pippy? I was at Westover with Pippy. You may know her as Phyllis," said Elaine.

"Have you met the Peases?" queried Flip, "the James Peases, that's Wendy and Jimbo. Jimbo was in my class at Yale. From Kennebunkport, but they winter on Captiva, the house next to Prentices, that's Kitty Prentice. Of course, the beach is practically gone on Captiva, so they're looking at Sea Island."

Mark deTerra with good temper denied Yale, the Peases, Captiva, Westover, and Pippy and Todd. "I've lived a dull life," he admitted. "Small town in Maine, small town in Florida, do a lot of volunteer work for David's church and tend to my business."

"Which is?" Sarah smiled to show that this was a question meant to show proper interest in a stranger.

She was ignored and the question went unanswered. Mark went on to describe his "dull" business life (business unnamed) and his love of sailing. He expressed his regret over the fate of Billy Brackett. "I met him down in the Keys, heard he'd been tossed out of Harvard."

"Harvard," said Elaine in a welcoming voice, as if even this hearsay connection of deTerra's with Harvard was better than nothing.

"Me," continued Mark, "I went to community college, night school. Business Ed. My parents couldn't hardly read, immigrants from the old country. Good hardworking stock, solid people but never had time for school. They spoke Italian at home but wouldn't let me. I haven't used the stuff in years. Don't even know how to say *buon giorno*."

This openness seemed, all at once, to charm the Chandlers.

Suddenly equality, simplicity of birth and schooling were "refreshing," in Elaine's words. "We're so bored with all this old school tie, this Ivy League talk. We do play the game sometimes, but we're sick of it."

"Sick to death," echoed Flip.

"So much of the summer scene in Maine is so absolutely superficial. And in Florida, too. You just never go beyond the surface. Summer people, visitors. And it's our own fault," Elaine added virtuously. "We're spoiled rotten, we don't make an effort, we don't meet people halfway."

Really, thought Sarah, the Chandlers are absolute windmills, all things to all people. They can't even be steadfast snobs. Before we know it, they'll be talking up the Teamsters or singing the "Internationale."

"Elaine is right," said Flip. "It's damn good to be with real people, people who do real things in the world."

Sarah tried again. "What real things do you do?" she asked the new arrival.

This time, Mark looked directly at her, and then shrugged and turned laughing to Elaine Chandler as if she had asked the question. "Oh I've done this and that. Rope horses, drill wells, tend the store, keep the old wheels spinning. Actually, my front is a hardware store, but at heart I'm a rolling stone."

Elaine laughed back and said that stick-in-the-mud people were what was wrong with this country. And so terribly dull.

David Mallory, having turned the wheel over to Tony, arrived at this moment, and after a brief discussion with Mark about the problems of distributing religious material to churches that didn't want it, brought up the subject of Mark's fieldwork. "Why don't you tell us about your experience in the Keys. Such a volatile population, it's hard to get a fix on the real needs."

"Their real needs," said deTerra, "would be hard to figure. Some would say clinics, others peace on earth, or at least peace in Key West. Me, I'd say love thy neighbor and use contraceptives. But hey, I don't want to bore these people with that stuff."

Elaine looked at Mark over her sunglasses. "I'm never bored, Mr. deTerra, not with someone new. Someone who has traveled, seen so much of the country, the west. Was it Oklahoma or Montana where you roped horses and drilled wells? Or Texas? I adore Texas. So much to find out about each other. Your mother and father, how they got their start in this country. And what you like to do for fun. Besides sailing. Do you play bridge?"

"Sometimes, but pinochle is more my game. Or poker. If you need another bridge player, I suppose I could fill in, but, hey, don't try any of those fancy conventions with me. I'll be left with egg on my face." He turned to Alex, abruptly. "You a doctor?"

Alex admitted that he was.

"Then I'll try and keep my big trap shut, because have I ever had trouble with the medical boys. Especially with my father and his condition. Talk about a runaround. I guess you'll tell me there are two sides to everything, but you can't prove it by me."

Alex, who avoided medical arguments like the plague, merely nodded in a distant way, and Mark turned back to David. "This boat is far out the best boat I've ever been on. All that wood and varnish, a mile long, cabins for everyone. It's like something the Rockefellers probably run around on. That *Simon Peter* got damn stuffy sometimes."

And to Elaine: "I'll bet you're a pretty good sailor. That sailing costume just sets off this boat."

Elaine melted. "It's an old thing I bought in Virgin Gorda. But I love to sail and I'm going to do my share. I mean to take my turn at the wheel this very afternoon."

"Over my dead body, Elaine," said David Mallory, leaning over Elaine and giving her a big hug. "Charming you are, but not a helmsman, or helmsperson. But thank you, Mark, for your kind words about *Pilgrim*. She is everything I've ever wanted in a boat."

Sarah growled to herself. Everyone was falling. Left and right. Even Tony, because Mark was now talking music with Tony. He'd brought his mandolin, perhaps they could get up some music tonight. Alex remained a holdout and sat, dark-browed and with arms folded. Medicine was his Achilles' heel, and he didn't take kindly to unsubstantiated complaints about "medics" who had given someone the runaround. She reached over and took his hand. Together, they would sneak up on Mark deTerra and tip him over the rail.

It was an easy sail. As the sloop came into East Penobscot Bay, the southwest wind let her run on a broad reach and then shifted slightly south, so with spinnaker set she ran before the wind, the water in a green surging wake behind them. David decided to stay out of harbor and float for a while toward Castine and then in the late afternoon turn and tack until he could swing east toward Bucks Harbor. Sarah and Alex, the two dissenters from the Mark deTerra fan club, sat on the deck somewhat apart from the others in the cockpit. Ezra had the wheel. David had left for the nav station; he wanted to chart a route for the next day and work on a glitch that had developed in the Doppler log sensor.

The cockpit, minus Gracie, who had also gone below, was the scene of jollity. The fact of Billy Brackett, dead or alive, seemed to have faded into history—a disagreeable incident not to be allowed to spoil a good time. Truly, Sarah decided, I was right. Shipboard is an escape. What is a corpse on the mainland to high life on the ocean? Elaine and Flip, for instance, seemed to have dedicated themselves to being the life of the party. Flip took a handful of paper napkins and folded them into swans, sailboats, and flowers, and then into a series of grotesque paper puppets. Elaine took charge of a curly-haired number and launched with Flip into a Noël Coward-like dialogue.

The audience responded: Tony and Andrea with a coda in kind if not in skill; Mark deTerra and Ezra cheered. Elaine and Flip, thus encouraged, launched themselves into a pseudo-Elizabethan argument full of references to naughty wenches, tattling knaves, and cries of "Forsooth, my pretty one" and "You lie, sirrah" and "Nay, I lie not alone, I lie with you, madam."

Sarah had to admire the effort. There was more to the Chandlers than had met the eye and ear. Granted, they were shallow as saucers and entirely too precious, but they were really clever. Sarah was again reminded of toy dogs with diamond collars and little ribbons, trivial but in their tiny sphere, oh so delightful. Elaine played with cocktail talk and flippant amorous references like a practiced habitué of the drawing room, and Flip had the talent of turning a smart remark on its head, to surprise, and to draw the others into the dialogue. His puppet appealed for understanding from Andrea, asked a nautical question of Ezra; Elaine's puppet demanded a song from Tony, a smile from Sarah. Alex, still smoldering, Flip and Elaine wisely left alone.

Sarah nudged him. "Forget it, that doctor remark. Relax. Everyone has trouble with doctors."

"What do you mean, 'everyone'?"

"It happens; people are sick and upset, doctors are human."

"I'm glad to hear you say so."

"Well, there are times I want to stuff my doctor into his own wastebasket."

"How lucky you're not my patient."

"Alex, stop it."

"I'm sorry, that Mark deTerra rubs me the wrong way, and the whole scene looks like a second-rate Broadway revue."

"I'm not wild about deTerra, but you're being a complete grump. Go sit by yourself and breathe deeply." And Sarah slid along the deck and joined the others in the cockpit in time to join puppets and the others in a chorus of "No wind that blew dismayed her crew or troubled the captain's mind, so I'm off to my love with a boxing glove ten thousand miles away."

Alex went to the bow and sat looking at far horizons.

Bucks Harbor was reached at tea time—"or drink time, which ever you want," said David as the big anchor dropped into the western part of Bucks Harbor and the *Pilgrim* swung slowly in the falling breeze.

The early evening was uneventful. Mallory closeted himself for a time with Mark deTerra and emerged jovial and smiling, one arm around the new crew member, and when dinner was over, the setting sun brought Tony on the banjo, Mark on the mandolin, everyone in the cockpit singing lustily, and in the middle of "Cockles and Mussels," it brought George Fitts in a longboat.

FOURTEEN

GEORGE CAME ABOARD WITH CLIPBOARD, NOTEBOOK, and an assistant in the person of one Mike Laaka from the sheriff's department. This individual functioned as a roving deputy investigator and more notably as the bane of George Fitts's life.

Where George was constrained, Mike was easy, irreverent, and outspoken. He was tall, with the fair-haired, broad-cheeked look of the northlands, proud of his grandparents' birth in Finland, and he often expressed the opinion that any progress made by the State of Maine was due to the strong backs and clear vision of its hard working Finnish population. Mike had set opinions regarding the upper economic reaches of the world, and as he boarded the *Pilgrim* behind George, Sarah remarked a visible curling of his lip as he glanced first over the boat's gleaming eighty feet and then took in the elegant Chandlers lounging in the cockpit, Elaine under a tiny pink silk parasol with fringe.

Mike regarded George Fitts as one of nature's aberrations, while George made it plain that Mike was a cross harder to bear than any fugitive felon. The fact that Mike preferred horse racing—and off-track betting—to the pursuit of malefactors was an added grievance. Sarah wondered why any police command would put two such ill-suited characters on one job—unless their chemistry together produced a useful equilibrium.

George centered himself in the cockpit and announced, "Mike Laaka here is my backup." He looked over at Mike with his usual expression of faint distaste. "He is the deputy investigator of the Knox County sheriff's department, on loan to us for the investigation. Mallory, I'll see you first, then the others. Clear up some points. Mike, have a talk with Sarah and Alex."

Mike stepped forward. "Okay, you two, how about a boat ride over to that island? That rubber raft there looks as if it could keep us afloat if no one uses a darning needle. I can fill Alex in and Sarah can look at the sunset if she doesn't want to listen to medical details."

"What's the idea?" asked Sarah, as she settled onto the soft rounded bow of the Avon. "You're not dragging us out in the middle of the harbor to observe the glory of a Maine sunset."

"Shut it down; you've forgotten that sound travels across water," said Mike. "Make for that island, what's its name, just ahead."

"Harbor Island," said Alex.

"I grew up on *One Morning in Maine*," said Sarah. "Robert McCloskey set some of his books here."

"I've read *Time of Wonder* and *Blueberries for Sal*," said Mike unexpectedly. "Unlike George, I had a childhood. We'll find a place to pull the raft in, get behind some bushes and have a chat."

"Were you a pirate in a past life?" asked Sarah.

"I wish. Or a fox, a seagull. Or Secretariat, the thunder of hooves, the roar of the crowd. But fate and the state police CID have hitched me to George's wagon." With that, Mike rowed skillfully and fast across the little stretch of water that separated Harbor Island from the mainland, pulled out of sight of the moored boats, and propelled the raft into a niche. They hauled the raft partway up a rocky incline and tied the painter to an overhanging branch. Together, the three scrambled into a damp pocket made up of sharp rocks and thorny shrubs and huddled well out of sight of the *Pilgrim* and her company.

"I've taken you both away," said Mike, "to give George a free hand in working everyone over. There's too much posing and deference and hovering over guests. He'll question the crew again and siphon off the Chandlers, send them to their cabin to reflect on their frivolous life. Those Chandlers could sabotage any questioning or influence any witness. Okay, with George's permission and in view of our past fun and games in the world of crime, I can give you some news. Billy had a skin full of booze, almost point ten. Several people at the church supper say there was undoubtedly something other than apple cider in Billy's glass, probably rum, since Mallory and the others on board ship say he avoided other stuff. Anybody could have given it to him or he could have had his own supply of firewater."

"But alcohol didn't kill him," said Sarah.

"No, though it didn't help his state of health, considering what happened to him after he left the supper."

"Was he taking drugs?" asked Sarah, mindful of the syringe and Mallory's conviction and Gracie's fear on that subject.

"Not as far as they can tell. No painkillers, no coke. Nothing. As Alex may have told you, Billy was hit along the chin—or he fell on his chin, which is also possible. But the mark was just right for a fist connecting. It wasn't a postmortem injury."

"But not enough to kill him," repeated Sarah. "Lord, it's like Rasputin. Alcohol, assault, and tossing in the water."

"Have you a line on his Florida medical history?" asked Alex.

"Quite a resumé. Our Billy was treated for drug abuse—quite a while ago. Once. And for unnamed psycho behavior. Half-way-house stay, but he went over the wall. Billy had tantrums, kicked up a lot of dust—probably including angel dust. Lately, he seems to have been clean. Last year, he was hospitalized for seafood poisoning, later picked up on a drunk-driving charge and checked for concussion. Hit a street lamp. God, Billy Brackett had everything but trench mouth."

"Poor Billy," said Sarah.

"And he was Mr. Allergic. To bees, yellow jackets in particular. Had several severe reactions to poison ivy—all blown up. And to some shellfish. Couldn't tolerate penicillin or sulfa drugs, which made him hard to treat. And he had been given a prescription for a kit with epinephrine and Benadryl tablets."

"With a syringe," put in Sarah. She shifted her position on her granite seat. The sharp boulder with its encrusted lichen was beginning to bite into her still-inflamed legs.

"Presumably. The one Mallory turned in probably came from a kit, and Billy may have used it for its proper purpose. Or he could have kept it to stick himself with something else."

"I wonder at Mallory even wanting him to spend ten minutes aboard his boat," said Sarah. "He was a walking bomb."

"Mallory—or Gracie for that matter—may not have known all of Billy's medical history," said Alex. "Besides, Mallory's into rehabilitation. He's got Tony aboard, too. For all we know, Ezra may have escaped from Sing Sing."

"Don't you mention Tony in the same breath with Billy," said Sarah fiercely. "And while you're at it, Mike, how about that grizzly bear, Mark deTerra? Talk about walking bombs."

"Our Florida connection says deTerra is a hardworking member of the Church of the Apostles."

"Mr. deTerra is not really from Florida," said Sarah. "He grew up in Maine, and he's barely polite to me, rude to Alex, and simply charming to the others. He's someone I'd never turn my back on."

"You can't expect to charm everyone, Sarah," said Mike. "He may come from a resistant strain."

"I don't like him," said Alex, "not because he doesn't like doctors, because people fighting with doctors right now are legion. I think he was deliberately antagonistic. So get on with it, Mike. You left Billy, drunk, with a bruise on his chin."

"Sometime after he left the church dinner, Billy must have made his way down to the shore. Which part of the shore, we don't know. Perhaps the float at the inn or the lobster dealer's float where he was found. Or instead of going on his own steam, he could have been carried down, though no one has claimed the honor."

"Maybe he was looking for a dinghy or the Avon raft to take back to the *Pilgrim*," said Sarah.

"He must have fallen, waded by accident or on purpose into the water, into the jellyfish, one of those big whoppers. Maybe he tripped, embraced the thing, fell on it; his shirt and jacket were off. We found them nearby. Anyway, the pathologist found multiple stingers on his chest and stomach. The guess is that he had one hell of a reaction and that he was just about dead when he went under. The medical examiner is tentatively suggesting that the primary cause of death is from anaphylctic shock complicated by alcohol ingestion and by immersion at the point of death in seawater. Time of death difficult to fix."

"But why was he undressed?" demanded Sarah.

"He was drunk. Don't ask me why drunks undress. Maybe he wanted to go swimming, to cool off. Maybe somebody undressed him."

"My Lord," said Sarah. "It *is* Rasputin."

"Oh, for the good old days, a single shot from a single gun," said Mike. "We're telling you both this because we've worked with you before. Mallory knows most of it, but the others, well, why mess up their heads? We're just saying Billy died from a jellyfish sting—which is probably true—and hypothermia."

"Do you think he was part of some drug group in Florida?" asked Sarah. "And Mallory took him on trust because of Gracie?"

"This much we have. Billy, who on Islesboro dodged the Bible-distribution business, had some bad-smelling pals on the island, one of whom owned a green pickup truck. That wake you up, Sarah? Billy or Billy's pal—if they did it—may have decided to scare the daylights out of you, not intending to do more than dump you in a ditch. Of course, we've been told that there are lots of green pickups on Islesboro, so we can't be sure."

Mike ticked off an item in his notebook and let his pencil drop to his lap. "About that truck, like the medical info, it's for your information alone. We especially don't want sister Gracie to have it on her mind. She's is tough to handle as it is and if she gets more so, she'll be zero help with the case."

"It's all absolutely disgusting," said Sarah vehemently. "The only reason you care about Gracie is that she might gum up your precious case—if you have a case."

"Billy Brackett's death is pretty disgusting," said Mike quietly.

Alex turned to Mike. "So, what are they ruling the death? Are you and George talking homicide?"

"That's on hold."

"I have a theory about Gracie," began Sarah.

"No," said Alex sharply. "Not now. Let that idea simmer for a while, because it's really out in left field."

"Yep," said Mike. "We've got enough at home plate right now. Keep your idea on reserve, Sarah, for a rainy day."

Sarah considered. Out here on this quiet island, the idea of Olive Oyl and wild man Billy Brackett in league over anything more serious than a change in the dinner menu seemed absurd. "Okay," she said. "On the back burner. For now."

There was a long silence and the shadows deepened into a single mantle of dark purple and slowly into denser blue-black. Then Sarah rose painfully from her rock, stretched her cramped legs, and lifted her arms. "Oh Christ." She sighed. "What a bloody mess."

Mike stood up and put his notebook into his jacket pocket, produced a flashlight and snapped it on. "Let's head back. George has finished his needle work by now."

Alex led the way to the beach, untied the Avon raft, now high and dry with the falling tide. The three carried the raft down to the water and boarded and Mike pulled for the *Pilgrim*, a graceful black silhouette polka-dotted with the lights shining from her portholes and from the riding lights high on the mast.

After several minutes of forward movement and splashing oars, Sarah gave a small rueful laugh. "I don't suppose," she said almost wistfully, "you have any proof that the Chandlers are cat burglars or are wanted in Monaco for jewel theft or forgery."

"Sorry," said Mike, "because I have not taken to the couple. George says they are what they seem. High society, proper schools, jets, yachts, and designer clothes. I met them in a question session over on the mainland. It was ever so la-di-dah. They thought police work would be 'fascinating,' 'such a challenge.'"

"You're sure Mark deTerra isn't an ax murderer?" asked Sarah.

"Sorry," said Mike again. "An ax murderer would liven up the summer."

Sarah closed her eyes and let the night air and the motion of the little raft lull her. She wanted her bunk and ten minutes of bedtime reading of *The Thirty-Nine Steps*. The book was pleasantly out-of-date, so that the scenes of thuggery and violence were fitted comfortably into a British world of old school ties and gentleman adventurers who with great daring outwitted sinister persons with German accents. The book was so restful that Sarah was always sent to sleep immediately. What she didn't want at bedtime was any more traffic with the contemporary world of police and anxious Gracie, of Billy Brackett and misplaced jellyfish.

In these hopes, she was much disappointed.

As the spot of Mike's flashlight touched the boarding ladder of the *Pilgrim*, they heard it: a low whine that trembled, then slowly rose to a soprano range, wobbled on sixteenth notes, and fell again to alto. To Sarah's ears, it sounded like the voice of her old cat Blackball when he had met an intruder on his domain. And yet it was human. She shuddered.

Mike jerked his head up. "What in hell is *that?*" Then he reached out and grabbed the boarding ladder, took the painter in one hand, climbed aboard, and secured the raft in one long, fluid movement. Alex and Sarah followed silently, hearing the sound again begin the scale, reach its top, waver, and cascade down again.

Sarah, climbing down the companionway into the lighted main cabin, later thought it was like that moment in the theatre when the audience goes from anticipation in the dark to the curtain rising on a lighted scene. And this scene was exactly like one of those tableaux so popular in the nineteenth century. Scenes from history and literature. The Warrior's Return. Betsy Ross Gives the Flag to General Washington. Mr. Browning Woos Elizabeth Barrett. The Lady with the Lamp. The Fatal Letter.

This was from the Fatal Letter. Except no letter. Ezra stood by the galley door, inclining forward, his face set in perplexity.

Andrea, with Tony behind her, was emerging from the galley with a glass of water. Elaine Chandler expressed horror by covering her face with one lovely hand, while Flip and Mark deTerra each stood in a manly posture with braced shoulders and tightened lips. George Fitts faced the long upholstered cabin sofa, his clipboard under one arm. David Mallory knelt to one side of George, a bottle of brandy held up. And in the center, on the upholstered sofa, Gracie. Gracie in an electric blue chenille dressing gown sitting stiff as a department store dummy, her feet in their black quilted satin slippers with pompoms sticking straight out. Gracie, her eyes rolled up, her mouth open like a fish without air, keening, crying, singing up and down the scale. Up, crescendo, waver, wobble, down. And up.

For a moment, Sarah stood at the bottom of the companionway, ice crawling down her spine. Then Alex took her roughly by the shoulder, shoved her aside, strode to Andrea, seized the glass of water, took four steps across to Gracie, and flung the water in her face. Then without a pause, he flattened his hand and brought it stinging against her cheek.

Gracie Mullen opened her eyes wide, gave a short yelp, and slid to the cabin floor—where she lay whimpering.

FIFTEEN

SARAH ALMOST JOINED GRACIE ON THE FLOOR. SHE
felt the slap as if it had smacked on her own cheek. However,
by taking several deep breaths she controlled herself and sat
down in a far corner of the cabin to watch the general effort
toward reviving Gracie. She found herself not so much upset by
Gracie's condition as by Alex's method of dealing with it. Yes,
she'd certainly read about hysterics and the necessity for forceful
action, but she'd never seen Alex in the capacity of a brutal
doctor before. But don't be a fool, she scolded herself, because
the water and the slap had done the trick. Gracie was now quite
quiet, sobbing gently on Mallory's shoulder.

While Mallory comforted Gracie, Alex went for his medical
bag, and Tony for a sponge and water for Gracie's brow, and
Andrea retired to the galley to make coffee. Mike Laaka moved
over to Sarah's corner, hands in pockets, whistling softly under
his breath, and George Fitts got out his notebook.

It was not until well after eleven o'clock that George finished
with them. In turn, he took the crew members into Mallory's
cabin for a final statement and, no doubt, a quizzing on the

recent outburst. The Chandlers made a particularly picturesque parade. Elaine, in a dressing gown of burnt-almond silk with lace panels, expressed concern by a charming lifting of both hands and a shaking of a beautifully tailored head. Flip, in a plum silk robe with black watered-silk panels, welcomed her back from her interview with a wide embrace, and together like two swans they floated back to their cabin.

Sarah was last to be seen. Gracie next to last. George made a visit of some ten minutes to Gracie's cabin and reported to Alex that she had settled down. "Give her that sedative now if you like. I wanted you to hold off until I could get some sort of sense out of her."

Stoneheart, said Sarah to herself as she made her way to Mallory's cabin. Unexpectedly, she found herself now in sympathy with Gracie, her suspicions of drug teams well to the rear.

Determined not to show emotion, to be as cold and nasty as possible, Sarah faced Mike and George.

"All right, what was that all about? Have you been torturing Gracie Mullen? Putting lighted matches under her fingernails?"

"Simmer down, Sarah," said Mike. "George isn't to blame. Not this time, anyway."

"Mike, I do not harass people, I question them," said George, indicating a small chair next to Mallory's bunk. "Sarah, I'm trying to find out what it's all about. I was just beginning to go over what Gracie knew of Billy's medical history, and I asked if he kept any prescription drugs in the refrigerator that we had overlooked or someone might have thrown out."

"George said she leaped up like a trout at that," put in Mike. "Apparently she hit the refrigerator running, came back crying 'It's missing, it's missing.'"

"Epinephrine, an extra ampule," said George. "Billy apparently kept it there in a little white box. No one else seemed to know about it except Andrea, who's in charge of the galley. Knew the box belonged to Billy, had his name on it. She cleaned the refrigerator yesterday and didn't notice it."

"Then Gracie started to slide out of control," said Mike. "George asked about anything else Billy had, on board, on his person, and she said he always wore his safety necklace, George asked, 'What necklace?' and she really flipped."

"Hysterics," said George with disapproval. "She began insisting that Billy'd been murdered. Then changed it to suicide. Said something about his being depressed and that maybe he hadn't wanted anyone to find him. I suggested to Gracie that suicide by jellyfish was most unusual, and this seemed to upset her further. By the time you arrived we were dealing with a full-fledged case of hysterics. If Alex hadn't shown up when he did, I would have used the water and slap treatment. It's the only way."

"Actually," said Mike, "there's a place on your shoulder, if you press it, it's so painful, the person just quits hysterics."

"You're a lovely pair," said Sarah, glowering.

George nodded agreeably. "You do what you have to. Anyway, she made no further contribution to what she'd said before when I saw her just now in her cabin. Sarah, if you'll bear with me, I'd like to go back to your statement about Billy Brackett."

"With the word *murder* ringing in our ears," said Mike. "Or *suicide.*"

"Wait, Gracie's right," said Sarah. "Billy did wear a necklace, or a silver metal chain. I never mentioned it; it didn't seem important. I thought Billy might have been Catholic, which is funny since Gracie was involved in the Church of the Apostles, which is Protestant—at least I think it's Protestant. A subspecies maybe. Maybe Billy was a convert, but knowing Billy, it might have been a hex sign or a medal from some satanic cult."

"There was no medal or chain on the body," said George.

"Nope," agreed Mike. "Nor in his clothes. As we told Gracie."

"Nor in his cabin," added George. "I'll look into it and see if anyone else remembers seeing it. Considering his medical history, I have a good idea that he was wearing some sort of ID. Now Sarah, anything else?"

"Oh, God." Sarah sighed. "I've told you everything."

"Think hard. Here's your statement. Look it over."

Sarah, longing for her bunk, wearily went over her description of dining with Billy and then nodded. "It's okay. I haven't left anything out about Billy that I can remember. Except he said *The Secret Agent* was his favorite Conrad novel."

"There you are, George," said Mike. "What more do you want? Call in the CIA. What's the thing about? Terrorists? Bombs?"

"Among other things," said Sarah."

"I have read the book," said George—surprisingly. "It isn't helpful in this case."

"Well," said Sarah, "maybe it fits in with what Mallory was supposed to be doing, looking for drug runners. Except he doesn't seem to be talking much about it since Billy died."

"Yes," said George. He laced his fingers together, turned them over, and examined the inside of the folded hands. "I was never happy about that, an idea concocted by the Florida police. I've told Mallory that the notoriety with Billy makes the *Pilgrim* less than a desirable surveillance vessel. Amateurs— even sworn deputy sheriffs—have no place in this business. The coast of Maine is not Dead Gulch, Wyoming, getting ready for a shoot-out. All right, Sarah, good night."

Sarah made it to the door, but then, unable to resist, said, "That Mark deTerra. I don't think he's safe. I know he's supposed to be a lay church worker, but there's something about him." Here Sarah became somewhat incoherent. "And I have this sort of hunch. That there was a working link between Gracie and Billy. Something to do with drugs, because Gracie is so vehement about Billy not taking them. I think she's overdoing it. And now deTerra has come to take Billy's place."

"Mallory chose to take on deTerra," George reminded Sarah.

"Yes, but." Sarah stopped and shook her head. "It's just a feeling. That if Billy and Gracie had something illegal going, well, she couldn't go on without a partner. And Mark deTerra turns up, one of the *Apostle* boat people. Who looks like a real thug. And, deTerra, he's, well, *antagonistic* is the word. With Alex and me, anyway. Although the rest seem to like him."

George paused, pencil in the air, and remained unmoving for a full five seconds, and Sarah saw Mike look at George and thought she saw the merest flicker of understanding pass between them. Then, George said, "Thank you, Sarah, I'll keep what you've said in mind."

Sarah found herself good for only five pages of John Buchan before she fell into a heavy sleep, only to waken in the early-morning hours to find the boat rolling and pitching. An angry siren wind whistled by her open porthole and the shrouds vibrated and shook and somewhere a loose object bumped.

"Wind's picking up," Alex observed unnecessarily.

"Will we leave tomorrow, then?"

"Of course. You haven't really sailed until you start fighting a forty-knot wind."

"That ought to separate the sheep from the goats," said Sarah, settling back on her pillow. Then as she was beginning to slip back to sleep, one foot now braced against the bulwark to prevent rolling, she had an idea.

"Alex, I've got it. Billy and deTerra and Gracie."

"What?" Alex grunted sleepily, and pulled the blanket around his shoulders.

"Listen, I tried to tell George and Mike. What if Billy and Gracie worked together in Florida and then aboard the *Pilgrim?* With Billy gone, deTerra has come to take up the slack, having made himself valuable to Mallory working with the *Apostle* boats."

"Sarah, go to sleep. Does anything about Gracie suggest a secret life in harness with such a loose canon as Billy Brackett? Being a sister—make that half half sister—is one thing, taking brother Billy on as a business partner is another. I think she's unhinged by his death and is going on about murder and suicide and drowning without knowing what she's talking about, a sort of scattershot response to emotional trauma."

"Forget Gracie then. For the time. What if Billy has been in touch with deTerra all along, working out of the *Simon Peter?* Billy was the odd man out on the *Pilgrim* and deTerra certainly seems a bit out of place on board, though I can't put my finger on why. Except for the cold-shoulder treatment."

"Are you trying to suggest that after Billy died, he rose from the dead, mailed a note to deTerra telling him to jump ship and join the *Pilgrim?* DeTerra is Mallory's colleague, another toiler in God's vineyards. Button up, my love. I've had to give Gracie a knockout dose; maybe you should try the same. Save your energies for the morning. There's going to be a big wind; we'll be ripping along the whole way. You can take reefs and pull sheets. Good for what ails you."

Sarah subsided and fell asleep with the sound of wind in her ears and the vision of Mark deTerra standing on an unknown wind-whipped waterfront, his dark hair blowing into his face, his ice-blue eyes looking straight ahead, a huge ax in one hand and a smiling Billy Brackett draped over his shoulder.

The next morning on shipboard was like another country. Even with the amenities of hot water and a beautifully furnished cabin, order went out the window . . . or rather, the porthole. And dressing on a bouncing boat, even a boat at anchor in a protected harbor, was a matter of grab and pull. Sarah bumped her nose on the bulkhead while washing her face and slipped to the deck on splashed water.

Alex, however, was exhilarated. He braced his feet, sang "Blow the Man Down," and decided not to shave. "Now we'll sail. Even on this big baby, you'll know there's a wind."

"Yo ho ho and a bottle of rum to you," said Sarah, catching at the side of her bunk and colliding with the swinging door from the head. "I was perfectly happy with the trade winds."

Breakfast was a matter of keeping coffee level in its cup and catching plates, which despite their rubber-rimmed bottoms slid around like poker counters. Gracie appeared, bundled in sweaters, hollow-eyed, subdued, but entirely sensible. She did not seem now to be a person given to hysterics and babbling wildly of murder and suicide. Sarah was relieved. Today weather and wind were the concerns.

The group was halfway through a breakfast of muffins and oatmeal when Mallory, Tony, and Mark deTerra joined them. "All set for Northeast Harbor," said Mallory, rubbing his hands. "We'll start off with a double reef in the main and our third working jib. Don't want to head out with too much canvas and blow out a sail. Do you know the lines in the Psalm—'They that go down to the sea in ships, that do business in great waters; These see the works of the Lord, and His wonders in the deep.'"

"That's a good one," said Mark. "Doesn't it go on about the

Lord's works and how 'He commandeth, and raiseth the stormy wind, which lifteth up the waves thereof.' We'll certainly know who to blame if we get into trouble."

For a minute, Sarah thought that David might reprove his new crew member, but instead, he frowned slightly and then turned to Alex. "So, Alex, this is a heavy weather shakedown for you and Sarah. And, I'm afraid, for the Chandlers. I don't think I've ever had them aboard in a big wind."

At this, both Chandlers, pale of face, wrapped as for a trek to northern Tibet, appeared, scanned the breakfast table with distaste, and headed topside.

"About time we had some fun," said Tony. "But where's Ezra? He knows more about the sail changes than I do. And he's terrific when it comes to reefing in a hurry."

Mallory was regretful. "Gone. Remember I told you that Ezra had a project in Castine. A real chance to bring two coastal churches under our distribution umbrella. I hated to let him go with this blow on, but he's the right man for the job. He'll meet us in Northeast."

Sarah nodded, impressed again by the scope of the *Pilgrim*'s mission.

"But," continued David, "we're plenty lucky Mark turned up."

Mark, who had been chasing a rolling bran muffin down the table and bringing it home in his hand like a soccer ball, looked up and nodded. "Glad I can help. It'll be a sail to remember."

"Like that book about the *Titanic*, a *Night to Remember?*" asked Sarah.

"Oh, it was sad, so sad, when the great ship went down," sang Tony.

"To the bottom of the sea," rejoined Mark in his deep voice. "Now, hey, Miss Deane, none of those *Titanic* jokes. We're a sturdy crew and *Pilgrim*'s a sturdy lady. And I'll bet you're a sturdy sailor with a good head on you." He grinned broadly and returned to his muffin.

What a switch. Now he's all buddy-buddy, thought Sarah. What's he up to? Yesterday he'd hardly look me in the face.

"Please not the *Titanic*," said Gracie. "I *am* superstitious.

Think of something positive, like those old shipboard movies. What was the one where Paul Henreid lit two cigarettes for Betty Davis? *Now Voyager*. And that Deborah Kerr, Cary Grant movie. *An Affair to Remember*, where Deborah got run over going to meet Cary in the Empire State Building and was crippled but he didn't know it until the end. They don't make movies like that anymore."

"How very sweet," said Andrea, appearing with a tray. It was said in a tone Sarah hadn't heard her use before. The change in the weather was altering some personalities. "I love old movies, too," continued Andrea. "Remember the one where a tidal wave hit the ship and Shelley Winters drowned?" Andrea began to snatch at the dishes and pile them together, one hand bracing herself against the table.

Gracie flushed. "Andrea, you said that on purpose. It isn't wise to mention accidents; we all have enough trouble as it is."

"So I shouldn't bring up *Macbeth*, either?" rejoined Sarah. It was said with deliberate intention. Her sympathy for Gracie had not derailed her interest in the secretary's activities. *Macbeth* had thrown Gracie off balance before. Perhaps she really did know something of a murder. Or a suicide. A brother's death.

And Gracie reacted satisfactorily. "I'll say it again, the Scottish play is not lucky. Please, Sarah."

Sarah bent her head over her oatmeal. Billy, Gracie, and Mark. The gang of three. David Mallory, how had she ever considered him as suspect? He was a monument to good sense and Christian charity. As for Andrea, well, anyone liking Tony or reading *War and Peace* couldn't be all bad. Ezra was the perfect sea dog, and the Chandlers, it wasn't entirely their fault if they were brought up to be social ornaments. Sarah silently apologized to them all. But for Gracie and Mark, vigilance and caution from now on. And make an effort to convince Alex that she was on to something.

It was time to get under way. Yellow foul-weather gear was brought out, rubber boots donned. Alex showed Sarah how to fasten a towel inside her jacket to keep out the spray, and Andrea went to fasten down hatch covers and portholes. Gracie, clutching a tartan blanket and a blue poncho, climbed topside and joined the Chandlers in an apprehensive huddle under the canvas dodger.

The diesel rumbled into life, the anchor was brought up, and the *Pilgrim*, bouncing in the harbor chop, pushed her nose seaward.

"Of course, we're not going very far," called Mallory to Sarah, who, intending to disassociate from the huddlers, was perched on the far side of the starboard cockpit, next to the wheel.

"We'll have to tack, won't we?" Sarah was proud of this perception. Certainly some of the distance was going to be in the teeth of the wind, which was now howling out of the northwest.

"Not now, wind's behind us, we'll go like crazy. A piece of cake through Eggemoggin Reach, but then we'll come out in the open and really feel it."

Sarah, the wind singing in her ears, saw the boom swing out, the mainsail fill, the storm jib fill, and felt the *Pilgrim* surge forward as if released from a catapult. Eggemoggin Reach wasn't exactly what Sarah would describe as a piece of cake, what with sudden gusts slamming over the land, but when they swept out of Blue Hill Bay and over the Bass Harbor Bar into the waters below Mount Desert Island, she thought she had never known what sailing was about until that moment. She felt the *Pilgrim* roll to leeward, right herself, bound forward, up over a swell, plunge down, and rear again. Then she set her keel, dove down and scooped herself into the trough of a wave, and, regaining her equilibrium, raised her bow and rose again, her wake boiling behind her. Sarah found herself shouting, and David leaned over and clapped her on the shoulder.

"Terrific," he called to her.

Alex, wearing the safety harness that all the crew wore that day, joined her, his slicker glistening with spray, his black hair wild.

"Yo ho ho."

"It really is," said Sarah. "I love it. For now, anyway. Not all day and all night."

"This is a luxury trip," said Alex. "I'll take you on a real workout in a twenty-foot boat someday."

"I like eighty feet."

"You're spoiled rotten." Then as the *Pilgrim* rose, bow to the sky, paused and dipped, her stern out of the water, Alex pulled at Sarah's wrist. "So marry me. Okay? A shipboard wedding."

"Anything you say," said Sarah. "This is too much fun for any argument."

Alex pushed her sou'wester off her forehead and peered at her. "Sarah, you mean . . ."

"Will you buy me a boat like this?"

"Exactly," said Alex. "How about tonight?"

"Oh, absolutely, on deck under full sail," said Sarah, but then to Alex's annoyance at this propitious moment, they were joined by able seaman Mark deTerra.

"Quite a blow, folks. Some fun."

She nodded, again puzzling why this creep was using such a cosy new approach. Now he was working Alex, talking sailing, gesturing, pointing out the set of the main, questioning whether or not they should douse the jib. And Alex, judging from the set of his mouth, didn't like this affability any better than she did. The ax murderer. Or the primo drug dealer come aboard. Perhaps into sabotage. Sarah had just seen him bent over Gracie whispering while Gracie, looking numb and unhappy, nodded. Of course, the Chandlers were within earshot, but from the color of their faces, they were both absolutely out of it, stupefied with seasickness. This was suddenly confirmed when Elaine rose with a ghastly expression and leaned far over the rail. Andrea appeared from nowhere with a towel and Flip helped his wife below.

Mark shook his head. "Shouldn't go below, make it worse. Now they'll both puke all over the cabin. Even Gracie feels rocky; she could hardly speak. The thing is, Sarah, in case you feel queasy, keep your eye on the horizon. It steadies you."

Sarah watched Mark as he made his way cautiously along the deck, checked the reefing of the mainsail, and then, secure as a cat on the wet deck, settled down next to Gracie.

"I still cannot like that man," she whispered to Alex.

"Not my favorite, but he pulls his weight. Hang on, there's a big one ahead." This as the *Pilgrim* rose as if sent from a springboard, hovered, bow in the air, at the top of a huge crest, and then swooped down as if she never meant to come up. Sarah, clinging to a stanchion, saw David, his jaw set, turning the wheel hard, then back again, felt the sloop shudder and then settle into the wave. Then he gestured at Mark and Alex.

"We'll need another reef in the main, we're getting forty-five knot gusts at least. Okay, there's the gong for the entrance to Western Way, so prepare to tack."

And the *Pilgrim* beat her way, starboard tack, port tack, until suddenly as she swept between Great Cranberry Island and the mainland of Mount Desert Island, all was tranquility. Comparative tranquility for what were a few whitecaps and a modified thirty-knot wind blanked by land to the gale the big sloop had been fighting.

"Let's get those sails down," shouted David. "We'll go in on motor. Sarah, take the wheel, keep her steady on the present course, and when I call, turn her into the wind.

Sarah, gripping the wheel, found that even in the reduced wind, handling a sloop like the *Pilgrim* was a memorable event. After a few overcorrections, she picked up the rhythm of the waves, the lateral thrust of keel, and learned to compensate for the sudden off-shore gusts that laid the *Pilgrim* on her side. She felt, just for those few minutes, as if she and the *Pilgrim* were larger than life, that they sailed as a team, Sarah bracing as the big sloop healed, then relaxing and spinning the wheel to center as *Pilgrim* righted herself. It was, as Tony might have said, a total trip.

So it was with a real sense of loss that Sarah saw the sails come down and David return to the cockpit to take over the wheel and chug their way into the harbor. It was like losing wings. She saw, almost with sadness, the harbor choked with boats, the forest of masts at the harbor floats, the town rising on the hill ahead.

The Chandlers emerged, pale and pinched of face, and Tony with Andrea on the foredeck began fastening halyards and coiling lines.

Alex rejoined Sarah and David in the cockpit. "Did you call

in for a slip? They're hard to come by at this time of year, especially in a big blow."

David laughed. "You don't really want to tie up in that zoo. Cheek by cheek with every boat off the Maine coast. I called the harbor master last night for an outside mooring and was told to pick up one of the orange balls with numbers. We've got two-ten over there by the little green schooner. I thought of anchoring, but Gracie and the cruise guides tell me to forget it, nothing will hold."

Sarah pulled off her sou'wester and loosened the buttons on her slicker. "Wouldn't a slip be safer, tied right up to the dock?"

"This is a safe harbor and we want to be somewhere quiet," David said as he swung the *Pilgrim* slowly behind two twin blue-hulled ketches and toward the designated mooring. "The noise and crowds would ruin our stay here. People, visitors, other crews coming down on the docks and looking into the portholes. It's life in a fishbowl."

"David's right," said Alex. "Northeast Harbor is a summer sailing mecca, not to mention traffic from the Cranberry Islands Ferry and the local fishermen."

"And it's a tourist trap," put in Tony, joining them. "Shall we leave the sail covers off, give the sails a chance to dry?"

"Yes," said Mallory, "but hose the saltwater off first. Now, I'm bringing her round, stand by to pick up the mooring." And the *Pilgrim*, humming on low throttle, circled up into the wind, and Tony with the boat hook and Mark standing on the bow fetched up the mooring line and made it fast.

Sarah found herself more and more in agreement with Mallory's ideas of peace. One look at the network of boats in the inner harbor, the congestion of sailboats, motor yachts, every shape and size of vessel, would make anyone flee for the outer perimeters.

"We'll make *Pilgrim* shipshape later," called Mallory. "We made terrific time, it's only just twelve-thirty. And now, before we go ashore, I want to talk to all of you. Except Gracie. I've excused Gracie; she understands."

In a few minutes, the crew and the passengers gathered in the cockpit, the Chandlers visibly bothered—they wanted to change their clothes—the others simply waiting. Perhaps, thought Sarah, always ready for a dramatic moment, he's going to unmask Mark deTerra as an imposter and has already called the police.

Not for the first time, Sarah was one-hundred-percent wrong.

"You have all noticed, I'm sure," said David Mallory, looking around the group, "how very distressed Gracie Mullen has been since Billy's death. Quite a natural reaction, of course. Well Gracie, as some may know, hasn't been close to Billy for quite a while—after all, she's a great deal older and grew up in a different situation. She caught up with him last fall in Florida, found out that his health was unsound, and felt he needed guidance. Needed to break off from a gang of bad-news punks. I don't know if she knew how closely involved he was with the drug scene. Or if she did, couldn't accept it. Anyway, she asked me at the beginning of the summer if Billy could sail with us to Maine. I wasn't happy about the idea. Billy was unstable, his health had been undermined from drug use, but I'm always willing to give someone another chance. Besides, Gracie is a longtime associate and Billy was her brother."

"Billy," said Flip Chandler in a severe tone, "was the universal bad penny."

Mallory's voice took on an ecclesiastical timbre. "I never give up on a single human. Never. I took Billy—though, of course, Gracie still felt responsible. Billy was never any real help as a crew member, but I still had hopes. Then came those not so funny jokes, that incident with Sarah and the pickup truck. Real instability, drinking too much at the church supper. Well, after I found the empty syringe in his cabin, it seemed obvious that Billy was still into drugs. But poor Gracie is denying the drug taking and still trying to protect him. And to rescue his reputation after his death."

"So sad, last night, that scene. Oh dear," put in Elaine. "Perhaps some time ashore. Shopping. A new dress for her. Dinner in a really good restaurant. We'll all try to help."

"Thank you, Elaine. I'm sure you will. Yes, Gracie needs understanding. She's begun to be anxious about everything. She even questioned Mark's presence here and whether Alex was a real doctor. I told her that George Fitts has completely cleared Alex and Mark and Sarah. Gracie also claimed Sarah had been looking at her strangely, and I told her that all of us have been looking at her, worrying about her, and that what happened to Billy had absolutely nothing to do with her; that she has been a good sister to him."

"And she's going to accept that?" asked Flip.

"I believe she is. Accept it, and enjoy as far as she can the rest of the cruise. Next week will be very difficult for her. The police will probably release the body by then and she will have to make the funeral arrangements. Now we can all try and be very kind."

Despite the general agreement on the advisability of avoiding crowds, it was amazing the interest aroused by the idea of going ashore in a busy tourist trap. Andrea wanted fresh vegetables and fruit and Tony said he always enjoyed choosing groceries. Gracie emerged and said she needed a roll of film. Sarah thought she looked marginally brighter than before. Mallory brought out an appointment book and said that he had deliveries to arrange: out to Great Cranberry Island and to some coastal missions that needed material. First, however, he'd take a look at the Maine marine and resort scene. The Chandlers, reviving like wilted plants after a rain, were now in full fig. Elaine had changed to a silk blouse and a flame-red chiffon sailor tie, its knot held in place by a simple diamond pin shaped like a curving feather. Her skirt was pleated silk, her feet in linen sandals. She was Mrs. Maine Resort personified. Flip in his blue-striped open shirt, his rusty-red canvas trousers, and his white boat shoes made, as always, a proper complement to his mate. Only around the eyes and mouth of both, Sarah decided, was there a sign of their recent bout of mal de mer. They spoke of shopping, offered to take Gracie, and mentioned the Asticou Inn.

"The Hunters are staying at the inn this month. Ellie and Kyla with their father," Elaine told Sarah. "Such great people; they're joining the Nevilles."

The motor whaleboat was lowered from its stern davits and, filled with the shore party, departed. Left aboard, Alex, Sarah, and Mark. Sarah and Alex would take the Avon raft, which was already bouncing at the side of the *Pilgrim*. Mark had said he preferred to stay aboard, that he needed time to unwind. It had been agreed that they would all explore on their own and meet for dinner on board.

Sarah and Alex went below to change for the trip ashore, pushed open their cabin door, and stood dismayed. The hammocks over their bunks had spilled their contents, the hanging locker door swung loose, and a pile of hangers and skirts and pants were scattered everywhere. In the head, the soap had traveled across into the shower and the towels were huddled under the toilet. Sarah stepped over the mess, hung up her skirts, and picked up her day pack. Then hesitated.

"We should stay and clean up."

"You thought that on a big boat like the *Pilgrim*, nothing would ever be out of place. Forget cleaning; let's hit dry land." Alex folded his pants back on their hangers, pulled on a clean shirt and dry jeans, and, followed by Sarah, climbed topside. For a moment, they stood and considered the afternoon. The wind was dropping fast, the sun was threatening to be a permanent part of the day, and Alex felt that with such a morning behind them and a hike ahead, he could bring Sarah safely back to the subject of a wedding.

They were already aboard the Avon ready to cast off when Sarah remembered her wallet. "No fun without a few dollars."

"You are dressed from head to toe in new clothes," Alex reminded her. "And we're trying to buy a house."

"Not clothes. I want to go to a bookstore. I always want to go to bookstores. And I'd like to replace the copy of the *Odyssey* that I knocked overboard. I'll only be a minute."

Sarah scrambled up the ladder, swung herself into the cockpit and down the companionway, and slammed directly into Mark and a stack of books he had clutched in his arms.

The books slipped to the deck. Off balance, Sarah had to grab at Mark who came to an abrupt halt. Sarah saw that one of the books was a Bible, a large-print edition of the New Testament. She found herself saying, "A little light reading, Mr. deTerra?" which as soon as it was out of her mouth, she regretted. If he was a dubious character, it certainly wasn't very wise to make a sarcastic remark.

Mark only smiled. "Afternoon devotions, what else? Actually, they're from the main cabin library. The bookcase came loose in the storm; everything's all over the place, didn't you notice? These got wet; a porthole leaked. I'm taking them on deck to dry. Least I could do."

Mark reached for one of the open books and showed her the ruffled pages. It did look damp—somewhat. He grinned down at her. "Hey, Sarah, that was quite a blow. The best battening down gets loused up. Even on this big mother. I'll bet some stuff in your cabin got loose."

Sarah nodded that this was so and made her way aft to their cabin. She found her wallet in a drawer and retreated to the companionway. Mark had disappeared, presumably to take the books topside to dry in the sun.

Sarah let herself down into the rubber raft and Mark, a pipe between his teeth, an open Bible in one hand, cast them off.

"Lots of good reading here," he called.

"What now?" demanded Alex, seeing Sarah frown. "You haven't lost your credit card, heaven forbid."

Sarah waited until Alex had pulled the Avon out of earshot. "It's Mark deTerra. Reading the Bible, now come on."

"He can certainly read the Bible if he wants to. He's from Mallory's church. For all I know, the church members may have to knock off a few chapters every day. Put themselves into a state of grace."

"Speaking of grace, or Gracie . . ."

"Sarah, my dear love, let us have this one beautiful bright afternoon untainted by thinking black thoughts about anyone, especially Mr. deTerra. Let's just float romantically about the streets of Northeast Harbor, buy you a book, and then get out in the country and find me a bird or two."

"You're probably right," said Sarah. "Sometimes you are. And I'm still floating romantically from that sail, so I may give up suspicion and literature and sign on for good. I had such a sense of power this afternoon coming into the harbor. I could feel the boat move right under my feet when I turned the wheel."

"Don't get too fond. Consider the cost of that feeling. Look around the harbor." This as Alex swung the raft toward the long series of slips and the thicket of boats.

Sarah was impressed. Again. Because now, as in Camden, she was seeing the yachting scene as a participant, from sea level, so to speak. Alex rowed around two enormous yawls moored next to each other, the *Quizzical* and the *Lapwing II*, the decks of which were crowded with noisy young men tossing water balloons at each other. On the extreme end of the farthest slip lay a yacht of the sort that Sarah pictured belonging to at least an OPEC chief. Afternoon drinks were being served on the afterdeck, a white-coated personage bending over a tray and moving from one elaborately dressed female to the next. As their raft slid past one rectangular porthole, Sarah could see into a living area that sported a fireplace complete with a heavy oil painting over the mantel.

"A fireplace," she exclaimed.

"You want a fireplace?" said Alex.

"Why not. With a Cézanne over the mantel. And men in white coats with drinks and soft music. Do you suppose the whole thing is owned by Saudi Arabia?"

"It's a New Jersey register," said Alex, pointing to the stern of the yacht, on which a huge carved wooden scroll proclaimed it to be *Casa Blanca* of Elizabethtown.

"Probably a front."

"You're incurable. Come on, let's hit town."

But they had no sooner tied the Avon raft into a nest of dinghies and skiffs at the town dock and climbed the ramp to the ground level than a young man stepped forward with a note. "Dr. McKenzie from the *Pilgrim*? Mr. Mallory said you'd be coming ashore. There's a telephone message just come in to the harbor master for you. You're to call this number. The phone booths are over there."

Alex strode away and returned minutes later looking grim. "My father, he and mother just made it home from Denmark when he had some sort of attack. They're going to put in a pacemaker. My mother's being brave and saying she can handle it, but I want to be there."

It was all settled in a minute. Alex would take a taxi to the airport and be in Boston by early evening. "Putting in a pacemaker is a simple-enough procedure, but I'll feel better seeing the whole thing firsthand. If everything goes well, I'll be back the day after tomorrow. I'll call into the *Pilgrim* tonight and check on your plans."

"Oh, Alex, I'm sorry."

"Yes, so am I. But I'm sure everything will be okay. Listen, this might give you a chance to see something of Tony. Even if Mark deTerra isn't all he should be, you've got your brother on board. And Mallory. You know David now; he's totally watchful and fatherly. He may even let you fool around with his boat again."

And Sarah would remember later how close Alex came to the truth.

SIXTEEN

ONE MINUTE, SARAH AND ALEX HAD BEEN PLANNING A contented morning of exploration in Northeast Harbor; the next, Alex was rowing hastily back to the *Pilgrim*. They sat in the little boat not speaking, Alex preoccupied with his father's illness, Sarah unable to think of anything to comfort him.

Mark deTerra took the painter of the raft and held it ready while Alex threw a few things together. Then Mark offered to row them in and they were off. To the dock, to the taxi stand, to the airport. In an hour's time, Sarah rode the taxi back to Northeast Harbor and had it leave her on busy Main Street.

She had a rather hollow feeling in some central part of her anatomy and decided the corrective for this condition would be to do as they had planned. The bookstore first and then a hike out of town to try and see, even identify, a few birds.

She walked briskly down the street, found the bookstore, and was happy in the discovery of a copy of the *Odyssey* with the same translator as the one that had gone overboard. She settled into a new small sidewalk café for a cup of tea and a biscuit. She had just launched herself into the scene where the old nurse recognizes the scar on Odysseus's thigh when she saw Mark deTerra staring into an opposite shop window. Why hadn't he returned to the *Pilgrim* to delve into an improving Gospel? The disturbing Mr. deTerra, even in the sunny summer crowd that thronged Main Street, looked, to Sarah's eyes, out of place. Somehow, although she couldn't quite put her finger on it, there was nothing about him suggesting the vacationer at his leisure. But why not? It wasn't his clothes. DeTerra was in a blue work shirt, khakis, and deck moccasins. Perfectly normal attire, yet there was something about him. He looked as if he had a purpose; he didn't slouch at the window in a tourist posture. He stood square and upright staring at his reflection. Or did he stare at the scene across the street? At the café with its striped umbrellas. At Sarah. He was watching her. Damn. That was it, not a tourist, a spy. Sarah ducked her head, reached for the bill, hailed a waiter, and turned and twisted her way through the crowd. DeTerra followed, slowly, discreetly on the other side of the street. Or did he follow? Was he just taking a stroll in the same direction?

Sarah reversed her steps and flung herself into a small shop marked BOUDOIR BOUTIQUE—LADIES LINGERIE, and reviewed her options.

She could go out and confront him. But why? What had Mark deTerra done except seem—now she could not be sure— to take an interest in her afternoon refreshment and march along the opposite sidewalk? Well, she could go out and, staying within hail of large numbers of people, engage him in fact-finding conversation.

Or she could ignore the man and search out David Mallory and unload her worries. But this meant tracking David down at some church—there were probably at least a half a dozen in the area—and interrupting him in the middle of good works and Christian endeavor. Plus Gracie would be in attendance, and arranging a tête-à-tête with David might be awkward. Gracie might suspect. Suspect what? That she, Gracie, was suspect. Well, scratch that.

Sarah could find Tony, detach him from Andrea if possible, and pour out her worries on the subject of the Gracie-Billy

Brackett-deTerra team, with special emphasis on deTerra. Or if Andrea proved immovable or Tony balked at being separated from his love, she could open her heart to both.

Or she could march out of the shop and go about her business and be followed—or not—and to hell with it.

"Madam would care to try on one of our robes?"

Sarah came to and found that she was staring at a long rack of fluffy pink dressing gowns with feathers, the sort that she thought had become extinct in the Hollywood of the thirties.

She pulled herself together and opted for bras. "A sport bra. For jogging."

The saleswoman—a well-upholstered female with glued-on eyelashes—took stock of Sarah's chest and suggested a padded underwire. "You can jog in it, I suppose, my dear, but the underwire will do wonders for the way you present yourself."

Five minutes later, Sarah, having turned down the underwire, opened the store door and scanned the street for Mark deTerra. Not present as far as she could make out in the passing throngs. She hopped to the sidewalk and ran down sloping Sea Street toward the harbor, Alex's binoculars banging uncomfortably against her hip. She had almost reached the Chamber of Commerce information building when she saw Mark in the telephone kiosk that stood to one side of the building. His back was to her and his position was one that suggested long conversation.

Here was an option she was neglecting. She would call Mary or Amos to see whether they had any new information about the *Pilgrim*'s crew. Even try for something on Mark deTerra, although this did seem a farfetched idea. The Bowmouth records had their limits. However, perhaps Mary could find Mike Laaka and see whether he would do a little independent digging, since there was little hope that George Fitts would exert himself over people he had already cleared.

To this end, Sarah waited in the shrubbery at the other side of the Information Center until she saw Mark leave the telephone and walk in a determined way down the gangway toward the row of tied dinghies and prams. Good, he was going back to the *Pilgrim*.

Sarah settled herself at the telephone.

Again Mary was in class. Again Amos was home. Sarah pressed him for the results of his research.

"I don't say you've improved my summer leisure time," said Amos. "I'm beginning to prefer student essays. A heavy diet of alumni bulletins and student periodicals becomes wearing."

"Did you find anything?" Sarah interrupted. "About Gracie Mullen in particular."

"You asked for Mallory, too."

"I'm not as interested in him now. I think he's okay."

"Interested or not, I wish to unload. Mallory was a very busy boy but did nothing as far as I can see that was harmful to anyone's health. I did some digging in the student news rag of his time—you know, *Bowmouth Speaks*. He was on committees and he arranged various entertainments. For clubs, fraternities—that's when there were fraternities. I daily praise the Lord that they are defunct."

"Go on, Amos. I'm in a telephone booth and it's hot."

"And I'm remarkably comfortable in a porch rocker with an extension phone and a piece of chocolate cake. All right, your Mallory was very much a PR man. He met visiting dignitaries, and he also sponsored and put on a number of events that in some cases reached out into the community. Lectures, string quartets, high culture. And, are you ready for this—he juggled."

"He what?"

"Juggled. At home and abroad. In college and out in the world. For a museum-benefit night, for the Bowmouth Follies. One year, he stayed for the summer term and performed for the Rockland Lobster Festival and on a float for the Thomaston Fourth of July parade. On a float yet. Also for a fundraising event for the animal shelter. That should reassure you."

"Juggled," Sarah repeated. "How funny."

"We all have our hidden talents. I took tap-dancing lessons one year and can play the marine hymn on the French horn."

"Okay, I accept juggling, though David hasn't offered to demonstrate."

"He's probably out of practice. Added note. For several of his juggling gigs, he added a ventriloquist thing with a dummy called Gomer Nerd—not a very original name."

"My God, we'll have to ask him to perform."

"You do that. What a fun group you have."

"And Gracie Mullen."

"There I drew a blank. Almost. I have located a Gracia Mullen Delancy, who for one season directed the Bowmouth Little Theatre Group. About twenty years ago. I think I should get an honorary degree for this effort. This Gracie—or Gracia—was a blonde. Thin, squeezed, and blond."

"My Gracie is thin, pinched, and gray."

"Women have been known to change their hair color."

"Was she on the faculty?"

"No, a pinch hitter. Only for the theatre productions, not drama classes. Our beloved Professor Vera Pruczak had broken her ankle showing a student how to do Peter Pan."

"And that's all?"

"That's a lot."

"What plays did she put on that year?"

"I can answer that. *Ghosts* for November, *Oedipus Rex* for February and . . ."

"Let me guess, *Macbeth* for spring."

"On the nose. A dreary sequence, if you ask me. Especially if done by amateurs."

"Is, was she a Bowmouth alumna?"

"No women then at Bowmouth. All it says in the student review is that it was lucky that Gracia Mullen Delancy could fill in and that she brought with her someone to take the role of the porter and a kid to play Macduff's murdered son. Of such are real troupers made."

"No credits."

"You mean experience in stagecraft or drug smuggling. No, Sarah. She may have gone to college or prison or anywhere, but such is beyond my scope."

Sarah sighed. If it was the same person, well what about it? Her reaction to *Macbeth* might stem from that one amateur performance and the scuttlebutt about it being an unlucky play.

It certainly didn't have anything to do with being part of a drug ring. She tried one more name. With little expectation.

"Mark deTerra. Our new crew member. From Florida but Maine originally. He knows how to sail, and I think he's a real thug."

"DeTerra?" Amos rolled the word around on his tongue. "A Bowmouth student?"

"He says he went to a community college. Maine perhaps."

"Maine has quite a few community colleges. DeTerra you say?"

"He says. He's very dark, big hands and feet, pale blue eyes, and looks like someone on a Wanted poster. I caught him reading the Bible, a large-print edition."

"I've known stranger habits. But deTerra, it seems to ring a bell. I had a student once."

"You've had lots. Probably a deTerra or two."

"I had a student once," repeated Amos in a speculative voice. "A student whose nickname was 'The Terror.' A high school student. Not too tall but rugged, craggy, thuglike. It wasn't that he was a terror in the terrorist sense, but he was always into some scrape. Hence the nickname."

"Drugs?"

"No. Not drugs. At least not when I knew him. You react to the possibility of drugs, Sarah, like Pavlov's dog. The boy called The Terror—only his friends said it in a heavy Maine accent: deh terrah—was named Terrant. I tutored him in Latin one whole hot summer. He was very bright, did a whole year of Cicero and Ovid, and made early acceptance into Middlebury. He was thinking about being a language major, but I lost track after he left for college. However, I've never heard anything bad about him."

"But it's possible. He might have become a criminal."

"And he might have become an arctic explorer or sky diver."

"Anyone these days can get into drugs. Or drug selling. It's the 'in' scene for some kids. How old would this Terrant be now?"

"Let's see. I tutored him the year before his father took retirement."

"His father?"

"Yes, on the Bowmouth faculty. Classics. I took the boy on as a favor. Tutoring in the summer isn't a favorite occupation. I'd say Marcus would be about thirty now. Near your age. It was a good thirteen or fourteen years ago."

"Marcus!" shouted Sarah.

"You're hurting my ears. Yes. Another reason to remember him. He was the late child of older parents. His mother taught Western Civilization classes from time to time, and his father, who must be forgiven, named him Marcus Aurelius Germanicus Terrant. Be glad your parents aren't classics professors."

"But the one I'm asking about says his name is Mark deTerra. And he says he's from an immigrant Italian family who never learned English, and he worked his way through a community college and took up with David Mallory's church in Florida."

"So your Mark deTerra may have nothing to do with my Marcus Terrant."

"Mine has a G. as a middle initial."

"Consider Giovanni. Or Guiseppe."

"Oh, Lord. Do you think he's the same? If he is, he's been lying to all of us, and he's moving in on some scam Billy Brackett had going, and Mallory doesn't even know. What will I do?"

"Keep your head screwed on. Don't jump. Verify. Do proper research. Base assumption on fact. It's what I tell all my students."

"Did your Marcus Terrant know how to sail?"

"At his father's knee. Professor Terrant—who was named Julius Octavius by *his* father—is a sailing nut. An old salt."

"Who speaks English as well as Italian? And is or is not an immigrant?"

"Who speaks Greek—ancient and modern—Latin, French, German, Spanish, Hungarian, Russian, and has made his way through the Middle East without difficulty. And was born in Portland, Maine, the son of another classics type."

"I guess it's the wrong deTerra. Or Terrant."

"Wouldn't you rather have Marcus be your Mark? Wouldn't you rather have a scholar aboard than a possible thug?"

"Of course, but it's a bit scary—the possibilities. Listen, Amos. I'll call you again and see if you can find out what happened to your Marcus. Alex isn't here—his father's sick—so I'm on my own with all my usual suspicions and paranoia."

"No wonder you're having nightmares. No one should be alone with his suspicions. I should send you Mary. She needs sea air. As a matter of fact, we both do."

"We'll be in Northeast Harbor for at least a day more, I think, so if you'd like . . ."

"We would both like, but I don't know if we can find a boy, goat and dog sitter rolled in one. But we'll try."

Sarah hung up and before she could start sorting out possibilities from her new fund of information, the sight of an elderly woman being slowly escorted along the road by the parking lot reminded her of Grandmother Douglas. She remembered the jolt of alarm when the message had come for Alex. She would call her now and see if all was well. Besides, she had a question to ask.

Grandmother Douglas disliked communication by telephone. She maintained that if one wished to say something, one did it properly: in person or by handwritten letter.

"Sarah, is anything wrong?" Her grandmother's voice suggested that only accident or illness could account for the call.

"I just wanted to see how you were."

"I am as well as I usually am. If it had been otherwise, you would have been notified. I hope you aren't wasting good money inquiring after my health."

"Yes, I am. Don't you want to know whether we're having a good time?"

"Are you?"

"Mostly. Though one of the crewmen died in a rather peculiar way."

"I read about it in the paper. I sometimes feel that you and Tony make very strange friends, and incidents like that are the consequence. I hope the boat is comfortable."

"Extremely. Grandma, did you ever know a Professor Terrant? Julius Octavius Terrant."

"Of course. He was a good friend of your grandfather, although considerably younger. A member of his whist club. He owned that old gaff-rigged sloop, the *Rubicon*. However, he was a Unitarian." This last said in a voice of disapproval.

"Was there anything odd about the family?"

"Beyond being Unitarian? Certainly not."

"Did you know the son, a Marcus Terrant?"

"I have seen the boy. An only son and, I believe, a disappointment to his parents."

Sarah could hardly contain her excitement. "How a disappointment?"

"I really don't know the details, except he did not go into academic life, which was a pity. Then there would have been three generations of scholars. But there are so many pressures and unseemly possibilities for young people these days."

"But you can't think of *what* he did? To disappoint his parents."

"No, I cannot. Professor Terrant was really your grandfather's friend, not mine. Mrs. Terrant was something of a free thinker and our paths did not often cross. And now, Sarah, that is enough time wasted on a telephone call. You must be paying long distance charges." There was a pause, a sort of sigh on the phone, and then, "Has Tony, have you, read the little notes I gave you?"

"Yes, Grandma." Well, Tony had read his and Sarah had read one of them, enough to know that further reading would infect the recipient a full hour after perusal.

"I do hope so. Particularly my second note to you, because I am always interested in your welfare. And now, good-bye. A letter or even a postcard would be more suitable if you can manage it."

And the line went dead.

Sarah, after the confinement by boat and telephone, suddenly felt the need for motion. Perhaps movement would counteract this nagging sense of loss she had felt since she had watched Alex's plane taxi down the runway. Was she growing more dependent on him, unwisely dependent perhaps? Or was it the natural ache she always felt when he left her for an undetermined length of time, an ache greater now because he'd left her to the company of strangers? What did Blanche what's her name say at the end of A *Streetcar Named Desire?* "'I have always depended on the kindness of strangers.'" Kindness of strangers? Mark, The Terror; Gracie, the unstable; Ezra, the absent; Tony and Andrea, the preoccupied. Never mind, there was David, Mr. Kindly; he'd fill the bill. Then, lest she begin to be sorry for herself, she took off at a strong pace, something between a jog and a run.

The feeling of exhilaration persisted all the way down a pleasant woodland path, along the main road to one of the area's primary attractions, the Azalea Gardens, part of a series of gardens that welcomed the public. Sarah had seen Gracie flourish a tourist bulletin describing the botanical wonders of Northeast Harbor.

Sarah entered the garden and slowed to a walk on one of the neatly laid-out paths, trying to put her thoughts in order. First, Marcus Terrant was a disappointment to his family. "Disappointment" could mean anything from the boy not taking up life as a professor of classics to being wanted by the FBI. Second, the name Mark G. (for Giovanni or Guiseppe?) deTerra and Marcus Aurelius Germanicus Terrant were not really close enough to warrant her suspicion. Although, on second thought, a boy who was known to his friends as "The Terror," pronounced "deh terrah" might, as an adult, have used that name for an underground identity. Confronting Mark with this might be dangerous, but perhaps she could lay some little verbal traps. Catch him out with a Latin tag or an offhand reference to one of the Roman emperors.

Sarah circled the garden paths, admiring the plantings of azaleas and rhododendrons and the formal patterns of greenery that followed the curve of a quiet pond, without having much idea of what she was looking at. It was a pleasant place, a good spot in which to collect herself and make plans. She looked at her watch. Almost three o'clock. Lots of time before she had to go back to the boat for dinner. But perhaps she'd skip dinner. Stay out on her own, a chance to find her own equilibrium away from all that bright chatter of the Chandlers and the cold eyes of Mark deTerra. She turned, meaning to explore beyond the present garden, when she saw, directly across her path, the man in question.

He seemed delighted. "Hoped I'd bump into someone I knew. Sorry that Alex's gone. Hope his father makes out okay. What'd you say about a hike out past town? I've heard there's a trail from here to Eliot Mountain."

Sarah fought a rising sense of panic. Mark was really moving in, really following her. All the way to the Azalea Gardens. She hastily edged over to a group of four people bending over a planting of yew. "I'm just leaving," she said. "Back to town."

Mark stepped between her and the little group and reminded her that this morning she had talked of walking, getting away.

"Shouldn't wander around by yourself," he added. "It isn't safe, even in these resort towns. I've got a pamphlet about this Thuya Lodge and the gardens, if you don't want to go up Eliot Mountain. What say we wander around there and take a look?"

"I honestly can't," said Sarah, moving sideways so that she was shoulder to shoulder with an elderly man with an umbrella.

"Sure you can," said Mark. He smiled and said, "Listen, Mallory sent back a message. He's made reservations for dinner at the Asticou Inn for tonight. We're to meet the others at five-thirty for drinks first. So we can take in the Thuya Lodge Gardens, because they're just up the road from the inn."

Mallory's dinner party gave Sarah her out. "Then I'll have to change my clothes, so I'll go on back right now. I won't be alone. I'll follow those people." She indicated the receding group of four just starting down the terraced path.

"You look fine for dinner," persisted Mark. "Those long shorts look just like a skirt, anyway. What do you call them, culottes? I think you should stick with me. One of your shipmates." Again he smiled and all Sarah saw were the pale blue eyes.

"Besides"—Mark lowered his voice to a whisper—"maybe you didn't know, but there was a murder around here a time back, a young woman. I don't know what she was doing, hiking, jogging, something like that. I think it happened early in the morning, and I don't know if they ever caught the person."

Was that a warning? A prediction? Sarah wasted no time. She

turned, looked wildly about, and saw a sturdy-looking couple—the woman looked like a weight lifter—just emerging from a planting of shrubbery. She walked quickly to their side. And Mark followed.

The couple, apparently happy to be joined, flourished their tourist maps and together the foursome trudged up Route Three to find the entrance to Thuya Lodge. The couple, who turned out to be the Braunwalds from Ohio, stimulated by their arrival at the formal gardens, engaged Sarah and Mark in detailed garden talk. The virtues of foxglove, problems with lupine, when to pinch chrysanthemums. Whether shade plants could stand the sun. Impatiens and verbena. Was candy-tuft worth the effort. Cow manure versus bone meal. They admired the globe thistle, the stock, cosmos, and the borders of Sweet Alyssum and Ageratum. They exclaimed over the presence of a Dawn Redwood, *Metasequoia glyptostroboides* brought from central China.

Sarah, trying to avoid even sharing a path with Mark, talked desperately of flowers but soon exhausted her small store of botanical knowledge. But Mark proved remarkably game. He claimed that an Italian background helped. His mother had loved her little garden. Names like *Mahonia aquifolium* and *Abelia grandiflora* rolled off his tongue.

Sarah, now almost frantic, began to wonder whether she could become a permanent part of the Braunwalds' vacation, when Mrs. Braunwald said they must be getting back to their rooms near the Asitcou Inn. Sarah, letting out her breath, said she would walk down with them and Mark agreed. Which was odd, thought Sarah, odd if he had plans for getting her alone, for doing away with her that afternoon. Perhaps time was running out. Or Mark was hungry.

The four, Sarah still keeping close to the stalwart Mrs. Braunwald, made their way back down the path and along the main road to within sight of the inn. The couple exchanged farewells and added to Sarah that her husband—meaning Mark—must be a great help in planning and planting.

Sarah said good-bye and hurried to fall in behind four Girl Scouts and a leader. Then, feeling somewhat secure, she again asked Mark about his business, his home. Something useful might emerge.

"I live," said Mark, "in an apartment outside of Sarasota. Two bottle bushes and a palm tree. The hardware business keeps me pretty busy but I like it. You know, all those solid things, wheelbarrows, rakes, shovels. Hardware doesn't go out of style much and I don't have to worry about spoilage."

"And you can go away and leave the business. Close up for a while without having everything fall apart."

"I have a good manager. And two clerks. But yes, I can get loose to sail, to work with the church."

And smuggle and sell, Sarah said to herself. Grab a berth on the *Simon Peter* to be ready in case Billy and Gracie get into trouble on the *Pilgrim*.

"Do you travel much?"

"Travel? Here and there. When I have a chance. Back to Maine to see my folks."

"Who live where?"

"In a little retirement community. They have two Italian neighbors, which is nice for them."

"And you're the only son of elderly parents?"

Mark looked down at her sharply but only said, "I have an older married sister in Iowa. I'm the only son."

Sarah was dying to say "the only son of a professor of classics" but bit her tongue. Safe haven in the shape of the Asticou Inn was just ahead and Sarah quickened her step.

David Mallory, with Gracie beside him, met them in the front hall. "Right on time. This is a marvelous old place. It's just us for dinner. Tony and Andrea have gone to a restaurant that has folksinging. Ezra was held up in Castine, a new congregation very eager to work with us. A shame Alex is gone, but I hope he'll be with us for the last leg. And the Chandlers are here but dining with their friends. Now Mark, you'll have to wear a coat and tie."

"Which I don't have. Not here, anyway."

"The inn keeps a closet full of loaners, though some of the jackets look like they came from Caesar's Palace."

Mark managed to find a blazer about one size too small, so

his muscular frame had a constricted look, which, coupled with an alarming necktie of silver and purple diamonds, did give him the look of a wealthy gangster. Dressed for the part, thought Sarah. They all trooped to the terrace and for an hour or so practiced general conversation, drank their drinks, and repeatedly admired the view of the harbor below. Then they made their way into the dining room to a reserved table by the window.

The energy spent at cocktail talk seemed to have exhausted the party. Gracie seemed distracted—it was becoming her normal state—and introduced several subjects without participating in the discussion that followed. Mallory, too, seemed preoccupied, and Sarah's thoughts kept wandering to Alex. Where was he at this moment? Probably with his father or having a dismal meal in the hospital cafeteria. Only Mark made an effort. He paid pointed attention to Sarah, spoke of their good time in the garden, the interesting couple they had met, and offered to spend future time hiking with her, adding that he was, like Alex, an amateur bird-watcher and would like some pointers from her.

"Alex is the expert, I'm not," said Sarah, and again asked herself what was it with Mark. Was she an easy target because Alex was absent? But a target for what? Certainly she wasn't showing charms not visible when he had first joined *Pilgrim*. Nothing about Mark suggested amorous intentions. So what the hell did he want?

But now David exerted himel. He spoke highly of the halibut, the virtues of a certain California chablis versus an imported Graves, and said he knew Sarah must be feeling a bit down about Alex leaving with his father's condition in question.

Gracie came briefly to life. She explained that certain fishes, halibut among them, made her sick, and then asked Sarah what Alex's father did. "Is he a doctor?"

"Old English, Old Norse, Old Icelandic. Linguistics. He teaches . . ."

"At Harvard," finished Mark. And then added, "At least that's what Alex said."

And I, thought Sarah, shall ask Alex whether he even mentioned his father to Mark. If not, that remark made slightly more probable the possibility of Mark being Marcus. Academic families knew each other, knew where the others taught. Mark may have tripped himself without any effort on Sarah's part.

And then the Chandlers and their party arrived and settled at a large round table across the room and became from that moment the center of animation.

David Mallory waved in greeting. The Chandlers fluttered napkins back. "Those are the Hunters," David explained, indicating two young women, one tall wearing dark glasses, the other short with light two-toned hair, each a walking ad for Laura Ashley. "Kyla and Ellie are great girls. Kyla is at Mt. Holyoke and Ellie just graduated from Princeton. Their father is quite a horseman. Polo, Palm Beach, Aiken. I think he has an eight-goal handicap. And the two girls, they ride anything with four legs. Elaine and Flip told me they're here for a big benefit horse show in Bar Harbor. They sail, too, transatlantic, last year."

As David expounded on the Hunters, another couple joined the Chandler table. The woman was glossy, hung with jewelry. Sarah could see the sparkle and glints from across the intervening tables. Bracelets, pins, rings. The man was in a pale suit and looked like Colonel Sanders. These new arrivals were considerably—Sarah searched for a word—well, more ruffled and decorated than the others, so that in contrast, they reduced Flip and Elaine to almost Quaker-like sobriety of dress.

"The Nevilles," explained Mallory. "They have a summer house here. Elaine went to school with Tsamara Neville."

Nothing that happened at Mallory's table from then on could equal the happy liveliness and the loud tinkle emanating from the Chandler corner. Finally, David, sensing that his own dinner party was proceeding in a depressed fashion, began to outline future sailing plans. "It's Friday night; we'll spend Saturday in Northeast and leave Sunday noon. Our distribution from the *Pilgrim* is just about finished, so we can be loose. Perhaps explore Somes Sound, look at the Cranberry Isles, and then put in at Eastern Harbor. I hope Alex can join us there. We'll make our last stop at Roque Island. I'm told it's a must—a wide, curving beach, wonderful walks. George Fitts will meet us back here sometime next week."

Here David paused and allowed his guests to be refreshed by the idea of wonderful walks, and the dinner wore monotonously to its conclusion with Mark describing in detail how he had helped the Key West Chamber of Commerce with its flower planting. Sarah almost wished she could join the Chandler-Hunter-Neville table, which still reverberated with jollity. Flip was now doing something clever with a fork and spoon; the spoon was bowing to the fork and the pair began a little fox-trot across the tablecloth. The dialogue was apparently humorous because the Hunter girls were in stitches and Tsamara Neville showed signs of apoplexy.

Sarah returned to consciousness of her group, to find that David was making plans for her morning. It was to be Bar Harbor by taxi—with Andrea and Tony. She began an almost automatic protest, but David would have none of it.

"Andrea particularly asked. With Alex gone, she thought it was a good chance to know you better. And she has some questions about college. She's thinking of going back and wonders if Bowmouth takes transfer students. And Tony complained that he hadn't had a good talk with you during the whole trip."

Sarah assented and with great restraint did not point out that it was not her fault that she and Tony hadn't had a chance to talk. The plan would keep her safe from Mark-Marcus deTerra, however, and she could see what ideas Tony—or even Andrea—had about the Gracie-Billy Brackett-deTerra team.

David turned to Mark. "Wouldn't you like to take a look at Bar Harbor? You must have seen most of Northeast today. I wish I could go myself, but the Church of the Blessed Sacrament called me last week. They're having a hands-across-the-faith meeting with the Episcopalians and Congregationalists. We've been asked to do a presentation of our distribution methods and put on a display of children's material. I have a rental car standing by."

Mark shook his head. "Think I'll skip Bar Harbor. I thought I'd take the nature cruise over to the Cranberry Islands. Sounds like fun. A chance to hike and look at the natives."

Gracie looked at David Mallory with an anxious expression, and Sarah had the sense that she was gathering herself to say something. During dessert, she had been entirely silent and looked altogether grim. In fact, the only cheerful things about her were her yellow blouse with its dotted green butterflies and the little yellow and white daisy watch fixed to her bosom.

"I would love to see Bar Harbor," she said.

"Oh Gracie, would that I could let you go. But this is important. We've never worked with the Catholics before. A chance to bring us closer. With your shorthand, I can't spare you. How about this? After the meeting, I'll drive you over to Bar Harbor and around Mount Desert."

Gracie tried again. "I could go in the morning with the others and meet you in the afternoon. The first part of those meetings are just the same old prayers and introductions."

"Those same old prayers are the Lord's Word. Gracie, I'm surprised. No, I need you, and I'm sure you'll get a lot out of the meeting. Never mind, we'll get you to Bar Harbor yet."

With this, Gracie subsided, but Sarah felt that a seething was going on inside the butterfly blouse. She thought back on all Gracie's odd moments and became even more certain that something secret and unmanageable, something beyond mere anxiety and grief, boiled inside the secretary's person.

But the conundrum of Gracie Mullen was not to be solved that day, and with considerable depression, Sarah heard David suggest an evening of bridge with the Chandlers.

And bridge that evening with David and the Chandlers brought home to Sarah her often-expressed view that inexperienced cardplayers should never have traffic with experts. Sarah had no choice; she was the fourth. Gracie, at Mallory's request, had gone off to check the last of the inventory.

They played three interminable rubbers. Sarah's total ignorance of the newer conventions made for misery. David smiled steadily, making Sarah think dark thoughts about Christian charity, and the Chandlers were patient, and play went on and on.

"Only two down," said Flip to Sarah as she played a last losing trick in a doomed contract.

"A worthwhile sacrifice; they might have had game," said David, entering into the general spirit of forgiveness. "But I always play that a response of two no trump is not forcing, particularly as I had already passed."

"Such fun," said Elaine, adding up the score.

"You have a flair," said Flip to Sarah.

This was such a patent lie that Sarah stared at him. "I have a flair for making hash," she said, "but I'm not usually this bad." She rose, said good night, and as she turned to go to her cabin, heard the indefatigable Chandlers make plans for a night spin outside the harbor.

"The Hunters just insisted," said Elaine to Mallory. "They have an old mahogany Cris-Craft, too elegant, and besides, they haven't seen our slides. Flip darling, will you find the slides? The trip to Norway last year and the Christmas ones."

Sarah found herself unable to excuse the bridge scene or what must have been an exercise of the Chandler talent for mockery. They deserved to be hung up on a ledge all night in that "too elegant" Cris-Craft. Really, they just play with people. They're both without substance or ideas. Cardboard cutouts. And even David tonight. No one should be that forgiving.

Sarah lay under her blanket and listened from her open porthole to the sounds of the arriving Cris-Craft, the laughing Chandlers, and Gracie calling out, "Shall I come with you? I've never . . ." and Flip saying, "Oh Gracie, sometime we'd love it, but tonight's all set. And Elaine, "Very, very soon, Gracie." And then "Flip, have you got our slides?"

The Cris-Craft came to life and sped away, leaving the *Pilgrim* rocking softly in its wake. Sarah turned over, pulled up her blanket, and closed her eyes. And then stiffened. A high, stuttering, mirthless laugh sounded from above her porthole; it spread, like glass breaking over a flight of rocky stairs, and died to a throaty sob. Then the rumble of a man's voice—David's—a sort of scuffling sound, a sob, a low whimpering. Footsteps moving aft on the deck above. And finally, the only night sound left was the comforting slap of small waves against the hull of the *Pilgrim*.

But Sarah was not comforted.

SEVENTEEN

A RESTLESS NIGHT BEGETS A RESTLESS MIND. AT FIVE the next morning Sarah's was not only wide awake but suffering an extra irritation of spirits over Gracie Mullen who had begun to assume in Sarah's mind a multiple personality. The many faces of Gracie. Grace Poole, Olive Oyl, Lady Macbeth. And oh yes, Gracia Mullen Delancy, sometime director of the Bowmouth Little Theatre. Gracie was more and more unglued. Unstable was too mild a word. But so what, it ran in the family. Look at brother Billy.

The night shadows had begun to lift leaving blurred images of the cabin's furnishings. Sarah could make out a towel lying on Alex's empty bunk and her jeans and shirt rumpled into a dark mass over the back of the chair. And the cabin was cool. She reached over to the chair, found a sweater and pulled it on. And then propping herself on her pillow, she tried to think.

What was it Amos had said. Don't jump. Collect facts. Verify. Something like that. Well, she had jumped like a kangaroo at every little event. Or at every little nonevent. As a graduate student supposed to be doing research she was a disgrace. So now. Be calm, think. But the trouble was her ideas, her guesses, her small collection of facts—so called facts—all jostled themselves into an unsavory jumble of contradictions and impossibilities.

The more she tried to review the events of the past few days, to assess the personalities of the ship's company, the more insistently the mocking face of Billy Brackett rose before her, and she heard again the sound of an unearthly chuckle.

Well, damn Billy. Druggie? Sadist or childish practical joker? The Joker? Allergic to everything that flew, crawled, or grew. Food freak. Where was the Benadryl from the fridge? And the Banabite insect kit? Or his stupid ID necklace? What had it said? Allergic to bees? A substance abuser—alcohol, speed, angel dust, LSD, smack, crack, cocaine, or you name it. Must avoid jellyfish? Return body, if found, to sister Gracie?

Maybe that was it. Billy took off the ID necklace because it was a humiliating object worn only because Gracie bugged him about it. Or, having decided on suicide (by jellyfish?)—remember those quotations from Baudelaire about Old Captain Death and drinking poison—Billy took off the ID so he could float unknown into the great unknown.

Or, since Billy was conveniently soused at the church supper, the murderer (or murderers) tapped him on the chin, removed the necklace so that what was left of Billy after the lobsters and fishes finished with him would not be identified because of an ID disk. But tide and time which wait for no man had washed him right back into shore to be discovered by Alex and yours truly. Sarah gave an involuntary shudder and pulled her blanket closer to her shoulder.

And now the morning sun was sending slants of light into the cabin, the first engines of nearby boats in the harbor were turning over and, damnation! Sarah said to herself, my head is still in a complete wuzzle. Oh shit.

She swung herself out of her bunk, collected a fresh shirt and made for the head. Washing her face, rubbing in sun lotion, she pulled on her green linen slacks—it was Bar Harbor day— and stood at the little mirror on the cabin door and brushed her short hair into a punk stand-up. Where had all these overheated

190

ruminations taken her? Nowhere. Gracie, a murderer? Or cheerleader for murder? Coming unstuck after the murder like that other well-known female, Mrs. Macbeth, whose very name she dithered at. But how or where could she have done it? Really only Ezra and Mallory had had a good opportunity, but why? Ezra of all the crew tolerated Billy best, and David was into making men out of boys à la Conrad. Murder didn't always need a motive but surely Ezra and Mallory weren't the sort to do in Billy in a fit of random exasperation, fishing around in the dark to find a jellyfish to put down a drunken man's neck.

As for the rest of the crew, Andrea was simply a healthy combo of sex bomb and artless junior college type who could sail and cook, and Mark deTerra gave her the creeps—a sinister unanswered question. Sarah flattened her hair with a final sweep of her brush and reached for the cabin door. And then she remembered. The Chandlers. My God, she'd forgotten the Chandlers. A slick duo indeed, who were roving about Islesboro the night of the church supper, although it might be questioned whether they had the energy or fortitude to do murder. Unless, of course, they could use something aristocratic like a stiletto kept up the sleeve or an exotic Turkish poison powder.

To hell with it. Or them. Sarah opened her cabin door, and made her way to the dining table. Here she found David and Gracie winding up an early breakfast and making ready to leave for pastures new, Roman Catholic pastures as yet untilled by the Church of the Apostles.

At eight o'clock, Sarah stood by the rail ready to wave good-bye as Tony loaded the church party into the Avon raft, but just as he was ready to cast off, Gracie stood up, clutched the boarding ladder, and held out an envelope to Sarah.

"Oh, Sarah, would you? A favor. I may not have a chance to mail it. To Aunt Phyllis. I promised to write and last night was the first chance."

Sarah nodded, leaned over the ladder and extended a hand, but David was there first. "Gracie, for heaven's sake, we can stop at a mailbox, we've got time. Thanks anyway, Sarah."

And they were off. Sarah's last view was of Mallory pointing out a large incoming yawl and Gracie clutching a briefcase.

Then Mark departed with the Chandlers in the motor whaleboat, he to make arrangements for his nature trip, the Chandlers to drive to the Bar Harbor horse show. Tony returned in the Avon and at nine Tony, Andrea, and Sarah rowed into the dock to call a taxi.

Bar Harbor was, Sarah decided, yet another tourist jungle. The taxi had left them off in the center of town, and now they moved in a stream of people past shop after shop selling everything from fine art and antiques to gimmick stores featuring T-shirts, miniature lighthouses, and plastic lobster salt and pepper sets.

With no particular direction in mind, they walked toward the waterfront and came to halt between two restaurants, the Chart Room and the Fisherman's Landing. Here Andrea produced a guide book and she began to read off the possibilities.

"We could go on a tour bus around Acadia National Park and see the top of Cadillac Mountain or we could rent canoes or bicycles. And there's Aqualand. The ad says, 'fun for all ages.'"

But Tony wasn't listening. "This is worse than Florida. Let's get out, I'm getting claustrophobia."

"The Jackson Laboratory," announced Andrea, "does a tourist show. Genetic research on millions of mice. Or there's a museum at the College of the Atlantic."

Sarah saw her chance. "They have an interesting program, Andrea. David said you've been thinking of going back to college. Why not stop in and see them. Tony and I can bat around for a while and give you a chance to look it over."

Andrea was not persuaded. "Yes, it's one of the colleges I was going to check out, but not today. There's not time to really visit. I'll need to set up an appointment for an interview and talk to some of the students."

"You could go and pick up a catalogue," Sarah suggested.

It was not to be. Andrea wanted to be with Tony. After all, this was his day off, too.

"All Tony's days are days off," said Sarah crossly, and then bit her lip. That was not the way to ingratiate herself.

"Thank you, Sarah," said her brother. "You sound more like Mother every day. And Grandma."

Andrea ignored this exchange. "I'll tell you what. Let's go to that camping place I saw on Main Street. I need a new backpack and I wouldn't mind looking at a tent. Tony, Sarah, I'll bet you have lots of experience with camping gear."

Tony admitted that he knew a great deal about tents and backpacks and Sarah subsided.

Opportunity finally came when Andrea, ambushed by a salesman, was urged to crawl into a model mountain tent set up on the floor of the store.

"Tony, I've got to speak to you alone."

"You're not about to put down Andrea because if you are . . ."

"No, of course not. Listen, for God's sake. What do you think of Mark deTerra. Do you think he's for real?"

"Sure. Why wouldn't he be? He's part of the church thing and he knows how to sail."

"Think, now really think. You don't think there's the slightest possibility that there was a drug selling thing going on, one involving Mark and Billy and maybe Gracie? You see I've talked to Amos."

"Where have you talked to Amos?"

"From the telephone booth in Northeast Harbor. And from Islesboro. He's found out that there was a Gracia Mullen Delancy who directed a little theatre series at Bowmouth."

"So. What's that got to do with being in a drug scam?"

"Listen, will you? Maybe she's just pretending to be the perfect secretary."

"She *is* the perfect secretary. Or she was. I've seen her take notes, follow Mallory around. Miss Sunday School U.S.A."

"That could be a front. She could be working with Mark who handled the Florida end, and then when Billy died—or was killed . . ."

"Come off it. Do you think Gracie swam to shore with a jellyfish in her handbag. Be real. I'm the one who wanted to kill Billy, but I never got a chance."

"Forget the details. Just listen. Mark, after he heard Billy was dead, knew Mallory was shorthanded and offered his services so he could take over where Billy left off."

"Sarah, go have a drink. It might sober you up."

"What's this about having a drink?" Andrea, becomingly flushed from her tent crawl, joined them.

"Sarah thinks there's something funny about Mark deTerra."

"I do, too," said Andrea unexpectedly. "Yesterday, he was humming something. I asked what it was and he told me it was from *Rigoletto*, and he's not supposed to come from an educated family."

"That's more confirmation of his story than anything else," said Sarah. "Italians are opera crazy. They grow up with it."

"Well, I agree with Sarah. Let's see if we can find out something about Mark. Tony, you're not subtle enough. You'd go right up to him and say something crazy. Put him on his guard."

"And," continued Tony, as if to show just how unsubtle he was, "Sarah thinks Gracie's not only weird but up to something."

Andrea shook her head. "No way. Not Gracie. What you see is what you get. Sort of a sad old biddy who's gone off the deep end because she's really shook by Billy's dying."

"Sarah thinks Gracie might be in league with Mark. And even that Gracie might have had something to do with Billy dying."

"Tony, I wasn't serious," said Sarah.

"Yes, you were," insisted Tony. "You were dead serious."

Sarah, now speechless, glowered at her brother.

And the salesman rescued her. "That tent's on sale," he announced. "Twenty percent off list price, and we throw in the stuff bag and a patch kit. If you like it, you'd better grab it. Easy-pitch geodesic tents are popular; we've only got two left."

Tony was safely distracted. On Andrea's behalf, he began a series of questions having to do with double seals, urethane coatings, ventilation, and support poles.

Sarah gave up. Walking over to the sales desk, she asked a clerk to deliver a message. "Will you tell that man and woman over there by the floor-model tent that Sarah has gone exploring on her own, to visit the library. That I'll see them at dinner."

The clerk agreed and Sarah departed. Tony and Andrea, intent on the purchase, did not turn their heads.

Sarah did not explore, nor did she go to the library. She walked rapidly to the nearest restaurant, asked for the phone, and called the local taxi service. Within ten minutes, she was on her way back to Northeast Harbor. Her conversation with Tony and Andrea had taken her nowhere. Well, there was only one thing left to do, confirm some of these suspicions or lay them to rest forever. No one was on board the *Pilgrim*. Gracie and David were locked up in an ecumenical meeting, Mark was roaming the Cranberry Isles, Ezra was still in Castine, and the Chandlers were busy with the Hunter-Neville equestrian scene. She would have the *Pilgrim* to herself. If Mark's and Gracie's cabins were innocent of anything untoward, she would do penance. She would pack it up. Amen.

As Sarah hustled toward the swinging doors of the dock gangway, she was waylaid by the assistant harbor master. Messages. The first from Alex. Everything was going well, but he would spend Saturday in Boston to keep an eye on things. Would call for *Pilgrim*'s location on Sunday night or Monday. Leave any messages at his mother's apartment in Cambridge. The second note came from Amos Larkin and Mary Donelli. They were taking the weekend off, had a room at Betty's Bed & Breakfast on the harbor, and hoped to catch up with Sarah early afternoon.

Sarah didn't know whether to be glad or sorry. Mary was blunt, Amos sardonic; they might come right out with all of Sarah's telephone questions about the probity of the *Pilgrim*'s crew and her face would be red, her name would be mud. The idea of everyone having a very hearty laugh at her expense gave her indigestion.

"Another message, for anyone coming aboard the *Pilgrim*." The assistant harbor master held out a third blue slip. It was from Mallory. As with Alex, it was family sickness. Gracie had just had word that her Aunt Phyllis had suddenly become ill, and Mallory had taken Gracie directly to the airport. Would someone from the *Pilgrim* be good enough to pack her things— her cabin was unlocked—and he would see to it that they were sent on to her sister's address.

Sarah untied the Avon raft and rowed rather slowly out to the *Pilgrim*. It seemed to her that if Gracie had anything to hide, she certainly wouldn't be allowing open season on her cabin and personal effects. Of course, Gracie might be the shrewd sort that operated without encumbering herself with incriminating evidence. Or she might be the innocent, grief-stricken old biddy of Andrea's description. Sarah looked at her watch: 12:30. Lots of time to pack Gracie's suitcase after a little looking around. She would try Mark's cabin first, although it was almost too much to hope that it, too, would be unlocked. But then—as if it was meant to be—she remembered she still had Gracie's master key, the one she'd found in Billy's cabin, and since the secretary had never asked for it back, Sarah presumed there were others.

When unlocked, Mark's cabin—originally Billy Brackett's—was a model of order. It reminded Sarah nothing so much as those pictures she'd seen of a West Point cadet's room. Everything lined up. Shoes at attention, duffel zipped and standing on end, the bunk blanket taut; she was tempted to bounce a quarter off it. Instead, she peered out of the porthole to check for any untoward movement in the *Pilgrim*'s direction. No one coming. She unzipped the duffel and confronted a folded green sweater, three rolls of socks, a pair of sneakers, and a small camera—a very small camera, about the size of a wristwatch. Cute. Or sinister?

The hammock and ledge along the bunk, so recently the repository for Billy's Brackett's eclectic reading matter, held only a copy of the *Atlantic Monthly*, a hand-sized book of Maine ocean charts, and a harmonica in its case. The last no doubt for Mr. deTerra to entertain them with Italian street songs or sea shanties. The hanging locker produced the mandolin, a wool jacket, a flannel shirt, and a green windbreaker; beneath the jackets, a pair of rubber-soled brown shoes and a pair of rubber boots. For lack of anything else to do, Sarah reached into one of the boots and hit something soft and furry. She pulled and out popped Rollo Rabbit. Rollo who, if properly wound, gave off with a child's version of the Ten Commandments. Had Mark stolen one? Been given one by David for some nephew and put it in as good a storage place as he could think of? After all, he wouldn't put it on his bed pillow and destroy the manly neatness of the cabin.

Sarah backed away from the hanging locker and without thinking found herself winding the little tab in the rabbit's back. Nothing. Not a sound. Not a Commandment. She shook the rabbit and tried again. Nothing. She turned the animal around and faced it and discovered that Rollo's head was now turned so that it faced in the same direction as his fluffy cotton tail. She took hold of the rabbit's head and twisted it toward its proper position and found that she had beheaded it. Rollo's head in one hand, his fuzzy body in the other—his hollow fuzzy body. Because in his stomach where a cassette or a recording apparatus should have been hidden was a space. Sarah could reach down at least six inches. Probing, she produced a white plastic cylinder filled with a little leather bag tied at its neck by a leather thong.

Drugs. Sarah had found Mark-Marcus deTerra-Terrant out. How clever. Ask David for one of the rabbits for a child's present, empty out the cassette and fill it up with—well, whatever. Whatever drug was the going item in these parts. With great care, Sarah untied the neck of the bag and, taking it to the light of the porthole, peered in. Something glistened. She felt the bottom of the bag. Something small, bumpy, almost sharp. One finger probe. Two fingers, and she had fished out as handsome a diamond and ruby earring as she had ever seen. She emptied the bag on the bunk blanket. A second earring and a matching ring. A large square-cut diamond flanked by four good-sized rubies. A pin in the shape of a seagull—diamond wings, ruby eyes.

Great God, Mark was a jewel thief. Or smuggler. Is that what Billy and Gracie were up to, or was Mark busy on a scam of his own? Jewels *and* drugs? Or just jewels? Or was it all a joke? No. Nothing about these earrings suggested a joke. Sarah turned on the cabin light and squinted at the gold mounting. Eighteen carat.

She turned back to the hanging locker, found and plunged her hand into the second boot, and found, crammed into the very toe the same small navy blue leather Bible with a pilgrim stamped in gold that she and Alex had found in their own cabin. Opened, it, too, was hollow, the pages having been rather crudely cut into a square container. And in the center, nestling on a velvet pillow, a pin: a pin set with three rows of diamonds and emeralds (she assumed they were emeralds) in a striking checkerboard pattern. Underneath the pin was a small card on which was printed NORTHEAST HARBOR, 11 P.M.

She had him with the goods. And were they ever goods! Who needed to sell drugs if they could get their fists on stuff like this? And Mark deTerra was off on his nature tour having stupidly put his goodies where any roving reporter could find them. But of course, like Sarah herself when she boarded the boat, no doubt he assumed she was safe in Bar Harbor and the rest were all ashore going about their planned day.

Now greedy for more, Sarah attacked the flannel shirt, the wool jacket, and came up empty. With the slicker, she hit pay dirt. Both deep pockets were filled. The right pocket, a commodious one, held a large-print edition of the *Song of Solomon*, the left with a volume entitled *Inspiration from the Gospels*. Both were hollowed out. The first held a series of braided gold chains that clasped in every third link a topaz circled by diamonds; the second, a set of earrings very similar to those in Rollo Rabbit. How handy this collection of Biblical material. The *Pilgrim* was full of it, cartons, piles, stacks no doubt lived in her belly as well as under David Mallory's bunk and desk. Slippery fingered Mr. deTerra could have eased his way into the stores and made away with a few volumes or a rabbit or two and have resealed the cartons.

Sarah considered. She could pocket the lot and hope to make it to the police without bumping into Mark. Or she could leave the treasure trove undisturbed and call the police in for a raid. The latter course seemed the most sensible. Let the police do the discovering. She gathered up the little bags and velvet squares and replaced them in the slicker pockets and the rubber boots. But Rollo Rabbit refused mending. Sarah had taken off his head so thoroughly that he was now permanently decapitated. Well, she would just have to hope that deTerra wouldn't look into his boot before the police nailed him. Then she remembered that Flip Chandler had walked about the deck laughing at the Rollo. Perhaps one was in his cabin as a souvenir of the cruise, a puppet to amuse his friends. Sarah took the master key from her pocket and made her way to the Chandler's cabin, which lay aft of their own on the starboard side. Rollo number two was at home, smiling blandly from behind the rail that surrounded the built-in chest of drawers. She relocked the cabin, returned to Mark's and, and stuffed the honest rabbit back in the other rubber boot, the earrings and ring beneath the animal. With luck, Mark wouldn't investigate beyond feeling inside the boot and noting the rabbit's presence.

Now she had to conceal the fraudulent Rollo about her person and later give it to the police. Or if she saw Mark deTerra coming—she no longer had faith that he was safely on one of the Cranberry Isles—she could jettison it somewhere. In the meantime, however, hiding a twelve-inch headless rabbit wasn't easy; it certainly wouldn't fit in her purse. Sarah made her way to her cabin and looked about for a possible container. Seeing none, she wondered whether Rollo in two pieces could be wedged into her pants. To this end, she jammed her hands down into her pockets and found her right hand closing on a crumpled piece of paper. She pulled it and smoothed its wrinkles. Grandma's second note, the one she had told her grandmother on the phone that she had read. All right, she said to herself, I won't be stuck with a lie. She put Rollo Rabbit carefully on her bunk and began to read.

"My dear Sarah," it began. "I would like to call your attention to certain lines from Scripture quoted by Mr. Mallory during our recent luncheon party. I think you should know that when he recited from the Psalms, he did so incorrectly. In fact, he mixed several psalms together. He claims to be a devout man spending his time in Maine bringing the Word to small and needy parishes. An admirable program. However, one would expect that he would know the words of Psalms, not only as a professed Christian and lay teacher but because he said those were his 'favorites.' I won't make too much of this since so many of the young—and Mr. Mallory is at least thirty years younger than I am—have learned imperfectly. I send you lines from the Fifty-fifth Psalm: 'Cast thy burden upon the Lord, and he shall sustain thee: He shall never suffer the righteous to be moved.' Your loving Grandmother."

Sarah, who, when she had reached David Mallory's name, had almost trembled, expecting some sort of bombshell—that David himself was a drug dealer, a jewel thief, an imposter—felt let down. Not that she wanted to find one more criminal aboard the *Pilgrim*, but after she saw that her grandmother was actually writing a letter that did not concern the Children of Israel, a personal letter, well, she had expected more. So David Mallory didn't quote some Psalms correctly. Honestly, her grandmother was the living end. How many ordained ministers today were letter-perfect in all the Psalms? She'd bet they only had absolutely cold the wedding, baptismal, and funeral services, and maybe a few prayers, verses, three or four Psalms. Even the priest at Mary and Amos Larkin's wedding had bobbled the benediction. People didn't memorize the way they did in her grandmother's day.

Shaking her head, Sarah seized Rollo and his head, hurriedly draped the sweater over him, and made her way topside. From the deck, she scanned the harbor for approaching fellow crew members, and finding it safe, rowed to the dock, tied the dinghy, and was about to set off for the police station when she caught sight of a terrifyingly familiar profile at the top of the Sea Street: Mark deTerra holding binoculars and scanning the harbor scene. He was standing in the street directly opposite the police station.

A moment of freezing panic and then Sarah remembered her plan for quick disposal of the headless rabbit. It had to be in a place from which the police could shortly rescue him. Easy. On one side of the parking lot stood two huge green metal Dumpsters, one marked FOR HOUSEHOLD ITEMS. Surely Rollo was a household item. This Dumpster proved to be almost full and Sarah, standing on tiptoe, deposited Rollo Rabbit next to a crushed Clorox bottle. But after closing the top, she decided that to be doubly safe—after all, Mark might be throwing away some of his own garbage—she would push Rollo out of sight. Looking around, she found part of a thin branch blown down no doubt from yesterday's wind. With this, she poked and pushed until she had the white rabbit under cover—first the body, then the fuzzy head with its pink glass eyes and long ears with the pink linings. Giving an extra hard push, she caught her branch on a piece of material. She pulled and up came a yellow blouse—a blouse decorated with an intertwining pattern of spotted green butterflies.

Gracie's blouse. Gracie's wet, crumpled, bloodstained blouse.

EIGHTEEN

SARAH LET GO OF THE LID OF THE DUMPSTER AS IF IT had been molten metal. It clanged down, catching a small corner of the yellow blouse as it fell shut, and the triangular piece of material pointed at Sarah like a tiny accusing finger.

She stood absolutely still looking stupidly first at the stick in her hand and then at the protruding piece of blouse. Although she could see two and a half butterflies, her mind rejected entirely the enormity of what she was seeing; instead, it busied itself with alternate scenarios and possibilities.

Someone else had a blouse just like Gracie's. Which someone had thrown away. Because it was outgrown, out of style, unsuitable, stained. But her mind veered away from the stain.

Gracie had tired of her blouse. Gracie had been robbed of her blouse. Gracie had given her blouse to the poor; the homeless. The Salvation Army. Which had rejected it. Which had remanded it to a garbage truck—a truck whose irresponsible driver had driven the load to the harbor and stuffed it in the Dumpster.

Or: The blouse was in no way like Gracie's. It was quite different, with a different species of spotted butterfly.

Gracie had been murdered.

Once Sarah had voiced this to herself, she found she could then think not only that Gracie had been murdered but that Gracie herself, in whole or in parts, was lying under the debris of the Dumpster. Or perhaps divided between the two dumpsters.

But the thought of Gracie deceased did not, could not, stir Sarah into sensible action. She was not going back into that Dumpster. Nor was she able to move a foot toward help: not to the harbor master, the police, David Mallory, Tony, To anyone.

Instead, she stood cemented to the pavement, and it was not until a man in a red shirt came up to her, opened the Dumpster, and flung in a bulging plastic bag that she was able to move her head. The man let the lid fall and Sarah found that the piece of butterfly blouse had disappeared back into the jaws of the bin.

She looked around and saw only the usual bustle of a busy harbor and tourist center. A green-hulled yawl nosed its way into a slip; a schooner hovered near the outer line of moorings; a red pram and a miniature dory emerged from the tangle of the dingy dock and rowed away; and what seemed like an entire girl's camp in green shorts, white blouses, and green ties marched down the gangway and advanced on a motor sailboat.

Sarah decided. The harbor master. Who more proper to deal with something frightful in the Dumpster? She forced herself to take a step toward the harbor office when her eye caught again, in the center of the road down to the harbor, Mark deTerra.

Mark deTerra. Of the stolen rabbit, of the jewel cache. Mark who might be Marcus Germanicus, a disappointment to his father. Mark of the gang of three. Later the gang of two. Now the gang of one. Mark the survivor of a game of three little Indians.

Mark stood still, apparently searching, as before, the scene below. Then, catching sight of Sarah, he waved and began walking down the hill.

And Sarah fled toward the harbor master's office, surely a place of haven. However, as she charged the entrance she was moved aside by a purple-faced man with a yachting cap, followed by another in a tan uniform—undoubtedly the harbor master. Together, the two men hurried down toward the float, where a large ketch had pushed its nose into its neighbor's mooring space. And the harbor master's office was empty. Sarah turned back. The telephone. Surely she was safe at a telephone in view of the entire harbor. She would call the police. The station was right up there on Sea Street. However, even a police force with wings couldn't muster itself or alert a squad car to make it down to the harbor in the few minutes it would take Mark to saunter down the hill. She wanted someone now. Rapidly, she ran down the list of other possibles, only to find them impossibles. Except. Except Amos Larkin and Mary Donelli, who had promised to be at Betty's Bed & Breakfast right next to the harbor by early afternoon. And, by God, it was almost early afternoon.

Sarah peered out from the row of telephones and found that Mark, although now more than halfway down the hill, had been stopped by a woman in a straw hat and was looking over a map with her.

Luck was with Sarah. She found Betty's number, dialed, and it was answered. A minute's time found Amos on the telephone.

"Telepathy?" said Amos. "We just drove in hot and dusty. Route One traffic was fiendish. Never again."

"Amos, I'm in trouble." Sarah almost cried over the phone.

"Not unusual. Is it murder or just suspicion of?"

"I'm serious. You've got to help. Now. Both of you. Mark deTerra—the one who might be your Marcus—has been stealing jewels and probably just murdered David Mallory's secretary."

"Come off it."

"I mean it. Come down to the dock. Both of you. Do something to distract him. He's wearing . . ." Sarah looked out of the booth again; deTerra was still dealing with map directions. "He's wearing a blue shirt, tan pants, black-haired. Has binoculars. Just distract or deflect him and give me time to call the police or get the harbor master. Do anything you can think of create a disturbance."

"This is on the level? Not some joke?"

"Amos, for God's sake."

"Okay, we'll be down." And the phone went dead.

Now Mark had returned the map to the woman and had started down the last part of the hill—straight for the row of three telephones. He must have seen her. What the hell was the emergency number? She pawed through the telephone book's front pages and came up with 5111. Then, as she turned to dial, she glanced up the street again and saw a shape like that of Mary Donelli burst from a small frame house just beyond the Information Building, followed by the red-haired figure of Amos. They pelted down the road on a dead run, and just behind, Mark deTerra went into action.

It was like a Punch and Judy show American style. Amos became a wild drunken figure, lurching into Mark, clutching at Mark's shirt for balance while Mary, playing the shrew, came screeching down and tried to belabor Amos.

Sarah, her finger on the dial, had to admire him. Amos as a former drunk certainly knew what to do. He stumbled, he grabbed, he fell on Mark. Mary—rather overplaying her part, thought Sarah—seized Mark by the sleeve, gesturing wildly. Together, they managed to move Mark away from the pavement to the lawn of the Information Building, where they both tumbled against him and bore him to the ground, quite a feat considering Mark's strength and build.

Sarah dialed 5111, effectively used the word *murder*, and the operator promised instant police help at the harbor. Then breathing hard, she leaned back in the telephone kiosk to await developments. Amos and Mary's efforts were nothing short of heroic and were developing into a monumental wrestling match on the lawn. Quite a crowd had gathered and several male figures began making snatching gestures at the struggling figures.

Then in a crescendo of action, a squad car, lights blinking, siren wailing, shot down the hill, jammed to a stop, and its two occupants erupted from the car. Sarah saw to her amazement that just as the policemen reached the thrashing bodies, Mark emerged victorious from the tangle, with Mary under one arm and Amos clamped under the other. In seconds, all three were quickstepped into the squad car, which turned and sped back toward the police station.

Sarah was now at leisure to leave the telephone and collapse on a bench. She must steady her thoughts and decide on her next course of action. She must go at once to the police station and warn them about Mark, tell them that he was at the very least an accomplished thief, at the most a killer. And she would tell them to hurry down and look at the dumpster and direct them aboard the *Pilgrim* to Mark's cabin. And she must rescue Mary and Amos.

But, since she had brought the police into action, it might be a good idea to find George Fitts or Mike Laaka. Let them in on developments, ask for help. She stood up and turned again toward the row of telephones.

"Sarah, for heaven's sake. Shouldn't you be in Bar Harbor with Tony and Andrea? Is something wrong?"

It was David Mallory. Big, kind David Mallory. David who had the solid kind of shoulder on which someone could collapse. Sarah almost burst into tears. David could take charge. David could go with her to the police station, tell them about the Dumpster and release Mary and Amos and accuse Mark.

David took her arm with real concern. "What's the matter, Sarah? You look like you've seen a ghost. Several ghosts. What's happened? Something in Bar Harbor?"

It all came out. About Mark deTerra, at least. Sarah decided to hold up any idea of Billy Brackett's or Gracie's complicity. First warn David about Mark. This she did, ending breathlessly in telling how she disposed of the headless Rollo Rabbit and found Gracie's stained blouse.

And David turned as pale as it is possible for a man with a deep tan to turn. Color drained from around his eyes, his mouth opened, he looked years older. He fumbled for speech.

"Mark? Mark deTerra? Stealing jewelry, using our books, our toys to hide them. In his cabin? I don't believe it."

But Sarah urged him to believe it; the headless rabbit was right there in the dumpster. And then in an exhausted voice, she repeated the possibility of Gracie's murder. The blouse. The stain. The message from the harbor master saying Gracie was off to see sick Aunt Phyllis and asking someone to pack her things. The note that must have been telephoned by Mark himself in order to establish a reasonable explanation of Gracie's disappearance.

Now David had command of himself. In fact, he even managed the shadow of a smile.

"You have absolutely shocked me, Sarah, and I didn't think anything could shake me that much, not since Billy's death. But, but"—and here David almost stuttered—"Gracie isn't murdered. Oh Lord, poor Sarah. No, no. Gracie and I stopped for a bite—she was going to miss lunch—at one of those little roadside restaurants, and she managed to spill a bowl of beet soup, you know, borscht, down her front. She was upset about Aunt Phyllis. The message came just as we were leaving the dock. Anyway, Gracie's blouse was ruined. She washed up in the ladies' room, just buttoned up her sweater, and asked me to see if Andrea could have the blouse cleaned. I brought it back and disposed of it in the Dumpster. It wasn't worth cleaning. Gracie is frugal to a ridiculous point sometimes."

Sarah felt as if someone was hitting her with a wet pillow. She clutched at the main point. "You mean Gracie is all right?"

"Gracie is just fine. It's her aunt who's sick. Suddenly and violently, a rash and a terrible diarrhea. I was the one who sent the message back here to pack her things. We missed our church meeting, of course. I took her to the airport, but we couldn't find a space on a plane. She found a man going to Bangor and paid him to drive her. She'll fly from there. To Harrisburg. Harrisburg, Pennsylvania. Sarah, Sarah, I'm so sorry you were worried."

Sarah allowed herself a moment of real humiliation, thought of Alex and all his remarks about an overheated imagination, and then she felt better. Rollo the Rabbit and his diamond earrings were real.

"But the jewelry," she reminded David, who stood shaking his head over her.

"Yes, absolutely, the jewelry. I'll do something about that right now. The town police, you say. I'll make sure they hold on to Mark." And David strode toward the row of telephones.

Sarah watched him dial, saw on his face a look of anger and harsh concentration. Heard him demand the chief of police or the chief of detectives or "whoever you've got in charge," and then say in a loud voice, "Hold that man, pay no attention to what he says. He's a thief and a liar. Send a man down here to pick up the jewelry and search his cabin. I'll stand guard here and make sure no one goes near my boat."

Mallory slammed down the receiver and Sarah met him with the question about Rollo. "I stuffed him in that Dumpster."

"With the jewelry in it?"

Sarah was just able to smile. "No, though I might have; my head was spinning. I put the things down in the same boot under another rabbit." Sarah didn't feel quite up to admitting that she'd entered the Chandler cabin and stolen their Rollo.

"And what exactly was in the rabbit? Stones, bracelets?"

"Earrings and a ring. And a seagull pin. Diamonds and rubies."

"Real diamonds? Real rubies?"

Sarah hesitated. "Well, they looked real. I could see the gold setting was eighteen carat. The stuff in the little pocket Bible, everything," she repeated, "looked absolutely genuine."

"You looked at the carat mark. I hand it to you, Sarah. I think I'll try to be there when the police search. I'll give my full cooperation, but you never know about the police. They could do a search job that might sink the *Pilgrim*. Oh, and I'll have to call again. I forgot to make sure your friends Professor Larkin and his wife are released." David returned to the booth and made a long call; Sarah could see him nodding, shaking his head. Then he dialed a second number, speaking with each, his big face expressionless.

He emerged shaking his head in disbelief. "Well, deTerra has clammed up. I still can't believe I've been made a fool of. A man I've worked with and trusted. Why, he was the second man on the *Simon Peter*. A jewel thief. I wonder if he's cleaned out half of Florida and decided he'd like a trip to the northeast."

Here, Mallory paused and indicated a woman tripping by, each wrist weighted with bracelets, her ears hung with teardrop amethysts. "I've never understood the passion for jewelry.

Elaine Chandler, yes, I know, she's covered with it, rings, earrings, but Elaine is Elaine. To me, jewelry is just nonfunctional. I don't see any civilized, any moral reason for the custom. Think of Gracie, so sensible. A little watch, a simple string of pearls or beads. Imagine the work our church could do with the money people spend on decorating themselves."

"Are the police going to search the whole boat?" asked Sarah, thinking to move the talk away from the sinfulness of liking jewelry—certain members of her own family were guilty.

Mallory nodded. "I told them to come right ahead and take deTerra's cabin apart, look over the *Pilgrim* and our inventory books if they want, but that any damage would have to be paid for. My God, Sarah, this cruise was supposed to be peace on earth, goodwill toward men. Anyway, your two friends are being released and will meet you at their bed and breakfast place any minute."

"I wish Alex was here" was all Sarah could say.

"So do I, but he will be soon. I've called his mother's Cambridge apartment to suggest he catch up with us at Eastern Harbor. And just now I've called Ezra in Castine and I'll try to find the others to tell them the news. It's best to warn everyone, because I've never trusted the police to hang on to a suspect even if they found him with a body and a bloody hatchet. DeTerra might just want to do something nasty."

Sarah hesitated, then decided to go for it. "David, was Mark deTerra at that church supper? During the time Billy disappeared?"

Again David Mallory looked aghast. He froze into position and his eyes widened. "My God, Sarah, I never thought about it. Of course, he was there. Almost the whole crew of the *Simon Peter* stopped in. Do you think he could have . . ." David Mallory looked almost ill and the word *murder* hung unspoken in the air. Then he shook himself like a big animal just out of the water, as if to rid himself of something so awful.

"Sarah, put that idea completely away for now. That business is for the police. Now why don't you go and meet your friends, have a nice cold drink together and then bring them back to the *Pilgrim* for dinner. Mark deTerra and the police can't ruin a good steak. We'll grill on deck and the good Lord willing, we'll manage to enjoy ourselves. For tonight, at least."

Sarah was about to start up the hill toward the bed and breakfast when she remembered.

"The rabbit. The one I took apart. It's still in the Dumpster. I'll get it out."

"Goodness, no, you've done enough. I'll get it or let the police fish it out. You've had enough grief for one day."

Amos and Mary were not in the best of humors. The three of them sat on the little front terrace of Betty's Bed & Breakfast sipping long, cool, sinister-looking drinks, Mary and Sarah's laced with rum, Amos holding a frosty beaker with a double dose of Irish tea. Mary had torn her new shirt in the scuffle, and Amos, his face even redder than his bristly hair, had wrenched a knee and bruised an arm.

"Marcus twisted it with an expert touch. He must have been practicing since he left college."

Sarah sat up and exclaimed. "Marcus! It was Marcus. Mark and Marcus are the same."

"The same. Not that I'm happy to find out that a former pupil, the son of an old friend, has chosen crime instead of graduate school."

"Did he know you?"

Amos looked thoughtfully at his iced tea, swirled it with one finger, and took a long sip. "He must have. He didn't say anything, but when I came raging down the hill doing my best drunken wild-West act, he did a double take."

"More than a double take," put in Mary. "He looked absolutely knocked out, outraged, revolted. In that order."

Sarah nodded. "The professor gone ape." She decided then and there not to bring up the real possibility of Mark as the murderer of Billy. Truth would out in good time and for now she could save Amos that unhappiness.

"He probably knew I was a heavy drinker even in those days, so he wasn't surprised. But, my God, what a hold that boy has. He could have tossed me forty feet in the air and not felt the strain. You said he'd murdered someone, a secretary. Probably a good choice."

"Amos," said Mary sharply.

"I made a mistake," said Sarah, her face coloring.

"Not a secretary?" asked Amos.

"No. I'd seen the secretary's blouse in the Dumpster. I'd just found that Mark—or Marcus—had been making off with jewelry, and I jumped to the idea. The blouse was stained, only David Mallory said she'd spilled borscht on it, and she really is on her way to see a sick aunt."

"A likely story," said Amos. "Couldn't she think of anything better? Gracie is probably working with Marcus."

"Yes, yes,". said Sarah excitedly. "It could be that. I mean now that's she hasn't been murdered by Mark. Gracie is working with Mark, and she has a briefcase full of earrings and plush rabbits and had someone make up a message about a sick aunt and had David drive her to the airport and now, poof, she's gone."

"*Has* she an aunt?" queried Mary.

Sarah shrugged. "Who knows. She wrote a letter to one and Mallory believes it. You're supposed to come for dinner tonight, and we can ask about the aunt and what's supposed to be wrong with her. If Gracie wasn't very specific, it may be a lie. It will be great to have you two loyal friends around, what with Alex away and Tony gone, maybe forever, to Bar Harbor with Marilyn Monroe."

"Your loyal friends are a bit battered, and is that a disagreeable note in your voice?" asked Amos. "Big sister doesn't approve of brother's bedmate. I assume that she's his bedmate."

"Undoubtedly, but that's not it. Andrea is gorgeous. She's adaptable, she sails, she cooks, she reads *great books*."

"So?"

"Oh, I don't know," said Sarah crossly. "It's just that I haven't been able even to talk to Tony. My parents have this unreal idea that I can find out if he intends to go on drifting to nowhere. But the only plan Tony has is to make Andrea."

"Your parents should have known better," said Mary. "If brothers listen to someone, it will not be to their sister—except in Victorian novels."

"Maybe I'm discouraged because I miss Alex."

"Very laudable," said Amos. He pointed toward the harbor. "The police have arrived. The search party, I presume."

"Do you have binoculars?" asked Sarah.

"Certainly not," said Mary. "You and Alex are the bird nuts."

"With my excellent vision," said Amos, "I can tell that a large gentleman in a yachting cap is handing over a white object to two men who by their depressing appearance must be plainclothes detectives."

"David Mallory with Rollo Rabbit," said Sarah.

The three friends watched as Mallory and the two men, each with a small carrying case, made their way down the gangway, hoisted themselves into the motor whaleboat, and moved off sedately toward the distant mooring of the *Pilgrim*. Then the talk drifted to the affairs of Bowmouth College, the eternal problems of the English Department, who was teaching what and why, who might be denied tenure, who was going on sabbatical, egregious changes in the degree requirements—all grist and gristle to be contentedly chewed over by the faculty. The sun sank lower in the sky and lighted the tip of the tallest mast, the mild breeze subsided and the harbor water beyond the line of moorings flattened into wrinkles.

Then the whaleboat reappeared and the two men climbed out and moved toward the gangway. Sarah jumped up. "It's time to go. Dinner. I said I'd bring you by six-thirty."

"Upscale dining aboard the yacht *Pilgrim*," said Amos, rising and wincing as he put weight on his knee. "I shall have to use a stick; damn Marcus Terrant and all his works. See if I ever tutor anyone's son in the summer again."

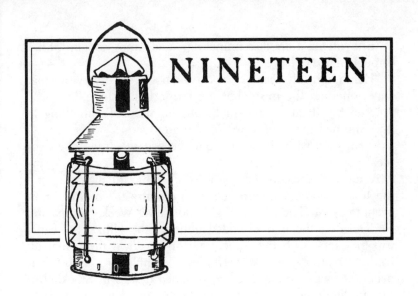

NINETEEN

DINNER FEATURED DAVID MALLORY AT THE GRILL WITH what appeared to be the side of a brontosaurus. The grill was fastened to the after rail and gave off dangerous sparks, which Sarah hoped would not ignite all the fuel systems of the entire harbor. Mary leaned back on the cockpit cushions, watching with half-closed eyes, and Amos tangled with the Chandlers. Or to be more precise, he led them on so that their bright verbal shuffle sounded more and more to Sarah's ears like a parody of a drawing-room comedy.

Amos, posing as an interested second banana, fed them openings that only Sarah—and Mary if she was listening—could recognize as having an ironic undercurrent.

"Do you enjoy Europe in the summer?" asked Amos. "Isn't it becoming absolutely overrun? Tourists, students, academic transients?" This when Elaine had murmured about catching the Edinburgh Festival at the end of August.

"The popular places, of course. You simply have to get off the beaten. But Flip just adores the festival; he claims he's got Highland blood coursing through his veins and goes all goose bumps when the bagpipes start squealing."

"But you are more discriminating," said Amos, looking at her through narrowed eyes.

"Edinburgh, oh dear me, it can be positively dreary, all that gray stone and the mists, but the music is smashing."

"And the theatre," put in Sarah, for want of something to say. She had never been to Edinburgh.

"That goes without saying, but the people, dear. The people."

Amos moved Elaine on, gathered Flip into the dialogue, and the two Chandlers leapfrogged from country to country, from event to event. The Isle of Wight and Cowes Week, Verona and *La Traviata*, the new extended hours at the Uffizi, the canal trip they took with the Malcolm Knights down the Canal du Midi. Ascot, Newmarket, Henley, Wimbledon, and Glyndebourne, wine in the Medoc, poached oysters in Stockholm, fun in Sardinia, seeing the Aga Khan on a yacht in Porto Cervo.

Amos, almost visibly taking notes, led them on. Sarah knew that as a lifelong fan and scholar of Jonathan Swift, the follies of the fashionable world were his meat. Perhaps this winter a small satiric piece under his name would appear in a review and his friends would enjoy a wicked chuckle at the expense of Mr. and Mrs. Chandler, whose names would be altered ever so slightly.

The shadows lengthened, Sarah and Mary began yawning, and Amos rose to his feet, well satisfied with his evening's work.

He had listened with pleasure to Elaine comparing the Taj Mahal to a biscuit box, and now drew Mary to the rail, thanked Mallory, and turned to Sarah and handed her a folded piece of paper. "It's the curriculum list for undergraduates. The one you asked for. I forgot to give it to you earlier."

"I asked for?" said Sarah stupidly.

"Last semester," said Amos firmly. "I meant to give it to you this afternoon, but the tussle with Mark put it out of my mind."

"Now don't lose it," said Mary. "Not many copies out yet."

Sarah, frowning, began to say that she knew the curriculum, but she saw Mary's eyebrows raised a fraction of an inch and was quiet.

Mary then turned to thank David Mallory, adding, "Sarah

told about your losing your secretary, who did so much of the organization work. I hope her aunt's illness isn't serious?"

"I'm afraid so," said David, shaking his head. "Her oldest living relative, they think it's Lyme disease."

Amos and Mary expressed appropriate concern and David suggested a plan for them to join the *Pilgrim* on Little Cranberry Island for a picnic and a look at the museum. "Of course, it will depend on the weather. I'll try to reach Ezra to delay his starting for Eastern Harbor."

"And I," said Amos, "may be overwhelmed suddenly with a desire to go home and see to my goats, Sarah's dog, and my son, not necessarily in that order. Besides our boy and animal sitter may become desperate after two days."

"Somebody call us tomorrow morning," said Mary, "and we can firm things." Mary turned to Sarah and gave her another look, which said as clearly as possible, You call from a phone booth.

David, acting as chauffeur, pulled in the Avon raft, assisted Mary and Amos into the boat, and as he rowed away, he called back to the Chandlers, "Bridge?"

"Love to darling, but we're going out in the Cris-Craft again. Such a ball, just drifting under the stars."

They're absolute night owls; how do they do it? Sarah asked herself as she made her way to her cabin. But then, the Chandlers had probably not tossed about in their berths worrying about the honesty of the crew. She undressed, took a fast shower, tumbled into her bunk, and reached for *The Thirty-Nine Steps*. One last chapter before sleep. Then she remembered Amos and his curriculum.

She found the folded paper in her pants pocket, unfolded it, and was about to read when she heard a soft rapping on her cabin door. The handle turned and a dark head with a black beard pushed itself into the room.

"Tony! What on earth?"

"Are you asleep?"

"Almost but not quite."

"Can I come in?"

"Of course." And then because it was an automatic reaction, she asked, "Where's Andrea?"

"We had a disagreement. She wanted to stay in Bar Harbor."

"And you didn't?"

"No, it's a tourist bin. I'd had it up to here with the place and I thought she had, too, and then suddenly I found out that she wanted to camp out, use her new tent, or go to an inn or something. She called Mallory, something about Mark deTerra being held by the police, and was told he wanted her to see about some church business in Bar Harbor. Something he'd forgotten."

"And?" Sarah sat up in her bunk. She couldn't imagine that Tony had turned down this invitation because Andrea was not a desirable bed partner.

He answered her question. "It's not that I didn't want to. But after all, we *have* been sleeping together, so it seemed to me that we could go on doing it here on the *Pilgrim* instead of being stuck in a campground with half of the American tourist population breathing down our necks."

"So she stayed and you came back."

"I told her Mallory's business could probably be done in a hurry and I'd go to the church with her, but she said no and that it was complicated. Something about a messed-up order, the wrong Bibles. Whatever."

"But you haven't really had a fight?"

"A cool spell. I think she's terrific, but she always wants to do what she wants to do. I don't want her to get the idea that everytime she bats her eyes I'll jump."

Which, thought Sarah, you've been pretty much doing since we took off from Camden. Well, if Tony wanted to talk, she wasn't going to lose the chance. The Andrea cool spell might not last long. Aloud, she said, prompting him, "You wanted to talk."

"Yeah, though not about Andrea. We'll settle what we have to by ourselves." Tony came all the way into the cabin, closed the door, and stretched himself on the opposite bunk, adjusting Alex's pillow comfortably under his head. "These cabins are posh; we crew get thirty-inch bunks. Anyway, it's about Mark deTerra."

"Do you know he's really Marcus Terrant, and he's a jewel thief? Or smuggler. Or worse."

"Andrea told me the whole bit. First, about Gracie leaving, then about Mark. No, it's her reaction. She turned sort of gray. She had called Mallory earlier when we were at a bar having a beer around two thirty and said we'd be late and asked whether she was needed to start dinner, and he said to have a good time, he'd cook steaks. Well, she told him she'd call him aboard the *Pilgrim* around five in case there was a change of plan and that's when he gave her the news about Mark being held by the police and the church's messed-up order. But she was rattled. I mean rattled. She looked as gray as an oyster and sort of stuttered. Said David was all shook up."

"Well, no wonder," said Sarah. "A trusted church member."

Tony looked reflective and slowly ran a finger over Alex's open book on the bed and displaced the bookmark. Then he rolled halfway over on his stomach and looked at Sarah. "I'm no one to get all steamed about a weird reaction, but Andrea's pretty steady and she was like blown apart by this. If Mallory was hit half as bad, well, what do you think? I know I sound like you playing your little detective games, but do you think this Mark-Marcus could have had some sort of hold over Mallory? And Andrea. Or over everyone on board. Like blackmailing or something."

"I wouldn't put it past him. But blackmailing about what?"

"I thought you might guess. You've been boiling over with suspicion since we took off, haven't you?"

Sarah was quiet for a moment and then said, "Tony, does Mallory know you've come back on board?"

"Don't think so. I didn't tell Andrea where I was going, so she wouldn't have called him. I made a big exit and said I needed fresh air, away from crowds. To let her think I'd gone mountain climbing or something. When I got to the harbor, I saw Mallory unloading Mary and Amos. I didn't feel like talking, so I hitched a ride in someone's dinghy going past our mooring and went down the crew's forward hatch."

"David thinks I've gone to bed. He wanted someone to pack up Gracie's things, so I could go to her cabin and do that, and when Mallory turns up, I'll say I couldn't sleep and thought I'd help him."

"You mean to find something that Mark would be blackmailing Gracie about? Or that fits her into a blackmail scheme *with* Mark?"

"I'm not thinking blackmail, but it seems like a last chance to find out about Gracie. You could report in to David, keep him busy, and I could take a look at the Chandlers' cabin, as well. They haven't come back from their evening cruise. If David joins me in Gracie's cabin, you can check his. And Andrea's."

"Christ, Sarah, I can't go into Mallory's cabin. Are you crazy? And Andrea would flay me alive, getting into her stuff. Besides, it would be an absolutely lousy thing to do to her."

"Were you serious about her reaction to the news about Mark? And to her view of Mallory's reaction?"

"Yes, but not serious enough to break into her cabin."

"Then you're not worried enough to do some looking?"

"Yes, but I do have some standards." Tony closed his eyes and Sarah could almost see an inward struggle taking place. He frowned, crossed his legs, flipped Alex's book up and down. Then he said, "I'm not going poking my nose in just anyone's cabin. Anyway, not Mallory's and Andrea's. But if you want to hit the Chandlers'—because they strike me as really flaky—and Gracie's—well, okay. I'll go with you. *Then* I'll tell David I'm back. If I do it now, he'll think up some great little chore like making new splices in the mooring lines or cleaning the life-jacket locker."

Sarah nodded, rolled out of her bunk, reached for slippers and a windbreaker to wear over her pajamas, and started down the narrow corridor toward Gracie's cabin, Tony following. Suddenly, she stopped. "Speaking of standards, I'm going to do this thing kosher," she said, and disappeared aft toward the galley and Mallory's cabin. She returned in five minutes.

"What in hell?" said Tony.

"I knocked on David's door and said I couldn't sleep and needed to do something physical and could I pack Gracie up now for him. He said sure, go ahead, and thanks."

"You *are* crazy," said Tony. "Obviously her cabin will be

clean. If there ever was anything in it, that is. Gracie would have taken any oddball stuff with her, or Mark would have checked her cabin out, so what's the point?"

"I do need to do something physical; you've stirred me up. David gave me her key, said he'd locked her cabin after the police went over it. He doesn't know I hung on to a master key."

"The police. The police went over it. Jesus, why are we going to look through a cabin the police have swept? And you have a master key? You're the one they should be investigating."

"Keep your voice down," said Sarah. "Here's the cabin. You go through the hanging locker. I'll start on the toilet articles."

Sarah found two navy blue suitcases in the storage space under Gracie's bunk and went to work while Tony scooped out a jacket, a cardigan, and two floral print dresses. They worked quietly, Tony draping clothes on the bed, Sarah alternating between folding these and collecting toilet articles and a collection of seacoast mementos. She packed a framed photograph showing the *Pilgrim* at anchor, another of David Mallory under a palm tree, and a smaller framed photograph of a younger, healthier Billy Brackett. He was standing next to a large tree wearing a kilt and holding a sword limply in one hand.

Sarah held up the picture. "Billy."

Tony peered over her shoulder. "Billy in drag; that figures."

"He's dressed up for some costume party . . . no, I've got it. He's Macduff's son, the 'poor monkey.' And Billy quoted from those lines, you know Lady Macduff and her son. Gracie is Gracia Delancy. And Mark is Marcus. And I think I'm going crazy."

Tony let out a whistle. "Forget Macduff and look at these."

He waggled a pair of black lace underpants in the bikini style at Sarah. "Sexy, sexy. From the underwear collection. A bra to match. Gracie, the porno queen. You never know what's under those old-lady print dresses." He was about to stuff the pants in the suitcase when Sarah reached over and examined the underpants.

Not porno queen, but they might have been classified as "alluring." Sarah found the label: Henri Bendel. The bra also.

Tony now was tossing frothy bits of underclothes on the bunk, shaking his head and repeating, "Sexy lady."

"Gracie is *not* sexy," said Sarah, picking up a camisole edged in coffee-colored lace. Saks Fifth Avenue.

"Underneath she was," said Tony.

"She wore Yardley's Old English Lavender for perfume," said Sarah. "I've just packed it in her toilet-article kit."

"And in her underwear drawer, I find ze Tiffany eau de parfum," said Tony, in a false French accent. "Also I find ze Oscar de la Renta's Ruffles eau de toilette. Oo la la."

"Just pack," said Sarah. "Unless you come across a big hunky diamond or a rabbit stuffed with jewelry, I'm not interested. Or drugs, or a big stash of cash. Otherwise, get on with it."

They got on with it, although Sarah did pause from time to time to wonder at the quality of the things Gracie wore next to her skin and the utter dreariness and frumpiness of her outer shell. No jewelry. No drugs. No gold, silver, or contraband of any sort. Not even a small quantity of brandy hidden in a perfume bottle.

Sarah snapped the second suitcase shut and placed it on the bunk. "At least we've done an honest job of packing."

"And found absolutely zip. I can't see old Gracie as anything but a twit. Now how about the Chandlers?"

Sarah paused. Fatigue was overtaking her. The exhilaration of the hunt, even with Tony's participation to sustain her, had faded. But since they were at it, well, why not?

"This way," she said, pointing across the passage.

"I know where," said Tony. "Who do you think keeps the teak bright and the portholes polished?"

The Chandlers' cabin—which was unlocked—was the absolute opposite of the extreme order of Gracie's quarters. "Yin and yang," said Tony, as they closed the cabin door behind them. Blouses tumbled out of the locker, neckties hung over the bunk hammock, men's shoes of all types mixed with Elaine's collection of canvas, leather, and silk footgear, pajamas and nightgowns trailed from a drawer, a straw hat sat jauntily over a light fixture, and ropes of necklaces trickled from an open cosmetic case.

"The beautiful people are pigs," said Tony, moving a canvas belt embroidered with mallard ducks with his shoe.

"Don't move anything," said Sarah. "Messy people usually know where they've kicked something. It's a survival thing, otherwise they could never get dressed. And the Chandlers certainly dress."

"Their reading matter makes me puke," said Tony. He hoisted an enormous black volume with red lettering: *The Social Register*.

"I didn't know anyone still looked at that," said Sarah.

"It's for all cities," said Tony. "All the proper cities. He ruffled through a few pages. "God, those Chandlers. Look, it gives clubs, and schools and country-house names and kids and colleges."

"Imagine lugging it on a cruise," said Sarah. "It must weigh at least ten pounds."

"I suppose Flip and dear Elaine wanted to be sure that everyone they met was in the good book. This cruise must have disappointed them."

"Except every now and then they're into equality," said Sarah. Then on impulse, "Look up the Chandlers."

"What city?"

"Isn't there an index, a locater or something?"

"I've got it. Baltimore. Fleance Rumsey Chandler. Married Elaine Hewitt Weatherby. He's St. Mark's, she's Westover. He's Yale, she's Mt. Holyoke. They don't have a summer house; they live in Captiva. They have no little juniors. How veddy, veddy boring."

"Put it back. Anything else?"

"*Town & Country*, and *Harper's Bazaar*, and *Gourmet*, and something called *European Travel and Life*. Boring, boring," repeated Tony. "Let's can it."

Sarah agreed. However, as they turned to leave, Tony spied an open large-leaf bound manuscript on one bunk. He reached for it, turned a page, and then replaced it carefully. *The Skin of Our Teeth*.

"They read," said Sarah.

"It's a script. Mrs. Antrobus's part is marked, so are some cuts."

Sarah digested this information and added to her mental folder labeled "Chandlers," but she was too tired to try and sort out the implications of Elaine Chandler as Mrs. Antrobus. She had not struck Sarah as the earth-mother sort, but then you never know. It was probably for some theatrical benefit in some expensive resort. She squeezed Tony's hand, thanked him, and said good night. "Think about it, will you, Tony?"

"It?"

"All of it. Andrea's reaction, Mark deTerra's diamond collection, Gracie's underwear, and Mrs. Antrobus. Good night."

Sarah sat down, ready to take off her slippers, when she saw the curriculum paper Mary had forced on her. She opened it and read without much comprehension the following:

Welcome Welcome Welcome or—Sanibel salutes the Fourth of July

HELP US CELEBRATE THE GLORIOUS FOURTH

A WEEKEND OF EXCITING EVENTS

SATURDAY: THE PANTRY PLAYERS—The third appearance of this accomplished repertory theatre group. To be presented by Darcy Mallory two plays: *As You Like It* and Noël Coward's ever-popular comedy *Private Lives*. Favorite actors returning for a two-week run are Mallory himself, who plays and directs, Gracia Delancy, William Brattle, Elvira and Fleance Chipperly, and many other familiar faces. Performances on Saturday, Tuesday, Wednesday, and Friday, and a Sunday matinee at two.

ALSO WELCOME AGAIN !!!! SHARKY GONZALES AND THE JAWS IN A BLUE GRASS BLOWOUT—SATURDAY AND MONDAY NIGHTS.

Sarah left the description of Sharkey Gonzales and the Jaws and tried to comprehend. What *was* this? Actors! David Mallory, who had been so popular at Bowmouth College juggling for benefits, might he not be the director-player, Darcy Mallory, certainly a name with more theatrical élan than simple David Mallory? And Flip and Elaine must be Elvira and Fleance Chipperly—Elvira had more zip than Elaine and Flip's real name was Fleance. There couldn't be too many Fleances in the world besides Flip and Banquo's escaping son. *Macbeth?* Why did that play keep popping up? And Gracia Delancy, of course, was the lady who had been such a help to the Bowmouth Little Theatre group, bringing her little brother to fill in the cast. This William Brattle? Billy Brackett wasn't much of a leap. She returned to Flip and Elaine. Actors! God, she might have guessed it, especially after the manuscript in their cabin. But they seemed so real, such perfect jet-setters. And Gracie, an actress? Miss Nervous Twitchet. Okay, a director, but not actually onstage. Nor David Mallory. Producer, yes, actor, no. His too-too-solid flesh would never resolve itself into an actor.

Sarah was too groggy to want to speculate further on the Pantry Players. Perhaps it would all come clear in the night. She climbed into her bunk and reached for *The Thirty-Nine Steps* like a drowning person reaches for safety and oblivion. She could not think tonight. Tomorrow it would all come together. Or fall apart. Or something.

She opened the last chapter and began reading, quickly skimming, then slowing, slowing, rereading. And then it all fell apart and came together at the same time.

TWENTY

BUCHAN'S HERO, RICHARD HANNAY, HAD MADE IT TO the seaside, expecting to pin down the evil Germans and save, if not the empire, some portion of British honor. To his surprise, the spot designated as the rendezvous of enemy agents with an offshore yacht turned out to be the very ordinary seaside residence of an old gentleman who was enjoying tennis and bandinage with a younger man and a visiting golfer. They were in the author's words "three ordinary, game-playing, suburban Englishmen, wearisome, if you like, but sordidly innocent."

Hannay suddenly remembered a discussion on disguises by an old friend who "laughed at things like dyed hair and false beards and such childish follies." What mattered was atmosphere. Here Sarah propped herself high on her pillow and read with growing attention:

> If a man could get into perfectly different surroundings from those in which he had been first observed, and—this is the important part—really play up to those surroundings and behave as if he had never been out of them, he would puzzle

the cleverest detectives on earth. . . . If you are playing a part, you will never keep it up unless you convince yourself that you are *it*.

Three pages from the end, Richard Hannay concluded that one of the agents "must have been a superb actor." A superb actor. Actors. A whole cast of superb actors. No, a whole crew of superb actors. Stanislavski aboard ship.

Elaine-Elvira and Flip-Fleance Chandler-Chipperly—an expensive couple taking a trip, visiting old friends, making bright conversation that sounded like vintage drawing-room comedy. In their cabin reading scripts. What parts were they really playing?

Ezra. Ezra with the shifting accent. The perfect seaman who could do *Juno and the Paycock* or play Pistol in *Henry the Fourth*.

And Gracie Mullen-Gracia Delancy. Former play director, currently acting the secretary. Perhaps boning up for Mrs. Danvers in a revival film of *Rebecca*. Or the *Turn of the Screw*; that had a nice servant part. And the frothy fancy underwear. Damn, of course. Gracie had given herself away with all that lace and froufrou. No one seeing her at luncheon would guess that under the butterfly blouse was a designer bra. Not until the contents of her drawers were revealed. But no one had stopped Sarah from packing Gracie's things. The police had not found her underwear collection strange. Nor had Mallory. He had encouraged the packing. Why? Easy. Because most men, unless they were in the garment trade, would not know whether bras, panties, camisoles, slips were in tune with the outer shell, the workaday dress. To Mallory and the police, women's underwear was probably just women's underwear. But Gracie was an actress, a professional. Her print dresses were her costume; but why sacrifice her body to old-lady underwear? Becoming your part was necessary, as John Buchan suggested, but it didn't mean you gave up lace and silk next to your skin. The frumpy dress, the arch-support shoes were quite enough.

Gracie was an actress flinching appropriately when the word *Macbeth* was booted about. However, she wasn't supposed to let on about her other profession. Had she blown her lines, forgotten her role? Been nervous at the wrong time, laughed once too often that unearthly high laugh? What *had* happened to Gracie? Had she really gone to take care of her sick aunt down with diarrhea and spots, that trendy disorder, Lyme disease? Sarah would call Alex and check on the symptoms. Tonight.

And Mark-Marcus deTerra-Terrant, was he a member of Pantry Players playing Caliban, or—why not—the new-made Thane of Cawdor. A thief playing the blue-water sailor and church member? Working with Gracie or murdering her? Murdering Billy?

What of Mallory? David-Darcy Mallory. Director, player, Gracie's appreciative employer. Gracie's fellow worker in the trenches of the church. Gracie's lead man? Uncle Vanya, Coriolanus? Creon in *Antigone*?

Oh my God. Sarah held her head. The Pantry Players. Actors. What was the *Pilgrim* crew, anyway? A floating rep company. Or actors on Godly missions. Or?

Billy Brackett, child actor appearing in *Macbeth*. Billy, who had shown how clever he was, what an accomplished mime. Billy as Puck, as Caligula? As Billy Budd? And Billy was dead. He blew it.

And Andrea? The ingenue? The little blond piece who always fell into the arms of the young male player—Billy? The ingenue currently playing opposite brother Tony, the fall guy.

Sarah, her head swimming, dangled her legs over the bunk. Tony. She had to talk to Tony. Tony was Tony. He wasn't an actor, he was her brother, and he would tell her that she was on the edge of a breakdown, that she was in some crazy fugue from reality, and to straighten up and fly right. Mellow out. Lighten up. With the playbill in her hand, she opened the door and hurried along to the crew's passageway, pulled open Tony's door, entered, and shook her brother awake.

Tony sat up staring while Sarah, wild-eyed, poured out her story. Her certainty that things were amiss on the good ship *Pilgrim*, and that they had all embarked on a voyage to a very dangerous never-never land.

Tony at first laughed. Then soothed. Then told Sarah she

was raving. Said he would call Alex; she needed help. A tranquilizer. It was what happened to academics. They were all too strung out. Overachievers living on their nerves.

But Sarah persisted. She took hold of herself and now spoke calmly and firmly. She presented evidence, the playbill, lists of notable facts, recollections of conversations. Tony resisted at first, particularly when Sarah cited her grandmother's warning about Mallory's imperfect memory of favorite Psalms, a warning at which she herself had scoffed.

"Come off it. So he slipped up on a Psalm. I'll bet even Grandma makes mistakes. Mallory is a lay preacher. He practically *is* that church; he always carries a little pocket Bible around. He's for real. So is that stuff, the cassettes, the braille books. As for sailing, he loves this boat. My God, he's a compulsive skipper. It isn't an act. You should have seen us off Hatteras."

Sarah moved away from Mallory. She had the sense not to mention Andrea, but instead presented the case for Billy, for the Chandlers, Ezra, Gracie as all being members of a well-known—at least in Sanibel—theatrical company. And she put the Fourth of July announcement in Tony's hands. "I don't know where Amos found it; he'd been doing some research for me."

Tony was silent. He studied the sheet, and Sarah could see him making the associations. Elvira for Elaine, Chipperly for Chandler. William Brattle, Billy Brackett. When he reached Darcy Mallory, he put the sheet down.

"It's weird. But I don't see . . ." He paused, and then said defiantly, "Not Andrea. No way. She couldn't act to save her life."

"Unless," said Sarah, "she was acting someone who couldn't act. The playbill says 'many other familiar faces.' That might include Ezra and Andrea. And Mark."

"Not Andrea," repeated Tony furiously.

"Okay," agreed Sarah, "but what about the rest of it?"

"Weird. The whole thing is weird." Tony picked up the playbill as if rereading it might bring order. Finally, he said, "Well, they could be actors and church people and sailors and secretaries, couldn't they? There's no rule against it. I know lots of people who do two or three things."

"Has anyone on the *Pilgrim* mentioned an interest in the theatre? Theatre people I know talk shop all the time. Incessantly. They can be very tedious."

"The Chandlers," said Tony. "They talk new shows, plays."

"As spectators. Plays as something to go to." Sarah did an imitation of Elaine's flutelike tones. "They say, 'Have you seen that wretched new *Hamlet* in London? Such a mistake doing it in Japanese costume—Gertrude in a kimono. Flip and I just adored the new A.R. Gurney because we just know those people. We had fourth row center. We always try for fourth row center.' That's what they say. Not a soul on the *Pilgrim* has ever suggested that he or she has any serious connection with the theatre, the legitimate theatre."

"Is Sanibel theatre legitimate? Besides, Flip does puppets."

"As a parlor game, not as a professional. But those cute little dialogues he and Elaine fool around with, well I kept thinking they were just like Noël Coward. Well, they are Noël Coward. Almost. Remember Elaine saying to Amos that the Taj Mahal was like a biscuit box? Isn't that *Private Lives?* They've been serving us drawing-room comedy, but because it was in character—it fitted the characters they'd established when they came aboard—we didn't notice. We expected bright, aimless chatter."

"All that stuff about Paris and Cannes and Yale and old friends called Pippy and Nippy and Skippy, you mean it's an act?"

"Yes and no. I'm sure they do know the Hunters and the Nevilles. And they do travel. But some people who go to Yale and Mt. Holyoke also go on the stage. They use Chipperly as a stage name."

"What do you mean yes and no? That *Social Register* volume and the garbage about 'our kind of people,' is it or isn't it real?"

"It's in character."

Tony sat up, his eyes wild, his hair ruffled. "Christ Almighty, what character? Why in character? Aren't they just themselves? If they've been in a theatre company together, why shouldn't they sail together? The Chandlers or Chipperlys are just rich actors on a cruise who know gorgeous, expensive, useless people. And Gracie's fucking brother, Billy, wasn't he just an actor who was allergic to everything that moved? And Mallory, he's a churchman and actor and a sailor. And Marcus what's his name. Was he playing something? Isn't he just a good old common criminal who knew a juicy setup when he saw it? God, you can complicate something, Sarah. Christ Almighty."

"Where *is* Gracie?" said Sarah quietly. How *did* Billy die?"

Tony frowned and appeared to be thinking when a small noise, a tiny splash distracted him. "What's that?"

"I don't hear anything," said Sarah, her ears still ringing from Tony's tirade.

"Shut up, listen."

They sat rigid on Tony's bunk, and then Tony reached over and carefully pushed his porthole open, and now a swish of water and a soft scraping sounded along the hull of the sloop.

"It's the Avon," whispered Tony. "Someone's taking it out."

"There's only one someone on board," Sarah said. "Mallory."

"Well, it's his raft," said Tony, "He can use it if he wants, though it's almost midnight and he usually turns in by eleven."

"Maybe the Chandlers need picking up."

"Yeah, that's probably it. That old mahogany cruiser may have hit bottom somewhere. It's probably fifty years old at least."

They were silent again, listening. Then Tony gestured toward the bow of the boat. "Someone's fooling with the mooring line."

"Can't you look out?"

"Not without being seen. If I poked out of a hatch, Mallory would spot me for sure. He has eyes like a cat."

And with that remark, Sarah knew Tony had accepted some small portion of her story.

They remained unmoving, and then Tony, his head cocked toward the porthole, said, "The boat's swinging. Just a little. Mallory must be checking the mooring."

"I thought these were big, safe moorings."

"They are, but something may be loose. Or twisted. Or there's too much slack, too short a line on the mooring."

"Can't you work your way forward and see?"

"No. Just sit still and listen."

Sarah subsided, hearing only the occasional splash from the bow. Then Tony poked her. "He's taking off, rowing. He may be just bringing the Avon aft and tying her up."

But Mallory didn't. They heard one or two minute splashes as the oars dipped, then Tony heaved himself up, opened the cabin door, and disappeared.

He returned almost immediately. "It's hard to see. He's rowing away from inner harbor, not making much headway."

"If he's really rowing out, I can call Alex with some questions and then we can look at Mallory's cabin."

"I said I wasn't going to do that."

"Even after everything I've told you?"

"Big deal. A bunch of actors go on a cruise. It's all probably some kind of joke. Or it's a religious acting company. Listen, how about this? DeTerra and Gracie were going to escape with the jewelry, but he knocked her off because he wanted it all, or her sexy underwear was driving him bonkers. There, do you like that better? More in line with S. Deane's calculations."

"Tony."

"Okay, okay, but ease up. Worse things have happened than finding yourself on a boat run by actors."

"I'll call Alex first about Lyme disease and you can stand guard while I take one quick look at David's cabin."

Sarah found that making an urgent telephone call from the coast of Maine at the end of July—the favorite cruising time—was a matter of total frustration. At least eight calls were stacked up before her. For twenty minutes, she and Tony stood by as requested by the marine operator, stood by hunched over and the radio-telephone listening to the boating population and its shore-based buddies. Businessmen discovering urgent reasons not to return to the office. Boyfriends calling girlfriends, girlfriends ditching boyfriends. Late drinkers calling those already asleep. Calls about moorings, leaks, balky bilge pumps, broken stays, broken rudders.

Finally, "*Pilgrim*, go ahead with your call." And then static. "Camden marine says I'm breaking up," said Sarah in exasperation.

"You're too far away or the radio's on the fritz."

Then after more crackling and static, Sarah landed Alex's mother, Elspeth, in her Cambridge apartment. Alex had gone out to say good-bye to his father in the hospital and then had planned to go straight to Fenway Park. "The Red Sox, you know how important they are to Alex." Sarah did know and felt a wave of frustration. Those damn Red Sox. However, she made the necessary inquiries after Alex's father, and Elspeth reported happily that yes, Alex's father was doing splendidly, then asked was anything wrong. Sarah tried for a middle ground between alarm and routine but made no headway beyond convincing Elspeth that the entire crew of the *Pilgrim* had come down with Lyme disease. The radio-telephone reception made Elspeth McKenzie sound as if she spoke from the bottom of a rain barrel.

"You poor things. Did you all have the rash or get arthritis or think you had flu? Alex says it can be hard to diagnose."

"Not us," Sarah found herself shouting. "One of our crew members has an aunt who might have it."

"The aunt has it, too?"

"No," said Sarah. "But do you get a total rash and diarrhea?"

"You sound very strange," said Elspeth, "but I hope you're having a lovely time even if you are sick. Alex says the boat is marvelous."

Sarah tried again, this time restricting her message to a request that Elspeth ask Alex about symptoms or whether there were ticks in Harrisburg.

"Are you interested in entomology now, Sarah?" asked Elspeth. "Alex will be pleased. He's always liked bugs."

"You'll ask Alex?" said Sarah desperately.

"Of course, though he'll be joining you sometime tomorrow if he can make the flight; he's on standby now. They're jammed up. July, you know."

Sarah said she did know, said good-bye, and thanked

Camden Marine, then, remembering her practice session, said, "Over and out, *Pilgrim* WRD 6677."

"And what was the point of all that?" demanded Tony.

"The point is, or was, to find out if a body rash and diarrhea are symptoms of Lyme disease, and if you come down with it all at once. Aunt Phyllis may have been just a handy decoy."

"Christ," said Tony for at least the tenth time that night."

"So watch for Mallory and I'll make a quick visit to his cabin."

Sarah's master key opened Mallory's cabin. She was surprised. No double security system, so Gracie in her role as housekeeper-secretary had access at will. Of course, if Mallory was the innocent dupe of Mark and his cohorts—if he had cohorts—he would not feel the need of an extra lock.

The cabin was very much as she had seen it when David had invited her to look at his supply of religious goodies. A miracle of businesslike organization. His desk held the secular part of his library: books on navigation, tide tables, engine maintenance, two new cruising guides. Above the desk was lined up evidence of the *Pilgrim*'s dual purpose: the Bibles, prayer books, tracts, a rack of cassettes.

She pulled out the under-bunk storage drawer David had shown her the day he demonstrated his wares and she found a considerably depleted row of Bibles and prayer books. She opened one or two at random and found them to be exactly what they seemed to be. Discouraged, she opened the hanging locker but found no Rollo Rabbits hiding in rubber boots or slicker pockets, no contraband, nothing but rather expensive-looking jackets, shirts, and trousers: heather-mix tweed, linen, Irish cotton, Viyella.

For a moment, she stood still looking around. The cabin with its curtains pulled across its large windowlike portholes had a almost cozy look. Except she remembered the curtains as being red. These were green. Had Mallory redecorated? If so, it was a mistake, because the green went poorly with the crimson carpet.

Then she shook herself. Back to work. Feeling absolutely loathsome, a person of the most despicable character, Sarah gritted her teeth and visited Mallory's shower, toilet, and sink.

Saw that he used an electric shaver, a red toothbrush, and some Calvin Klein products in an array of bottles. Pears soap. Crest toothpaste.

Retreating to the cabins, she examined the cabin sole under the rug. Nothing. The bunk, blankets, comforter, curtain yielded only a sense of violation as Sarah tugged and pulled, then retucked and smoothed her way through David Mallory's hangings and covers.

Discouraged, she was about to go when she saw at the bottom of the wastebasket several wads of printed paper. Reaching down, she came up with a crumpled handful: Joshua, Judges, Ruth, and First and Second Samuel, First and Second Kings, and a small section of First Chronicles. Not whole chapters, the guts of chapters—tiny printing on small sheets of India paper.

Puzzled, Sarah turned the loose pages. Bits of Delilah and Sampson and his fatal haircut, then Ruth, Samuel, and the trouble with the Philistines, David and Saul, and ending abruptly with Nebuchadnezzar in II Kings.

Why was that son of the church, David Mallory, scissoring his Bible? Or Bibles. Because this couldn't be some innocent educational project for island churches?

At this juncture, Tony poked his head in the cabin door. "I think I hear someone coming. Clear out, will you."

Sarah looked frantically around and then saw just poking from the bed pillow the pocket Bible that Mallory always carried to church meetings, identical to the ones left in the guest cabins, to the one Sarah had found in the bottom of Mark de-Terra's boot.

"Get out of there, Sarah. Oh Christ," said Tony.

Sarah squeezed the little Bible and its cover gave immediately to the pressure of her fingers. She opened it and flipped the pages, tearing a page in Exodus in her haste. Yes, there was the hollow. Joshua, Judges, Ruth, and right on through to II Kings. An square empty space. And in the bottom of the space was a snug velvet nest. A nest just waiting for a pair of diamond earrings. Fumbling again in the wastebasket, she pulled up pieces of Amos, Obadiah, Jonah and Micah and Zephaniah.

She pinched the Bible shut, pushed it back under the pillow, stuffed the pages back in the wastebasket, flew to the door, closed it, and grabbing Tony by the arm hauled him forward, through the living quarters, past the galley, and propelled him into the passageway that led to her cabin.

"God, Sarah, let me go. I think Mallory's boarding now. He may have heard you."

"Into my cabin. Please, Tony. Don't argue."

Tony allowed himself to be shoved into the cabin.

"Listen and don't say anything. Mallory. He's chopped a hole in his pocket Bible and put a velvet pad in it. Just like the Bible I found in Mark's cabin. I found the pages. Mallory's part of the whole thing, the whole damn jewelry thing."

Tony held up a hand. "Hold it. Say that again."

"Mallory's in it with Mark deTerra. And probably the whole damn shooting match. Everyone. Even Ezra. Maybe Andrea."

"Stop it, Sarah. I won't get mad about you saying Andrea. Not now. But may I point out"—here Tony's voice had an edge—"may I point out that one cut-up Bible doesn't make a jewel thief. And does it occur to you, sister dear, that Mallory probably found this Bible and the pages in Mark's cabin? *He's* the proven sticky finger. Mallory probably searched after the police did. He looked where the police didn't and found the Bible and means to turn it into the police tomorrow. Now that makes sense."

It did. Almost. Sarah climbed up on her bunk, her breath coming more slowly now. And then she heard a tiny click. A click in the passageway.

Tony heard it, too. He twisted his head in the direction of the passageway and then unfolded himself and tiptoed to the door, slipped out, and silently made his way forward. Sarah, listening, remembered her brother's success when they played Pathfinder and Mohawk as children.

He returned, slipped inside, and closed the cabin door without a sound. "The passageway. It's locked."

"What?"

"We're locked in. Or locked out. From the aft part of the boat, anyway. Of course, there's the forward hatchway, where the crew goes down."

"Try it."

Tony left and returned. "Fastened. From the outside."

"Any other way out?"

"Hatch covers." Tony reached up and loosened the screws that held the translucent cover in place. "It's fastened down from outside. Mallory has a double system so you can batten down without going below."

Sarah felt an enormous cold shiver take her from her head to her toes and shake her so that her teeth began to rattle. Tony reached over and took her hand.

"Take it easy."

"I'll be all right. But it's just hit me. The whole blessed business. We're it. Like tag. We've been living it up, fooling around and not paying attention, and they've been playing with us. Using us. You, me, Alex. Maybe Ezra. Maybe Andrea. Hiding behind us. And now we're it. Right now, you and I are it."

"Mallory probably saw us or heard you leave his cabin," said Tony. "That's why we're locked up. Or a storm is coming that I don't know about. Or . . ." His voice trailed off.

Sarah, still shaken, persisted. "When I mean we're it, I mean we're like Billy. We've done something to draw attention to ourselves. Just as Billy did, drinking, spouting off, imitating everyone. And you and I went sneaking into Mallory's cabin."

"You sneaked," said Tony. "I thought it was a rotten idea."

"Are you sorry I found what I did?"

"Yes. No. Hell, I don't know. The Bible may have been part of Mark deTerra's little caper. Like I said. But being locked down here. Shit, I can't figure it."

Sarah made her voice soft and insistent. "We'll have to do something. Get out. Go to the police. Something."

"You think he heard you ask Alex's mother about Lyme disease?"

"How could he? He was out rowing in the harbor somewhere. I hope. Now, Tony, think. Work at it. We have to get off this boat. Soon. Before we become allergic to jellyfish or go and visit a sick aunt and leave our shirts in the Dumpster. Think."

"I am, damn it." Tony scowled, leaned back on Alex's bunk,

and looked resentfully up at the heavy translucent cover. "We could break that, but Mallory would hear."

"He certainly would."

Tony searched the cabin as if looking for secret passages and hidden panels. Then he focused on the porthole. The oversize porthole. "Sarah."

"Are you thinking?"

"I'm thinking I'm damn glad you're underweight and scrawny."

"Thank you."

"I'm also thinking how great it is that Mallory had those super-big portholes put in. A special order, the kind you see on some motor-sailors. Listen, you can make it through that porthole. Sideways. If I push. If you strip down."

Sarah studied the porthole over her bunk. "Yes, I might. Just. But you can't."

"You can unfasten the hatchcover when you get out."

"And Mallory would be on my neck. And on yours."

"Distract him. Make a noise. Throw something overboard."

"We can't do anything to distract him long enough."

"Start a fire." Tony looked about the cabin for flammable objects. "Blankets, sheets. Have you got a match?"

"That's a terrible idea. We'll die of smoke inhalation." Sarah reached over the bunk and switched off the cabin light. "Let him think I've gone to sleep. Now try and come up with something that won't kill us. If we can make it to the deck, we can take the Avon and row into shore. Go to the police."

"It's your turn to think," said Tony. "Get us both on deck."

They sat unmoving in the dark. In Sarah's mind, images and sounds of the cruise raced one after the other through her mind. Billy talking in Mallory's voice. Gracie and that laugh. Mallory saying grace before dinner, thanking the Lord for new friends and old companions. Andrea and her plan to read *War and Peace*. Gracie, Mallory, and the syringe. Gracie mopping up Sarah's overflowing toilet. The toilet. The typed message tacked over the toilet about pumping the head dry. About closing the valve. Because leaving the valve open could flood the cabin. Leaving the valve open could flood the whole bloody boat. It could sink the boat.

Or if not sink, it could frighten the owner. Send him scurrying for pumps. Distract him.

So they could escape.

"Tony, listen."

Sarah explained.

Tony was silent for a moment and then said, "It's better than nothing."

"You're goddamn right it's better than nothing. How many toilets aboard?"

"You have one. The Chandlers have one. There's one in Gracie's cabin. Mallory has one. And the crew share one."

"We can hit all but Mallory's."

Tony sat absolutely still and then reached over and shook her hand. "Right. We'll open the seacocks on those toilets, then you come back here and strip down. I'll push you through this cabin porthole. I'd rather do it up forward but the crew quarters have small portholes. I'll bring your clothes up after you've unfastened the hatch cover. We'll launch the Avon, cut her loose if necessary, in case Mallory's done something fancy with a lock. I've got a knife. Bundle up a jacket or sweater; I'll grab two life jackets—we've extras next to the anchor locker."

Sarah didn't answer; she was already bent over their cabin's sea toilet releasing the closing valve.

TWENTY-ONE

They sat facing each other in the dark, Tony sitting hunched on Alex's bed, his arms around his knees. Sarah could just make out his shadowy outline in the faint light that came through the hatch cover and the porthole. There was a half-moon, she remembered. Sarah herself sat bolt upright on her bunk, both hands clutching the mattress edge.

It was odd there was so little noise. It was July, the harbor was packed with people encapsulated in their boats, lounging on decks for a late drink, or returning from late-evening visits. However, except for the tiny buzz of a small motor or the occasional thud of a dinghy landing against the hull of a yacht, the harbor kept its counsel. It was quiet enough for Sarah to hear a passing boat's wash against the *Pilgrim's* hull, followed by the lapping of little waves. Then these comforting sounds were joined by new water, at first a sort of light trickle, then a heavier sloshing.

"Do you think he'll even notice?" Sarah whispered at last. The waiting—although probably only ten minutes had passed—was becoming unbearable.

"Mallory knows this boat like his own face. He'll know when she isn't riding properly. But it'll take time."

"How much do we have?" To Sarah, it seemed that morning must be well advanced.

"Should be well after midnight. One maybe. Now Relax. You've started this mess, now enjoy it."

"Tony, if you think . . ."

"Relax, I said. I was joking. Sort of. Well, I mean here you are ruining a perfectly good job, trying to sink one of the most awesome sailboats I've ever put my foot on, probably ruining any chance I have with Andrea."

"Be quiet. I hear someone. On deck."

They listened but the only sound was a slight ping from one of the halyards slapping against the aluminum mast.

"Shit," said Tony. "That's my job. Making sure the halyards are tight. Mallory blows up when they're loose and slapping, says it wakes everyone in the harbor. He may try and fix them."

After another period of silence, Sarah said, "Now the water is flowing out of the cabin."

"I'll check the passageway."

Tony, or rather his shadow, detached itself from the opposite bunk, moved to the door, and disappeared. Sarah could just make out a faint sound rather like an animal moving softly through a creek.

He returned. "It's flooding. It'll be through to the main cabin and into the galley before you know it. Now if Mallory does any sort of routine check, he'll react like crazy."

"He'll check the heads, the toilets?"

"No, he'll think he's got some sort of major leak. A split in the hull, a separation of some seam. He'll hit the pumps."

"And while it's pumping, we hit the deck."

"You hope." Then reflectively, "If I could only screw up the system, he won't be able to use the power bilge pumps, he'll have to use manual. But we're locked in. I could break down the passageway door but Mallory would hear."

"Yes."

"Never mind, I've got it. There are four bilge zones, Mallory's own idea. Separate for safety."

"Like the *Titanic*."

"More like the Panama Canal. The bilges can be opened to shift water, to keep stability, or closed to contain the water that's in them. Mallory worked on a special electric design so he can pump them together—or separately, lowering the water level one by one. Stay right here."

Tony vanished and returned in less than five minutes. "We have access to the two forward bilges, so I pulled a few wires, messed up the pump switch. That'll keep Mallory busy. Of course, the computer readout will show him the two aren't working."

"Which will bring him right down on our neck."

"No, by then we'll be through the porthole and gone."

Sarah climbed across the bunk, lowered herself, and reached down to the cabin sole with one hand. "The water isn't very high."

"It's still leveling out, getting into nooks and crannies. The utility locker, all the crew cabins."

"How will we know when to take off?"

"You'll hear Mallory stamping around."

"No, he'll be quiet. We're not sure he even knows you're back on the boat, and he wouldn't want to wake me because I might find out I'm locked in. Then he'd know I knew and if he knows . . ." Sarah, now incoherent, paused for a breath.

"Yeah, yeah, I get the point. Okay, find a jacket, a sweater, some jeans. I'll take it with my stuff. You start stripping. I mean really stripping, because it's going to be a tight fit."

In the dark, Sarah shook her head. "I don't believe this scene. People don't do things like this unless they're characters in *The Thirty-Nine Steps*."

"The what?"

"The book I was reading."

"Never mind books. Strip. Someone's moving around on deck."

"Mallory can't see the toilet water from the deck."

"I said he'll know the minute she's not riding right." Tony sighed and said in a tone of genuine admiration, "He's an absolute genius when it comes to the trim of a boat. He can sniff out a problem before anyone has any idea that anything's wrong."

The steps above their heads moved softly forward, stopped, turned, and then hurried aft to the companionway ladder.

"He knows something's up," whispered Tony.

"And when he goes below, he'll see the galley, the navigation station afloat."

"Not afloat but at least four inches by now. It should be seeping into the passage to his cabin. He'll try the pumps. Listen for a sucking noise."

And, as if on command, they heard the sucking noise somewhere far below, toward the stern of the boat.

"He'll find out fast enough that the whole system is screwed up. He'll pump the aft sections dry and go to manual for the rest. Now, hit the porthole while he's working on it."

Sarah in bra and pants, shivering from a combination of the damp and excitement, got to her knees and found Tony beside her unscrewing the nuts holding the oval bronze porthole bolts closed.

It was more than a tight fit. Sarah felt exactly like a dog being pushed through a too-small dog door. The metal edges of the porthole scraped against her shoulders, tore skin from her shoulder, her back, and she knocked her knee on the brass bolts. Headfirst she wiggled, reaching for something on the upper deck to hold. She found a grab rail, a stanchion, a coil of line, and, in terror of being found by Mallory, she stayed still for a full minute, then cautiously pulled herself to a sitting position.

Tony poked his head into the porthole space. "God, get going. Unfasten the forward hatch cover, not this one here, the one nearest the bow, it's farther away from the action and stay down."

Which Sarah did, inching her way on her stomach along the cold, moist deck, over lines, past dorades holding ventilation funnels, catching her underpants on a cleat, until at last, fumbling in the dark, she found the large forward hatch cover.

It was all accomplished in a minute. Tony reared out of the hatchway like some bearded sea monster and crawled to the edge of the rail.

"I won't try and untie the Avon from the deck. I'll let myself down into the water, swim around, cut it loose, and come back for you. Keep flat on the deck. Here are your clothes. You'll have to let yourself down by hanging on the outside of the hull; I'll guide your legs. Don't make any noise."

Tony dropped over the side and went through the water like a porpoise. Praying that Mallory was busy with his pump system, Sarah gathered her clothes in one arm, pulled herself under the lifelines, and waited.

Several centuries later, the Avon appeared below her, a dark rectangle. Sarah let go of the clothes, heard them make a soft thud, then turned so that she hung over the edge, her hands clinging to the rail. It was a nasty drop into black space. She could hardly make out her brother's outstretched arms reaching for her ankles.

"Drop," he commanded. "I've taken out the floorboards. It's a safe landing."

And Sarah dropped. Straight into the harbor. Splat and splash. Even as she sputtered to the surface, she felt she'd made a crash like a falling airliner.

"Fuck," said Tony succinctly. He grabbed; Sarah scrabbled and finally rolled and wrestled herself over the soft rubber rail.

"Okay, push off," said Tony. "I've got the oars. I think Mallory's so compulsive, he won't pay attention to anything else when he's trying to pump the boat out."

"Where to?" gasped Sarah. Shaking from the cold water, she sat hunched on the stern seat of the Avon. Then she asked, "Has he a gun?"

"I don't know. Maybe. I heard him say once that he wouldn't look for trouble but he was ready if it came. Anyway get flat, right on the bottom. I wish I'd brought a chart, but they're all in the nav station. We'll try for the nearest land and head for the police. And get dressed; do you want to get any colder?"

Sarah, shivering so hard that speech was impossible, obeyed. Her brother seemed to be in full command, at least of the nautical phase of their escape. Lying on the rubber bottom of the raft, she struggled with clenched teeth into very wet jeans and jacket, both having been lying in a puddle on the bottom of the raft.

And then it happened. A crack and a simultaneous *poof* and a heavy sigh from one side of the rubber raft."

"Shit, he's shooting. Are you all right?"

"He got the raft, one side of it. It's losing air fast." Sarah reached over and felt the wrinkled, deflated side of the Avon.

"Never mind, that was a fluke. He can't see us and he won't dare try to put up a flare. We've got air in the other raft compartments. I'll get us behind some other boats." Tony, as if he was finishing a race, pulled like a madman, and Sarah concentrated on trying to force her hand over the gaping hole in the port side of the raft.

It was still an awkward passage. The Avon moved in a lopsided way, rippling awkwardly across the water to the dark land mass that made up the eastern shore of the harbor. Then Tony, giving two last tremendous pulls, shot the raft into an narrow space between two rocks, jumped out, and pulled it into a nest of brambles and shore bushes. "Okay, out," he said softly. "Help me haul it out of sight above the tide line."

Together, they tugged the crippled raft—Sarah thought in the dim light it looked like a deflated rubber elephant—up a rocky incline well out of view of passing boaters. Tony, always careful in matters nautical, took the painter and looped it around the nearest bush, and Sarah, breathless, subsided on the still-inflated side of the raft—and slipped sprawling into the center of the boat. Trying to save herself, she reached out for the seat, missed, spread-eagled on the boat's bottom, and propelled her right hand under the now-collapsed side of the raft. Her hand closed on something small, hard, and sharp. With a yelp of pain, she wrestled herself into a sitting position and peered in the dim light at the object in her hand.

"I've stabbed myself." Sarah held her middle finger in the air. "It's got a pin."

"Come on, we don't have time to klutz around here."

Sarah turned the offending object around in her hand, testing its surface gingerly with her fingers. "It's too dark to see, but it feels like some kind of jewelry."

"Let's hope it's some fancy jewelry deTerra's been making hay with and our fortune is made. Probably fell out of his Bible.

Stick it in your pocket and let's get the hell out. If Mallory gets the *Pilgrim* pumped out, he may come after us with the motor whaleboat."

Sarah stood up, pushed the piece of jewelry into the pocket of her jeans. "Where to, the police? Or should we call from someone's house?"

"See what we hit first, a house or the main road."

What they hit was a barn, its door open in an inviting manner, and in the dark beyond the door there appeared to be a jumble of summer furniture and pieces of stacked latticework.

Sarah stepped cautiously into the barn and sat down abruptly on the edge of a wheelbarrow. "Hold up, Tony. Give me a breather; I can't seem to get warm. It won't hurt if we take a break."

Tony considered and then said generously, "Okay. We'll take ten minutes and get warm. Wave your arms, do sit-ups."

Sarah stood up and began making windmill motions with her arms and then stopped abruptly. "What do you really think Mallory will do?"

"He's very sharp, very with it."

"And?"

"Well, he might be tricky. That's if he's as you think, the crime boss of a jewelry operation."

"How tricky?"

"If he doesn't come after us in a boat, he might go to the police. Report us as criminals or drug dealers. Or something."

"George Fitts would put a stop to that."

"George Fitts isn't in Northeast Harbor," Tony reminded her. "You told me Mallory said he tried to call him about Mark deTerra, and he was off somewhere. Mallory's probably policeman's pet since it's thanks to him that they've got their hooks into deTerra. We might be the next link in the chain."

"Tony, sometimes you make sense."

"I usually do," said her brother complacently. "But no one gives me credit for it. Now let's shove off. We can make the police believe us."

"You know," said Sarah thoughtfully, "I think I'll even be glad to see George Fitts, so I must be desperate. Never mind, in another hour it will be all over."

Which statement was another in a long line of statements that Sarah regretted making.

When Tony, with Sarah behind him, emerged from the barn, in the early dark hours of Sunday morning, a slight drizzle had begun and a foghorn sounded from somewhere far away.

They made their way swiftly up a long driveway, past a silent shingle cottage with the curtains pulled, and onto the main road. Route Three. Or what Sarah hoped, in the general loss of direction caused by fog, was Route Three. They had landed, she thought, on the eastern shore of the harbor, a substantial distance below the Asticou Inn and below the terraces leading to Thuya Lodge Gardens. Route Three, then if followed properly, should lead north along the ocean until they could turn south to Northeast Harbor and the police station.

"You don't think Mallory will have mustered his troops?" asked Sarah as they squelched along in the dark at the extreme edge of the road, ready to duck into the brush.

"Troops? What troops?"

"The Pantry Players. They might try to cut us off."

"Cut us up, you mean."

"Yes, why not? We're not people they want alive and kicking."

"If it's alive you want, move it." Tony gave his sister a little push. "Try a jog and be ready to take a dive if you see a car coming."

Three times, they had to do just that. Headlights from an approaching car and then two small trucks made them slam themselves down below the roadside rail, cling to the clifflike verge, flattening themselves into a sludge of weeds, paper throwaways, and old bottles.

Sarah on the third time down, as the moisture seeped into the few dry spots she had left on her body, began to wonder whether, by her suspicions and imaginings, she had actually caused things like this to happen. If she had kept her nose clean, her mind in neutral, wouldn't she soon be waking up in her cosy cabin on the *Pilgrim* ready for some of Andrea's French toast and blueberry muffins, happy in the thought of Alex's return? At breakfast, David Mallory would be planning a picnic on one of the Cranberry Isles, Ezra, returned from Castine and distributing Bibles (or Bibles with diamond earrings in them) would be full of good cheer, ready for the day's sailing. And Gracie . . .

But at Gracie's name, Sarah stalled and her brief moment of regret evaporated. Gracie, Billy Brackett, Mark deTerra: They couldn't be swept away by a wave of nostalgia. Sarah, stamping along in sodden sneakers, had never felt quite so miserable. "Oh hell."

She said it loudly and angrily and Tony, ahead, stopped and turned. "Hold it down; we're getting there. We've gone by the Thuya Lodge entrance sign."

"Well, good," said Sarah. "Then the inn's just ahead and there's a shortcut trail to the harbor beyond. And we won't just march into the police station; we'll check around a minute."

"You mean make sure Mallory isn't hiding behind a hydrant."

They reached the trail's end, which gave out into a corner of the harbor, and saw the police station which stood almost at the foot of Sea Street, with a fine view of any trouble that might arise from the tennis courts, the harbor, and the parking lot. Sarah and Tony took their last few steps with caution, sliding around to the front of the building then almost hurling themselves into the front door.

Blinking in the lighted entrance hall, neither saw the man seated on a bench just inside the entrance.

"Hey, there. Sarah. Tony. I've been waiting. Thank God."

But Sarah and Tony didn't wait to find out why Mark deTerra, alias Marcus Aurelius Germanicus Terrant, was thanking God.

Tony seized Sarah by the elbow, spun her around, whipped open the police-station door, and together they ran through the quiet Sunday-morning streets of Northeast Harbor.

TWENTY-TWO

MARK DETERRA MUST HAVE BEEN CAUGHT BY SUR-
prise because for a few seconds Sarah and Tony had the street to
themselves. They pelted down Sea Street, then doubled back
behind a series of shops to Main Street, ran across the Old Fire
House Museum driveway, crossed the street, and ducked into
an alley by Mrs. Pervear's shop (Crafts and Notions), passed the
bottle Redemption Center, then as they turned and headed for
the backside of Pine Tree Liquors, they heard Mark pounding
behind them. Calling. Shouting.

"Faster," yelled Tony in Sarah's ear.

"I can't," she called back. But she did. Sarah pushed every
unhappy muscle, and together they looped around a white
frame house, waded through a vegetable garden, shot onto
Route 198 and headed north, while behind them sounded
shouts of "Hey, hey there. Sarah! Tony! Come back. You goddamn fools, come back!"

"Head for a driveway," Tony panted. "Hide in the bushes."

"Is he alone?"

"I think so. Come on, push it."

For the briefest moment, Sarah turned her head and saw the dark shape of Mark deTerra, only a few yards behind, his hand raised as if he carried an invisible spear.

"Christ Almighty," yelled Tony, and he wheeled suddenly at a turn in the rising road, grabbed at Sarah's arm, and plunged down a sloping driveway. They had run about twenty steps when Tony spun Sarah into a planting of yew and pulled her head out of sight.

None too soon. Mark deTerra loomed at the top of driveway under a street lamp like some giant about to begin trampling villages and farms.

"Don't move a muscle," commanded Tony in a loud whisper.

"Quiet," said Sarah. She felt, like the scraping of a thousand razors, the clawing and prickling of the yew branches against her back, her shoulder, her ankles.

"Jesus, he's coming down. He's got a flashlight. Fucking Boy Scout." Tony by some miracle of muscle compression managed to reduce his length into a dark lump and by clamping a hand on Sarah's shoulder kept her steady and low. Sarah wondered how Mark could miss both of them; if he couldn't see them, surely he could hear them breathing like twin steam engines.

The flashlight circle of yellow swung back and forth across the driveway and then moved over the shrubbery, probing here, penetrating yew, azalea, and then arching over rhododendrons, moving along the branches of a heavy spruce, lighting an urn of geraniums, and then, abruptly, it switched off.

"Damnation," said Mark deTerra loudly, and so close was the voice that Sarah, if she had not been held by Tony's hand, would have jumped out of her skin. "Damnation," Mark repeated, now in a resigned voice. Then, "Look, Tony, Sarah, if you're in there, come on out and go down to the station. I can explain everything. George Fitts can. It's okay. We know about Mallory." Then, almost pleading, "Come on, save us the trouble or we'll have to turn out the troops to find you."

Sarah turned to Tony and heard him whisper, "No way."

For a moment Mark stood irresolute, then turned, said "Damn you both" to the night air. Then Sarah and Tony heard his footsteps retreat toward the top of the driveway.

"Stay put," said Tony as Sarah began to writhe out of her crouching position.

"He's gone."

"No, wait."

They waited, Tony jiggling his knee with impatience—or nerves—Sarah increasingly uncomfortable with wet clothes, leg cramps, and the scratchy embrace of the spreading yew.

Finally she stood up. "All right, now what?"

"We go." Tony pulled himself loose from the bush and began pulling small pieces of broken greenery from his shirt. "We go somewhere deTerra and Mallory aren't."

"I think we're out of our heads. Why didn't we stay at the police station and explain? Why this chasing about? We're the good guys. There must have been police in the police station. Mark or Mallory couldn't have murdered us there on the front steps."

"Listen, Sarah, I've had—my friends have had—some very bad experiences with the police, and deTerra seems to have them in his pocket. He probably lied his way out of custody."

"I suppose you're right," Sarah muttered, "though some of your friends probably deserved the police."

"And," added Tony to clinch the point, "he's going to bring someone to look for us. Does that mean police or the *Pilgrim*'s crew? You talked about Mallory's troops."

Sarah considered this and then remembered Mark's pleading voice, a voice that bordered on desperation. "Tony, you know he sounded sincere, and if he hadn't been giving me the sincere treatment yesterday in the garden and at lunch, I might have been fooled. Because it's just dumb luck I found that rabbit in his cabin or he might have us right by the neck this minute."

"Yeah," agreed Tony. "A real con man, he had me fooled, too. He's a better actor than that whole bunch."

"George Fitts," said Sarah firmly. "We've got to find him. And I've had it. I may drop dead at your feet."

"Hang in. It'll be getting light pretty soon. We'll keep out of sight and head for those woods behind the Asticou Inn. Just in case deTerra really does find a search party. Later, when we can see better, we can work our way back into town away from the police station and make for the telephone."

"You know," said Sarah, as once again they started along the border of the road toward the Inn, "I'd swear that Mallory was just as shocked as I was about the jewelry in deTerra's cabin."

"Which means that deTerra was dipping into the main supply, went into business for himself."

"I guess. But I can't see where Gracie and Billy fit in. Maybe as moles digging into Mallory's operation. And deTerra had to kill Billy because he was messing up. And Gracie was upset, but now she's off somewhere selling the goods. Maybe her sick aunt is a fence." Tony nodded and for a while they half-walked, half-jogged in silence. Then as they climbed into the wooded hillside above the Inn, Sarah took him by the shoulder.

"Listen, could we just hole up for a while?" Sarah pointed to a cave-like hollow under a large granite boulder. "I'm not superwoman."

Tony nodded, and Sarah led the way to the welcome shelter. The ground was quite dry, and Sarah sank down gratefully. Tenderly she pulled off her sneakers and stretched. "It's almost comfortable."

Tony nodded and pulling off his sweat shirt handed it to his sister. "I don't need this," he said gruffly. "I'm hot, all that running. Glad to help the weaker sex."

Sarah was too tired to take the bait. Instead she pulled on the sweat shirt, and then said, "I've an idea. We wait until it's light, then we sneak back into town and hit Betty's Bed & Breakfast— sometime around seven. You have your watch, don't you?"

Tony nodded. "Waterproof, works no matter what."

"Good. Betty's B & B will be our safe house. We'll find Mary and Amos and take it from there. Now, I'm going to try to sleep." And Sarah slumped down to the ground and put her head on her arms.

A great while later after a number of disconnected dreams

involving pursuit and immersion in cold water, Sarah opened her eyes to find that morning had come. The air had cleared and only wisps of fog swathed the tops of the spruces above them. Tony sat beside her, knees drawn up, frowning, his angular face so much an exaggerated likeness to her own. She studied her brother for a moment, thinking that at times she didn't know him at all, that he'd grown into a stranger. Then she remembered how much she had wanted to find him alone, to have a serious conversation. Despite the unlikeliness of place and circumstance she decided to plunge in. After all, in another thirty minutes they might be back in the town playing fox and geese. Or being debriefed by George Fitts which was not unlike going to the dentist. It was necessary but it hurt.

"Tony, could I talk to you. Before we go galloping back into town and into all that mess."

He looked down at her and frowned. "Watch it, Sarah, you're sounding like Mother again."

"I mean it. I'm not going to talk about Andrea if that's what's worrying you."

"You're so right. You're not."

"We agree. No, it's about what's going to happen after this cruise. This so-called cruise of ours that is about to fold up. I mean, have you thought about what you're going to be doing?"

"You mean in life? Yes, every now and then it flits across my poor brain and I brush it away."

"I'm serious. I mean about a commitment to some sort of plan, a way of going on. Does that make sense?"

"Coming from you? I don't know. Because who are you to talk about commitment? Okay, you're teaching and in a graduate program. Fine. But what about a human commitment? What about Alex? Is he just sort of an appendage you like to have around?"

"I think," said Sarah in an austere voice, "that we will leave Alex out of this."

"I've heard him make his little marriage jokes. Like he wants to be married and you can't bring yourself to be serious about it because the career woman might be derailed."

"Tony, stop it. That's not true. It's just because, well, it hasn't worked out for me before, and . . ."

"And you're scared. Try a little trust. Take a jump, get wet. Or quit. Fish or cut bait. Don't string someone along. I've been strung along and I don't like it. Alex is a good guy, but he can't want to be hung up forever. He wants commitment. Just like Mother and Father do. Think about it. Me, what I do with my future is my business, but I won't hurt anyone, string them along. So my beloved sister, no more quizzing. I will report to Mother and Father that you've done all you could with wayward, wandering Anthony Deane. And that's an end to the subject. I admire you for your restraint on the subject of Andrea and I love you very much, but bug off."

Sarah started to speak, thought better of it, snapped her mouth shut, stood up turned away from Tony and jammed her hands into her jean pockets. And closed her right hand on the piece of jewelry she had found under the collapsed side of the Avon Raft.

Slowly, she opened her hand and in the increased daylight the object was perfectly clear. A familiar object seen many times a day on the cruise of the Pilgrim.

Gracie's watch. Gracie's flower watch with its white enamel petal collar studded with tiny diamond dewdrops. The little old-fashioned pendant watch Gracie never took off, the one that had hung from the butterfly blouse the previous morning and before had held pride of place on a Liberty floral and the lettuce-leaf print dress. "Tony," said Sarah quietly. She extended her open hand.

Tony whirled around, his expression giving every indication of a willingness to continue the argument. He saw the watch and frowned, puzzled. "That's Gracie's." Tony lifted the watch up and with one hand ran his finger around the petals. "She said it was like a daisy because the face was yellow."

"She told me," said Sarah, "that it was her mother's, that they'd gone to the same school and the school flower was a daisy. Miss Somebody's. Gracie had a scholarship. And the watch was *not* an affectation, not part of her secretary's costume."

"Yeah," agreed Tony. "It was her good-luck charm. She said so in Florida, and she had it on yesterday morning. I know because it caught in her sweater and she re-fastened it on her blouse when I was rowing her with Mallory to the dock. She had it on when she left."

Sarah retrieved the watch and turned it over. "The pin's still fastened. I suppose it was on her blouse when she spilled that so-called beet soup, and she forgot about it when she took the blouse off. And Mallory rescued it. At least that's his story which I no longer believe a sentence of. We'll give it to the police and let them do the guessing. I've had it with everything. Let's find a back path to Betty's Bed & Breakfast."

It was something after 7:00 when, after a certain amount of trespassing, shore scrambling, and avoidance manuevers, Betty's modest cottage was reached. The town itself had come to life and a small bustle had begun. An early doubles match was under way on one of the courts, and several yachting types were trooping up the harbor hill in search of breakfast on dry land. Tony and Sarah entered Betty's by the back door, surprising that person in the middle of scrambled eggs.

Yes, Mr. Larkin and Mrs. Donelli-Larkin were in their room. In fact, a visitor had arrived that very morning looking for them at the ungodly hour of six.

"I had to go down in my wrapper and let him in. An old gentlemen and bossy with me," said Betty, who still wore the same wrapper, now circled by a large checked apron. "Yes, you can go right up. It's the second room on the left. I call it the Harborview Room. I name all my rooms, and if you want breakfast let me know, because I'm just putting the biscuits in." Then, looking dubiously at Sarah and Tony's mud-stained condition, she added, "You can wash if you want, but don't use the little towels, they're embroidered by hand." And Betty returned to her eggs.

Sarah, a great weariness turning her legs to lead, hauled herself up the stairs. Tony followed, even his step was slowed by the morning's exertions.

Sarah knocked and called at the same time and in a minute

Mary, wearing a raincoat over a nightgown, opened the door, took one look, and pulled Sarah in. Tony followed.

And they both stopped cold.

In a large wicker chair by the window sat an elderly man holding an umbrella, his mackintosh draped over the nearby radiator. Next to him, a map unfolded over his knee, Mark deTerra.

Amos Larkin rose from the foot of the double bed that half-filled the room.

"Sarah, Tony, I'd like you to meet a colleague. Professor Julius Terrant. And his son, Marcus Terrant. I believe I've told you that he was once a student of mine."

TWENTY-THREE

I T IS AMAZING WHAT A GOOD BREAKFAST, A HOT BATH, and dry clothes can do for the depleted human body. Sarah, after these refreshments, was able to rejoin her friends and contemplate the rest of Sunday in Northeast Harbor with nothing more violent than astonishment.

They sat once again on the little back terrace of Betty's: Amos, Mary, and Professor Emeritus of Bowmouth College, Julius Terrant, who sat next to his only son, Marcus, late of the sloop *Pilgrim*. It was, Sarah remembered, the same view of the harbor that she, Mary, and Amos had enjoyed yesterday afternoon after her friends had been sprung from the police station. Sprung by that upstanding citizen, sailor, man of the church, and Bible shredder, David (aka Darcy) Mallory.

The same Mallory, Sarah reminded herself, who had told the police that the *Pilgrim* could be searched, who had escorted the police aboard the sloop and perhaps assisted them in examining deTerra's cabin. David Mallory who promised that the criminal deTerra would be held in custody.

Sarah, holding tightly to the thought of George Fitts as to a sheet anchor in a heavy wind, spoke into the low murmur of conversation. "George Fitts. Is he coming? He can straighten this out, can't he? Otherwise, I may explode."

"No, you won't," said Tony. "I tell everyone I have one tough sister, so don't embarrass me."

Sarah sat up straight. "Tough sister is on the edge. Hard night, soaking wet, running all over the Maine coast."

"I wish," said Marcus Terrant, "I could have saved you some of that running. I tried this morning but you didn't listen."

"Excuse me," said Tony, standing up. "I've heard all this when you were in the bath, Sarah. You can fill me in on the nitty-gritty later. I want to hunt up Andrea. She may be still in Bar Harbor or hiding out since the police have taken over the *Pilgrim*."

"Tony," said Marcus, with a new authoritative note in his voice, "remember the police also want to hunt up Andrea. She's wanted for questioning. So if you find her first . . ." He didn't finish the sentence but his look was a command.

Tony shifted from one foot to the other—Sarah could see he was considering a retort—but then he shrugged. "Okay, okay, but I'll be damned if she had anything to do with this whole stupid scene. I'll see you all later. Sarah, you take care." Tony took two long strides to the little picket gate enclosing the terrace and was gone.

"Tony may well be damned," put in Amos. "All right, Marcus, put Sarah out of her misery."

"First," said Mary, "support is on its way. George Fitts is at the police station, and Alex will be here by afternoon."

"How do you want to do this?" asked Marcus. "Twenty questions or a complete confession? On my part. And yours, Sarah, because you must have things to tell us. The Larkin-Donelli hit squad that you put into action almost frightened me out of a year's growth."

"You could do with losing a year's growth," said Amos. "My knee is damaged beyond repair."

Marcus grinned. "Then we're even for a summer of torture by Latin."

"You lead off, whoever you are," said Sarah faintly. "Since you're not in jail and no one is worried about it—except me."

Marcus leaned back in his chair, lifted a coffee cup, sipped it, and then put it carefully back on the little wrought-iron table at his side. He reached over and touched his father's hand. "To begin with, Sarah Deane, I'm a disappointment to my father."

"No, no, my dear Marcus," murmured the old gentleman in the high-pitched voice of the very old. "Never a disappointment."

"I was building my 'case,'" said Sarah, "if it could be called that, on your being a disappointment. It was sort of the keystone to my whole idea. It was my grandmother's description."

Professor Terrant nodded, his white head bobbing on his thin neck. "Mrs. Douglas. From Camden. I knew her husband, Angus, well. We played bridge in the old days. Mrs. Douglas always had strong opinions. I believe she thought the Terrants were heathens."

"Sarah—I can call you Sarah without you giving me one of your looks?" asked Marcus. "I would have given a year's salary to have told you what I was doing aboard the *Pilgrim*, but George Fitts said absolutely no. I've been working on the Church of the Apostles for a long time, and George didn't want me to come north just to wreck the whole setup. Not until everything was ready."

But Professor Terrant was still brooding about his son. "Not a disappointment, Marcus, my boy. But you had such a gift for languages. Such a waste, however, I *am* proud of you. Someone must deal with anarchy in the modern world. And now it is time I took a rest. At my age, I travel very seldom and this trip has taken its toll. Marcus, your arm, please? I expect, Amos, I may use your bed, may I not?"

With a great effort, Sarah stifled her questions and watched Marcus assist his father into the house. With his cloud of white hair rising in the slight breeze and his bent match-stick body, Sarah thought that but for Marcus the professor might levitate into the upper atmosphere, and for a moment she remembered helping Grandmother Douglas up the lawn to her nap.

She turned to Mary and Amos. "Professor Terrant, what is he doing here? Giving a seminar or is he rescuing his son?"

"Rescuing his son," said Mary. "Amos started going into a lather about Marcus turning into a criminal, being held at the police station. Thought the old boy should know, even though the shock might kill him. Mrs. Terrant wasn't up to the trip, but the professor is a strong old bird despite his looks. Amos called him and the professor climbed into his trusty Packard—"

"Packard!"

"Packard," repeated Amos. "He believes that if you've found a car you can trust, you keep it. Professor Terrant trusts Packards. Anyway, he turned up at dawn, shouldered our landlady out of the way, and was about to call the White House or the CIA when Marcus appeared after losing you and Tony in hide and seek. He reassured his father and they had a touching reunion. Papa Terrant has been urging Marcus to quit his present dubious line of work and rejoin the world of classics."

Sarah was digesting this information when Marcus reappeared. She leaned forward and almost shouted, "You and George Fitts. George Fitts wouldn't let you tell me. Tell me what? Wreck what setup? Are you a jewelry dealer? The Mafia? Or the IRS? The FBI? Or are you doing some sort of plea bargain?"

"None of the above. And I before I go any further, I want to contradict my father. Knowing languages has been a terrific help. Especially wheeling and dealing."

"Wheeling and dealing in what? Where?" demanded Sarah.

Marcus pulled his pipe out of his pocket, looked at its interior with suspicion, and then began to fill it, slowly, methodically. "Hope you don't mind my pipe." Sarah shook her head and repeated, "Dealing in what?"

Marcus's look was sympathetic. "Poor Sarah, you still don't know what this is all about."

"Don't you 'poor Sarah' me, Mark or Marcus, or whoever you're pretending to be. Spit it out or I'll make a citizen's arrest."

"And she would, too," said Amos. "She tried it on me once."

"Wheeling and dealing with gems. Diamonds, rubies, tourmalines, amethysts, emeralds. Mounted and set. Or unmounted. Sent stateside. From South America. Brazil. Colombia. Colombia has the best emeralds."

"As Mallory's partner? Or working for yourself? Are you out of jail because you've turned state's evidence?"

"No, don't you get it? You kept asking the right questions. Professor Larkin here says you were boiling with suspicion and Tony tells me you took in the whole scam. The theatre of smugglers. Actors playing sailor and church do-gooders. In fact, Tony claims you thought up a way to sink—or half-sink—the *Pilgrim* and get away. Three cheers, you were terrific."

"I had you and maybe Billy and Gracie down as a sort of gang. A cell within the cell." Sarah stared at Marcus sitting there, sucking on his pipe, looking so solid, so reliable, now so unlike a felon. "You mean, you knew all along? And George knew you knew? George, you work for George. Damn it, you work for George."

"Bingo! I work for George. I am George's mole. Not Gracie's or Billy's mole. Or Mallory's. To be exact, I'm working for two outfits, the Sarasota police and the Maine State Police. The Feds are also interested. I began infiltrating about two years ago. The Church of the Apostles is always looking for new members."

Sarah shook her head back and forth in disbelief. "The Church of the Apostles is a front, a fake front? All those Bibles. Cassettes, pamphlets, Rollo Rabbit and the Ten Commandments. Oh, come on. I saw that stuff. It was real. And so were the churches. All those Saint Something of the Islands."

"A front, but no fake. The scheme wouldn't work with a fake mission church. You have to hand it to Mallory. He started out a long while back with a little rep company touring Florida, sometimes moving into Louisiana, Texas, Arizona. Not much cash flow, not with small-time theatre. Then he settled into the Sarasota area, tinkered with real estate, invested in local banks. Bought up land, got into condominiums and beach resorts. Did well, made big bucks. But Mallory loved to sail. Loved to act. Being a theatre type, he was probably bored with business. Sometime or other, he made a series of trips to South America and came up with an idea for extra income that would allow travel."

"Not drugs? Jewelry."

"Right, jewelry. Though he wanted you all to think he was a citizen drug hunter. Working with the police—which he was. Sort of. Talk about fronts or distractions, drugs will do it everytime. We all believe in drug smuggling because we see it every day. People make money from drugs; they die from drugs. It's the number-one business in Florida and points north."

"And," said Sarah slowly, letting the whole idea slowly fall into place, "Mallory figured out how to combine sailing and smuggling and acting. And he found the perfect vehicle."

"The Church of the Apostles," put in Mary, rousing herself from a wicker swing with many cushions. "Mallory could run a missionary outfit, bring the Word, send all the little boats around with, with what? Marcus, did the little Apostle boats like the *Simon Peter* do jewels or Bibles?"

"Both, depending who was in charge. Sometimes they were absolutely pure, sometimes with the right person aboard they carried a mixed cargo, real Bibles and hollow Bibles. Separately marked cartons to imaginary churchs. Those special congregations that need special material, a spiritual boost from Father Mallory and Sister Gracie."

Sarah nodded remembering *Pilgrim*'s program of reaching out to isolated island churches. Islands and isolation were the sine qua non of passing and selling interesting material. "And you were actually working in Florida on an Apostle boat?" she asked.

"I went aboard after I'd made the right friends in the Church. We met couriers from Mexico, the Bahamas, Virgin Islands, from all over South America. And believe me it was good goods. Mallory had set up some independent—very independent—jewelers who sold the unset stones, or mounted them. We brought the stuff to Mallory and Company, he with his executive team—Gracie, Ezra—packaged it, distributed it, mixed it in with the legitimate cargo."

"And he really trusted you," said Sarah.

"As far as he trusted anyone. I was part of the Key West-based operation and I had fine credentials because of bringing in loot from South America."

"And then," said Sarah, clenching her teeth, "when you came aboard from the *Simon Peter*, he told you he'd killed Billy."

"No such luck. Mallory isn't stupid. George will fill you in on the probable murder. That's his department."

"And the *Pilgrim* wasn't just bought as a pleasure boat?"

"That yes, but also so Mallory could extend his sales and keep an eye on the little Apostle boats. When he visited a genuine church group, he was the good Christian, David Mallory, but the meetings with the church fathers were often coordinated with sales meetings with people he'd trained in Florida and placed along the coast. Dealers and distributers."

"But," said Sarah puzzled, "I don't see how this little rep company knew enough about jewelry to pull it off, the distribution business, getting the loaded Bibles into dealer's hands."

"They didn't have to. The crew just handled the *Pilgrim* and shared in the profits. The dealing took place only under Mallory's and Gracie's supervision. With some help from Ezra. You don't need many hollow Bibles and rabbits for jewelry. A little space hides a lot of sparklers, as does a nice pocket Bible taken everywhere with you. Just like the ones given to the guests."

"And Andrea and Billy, how did they fit in?"

"Handpicked crew. Andrea genuinely useful, Billy forced on Mallory by Sister Gracie—maybe she threatened him. Take my brother or else. Billy had acted with Mallory's Pantry Players, but his record was against him being anything but trouble. The *Pilgrim*'s trip northeast was a trial run—to see if Mallory could pull in the whole North Atlantic seaboard. We nailed Ezra early this A.M. and he's decided to 'cooperate.' He told us Canada was on the drawing board, the Maritime provinces. Mallory thought big. And you, Sarah, Alex, and Tony were all part of the picture."

"You mean?" Sarah looked around the group for confirmation of what now seemed a scheme so simple as to be ridiculous."

"He means," said Amos, "you and Alex were set up. You were part of the cover. Two good, honest people, three if we include Tony, were the ones to make the trip absolutely legitimate. And it would have worked if you hadn't been pathologically suspicious of good things. Now, frankly, I smelled a rat the minute I heard about Mallory wearing those white patent-leather shoes."

Mary looked at her husband. "Amos. You did *not* smell a rat."

"Why do you think I allowed myself to be hauled through Route One traffic to a town devoted to tourists and oversized yachts? I smelled a rat."

Mary stood up and pulled at her husband's arm. "Let's give Sarah a break. Alex will be here soon. And George Fitts."

"Wait a minute," said Amos. "One question, Marcus. Did you recognize me when Mary and I came slamming into you— per Sarah's orders?"

"Of course. I mean I spent a lot of time with you that one summer." Marcus looked embarrassed. "But, well, you fooled me."

"You thought it was just old drunk Amos Larkin ruining your career as a mole."

"Yes, I did. I'm very glad to find it was just a gag."

"Not a gag," said Amos, rubbing his knee. "But why didn't you tell the police in the Northeast Harbor station who you were? They would have let you go and saved us all a hell of a lot of trouble."

"George wasn't around and if I'd blown my cover without his permission, he'd have had my hide. I didn't get an okay until this morning after Mallory began trying to leave with the *Pilgrim*, and Sarah was on the loose with Tony. No okay, until the whole business came out in the open. When we found Gracie's body."

Sarah bolted out of her chair, "Gracie's body! Gracie! She's dead? Really dead. Oh my God." Then, remembering, "In the Dumpster?"

"Those details are for George. I'm going down to the police station. We're still working Ezra over."

"But Gracie," faltered Sarah. "Her blouse, you mean?"

"She was murdered," said George Fitts, opening the gate to the terrace and walking up to Sarah. "She was murdered yesterday afternoon and disposed of last night."

TWENTY-FOUR

MARY AND AMOS, WHO HAD BEEN ABOUT TO LEAVE, subsided again in their chairs, the word *murdered* holding them like glue.

Marcus stood up, looming for the moment over the seated group in a way that reminded Sarah that she had thought him intrinsically dangerous. For a moment, he surveyed the three, his face impassive, his hands folded across his chest, and then he turned to leave. "They're all yours, George. I've spent most of the time cleaning my own slate." And to Sarah, "Forgive me. Okay?"

When Marcus had closed the gate to the terrace, Sarah whirled around to George, who was settling himself in the chair vacated by Professor Terrant. "George Fitts, how could you? You planted Marcus. You planted him and never said a word. And what was all the crap about Mallory looking for drug dealers? And Gracie. What happened to Gracie? Or is she one of your spies who didn't know enough to come out of the cold, so you put her in the Dumpster?"

"Whoa, Sarah." Amos Larkin held out a restraining hand.

"You're in overdrive. Slow up. One question at a time. Let Sergeant Fitts defend himself. Mary, come along. Leave Sarah to her fate. We will go into town and examine the tourists."

"George had better explain himself," said Sarah, breathing hard. "Letting Alex and me go off as happy cruising passengers on a criminal ship with a police spy."

Mary and Amos vanished in the direction of Main Street and George removed his rimless glasses, huffed on them, wiped them carefully with a folded white handkerchief, and then rested the tips of his fingers together in a characteristic gesture. He looked mildly around him. "These bed and breakfasts places with a view of the harbor are on to a good thing. I met the landlady a little while ago. I think we could use her in the state police."

"George," said Sarah in threatening voice.

"Sarah, your annoyance is justified. I have explaining to do. And believe me, it took an argument to make Marcus agree to keeping you and Alex out of it. Mike Laaka, too. He really wanted you on the team, but I can't mix amateurs and police."

"Mike! Mike knew and he didn't say a word." And then Sarah remembered the look that passed between Mike and George when she had tried to warn them of the danger from Mark deTerra.

"I made a mistake with Marcus," said George, who rarely used the word *mistake* in connection with his work. "I told him not to be too friendly with you and Alex. It might make Mallory or the others suspicious. He overdid it and you reacted."

"He was as rude as hell. And nasty about doctors."

"I straightened him out when we were in Bucks Harbor, and he said he would try to be more pleasant from then on."

"And when he did, I was sure he was a thug or a rapist."

"He also had orders to keep an eye on you. After Billy's death, we were ready for more trouble. Marcus called me when Alex left, and I told him not to let you out of his sight unless you were with Tony."

"That's why he was trailing me all over Northeast Harbor into the Asticou Gardens."

"Exactly."

"But Gracie, what happened to Gracie? Did she have a sick aunt with Lyme disease?"

"No sick aunt. As far as we know."

"Please put me out of my misery," said Sarah. "Is she, was she in the Dumpster?"

"No. We tracked down the contents of the Dumpster in the town disposal site and found a stained blouse, a sweater, and a skirt. Ezra identified them as Gracie's. But no body."

"You're sure there is one?" asked Sarah. "But," she added, reaching into her pocket, "we found her watch, the little daisy watch. With the pin closed, in the Avon raft."

George accepted the watch with an expression that for him bordered on excitement. "Very, very helpful. We needed something like this. Mallory probably took it off her clothes and it fell out of his pocket into the Avon raft when he was towing the body."

"Towing the body?"

"Let me explain. Gracie probably died of multiple stab wounds. The clothes tested positive for bloodstains. We're waiting for the complete report from the medical examiner. Her body was recovered on a ledge off Bear Island by a lobsterman early this morning. An attempt had been made to sink her with a small anchor belonging to the *Pilgrim*, but it pulled loose. We judge Mallory had the body hidden somewhere near the *Pilgrim* last night—he wouldn't have had time to do anything about it—even get the clothes out of the Dumpster—after you turned up unexpectedly from Bar Harbor and forced him to call the police about the jewelry you'd found in Marcus's cabin. And he had to release Mary and Amos, and at the same time make an effort to keep Marcus in custody. He was lucky, because Marcus was not allowed to identify himself without permission— which he didn't have."

"But," protested Sarah, "everything went on as usual. Mary and Amos came for a cookout on deck that evening."

"Damage control. But Mallory must have been worried. He didn't know whether Marcus was working for someone—the police perhaps—or doing a free-lance. And there was Gracie's body."

"Wasn't he afraid that Tony and Andrea would come back?"

"Marcus debriefed Tony while you were taking a bath. I understand that Andrea tried to keep Tony in Bar Harbor. Mallory didn't want him around when there was a body to get rid of. With Tony gone, you in bed, the Chandlers on an evening cruise, there wouldn't be any interruptions. As it happened, Tony came back without Mallory knowing. He told us Mallory went out in the Avon raft late last night."

Sarah, feeling sick, nodded. She remembered the faint undulations of the *Pilgrim* while Tony explained that Mallory must be checking the mooring line. "Mallory tied her body to the mooring line, down under the water?"

"Weighted with the small anchor," said George. "Probably. Then when he thought you were asleep, he towed the body out. He would have been in a hurry because he couldn't depend on not being spotted in that crowded harbor even in the middle of the night."

"That poor woman, her nerves shot to pieces."

"Nerves," said George, "can ruin any enterprise."

"George, you have no more blood than a turnip. Her nerves didn't get Gracie killed."

"It may have hastened her death, Sarah. We think we've got the pieces together, why she and Billy were killed. You and Alex can fill in the gaps." He snapped his notebook closed and rose from his chair. "I've got to go down and check the searching of the *Pilgrim*. Come with me and I'll give you what answers I can." His voice implied that only some answers would be given to the amateurs, no matter how involved they were. Or used.

Sarah hesitated, two sleepless nights and a cross-country run beginning to make themselves felt. She was bone-tired.

George offered his hand as to an invalid incapable of rising on her own. "Alex's plane should have landed a half an hour ago, and he'll be down on the dock looking for you."

That was enough to move Sarah out of the gate and down the road, if not with alacrity, at least with steady forward steps. George followed, pacing firmly behind her, his bald dome shining in the afternoon heat.

They arrived at the top of the long ramp leading down to the series of floats and slips that made up the public landing. Sarah looked rather wildly around as if expecting Alex to materialize suddenly beside her. He was not in sight.

"How do you know Alex's plane landed a half hour ago?"

"We checked his flight in Boston, made sure he had a seat. We left a message telling him to come directly to Northeast Harbor."

"And told him about Mallory? And Gracie?"

"We kept it simple, just signed it *Pilgrim*." George pointed to the end of the long series of floats. "She's down there. We've blocked off access. The harbor master isn't happy, but I've promised we'll have her out of here by tonight."

"Have you found anything? You know the Northeast Harbor police did search; Mallory even invited them."

"Which meant that he had cleared everything out—except that hollowed-out Bible Tony told us you found in his cabin. Careless, but he was under pressure last night. We haven't found anything yet, but we must do a routine search. From what we can make out, Northeast Harbor was the end point for jewelry deals."

"And the rest was going to be pure cruise. Happy times on the bright blue sea. Eastern Harbor and Roque Island?"

"Apparently."

"So we won't make it to Roque Island, and what the devil are they doing to the *Pilgrim*? Hello Sarah, hello George."

"Alex!" Sarah whirled around and found herself pulled into Alex's arms—where she collapsed with a cry of relief. For a moment, Sarah rested, her head against Alex's chamois shirt, and then she hugged him with the strength of ten, hugged him as if her life depended on not letting go.

"Sarah, for God's sake. What's the matter, what's going on? Are you okay? George, what have you been doing to Sarah?"

Sarah loosened her grip and looked up at Alex. "I'm all right, but everything's all shot to hell, and last night was pure murder." And as she said *murder*, she stopped, took hold of Alex's hands, and stood there shaking her head.

"Murder?" repeated Alex stupidly.

"Gracie's dead, and Mark deTerra—only he's really Marcus Terrant—was working for George, and last night Tony and I found out that Mallory was in on the jewelry business, and I'd thought it was Marcus hiding earrings in Rollo the Rabbit, so Tony and I had to get off the boat because we were locked in, and then we tried to sink the *Pilgrim* by flooding the heads— you know, opening the seacocks like the sign over the toilet said not to—"

"Stop, stop. Gracie dead? What jewelry business? Sinking the *Pilgrim*? I may fly right back to Boston and try again and see if this is part of a bad play."

"Play is right," said Sarah, detaching herself from Alex and gesturing at the *Pilgrim*. "The whole bloody boat was a stage. And everyone was an actor. Pantry Players. Amos found a play-bill. Leading man and woman, ingenue, supporting characters, the whole cast. Except us. We were the audience and we didn't know it."

"Sarah, could we all simmer down and have a sensible, chronological rehash."

"I have a suggestion," said George quietly. "We'll go down to the *Pilgrim*—you have to pack your things—and put a scenario together that might make sense to Alex and even to the district attorney. Mike is coming down there shortly."

So by general agreement, George leading the way, the three moved down the long ramp and made their way to the *Pilgrim's* last berth. She lay at the far end of the dock, and, even at a distance, Sarah could see that she had been stripped of her dignity. She looked humiliated, violated.

Her tan cushions ("Fawn is so practical" Gracie had said) from the main cabin were stacked on the dock with a pile of life jackets—all of these slit open at the seams. Her sails and sail covers lay in a rumpled heap just beyond the cushions, and, loaded into wheelbarrows, or lying along the length of the roped-off walkway, was a miscellaneous heap of objects that had made the *Pilgrim* a vessel of comfort and luxury. An ice bucket stood guarding a case of wine, three large serving dishes sat upon a backgammon board, and several books—Sarah thought she recognized *War and Peace*—were stacked on the top of the main cabin's VCR.

A perspiring uniformed policeman emerged from the companionway. "We're coming along, three-quarters finished. The lab's done the photographs and the latents"—"That's fingerprints," explained George to Sarah—"we've tagged everything—location and ownership, if we know it. She'll be ready to tow off by evening."

"Good," said George. "Alex, you and Sarah can come into the cockpit. It's private enough and comfortable. They haven't taken the cushions yet."

With that uneasy feeling that comes when a familiar place becomes strange and unaccountable, Sarah and Alex took their place on the port side of the *Pilgrim*'s cockpit, while George, notebook open, placed himself, appropriately enough, behind the big pedestal wheel. Sarah, looking around at the dismantled deck, the uncoiled lines and sheets, thought it was just like going back to a house in which one has spent some memorable moments and finding that it has been sold and the movers have come.

But George, immune to sentiment, opened his notebook and said, "Billy was probably murdered. Gracie *was* murdered, and thanks to the watch you found, we have solid evidence. Mallory is in custody and will be charged with her murder and with importing and selling jewelry without paying duty or taxes, with intent to defraud the Internal Revenue Service. Ezra Coster will be charged as an accomplice to the latter, and we may be able to connect him with Billy Brackett's death. We are looking for Andrea Elder in the Bar Harbor area. The Chandlers, Elaine and Fleance, are missing."

Sarah looked up. She had forgotten the Chandlers.

"The Chandlers," continued George, "landed early this morning in Southwest Harbor in an old mahogany cruiser and left in a gray Jaguar driven by a woman in a large hat."

Sarah looked at him bewildered. "But they were just out for a late-night ride in that Cris-Craft. They expected to come back on board; they said so."

"Do you see those curtains?" He nodded to a man in coveralls who was climbing the companionway with an armful of folded red and green material that Sarah recognized as the handsome curtains from the master cabin. "A simple device," said George, almost in admiration. "Green is come ahead, red is danger."

"What?" asked Alex. "You mean signal flags."

"Mallory's cabin," said Sarah. "The red showed inside the cabin and matched his Oriental rug. Except last night, the green showed inside."

"Reversible," said George. "When I visited at Bucks Harbor, the red showed inside, this morning out. Anyone approaching the boat would see the red and know to keep away. Last night, the Chandlers must have seen the curtain signal and taken off. Last seen heading south. We've set up roadblocks, but they'll probably get away. Change cars, cut through the White Mountains to New York, or circle back and hit Boston."

"And then to fly far, far away," said Alex. "Using whatever name is handy. Now George, give me a three-paragraph summary of what the hell's been happening. I turn my back on a pleasant if somewhat troubled summer cruise and come back to mayhem."

George, closing his notebook, gave Alex a crisp two-paragraph summary, ending with the fact that Mallory had been picked up when he brought the *Pilgrim* into Clifton Dock on the west side of the entrance to Northeast Harbor. "After he took that quick potshot at the Avon, he wrestled with the bilge pumps a good part of the night, so it wasn't until early morning that he turned up. Wanted diesel and water, said that he was going to do some offshore sailing. The man at Clifton's looked around and didn't see anyone else on board, and he wondered if Mallory was alone, because he thought the *Pilgrim* was an awfully big boat for one man to sail single-handed, even though a self-steering system had been rigged up. Anyway, he gave the police a call, stalled Mallory with the refueling, and we came down and nailed him."

"Mallory didn't object?" asked Sarah. "After all, he thought he was in the police's good books because of turning in Marcus, plus letting them search the *Pilgrim*."

"He objected," said George, "but by then Gracie's body had turned up. And a letter in his pocket."

"Letter?" demanded Sarah.

"George, you're wanted. I'll explain the letter." It was Mike Laaka. He heaved himself onto the deck of the *Pilgrim.* "And I'll finish the debriefing. The medical examiner is waiting. Gracie was probably killed with a sailing knife—the kind with a big blade and a marlinspike. And just such a knife has turned up in Mallory's pocket. The fool didn't throw it away. Washed, rinsed, yes, but not thrown away."

"Sailors feel naked without a knife," put in Alex. "The blade for emergencies, to cut lines in a hurry, the marlinspike for splicing. Mallory wouldn't think of taking off without his knife."

"For that, the lab is grateful," said Mike. "Good-bye, George, I won't be indiscreet. Besides, Alex and Sarah probably know more than we do."

George rose, gave Mike one long look that combined distrust and general irritation, and left the *Pilgrim* on, as Sarah said later, "little cat feet." Almost everyone who knew George agreed that if George hadn't chosen the law for his occupation, he would have brought criminal stealth of movement to a new perfection.

Mike Laaka settled himself on the sea-green cockpit cushions and stretched luxuriously. He seemed happy and healthy, his fair skin now deeply tanned, his hair turned almost white in the summer sun. He seemed much more at ease on the sloop when she lay in a state of dismemberment than at Bucks Harbor when, watched by the Chandlers and David Mallory, he had come aboard the boat with everything all spit and polish.

"Okay, my friends," said Mike. "Who has the ball? Shall I kick off?" He opened a notebook, the replica of George's, but Sarah could see scrawl and random arrows and question marks, while George's notebook was filled with neat miniature hen tracks.

"Two murders?" demanded Alex. "How in hell does jewelry theft, or smuggling, or whatever, add up to murder?"

"Yes," added Sarah. "Bringing jewelry into the country illegally is harmless if you compare it to drugs. Maybe you're defrauding the IRS, or breaking import laws or trade balances, but killing people isn't usually part of the action."

Mike consulted his notes. "Here's what we have. Billy first.

Billy Brackett was bad news, but Mallory probably thought he could put up with Billy—he needed Gracie, and anyway, Billy was one terrific actor and could fit into the crew's cast of characters."

"Yes," said Sarah, "he proved his acting ability."

"Which finally must have frightened Mallory. Billy couldn't stop showing off and that cute tricks like the pickup truck business, scaring Sarah—if Billy was behind it—was one more strike against him."

Mike flipped his notebook over and made a note, and Sarah watched while two men passed a series of cartons top-heavy with kitchen utensils across to a waiting wheelbarrow on the dock. She could make out two omelet pans and a copper mold in the shape of a curved fish. Where, she wondered, was their gourmet cook now? In Tony's arms safe in a cave on Roque Island, on the lam to Canada, or heading west with an armful of white plush rabbits?

Mike Laaka interrupted her speculations. "Okay. Getting down to it. You remember your jellyfish sting, Sarah?"

Sarah winced. "Distinctly."

"It fits in. The lab found the dried remains of nematocysts on the floor of the Avon raft, also in the strings of that mop you sat on. Alex told George you'd both heard sounds of hosing the night that Billy left the church dinner."

"Yes," said Sarah, "Alex told me all good sailors make sure their equipment is rinsed, that seawater rots things."

"Mallory—and Ezra, because Ezra must have helped—probably thought they'd rinsed the raft. And mopped it. But those long stingers are the devil to get rid of." Mike smiled, obviously enjoying himself. "Now, what were the stingers of a lion's mane jellyfish doing in a rubber dinghy? And in a mop?"

"Cut it short, Mike," said Alex with irritation. "I suppose there was a jellyfish in the dinghy."

"Absolutely. Put in by someone who knew Billy was superallergic. And there were plenty of someones aboard who knew that. Billy'd been a member of the Pantry Players, and some of his medical history must have come to light. There probably had been a jellyfish episode—Florida waters feature jellyfish.

Okay, who's with Billy at that supper the night he died? Answer, not the Chandlers, we've checked. Marcus was there and he left to tail Billy but lost him. Who else? Mallory and the first mate, Ezra."

"I thought of that," said Sarah, "but I couldn't think of a motive. And when I heard that Mark—or Marcus—was at the supper, I was sure he did it. I said so to Mallory and he seemed to agree."

"I'll bet he did. Now that Marcus was in jail as a jewel smuggler, why not try to pin the murder on him? But there was a whale of a motive. Billy, the wild card, is now a hazard to the whole operation, so he must be dealt with. Mallory and Ezra get him to the church supper, provide him with rum, let him leave early to find his buddies, leave themselves—one at a time according to witnesses—saying they're going to hunt him up, poor wandering boy that he is. They find him staggering around and . . ."

"And hit him on the chin, knock him down," added Alex.

"We guess," said Mike. "Take his shirt off and plop him down in the Avon right on a waiting monster lion's mane. Squish!"

"Stop, it, Mike," exclaimed Sarah. "You're talking about someone dying."

"Okay, Sarah, not squish. But sting. And, probably, as Alex and the medical examiner surmise, death by anaphylactic shock. Billy was likely dumped in the water when he was gone to make it look like drowning. Naïve. Mallory was medically naïve. Mallory didn't know that if someone is dead before he goes into the water, his lungs won't be full. You were supposed to think Billy was a rummie and a druggie who drowned. Marcus is kicking himself all over the mat for losing Billy."

"But what was all that business with the syringe?" broke in Sarah. "Mallory said the syringe proved that Billy was into drugs."

"To repeat. Mallory was medically naïve. He didn't know allergy kits have a special kind of syringe, one that has two jolts if you twist the barrel. To him a syringe was a syringe."

"But Alex told me that the allergy kit syringe *could* have been used for drugs," said Sarah.

"Sure," agreed Mike. "It could have. And Billy may have been using other stuff, although, as I've said, the lab hasn't found any traces in his body. But where was the allergy kit with the tourniquet and Benadryl tablets? We've checked with some of Billy's past associates, and with his doctor, and Billy always carried a kit with him and kept the prescription up-to-date. The police are guessing that Mallory tossed the kit overboard and rinsed the epinephrine out of the syringe, ready to make a case of Billy as an addict who drowned from a mix of alcohol and drugs. As you know, Gracie said Billy also kept an extra ampule of epinephrine in the fridge, but it was gone when she went to look."

"Mallory emphasized drugs as a cause of Billy's death," said Alex. "And Billy looked like a perfect candidate for addiction."

Sarah suddenly jumped in her seat. "I remember something. When I was looking for a mop to clean up my toilet overflow, I found Mallory with the syringe and Gracie by Billy's cabin. We went back into the cabin and the porthole was open and Gracie said she'd found it that way. Mallory must have opened it and thrown the kit overboard. And the ampule. And heaven knows what else."

"You know," Mike said in a reflective voice, "Mallory was some confident. He must have thought no one was going to tumble to a few hollowed-out prayer books and stuffed rabbits because he was running a legitimate Bible-distribution mission, and besides, he had that good-citizen idea of keeping an eye out for druggies along the coast."

"But that was a smoke screen?" said Alex.

"Not entirely," said Mike. "If Mallory had actually seen someone moving drugs, I'm sure he'd have called George. George hated the idea of Mallory playing policeman, but our Florida buddies thought it was a great way to keep tabs on the *Pilgrim*; that's why they had him sworn in as a deputy. And Mallory went right along with it; looking for dealers worked as smoke screen number two along with the smoke screen number one, the church scenario."

"What complications," complained Sarah. "Layers and layers."

"Sure," said Mike. "Mallory'd staked a fortune on this jewel business, on buying and fitting out the *Pilgrim*, and nothing was too complicated to make certain it worked. But when Billy died, George had Mallory drop the drug watching. Then we had a personal representative, so to speak, aboard when Marcus from the *Simon Peter* was asked to be the replacement for Billy."

Sarah held up her hand. "Do you mean the police in Florida *and* Maine knew about the jewelry from the beginning? Everyone knew. Everyone except those dumbos, Sarah, Alex, and Tony."

Mike smiled again, a smile with a touch of pity in it. "We wanted everything to be as normal as possible, for Mallory to be at ease. And Mallory was at ease knowing that you three, being innocent, common garden-variety passengers gave the whole *Pilgrim* scene the authentic touch. Of course, the Chandlers did the same thing for him—on a classier plane, but they were part of the scam."

"Didn't you all have a lovely time," said Sarah with growing anger. "The question is, who was using us more—Mallory or George? Or you?"

"You were much safer not knowing," said Mike blandly. "But we never thought it would come to murder. We didn't want you two to work as spies aboard the *Pilgrim*, all whispering and taking notes. You might have ended up just like Billy. Or Gracie."

"I certainly wouldn't want Tony as a spy," said Alex grimly. "But you could have saved your concern about Sarah. She decided to branch out on her own. A spy without portfolio."

Mike groaned. "Sarah, I never knew anyone who could bring so much complication to an already fouled-up mess."

And Sarah blew up. "Damn you! I know Marcus had the evidence, the rabbit and the jewelry, but who found Mallory's hollowed-out Bible? The rest of the boat was cleaned out because Mallory let the police search. Listen, Mike Laaka, if you and George and Marcus had waited for everything to ripen perfectly, David Mallory would have thrown out his hollow Bible, emptied his wastebasket, and sailed off to Roque Island as pure as Saint Peter. And talking about evidence, it's lucky I sat on that damn mop, because no one would have connected Billy's death to the *Pilgrim*. It would have been an accidental death. And if I hadn't left Bar Harbor and come back to the *Pilgrim* as suspicious as hell—"

"Suspicious about Marcus," put in Alex. "You *trusted* Mallory. Actually you exposed Marcus to Mallory."

Sarah waved away these details. "I turned up at the Dumpster and scared Mallory. I know it was dumb luck, but if I hadn't come back to the harbor, why then Mallory would have had the whole afternoon to clean up his act and get rid of Gracie safely. And Gracie's watch. George said Gracie's watch . . ."

Mike reached over and took hold of her arm. "Okay, Sarah, you've had your moments, but if you and Tony had skipped the cabin search party and sat tight, based on Marcus's information, we would have moved in on Mallory this morning when you were all eating your blueberry pancakes or whatever that sex bomb Andrea gave you for breakfast. And listen to me, sneaking around on a boat, a closed environment, it's risky no matter how you slice it. You're damn lucky you made it off the boat into the harbor."

Sarah was indignant. "Not luck. I knew about the toilets. How to almost sink a boat."

"I said damn lucky," repeated Mike. "And second, that little radio-phone call you made to Alex's mother asking about Lyme disease was listened to by the whole coast."

"Well, I know that," said Sarah. "It was a risk, but not much of one."

"Ezra tells us that Mallory often took with him a little portable radio that picks up marine calls. I'll bet he heard you."

Sarah felt a familiar prickling of her skin. "You mean?"

"You told us you and Tony were locked below deck."

"I thought he'd overheard me fooling around in his cabin."

"Oh, he may have, but the telephone call just set you up."

"Sarah," said Alex, "from now on, to quote your grandmother and David Mallory and the Book of Ruth, 'Whither thou goest, I will go; and where thou lodgest, I will lodge.'"

Mike chortled. "Alex, if you goeth where Sarah leadeth,

you'll end up at the bottom of the sea in a block of cement. And here's something for Sarah to put in her diary. I'm a fan of Sherlock Holmes and I've just remembered that he solved a jellyfish murder called the "Adventure of the Lion's Mane." Trouble is, Sarah, you college people don't read the right books. Now, I've another question for you both. How did Mallory get away with it, the whole bit? Why did you two fairly intelligent worldly humans bite on this cruise and then not have any idea that something was screwy?"

"My parents pushed it," said Sarah. "And I hadn't seen Tony in ages. And I'd never been on a big sailboat."

"And I," said Alex, "was talked into it because Sarah wanted to go and I do love to sail. It all sounded plausible. The *Pilgrim*, she's a beautiful boat, perfectly equipped, Mallory was a knowledgeable skipper. And don't forget George had cleared him—to us, anyway. And the Church of the Apostles."

"Sarah?" asked Mike. "Was it Love Boat at the start?"

"At first. Except Billy, he was always odd man out. But I'm by nature unnerved by too much perfection. I started to grumble and Alex was ready to throttle me. I thought it was all too much, and I've always distrusted those hotels who leave so-called hospitality packages, chocolates and little baskets of wine and cheese. Usually, there's a fat bill to pay later. Besides, early on I'd heard very strange laughs—Gracie, and Billy I realized later. And Billy didn't improve on acquaintance. George kept asking me what Billy had said to me, and I've just been remembering that he spoke about everyone as if they were part of a cast of characters. Mordred, Arthur, Gawain, and Will the Brackett. He said something like 'Right out of the Old Vic.' He gave the whole theatre thing away but I wasn't listening. I told George the part that stuck in my mind was Billy reciting poems about death and drugs."

"Okay, so they were actors," said Mike. "But how about Gracie, that hysterical scene in the cabin when Alex slapped her? If that was acting, she deserved an Oscar."

"I'll stake anything she wasn't acting," said Alex. "I think she was devastated by Billy's death."

Mike Laaka's face went suddenly tight and he spoke with

hardly contained rage. "Why shouldn't she be devastated? My God, after Billy was found, she must have realized that she wasn't on some jewelry-smuggling toot with lots of cash, good food, and fun."

"But why was she killed?" demanded Sarah, now caught up in Mike's anger. "She was pathetic, really, not dangerous."

"Don't be so sure," said Mike, "Remember the chain around Billy's neck that Gracie called his safety necklace?"

"I thought it was an I.D. thing and that either Billy had committed suicide and didn't want to be identified or the murderer took it off for the same reason, hoping Billy would just go out to sea. But was it smuggled jewelry? A big diamond?"

"Wrong. George guessed at once and checked with various manufacturing outfits that make these chains. And bracelets." Mike stood up, reached deep into a back pocket, and fished out a thin metal chain with a rectangular tag that hung from its center. This he swung in front of Alex's nose. "Recognize, Dr. McKenzie?"

Alex sighed, a regretful sigh. "Of course. Of course, Billy would have had one of those."

"One of what?" demanded Sarah. She seized the swinging tag and peered at the red enameled caduceus, the words *Medic Alert*, and then turned it over and read that the wearer, G. Mullen, had been allergic to penicillin, seafood, and peanuts.

"This is Gracie's," exclaimed Sarah. "Where did you get it?"

"Ankle of the deceased. Hidden under her stockings. Mallory missed it, but he—or Ezra—must have gotten rid of Billy's. They're like army dog tags, I.D.s with medical information. They don't come off; they're taken off deliberately."

"Gracie was allergic, too?" said Sarah, then added, "Of course, she's Billy's sister. I remember, she said halibut made her sick that day at the Asticou Inn."

"Hence the hysterics," said Alex. "Gracie knew the Medic Alert chain was missing, the epinephrine was gone, and that Mallory was hot for making out that Billy was a drug addict. She must have known that night that Billy had been murdered. Or killed himself. But she was afraid of Mallory now. He wasn't just your friendly Captain Smuggler anymore; he might have killed her brother."

"And," added Mike, "she was probably scared shitless of Marcus and Ezra, too, since they'd both been at the church supper."

"Three against one," said Sarah. "Enough to bring on hysterics. I can see why she wanted to go to Bar Harbor with us, not to the church meeting with Mallory."

"She must have finally understood that she might be next on the list. That day Ezra was still safe in Castine and Marcus was supposedly off on a nature tour—actually he was hanging around the harbor watching for any unexpected returns—so Gracie's real danger came from being alone with Mallory. But that female didn't know what the word *careful* meant. Granted she was unhinged, but she bucked Mallory all along the way. Instead of being wary, she contradicted him, made herself conspicuous, and, who knows, she may have accused him of stripping the Medic Alert from Billy's body, getting rid of the extra epinephrine, throwing out the insect-bite kit. She may have threatened him, all the while knowing that Mallory was about as safe as a king cobra."

"But she really had gone psycho by then," said Sarah.

"You're right," said Mike. "And a psycho sister is a damn sight more dangerous than a secretary. And foolhardy. Tony tells us she also wanted you to mail a letter for her."

Sarah nodded. "To her aunt. The non-existent sick aunt. George said that he'd found a letter on Mallory."

"Correction. Envelope, not letter. Addressed not to Auntie but the Northeast Harbor police. He had the sense to throw the letter itself away, so why not the envelope? Found in his pocket. Wanted to save an unused stamp maybe. I'll never understand criminals. I suppose the letter was full of accusations, something to pin Mallory and the *Pilgrim* to the wall. When Mallory grabbed the letter and saw the address, he knew that he had to take care of Gracie for good."

Mike paused and then slammed his fist into his hand. "Goddamn, that poor over-the-hill actress. Jesus, I could put a few holes into Mallory myself. We may never pin him with killing Billy unless Ezra limbers up, but we sure as hell will nail him with Gracie. That bastard with his great little Atlantic-seaboard gemstone racket fixed so he could sail on a beautiful boat and play God's gift to God to a bunch of sucker churches."

Sarah and Alex sat, not interrupting. Mike was doing a pretty fair job of expressing their own distress. Then Sarah made a correction. "The churches weren't suckers; they got real stuff. The Church of the Apostles was a terrific working cover. Mallory loved playing the man of God; he loved the *Pilgrim*. Maybe he loved jewelry. But that was all he loved. The rest was an act. He didn't give a damn about people. He's a handsome, cheerful, friendly play director and an actor and a sailor. And a goddamn butcher."

For a moment, the three sat unspeaking. Then Mike uncoiled himself, stretched, stood and loosened his shoulders, and swept a hand across the *Pilgrim*'s deck. "I'd love once in my life to take one of these big babies out in a good wind and let her rip." He sighed regretfully. "But what I'll do is see her into dry dock, I'll watch her hauled out, and later, if we get a conviction, I'll hear she's been sold at auction."

"Maybe some good honest skipper will buy her," said Sarah.

"Maybe," said Mike. "Okay, go below and get your stuff."

Sarah and Alex made their way to their cabin and began packing. Their bunks were stripped, the sheets and blankets with the running script PILGRIM had disappeared, the six-inch foam mattresses were rolled and tied, long slits in the mattress covers.

"George probably thinks *we* were hiding jewelry," said Sarah with annoyance.

"No, but the center of a guest's mattress might have hidden some emerald earrings," said Alex. He looked around the cabin with something like regret. "You know, she did sail like a dream."

Sarah nodded, remembering for a moment the *Pilgrim* turning toward Mount Desert, cutting the ocean like a giant knife. Then she seized her new jacket and folded it together with her new white cotton trousers. "Damn," she said to no one in particular. She grabbed a sweater and her pajamas and wedged them into her open duffel. Then hands on hips, she surveyed the cabin. Now it was only a container. No little touches of welcoming hospitality. The bunks bare, the bookcase empty, the radio system pulled out, drawers standing open. And no navy blue pocket Bible with the image of a pilgrim stamped in gold.

Sarah, feeling as empty as the cabin, reached for her toilet-article kit and jammed it on top of her new jacket. "I know David Mallory is exactly what I said, a butcher. But I was beginning to trust him. And like him. After I found Gracie's blouse in the dumpster and he turned up, well, I almost cried all over his shirt.

"My shirt is always available," said Alex. He leaned over and kissed her lightly on the back of her neck and then picked up his canvas bag. Sarah hoisted her duffel to her shoulder and for the last time the two guest passengers of the *Pilgrim* made their way through the main cabin, up the companionway, through the cockpit, across the deck, to the float, up the gangway, and onto dry land.

For a moment, they stood at the top of the dock looking down at the harbor: dinghies shuttling back and forth, big and little boats turning into slips, picking up moorings, a few casting off lines and heading toward the outer harbor. The day had turned fair, the sun was bright and the afternoon breeze was strong and southwesterly. Everything promised fair sailing.

Then Alex turned away from the harbor and took Sarah's hand. "Okay, let's blow this joint."

TWENTY-FIVE

EXACTLY ONE WEEK FOLLOWING THEIR RETURN BY automobile from Northeast Harbor, Alex and Sarah found themselves retreating from a stringent visit to Grandmother Douglas.

"Your grandmother seems to be remarkably strong," said Alex.

"Yes," said Sarah, sighing. "And she loved having the last word. Saying she knew Mallory was a fraud, that successful men often are. Because of misquoting the Psalms, of course, but that we were too poorly educated to realize it."

"She seemed pleased by Tony's call."

"You never can tell about Grandma. I would have thought the news would have sent her into a fit."

Sarah repeated this observation to Mary and Amos later that evening. They sat rocking on the porch after a late supper. The evening was still warm from the hot summer sun and thunder rumbled pleasantly in the distance. The scene was, more or less, a recapitulation of their earlier dinner on that same porch, except now the field beyond the farmhouse was enlivened by the shadowy figure of Amos's eight-year-old son, Terence, being dragged about by Sarah's Irish wolfhound, Patsy. From time to time, shouts of "whoa up" and "mush" racketed up to the porch sitters.

"I think they deserve each other," observed Amos. "What's this about Tony? He has a new job? What now?"

"It's very strange," said Sarah. "Tony called from Bar Harbor. The police had caught Andrea leaving town on a Greyhound bus. She's been charged with being part of the jewelry business and is out on bail. Tony has dedicated himself to her defense."

"That's not exactly employment," observed Mary. "Your grandmother is buying the idea?"

"Grandma seems quite happy. She feels defending Andrea is halfway to becoming a lawyer. She's already sent him a list of law schools and called my mother and father with the good news."

"However," added Alex, "Grandmother Douglas is also wondering whether Andrea and Tony are living together and is busy finding admonishing quotations from Scripture." Alex pushed himself out of his chair and opened the door into the house. "The Red Sox," he explained. "They were behind; I'll just check."

Sarah was still thinking about Tony. "I wonder about Andrea. Whether she was on board to distract Tony, or was a sort of a useful innocent. She may just dump him. Use him and dump him."

"He'll bounce back," said Amos. "I think Tony has great recuperative powers."

"I envy him," said Sarah. "He's a sort of junior Micawber. He always thinks something—or someone—will turn up. And it usually does."

Alex returned, announcing, "Boston ahead, four to three, with two men on. Seventh inning. They really look good this year."

"I'm beginning to hate the Red Sox," said Sarah. "You were at Fenway Park when I called to ask about Lyme disease. I never did find out. Did Mallory get his symptoms right?"

"As Mike said, Mallory was medically naïve. He should have said flu instead of trying to be fancy. Lyme disease is a tough diagnosis sometimes. To my knowledge, it never presents suddenly with a terrific bout of diarrhea. And rarely with a complete body rash."

"So I would have known he was making it up and that something was going on. And gotten out."

"Then you wouldn't have had the fun of flooding the *Pilgrim*, which I imagine was quite satisfying," said Amos. "Now I want to know about the Chandlers. I quite took to them."

"Such a happy ending," said Sarah. "I ran into Mike Laaka yesterday. Mr. and Mrs. Fleance Chandler have arrived in Zimbabwe for an extended visit—from Monaco. They are staying with old friends and will soon start rehearsals. A revival of *Skin of Our Teeth*, with three benefit performances for Zimbabwe Little Theatre. Buy next month's *Town & Country* and you'll probably see pictures."

Alex nodded. "Dear Flip, dear Elaine. Guess what was found in that nice old mahogany CrisCraft? One shoe box, one large photograph album. One marked SLIDES FROM TRIP TO NORWAY, the other, CHRISTMAS IN CANNES. Nice items, real photos and slides, but with a center area cut out and stuffed with you know what."

"Precious, precious jewels," said Mary. "Set with exquisite taste. Emerald-cut diamonds, diamond-cut rubies, ruby-cut sapphires. Sapphire-cut emeralds. Thousand-carat gold."

"And a list of old friends and their want lists," added Alex. "Flip and Elaine handled what you might call the retail end of the jewelry business. They filled orders, had gracious little show-and-tell parties at inns and beaches and summer houses. The customers were happy and kept their lips buttoned because they got good stuff at good prices."

"And the Chandlers," put in Sarah, "were happy because they made enough money to support their traveling habits and their designer wardrobes. They worked between engagements, so to speak. Aren't actors often 'between engagements'?"

Amos, restless as ever, pushed himself out of the rocker and moved toward the porch rail, swiveled around, sat on it, and faced Sarah and Alex. "What I don't understand, even now, is how Mallory fooled you. Didn't he ever look out of place?"

Sarah frowned. "Mike wondered about that. But it was the whole look, L. L. Bean, Brooks Brothers, upscale East Coast summer scene. He fitted in. As John Buchan said about acting, he had grown into what he was doing. He lived his character's life. And he chose roles that enhanced pleasure, those glory roles. The captain of the ship, the successful smuggler, the man of God, the bringer of good things that shall be to all people."

"He was certainly the perfect skipper," said Alex. "Tony and I did very little navigation work, although that's supposedly one reason we were there. As Sarah said, he fitted in."

Sarah gave a violent rock in her chair and sat up. "Just like he fitted into Florida. White plastic shoes, flowered shirt. He was in costume. He was an actor in costume. And," she added excitedly, "he was a chameleon. Everything blended. The *Pilgrim* even blended. Sea-green paint, sea-green cockpit cushions."

"And her spinnaker," said Alex. "Some spinnakers are gaudy, stripes, designs, easy to remember. The *Pilgrim's* spinnaker was the same sea-green, and now that I think of it, she never carried an owner's or a yacht club pennant."

"That day we left Camden, remember," said Sarah, "Because what a giveaway. David Mallory pointed out that some cruising people had been picked up for drug dealing because they didn't take moorings, anchored way out on the edge of harbors, paid cash and made themselves conspicuous."

"Which Mallory never did," agreed Alex. "Totally in control."

"No, wait." Sarah turned to him. "Once I saw him lose it. That morning when the propeller caught in pot warp and there was seaweed glop all over the deck. He came unstuck and I said here's Captain Bligh. Or the real David Mallory."

Alex nodded slowly. "He didn't lose his temper just because of the seaweed. He probably made that early start to put the *Pilgrim* and all of us at some distance from the place that he and Ezra had killed Billy, but with the possibility of a bent propeller, he had to turn back."

Sarah grimaced. "And Mallory didn't dare say no when you asked to go ashore to buy lobsters, but the last thing he must have wanted was for us to stumble across Billy, in case he'd washed in near the Islesboro Inn. With luck, we would have been in Bucks Harbor before the body turned up, or at the worst, we would have been in another cove completely disassociated from what Mallory thought would be called a drowning accident."

Sarah was silent for a moment, then she added, "You know, all of them, they were damn good. No one flaunted jewelry. Mallory just the perfect sports watch and telling me he couldn't understand the passion for the stuff. Ezra was clean; Gracie only her mother's watch; Andrea, that single perfect red stone on a gold chain nestled into her breast works. The Chandlers, of course, dripping with it because that was in character."

"Why do you think Mallory went in for jewelry?" asked Mary. "Drugs bring in the big bucks. Much wider clientele. And hungrier."

"You're forgetting," said Alex. "Mallory ran a class act. Jewelry is classy. Drugs are sleazy. Drug dealers come home with holes in their chests. In body bags. Jewelry movers can sail on yachts, wear beautiful clothes, and inhabit classy circles."

"You call two murders classy?" demanded Mary.

"No," said Alex, "but from Mallory's peculiar point of view, they were necessary to keep the operation that way."

Mary made a noise suggesting disgust, and for a moment the four on the porch sat quietly listening to the night sounds mixed with the boy's shouts and the low woof of the dog.

Then Sarah said to no one in particular, "For all that Mallory was supposed to be a sort of sea-going 'Good Shepherd,' there was never any real, any thoughtful discussion of religion. It was all window dressing. Costume and setting." She turned to Amos and asked, "Speaking of which, where on earth did you find that playbill announcing the Pantry Players?"

"The alumni file from the secretary of Mallory's class," said Amos. "Someone had sent it in, probably not Mallory, but who knows, he may have been honest then. Anyway, it was supposed to go into class notes but never did. Just filed with a bunch of other dead items. But the Larkin-Donelli research team missed one item. Guess what David Mallory majored and minored in at Bowmouth."

"Marine biology and the history of smuggling," said Sarah.

"Almost. Geology major, thesis on gemstones, and a minor in theatre. And I have a message from Marcus Terrant. He said he blew it when he identified Alex's father as teaching at Harvard. As Mark deTerra, he wasn't supposed to know things like that."

"I was going to ask Alex," said Sarah, "but everything happened too fast."

"As a genuine Italian female," said Mary, "I would have caught Marcus out in ten minutes. I knew I should have gone on the cruise with you. And now, Amos, it's time for Terrence to come in. And Patsy. His mother probably wants her dog."

"Yes, I do," said Sarah. And then, after making a little face at Alex, she turned to Mary. "Are you two free sometime this fall, or this winter, or this spring? Whenever."

"Free?" said Mary. "Free of what? Classes, school, research, penury, plumbing problems?"

"Free for a wedding. A nice old-fashioned Italian-style wedding."

"Whose chief participants," said Alex, "are not Italian."

"But we loved your wedding," said Sarah. "We thought we'd clone it. Dance and sing the fandango."

"That's Spanish, you fool," said Mary. "Leave it to me. I'll give you an Italian wedding that will put you out of action for a week."

"Sounds good," said Alex.

"Sounds frightening," said Amos. "Go away both of you, it's my bedtime. *Buono notte* and good riddance."